Joyce –,
to my Minneapolis signing

Chocolate Rabbit

BY

PETRA SABINE MANNING

Petra Sabine Manning

DORRANCE PUBLISHING CO., INC.
PITTSBURGH, PENNSYLVANIA 15222

This is a work of fiction. Names, characters, places, and incidents are either the product of the author's imagination or are used fictitiously, and any resemblance to actual persons, living or dead; events; or locales is entirely coincidental.

All Rights Reserved

Copyright © 2008 by Petra Sabine Manning
No part of this book may be reproduced or transmitted in any form or by any means, electronic or mechanical, including photocopying, recording, or by any information storage and retrieval system without permission in writing from the publisher.

ISBN: 978-0-8059-7817-9

Printed in the United States of America

First Printing

For more information or to order additional books, please contact:
Dorrance Publishing Co., Inc.
701 Smithfield Street
Third Floor
Pittsburgh, Pennsylvania 15222
U.S.A.
1-800-788-7654
www.dorrancebookstore.com

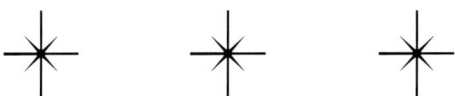

I would like to thank my friend Marilyn Jakes Church for her encouragement and help to get this book written. She has great computer knowledge, and we spent many afternoons sipping our way through a bottle of Chardonnay, me dictating, her typing away. She taught me how to use a computer and that put me on my way to write on my own. I thank you from the bottom of my heart, Marilyn.

To my wonderful husband Marty, my best friend and number-one supporter of anything I try to accomplish. Without you, I would not have gone forward with this project. I thank and appreciate you!

Love, Sabine

Section One

Once There Was a Little Girl

"What man doesn't understand, he doesn't have." —Goethe

Chapter One

Prologue to Decision

Nikki knew she was going to buy the rabbit as soon as she saw it. She didn't want it. But she had to have it. And Paul Peterson was to blame.

Trying to walk away from the shop window was useless. It was, after all, the day before Easter. Ignoring this particular rabbit might be possible, but how many other stores between here and the subway entrance would also be displaying the confections of the season? Nikki Fisher could not hope to elude them all. And Monika Groebel was demanding the purchase.

Normally she could control Monika. Not this day, however. Paul's offer had nearly liberated that other individual with whom Nikki shared body and mind. And since it was the Easter season, shoving her child-self back into the imprisonment of what was past and done would be hard, much more difficult than usual. Therefore, it seemed almost prudent to allow Monika to enter the door on which black script proclaimed "Fanny May."

The store's interior was uncomfortable. Central heating for the Loop's stores and offices was still active in early April. The sunshine and the breeze from the south, however, were unusual for this time of year. All the warmth made the aroma of chocolate cloyingly aggressive. For a moment, Nikki had to fight for breath. Monika's recollection insisted that chocolate had not smelled so strong last time. Had there been any smell at all? Monika wasn't sure.

Nikki stood just out of the collision zone created by the customer presently being served. He talked with a flatness that indicated he was a native Chicagoan, but his gestures suggested that his parents had not been.

As if to prove his status as native son, he turned with his purchases to give Nikki a view of his outdated "Re-Elect Daley" button. Perhaps he saw no point in removing it. Hizzoner's candidacy was as regular an occurrence as the College All-Star Game.

The one clerk behind the counter next turned her attention to a woman. Kidskin-clad fingers indicated a pair of baskets wrapped in lavender cellophane. Somewhere in the back of the building, metal trays were striking metal racks. A radio was playing, too low to distinguish words. Nikki looked at her watch. It was three o'clock. The news of the hour was coming on. The first item was detailing continuing efforts to reach the U.S.S. Thresher. One could tell by the announcer's funereal tones that the news wasn't good.

"Help you?" the clerk inquired as the two Easter baskets rustled toward the door, leaving a wake of Elizabeth Arden's Blue Grass strong enough to block out the candy smell.

Nikki stepped forward, moving from the white hexagonal tiles to the black and white border that marked the perimeter of customer space.

"A chocolate rabbit, please."

"What size?" The woman lifted a hand and plucked the edge of her hair net away from her forehead.

"Like that one," Nikki pointed to a twin of the creature in the window.

"Hollow or solid?"

"Solid, naturally."

The clerk didn't see it as "naturally" at all. She named the price without making a move toward the candy.

"That's fine," Nikki agreed. She'd saved out ten dollars to buy a new blouse, but she could live with her present wardrobe. Anyway, she didn't feel like shopping. What she really needed was time to think, about both herself and Monika, about Paul Peterson, about their future.

"That bunny down there in foil is just like this, and the pretty colors are only a dime more," the clerk suggested. "The paper'll keep it from melting, too. Awful hot out today."

"I don't want a wrapped rabbit. Give me that one. Put it in a sack."

"Can't do that. It goes in one of these here boxes with paper grass." The salesgirl held it up for inspection. "Nice, huh?"

"I do not want a box with grass in it." The petulance of a seven-year-old Monika broke through. "Just my rabbit."

"Well!" the clerk sniffed and appealed her rebuff to a waiting customer. Nikki didn't bother looking to see what the verdict was. She was feeling a bit red-cheeked, but she wasn't going to take time to apologize for the anxiety that Paul and Monika had raised within her. The clerk had no trouble taking her money despite the insult, but Nikki had to struggle to keep Monika from grabbing the proffered paper sack.

* * *

Usually it was cooler in The Loop than elsewhere in the Chicago area. Even in the summer, the tall buildings provided canyon walls to shade the sidewalks. Today it was different. The Windy City wasn't.

Nikki shrugged out of her beige suit jacket and slung it over the arm that bore the handbag and rabbit. She was grateful for the lack of sleeves in the paisley-print shell she had donned in the morning. At least her arms were cooler. Her nylon stockings and slip seemed to be armor that held body heat beneath her skirt. The warm moisture along her hips and thighs disgusted her.

Of course, she'd dressed in her best for the meeting with Paul. A junior in journalism did not enter the portals of a potential employer in jeans and trailing shirt tails. People in print media possessed notoriously long memories.

Her plans for a future as a journalist had been premised on entering the working world a year hence. She'd thought that, with luck, the appointment with the part-time instructor at Northwestern could result in a temporary job with the local media. Paul's proposal, however, would have her at work by mid-June, leaving her senior year for some later date. He had to have known that his offer was scary. Yet her request for time to consider had left him obviously annoyed.

The department store display window slowed Nikki's progress. One of the mannequins wore a chestnut wig that was approximately the same shade as Nikki's hair. The dress being exhibited was pink. She examined the result closely, wondering if she could indeed wear that pastel. Her eyes slid away as she identified her own reflection in the glass.

The results of the heat were not nearly so bad as she had expected. There was no visible perspiration on her uptilted nose or the cheeks and forehead framed by fluffy bangs and tendril curls.

"You're too critical of yourself," she scolded mentally as she moved on, repeating the same words her family and friends used to build her confidence. Today, especially, she should have known her appearance was acceptable. Paul had spoken praise, and she had seen affirmation in his gaze. Sometimes she wished she were older or he was younger. Paul Peterson was the most comfortable man she had met since Gerry, and she was sure that Paul would never betray her and hers.

She stared in amazement at the building in front of her. It told her conclusively that, while she was thinking about Paul, Monika was guiding her steps. Other people besides herself also had this as a destination. She frowned as she watched two women come out of Old St. Mary's carved doors. Newer commercial construction in the area nearly concealed the historic church. Its conservative reader board was lost amid neighboring signs in gilt and neon.

An old man hobbled, cane aided, toward the panel that was now swinging shut. Bolting ahead, she caught the metal handle and pulled it open again.

"Ye're a good lass," he told her with a Celtic grin as he slid past.

She peeked into the narthex. None of the individuals she had seen was dressed for a wedding. Yet what else would fill a church late on a Saturday afternoon.

"Confession," Young Monika supplied inside her mind. "You must be shriven before Easter Mass."

Nikki nodded her head at the thought. Probably Doro's phone call, a note of which she'd found last night in her box after she returned from a movie with Mark, had been a reminder about confession. A "best friend" from both sides of the Atlantic, Doro considered herself Nikki's parochial mentor, positive that the adopted Roman Catholic daughter of Reformed Jews required a spiritual guide.

That really wasn't so. Donna Fisher also took a serious view of her legal daughter's religious obligations. Surely there would be another call-back slip on the same subject. So why not get a jump on both of them? Nikki took a firmer hold on the candy sack and ducked into the structure's cool darkness.

Whether confession was really good for the soul, Nikki wasn't sure. She still struggled to determine what should and should not be confessed. Maybe all converts had that problem. At the time of her instruction in the Church, she had found that many errors in thought and deed that she deemed serious were not expected, by the clergy, to weigh heavily upon the Catholic conscience. She had yet to experience a penance that extended beyond a handful of prayers.

Lines before the Old St. Mary confessionals were long enough to allow Nikki to make her decisions. When she was on her knees at last, she had identified several exaggerations as full-fledged lies and dodging a babysitting assignment with the Fisher offspring was categorized with failure to honor one's parents. The priest, Monica, Doro, and Donna had been satisfied. Nikki hoped that Christ felt the same.

As the northbound train climbed out from the subway tunnel to the sundazzled elevated track, Nikki felt both blessed and in charge of herself once more. Monika waited quiet within for the time when the chocolate rabbit would be consumed. Paul's words, however, were biding for further consideration. Nikki knew that any journalism student, especially a female, should be thrilled to death with the opportunity.

"You'll be assigned as my assistant, mostly to translate during my stint in Europe. We've had trouble lately using native speakers. They keep telling us what they or their government think we should hear," Paul had explained, his grin erupting into a chuckle. "But I'll see you get chances to write, too. Mostly you'll go where I go, all over Europe."

His sandy eyebrows rose, nearly colliding with a forelock that never seemed to know its place.

"Granted, I can manage the British Isles on my own and I probably won't starve in Scandinavia. Anywhere else, I am in trouble."

"What about my senior year?" Nikki had inquired.

"Hang your senior year. With the experience you'll get on this job, no future employer is going to care whether you have a degree."

"David will care," she reminded him. Her stepfather, former editor of a *North Shore Weekly* and current head of the print media training at Medill School of Journalism, had guided her college course selection, a combination of writing and foreign language with history and political science on the side.

"No, he won't. I've already talked with him." Paul paused in filling his pipe bowl to level a glance at her.

"Then you know about…"

"Your German parents are dead, Nikki. Your name is Fisher. You are an American citizen. That may not be good enough to get you into Moscow, but I doubt if I could get there either. My esteemed employer has not exactly made himself popular with the Soviets and most especially with Comrade Khrushchev."

Nikki had smiled with Paul. The Colonel's editorial stance on Communism had made him a favorite of Joe McCarthy and the despair of the American State Department. He had died before she came to the United States, but David and Donna had regaled her with Colonel stories. And according to Paul, the paper's current management perpetuated its predecessor's foibles.

"We could be a great team, Nikki." Paul lurched across the office area with that body-twisting limp caused by his prosthesis. His hand rested lightly on her shoulder and felt good. "An overseas Drew Pearson and Jack Anderson."

"How ghastly!" She laughed at him. "But I can't say 'yes' now. I have to think about it."

Paul's fingers had stiffened before his grasp was released.

When she changed trains at Howard Street, Nikki saw that a grease mark was growing on the outside of the striped candy sack. She hung the jacket over her shoulders and changed her grip on the bag. It should have been the foiled wrapped bunny, regardless of Monika's preferences.

Despite the fact that her appointment with Paul Peterson had taken place in the tower most Midwesterners considered the symbolic of journalism, Nikki always sensed more tradition in Evanston, hometown of Northwestern University and its renowned Medill School. She begged a mental pardon for having laughed at Paul's reference to Drew Pearson. After all, Evanston was Pearson's home town. The walk from the Rapid Transit station to her dormitory was a traditional route.

On a quiet day such as this Easter eve, she could imagine others who walked this same way, who had become and were becoming legends in their own time. David Fisher, whose alma mater was Medill, told her stories about those outstanding individuals. Perhaps that was why he and Paul agreed that

Nikki should go to Europe. Somehow she couldn't quite see herself as a legend. She shivered at the notion of leaving the United States to return to what she had known earlier. David and Donna, who knew a great deal about her past, sometimes tried to get her to talk about the early days as Monika. When she tried to explain that the past was behind her and she was content to be Nikki Fisher, David would take on his wise Jew demeanor.

"We are what we have been, young lady. As you accumulate years, you will learn the truth about the universe. We know now that Copernicus was correct in his hypothesis that the Earth revolves around the sun, although men of his time thought the sun spun around the Earth. Most of us, however, begin life with the concept that the Earth revolves around us. And the wisdom comes at last with the realization that it is Jehovah that centers his universe. What we are given in experiences are neither earned nor merited. There is a purpose beyond our needs and wants."

Doro, who knew a lot more about the past that did David, never pushed in the same way. According to her, the wheel had stopped spinning on their number—hers and Nikki's. The payoff was life in the United States of America. Their winnings were to be spent wisely, to accrue more fortune.

So Dorothea Braun Kneipp, former resident of Wiesbaden, became a prototype suburban housewife. Without a backward look, this mother of a son whose precocity was a constant divided her time among maintaining a House Beautiful tract home, fulfilling the obligations of membership in the parish altar guild, and being show secretary for a local riding club.

"There are times, Nikki, when I wonder why there is anyone left in Germany at all," Doro decided one evening as they sat on the screened patio drinking daiquiris. "Just think! There are seven rooms in this house. That's more than two rooms a person. In Wiesbaden there would be at least one more family living with us. Maybe two. No way I would ever go back to that. Not even to visit. If anyone wants to see me, they can come here. You want to come with us Sunday to see the Cubs play? Joe has four tickets for the company box."

Nikki usually agreed with Doro. But there were times she had doubts. She stood at the corner, waiting for the Orrington Avenue traffic to give way to pedestrians. In Europe, buildings stood for centuries, surviving natural and manmade disasters. Some were so old that people could only guess at their origin. Yet on the opposite corner, the wrecking ball was destroying a brick building that was less than a century old.

Once, long ago, the aging Swiss cook had explained the phenomenon to small Monika.

"Ja, ices taste better than dried beef. But dried beef lasts. It will feed you tomorrow. The ice is only for today and this moment."

Arriving at the dormitory at last, Nikki shouldered her way past a cluster of residents to get to the small room. One of the girls jumped back as the corner of the candy sack brushed her arm.

"Oh, God, Nikki. What is that messy thing?" Her finger pointed at the oily brown stain that was radiating on the sides of the sack.

"My...I mean a chocolate rabbit. It's not wrapped in foil." Nikki managed a crooked smile, as if apologizing for the condition of the bag. She held it above her head to avoid rubbing against her dorm mates.

"Better put it out of its misery," one of the girls suggested. "It looks done in."

Nikki grabbed her messages from the mailbox and ran for the stairway. In the privacy of her room, she tore open the sack to examine the chocolate rabbit's condition. The temperature had made its molded lines indistinct. As she touched it, her fingers stuck to its surface. The animal's head sagged, and its ears fell off.

She sat down at her desk, staring sadly at the mess. Just what had happened to that other chocolate rabbit from the other land and life? Memories flooded back with Nikki's tears.

* * *

"I need clean water, Peter. You pump."

Monika scrambled up from the grassy hammock defined by the oak's gnarled roots. At seven years, she was accustomed to being obeyed, but Peter Walz, the bookkeeper's son, merely nodded. She frowned as the youngster carefully closed his knife. It made no sense. The blade tip had been missing when the knife was handed down to the boy.

"Slow poke!

Peter brushed at his shorts, then came to swipe his hands at her skirt. He led the way along the path that bisected the rhubarb patch, a shortcut etched by many feet over the years. As they reached the garden pump, the pair moved out of the oak's shadow. Brilliant light made both youngsters rub at their eyes. The heat in that spot made it hard to breathe.

Peter took his place at the handle. Monika remained on the edge of the stone slab, waiting for the first gush of water to explode from the faucet. In earlier years, she'd broken a paint jar when the water swept the glass from her small hand. Then she had cut her finger trying to help clean up the splinters. And Mutti had insisted that Hanna take her to Dr. Bindau's office for a hateful shot.

"Slow poke," Peter echoed. The water was flowing at a regular pace.

Monika emptied the dirty water over the leaves of the rhubarb and approached the spigot. Only one stroke of the handle was needed to fill it. She twirled the container until she found a clean edge and put it to her lips. Then she slid the jar back under the pump, waiting for Peter's continued effort.

"Do you want a drink, too?" she asked. "I'll pump."

She had to keep her back to Peter as he walked to the front of the slab. When he was in position, bent over the spigot with face near his cupped hands, she swung heavily down on the handle. Water spewed, droplets catching the sunlight and creating a halo of diamonds around his head.

Monika smiled, but did not laugh aloud, as Peter shook himself. She also avoided comment about the wet spots on the front of his shorts. This was her only playmate for the summer. In the fall, it would be different. School would mean many friends with whom to play. Then she might risk an insult, but not now.

"Mouse turd," he shouted, once he stopped choking on inhaled water. Then he threw back his head and laughed. Now she was free to giggle in response.

"Will we be taught painting in school?" Monika asked as they returned to their places, she with her small block and water colors, he with the chunk of wood on which he was whittling. Her sister, Hanna, had already assured Monika that painting was an important subject for first-year pupils, but it had been thirteen years since Hanna had begun school. She might not remember clearly. Peter, on the other hand, had cousins currently enrolled in the village school.

"Of course," Peter agreed, using his teeth to reopen his knife. "But it won't help you any because you are already a good artist. So why are you painting a picture of the old wolf?"

He glared across the grass strip to the kennel in which Harry roamed the fence perimeter. The German shepherd-wolf crossbreed growled shared dislike back at the boy.

"It's a secret. You have to pledge your good luck," Monika told him, enclosing her thumb within bent fingers, fist raised toward him.

Peter took a moment to survey the area. There were no adults nearby so he made the required signal. Lutherans weren't supposed to believe in good luck, but to trust only in grace. At least that was what Tante said.

"I'm doing this painting for Vati. It will be his Christmas gift."

"It's summer," he said impatiently. For this information he had risked exclusion from the church and subsequently from heaven!

"Stupid," she retorted, then eased the name with a grin and extended three fingers, using the paint brush handle to tick off her points. "First, I cannot paint blue sky if I wait until winter, and Vati likes blue best. Next, Mutti will have it framed when I am finished. That takes a long time because she has to go to Leipzig. Herr Gunter could have done it, but he went West. Finally, who wants to sit out here when it's cold and rainy to paint a picture?"

Peter nodded. Now he understood, except why she was painting Harry. Herr Groebel wasn't that fond of the dog. He'd heard the master of the estate curse the animal when it snarled. Harry liked only Monika. She could approach him and pet him. With her, he never growled or barked. Some of the people who lived on the estate said that she and the dog talked together. The dog's speech was a whining sound that came from the back of the throat.

Monika stopped dabbing color on the page to look at Peter. He was giving her that odd look that she often saw on the faces of many residents of the estate. The superstitious among them claimed that Monika understood Harry's words because she was a changling, daughter of a witch. That was because, Monika had heard the woodsman's wife insist, Frau Groebel had been too old to bear a child. Everyone knew, according to that same source, that the Groebels' unborn infant died when the Nazis threw the Frau down the villa's long stone stairway.

Peter grinned suddenly, asserting without words, that Monika was no witch. She was too pretty. Not beautiful like her mother or sister, perhaps, but nice to see. And she was his friend.

Monika smiled back. There weren't many young children on the estate. The man who fired the boiler had two sons, but their noses were always running. And they lived in a hut. Peter naturally preferred being friends with the child of the villa, even if she was a girl.

"Onkel Wilhelm is helping the Russians solve a case. If you pledge your good luck, I'll tell you about it."

Monika didn't bother to determine whether there were observers. Despite Vati's wishes, Mutti was Catholic. Of course, she never attended Mass in the village, but the priest regularly came to the villa. A daughter of a Catholic and a Lutheran could believe almost anything she wished.

"So tell me," she demanded.

"There are these outlaws...crooks...and three days ago they went to Herr Schwartz's house and robbed it. Herr and Frau Schwartz weren't home, but they knocked the maid over. She thought they were the secret police. That's why she let them in when they knocked."

"Did they have uniforms and badges?" Monika frowned at her work. Harry's eyes were too kindly. She often saw the gleam of love, but others did not. That was between her and the dog.

"No. Just dark suits, and they showed her a card."

"And she let them in?" She added a deeper brown to the pupil. That made Harry look more savage. "Surely she knew better."

"Why? Do you know what secret police look like?" Peter objected. "Not like Onkel Wilhelm and the village constabulary. They wouldn't be secret if they did."

Monika considered the thought and her picture simultaneously, and decided both were accurate. She nodded and dropped her brush into the container of water.

"What did the robbers take?" she inquired idly. She had been in the Schwartz home and couldn't remember anything very valuable. They had a marvelous cat with long soft hair, but she doubted thieves would be interested.

"Paintings. Four of them. Herr Schwartz had hidden them during the Nazi days by stapling old tapestries over them. Now, after all that care, they are gone. Onkel Wilhelm says Frau Schwartz cries all the time. It is bad, he says, that decent people cannot enjoy their beautiful things in safety anymore. First Hitler and now the Russians."

"Maybe I should paint something new for Frau Schwartz," Monika decided. "Then she wouldn't be so sad."

"And I can build a frame for it," Peter offered.

"No, silly. Mutti can get one in,..."

The scream that came from above them ripped the knife from Peter's fingers. In her hurry to scramble to her feet, Monika kicked over the paint water. Above them, the casement window on the villa stairway had been thrown open. The figure leaning out and screaming again and again looked like a picture from an old-time book. But the face and shoulders, the dark hair torn loose and hanging wildly, belonged to Mutti.

"Look," Peter pointed. "Frau Groebel is bleeding."

To Monika it seemed her parent's face had been ripped away. Some miracle, therefore, made her understand the babbled message that replaced the screams.

"Thieves! Stop them!"

Afterward Hanna had explained that Mutti had not been seeking the children's aid. The distraught woman had hoped some factory worker would answer her plea. But as the screams increased, Monika was sure that she and Peter were the only possible salvation.

"Find your Onkel Wilhelm and have him bring the constables," she yelled at Peter. "I'll let Harry out."

It was Harry's name, Monika was sure, that made her friend run so fast. He was beyond the estate gate before she managed to open the three separate latches on the animal's cage. The wolf dog had stood back patiently while she worked. Freedom was promised. As soon as she was clear of the doorway, he lunged.

Less quickly, she followed the dog around the house. All the noise—the screams, the barking—was in the front. At the corner of the drive, she surveyed the scene with pleasure, her face brightened by a toothsome smile. Harry was doing his job well.

One man rolled on the ground, howling and clutching at bloody flesh. She frowned, trying to decide where the dog had attacked him. And then she giggled. The robber had a very sore backside and not much left of his trousers. Satisfied, she turned her eyes away. A lady did not keep looking at a naked man. Hanna said so.

The downed robber's companion had made it to the car, but could not climb in. Harry had his leg and was pulling. Once, the man's frantic kicks caught the dog's ear and caused him to lose his grip. The slathering jaws found a new site at which to set teeth.

When Onkel Wilhelm and his constables arrived, the scene had changed little. The man who attempted to enter the vehicle finally fainted. He lay bleeding on the gravel driveway. Harry contented himself with gnawing at a forearm. The other man was stiff, his eyes rolled back.

Two officers raised rifles and swung them toward the animal.

"No!" Peter shouted from behind his uncle. "Monika, call Harry."

When she spoke his name, the animal rose immediately and ambled toward her. Obediently he padded along at her side to the cage, entering without protest.

"Peter," she called to the boy after Harry was locked safely away. Peter had his head cocked to the side as he watched the officers jerk at the shattered thieves. The youngest of the constables was still vomiting in the flower bed nearest Harry's first victim. "Peter, we should go inside and help Mutti."

The children discovered, however, that Wera Groebel did not require their attendance. Although her hair was still straggling around her elegant face and her emerald satin dressing gown bore brown splotches of dried blood, Mutti appeared composed as Onkel Wilhelm, Cook, and two maids fetched cologne-soaked cloths, brandy, and cushions for her comfort. Monika watched for a minute before turning toward the door, pulling at Peter's arm as she moved.

"Help me pump some water for Harry. He is very thirsty. And there's blood all over his face. I want to wash him off."

* * *

"We will sing our song about the farmer," Herr Schlauch, the music master, told the first-year pupils. "Farmers are very important in the German Democratic Republic. They work very hard to meet goals for food. And their job is made harder because so many lazy ones run away to the West. Farmers are heroes. I want those boys and girls whose fathers are farmers to stand up while we sing. And then it will be time for our very good hot lunch."

Eight youngsters—five boys and three girls— rose to attention at their desks. None of the others were surprised at this revelation of their parentage. They were remarkable by the dirt ingrown on their knees and the mud that rimmed the jointure of sole to heavy high boots.

"Aren't we proud to have these children in our classroom?" the teacher asked before sounding the pitch on the glockenspiel that he carried from class to class.

Monika wanted to shout back "No," but she had learned better. After four weeks in school, she knew that a student should be seen but not heard except when called upon to recite. More important, she knew why. The principal tiptoed through the halls every day, listening outside of the classroom doors. Sometimes there were Russian advisors who accompanied her. If they heard voices other than those of teachers, the offending teachers received notes reminding them of who was in charge.

Obediently, Monika joined her tones with her classmates' in the salute to farmers. Her volume rose as the teacher, who had been singing loudly, fell quiet as he came to her desk.

Herr Schlauch wore the pin that Vati was refusing to don. It meant, she thought, that he was a friend of the Russians. Vati said that friendship had little to do with it. No man should wear the mark of another.

When Hanna had asked why he had worn a swastika, he quieted her with a glance. There was that photograph, Monika remembered, of Vati and Mutti bringing her from the hospital after her birth. Vait held her because Mutti was bandaged and on crutches. And there was that uneven line where Vati's upper arm had been torn from the picture.

"And now you may bring out your bowls and spoons," the music master proclaimed as, after many verses, the song ended. "How good lunch will be. I can smell it. Can you smell it, boys and girls?"

A chorus of "ja" responded. There had to be something wrong with the teacher's nose, Monika decided. Otherwise he would be well aware of how awful lunch really was. She suspected that he didn't have to eat it. Since the teachers spent the day moving from room to room, they had nowhere to keep their bowls and spoons.

The din of metalware filled the room. Monika sat motionless. After the children lined up by the door, she pulled the lunch she had brought from home from her rucksack. There was liverwurst and cheese on the bread. A little package smelled sharply of pickles. First, however, she wanted to eat one of her pieces of chocolate before her classmates returned to suffocate her with the hateful smell of the noodle-laced gruel.

"Not joining us, Fraulein Groebel?" the music master asked as the pupils filed out.

"No, thank you, Herr Schlauch." She thrust her chin forward to keep her words firm.

"Nor you, Master Walz?"

"Not this day, Herr Schlauch."

Monika whirled to see Peter calmly unwrapping slices of brown bread and cheese. He winked at her as soon as the man's back turned to them.

"Who made your lunch?" Monika asked as soon as they were alone. Peter's mother was dead. Tante Walz, who did for him and his father, was fat and lazy. She would not have put the boy's lunch together.

"I did. It's not hard. And you are right. It is pig slop they serve." Suddenly aware of the blasphemy, he swept the room with his eyes.

"You must not say that in public," Monika chided. "I have pickles. Would you like some?"

As their classmates returned, they ended the conversation. The first to enter was Heidi, Monika's new playmate. Like Peter, she had no mother. Heidi's brother, Hans, was an apprentice engraver in Vati's Leipzig jewelry shop, Haus Groebel. Vati said that Hans was very talented. He must be, Monika decided, for Vati to overlook the fact that Hans had belonged to a Hitler youth group.

Vati had arranged for Heidi to return to the villa with Monika at the end of each school day. Hans picked her up before dinner and took her home to their factory house. Hans was a stupid boy, Monika thought, but his motorcycle was lovely. One of these days, he and Heidi were going to let her ride in the sidecar. She'd see to that.

"Our stew is very good," Heidi declared in a loud voice as she turned around in her seat to see what Monika had left from her meal. "Can I have that pickle you can't eat?"

Monika passed it over, wondering why she couldn't eat it. But it was wiser to do it that way. Otherwise, Heidi would announce to all the students in the school the contents of Monika's home-packed lunch. How good it was that the remainder of the chocolate was already out of sight.

Everything grew bigger when Heidi described it. Two pickles became five. An apple, just fitting in a seven-year-old's hand, was huge, glossy, and large enough for four people to eat.

"Of course, Monika's family is very rich," was Heidi's explanatory tag line.

A person would think she hauled tons of food to school, Monika thought. But she also saw the eyes that swung toward her during Heidi's commentary. They were speculating. How much? How good? Why Monika? Was it witchcraft?

"Very well done, young Monika," Frau Haufe nodded as she examined the drawing of the flower. "You work neatly, and your eye sees much."

Monika lowered her head and smiled at the paper in front of her. In the first week of classes, she had loved the art teacher's praise. Now she was less enthusiastic. For one thing, she felt the woman's comments at the end of each afternoon caused trouble on the way home. Older students who had not heard the original words would fling them back at her, often in fine imitation of Frau Haufe's nasal tones.

More than that, however, Monika doubted that the woman truly knew art. In the entire month of September, the first year students had drawn nothing but circles and squares. Flowers had just been introduced. Certainly they should be further than that in their artistic development.

"No, no, friend Max. The petals are not straight lines like railroad tracks," the teacher scolded from the rear of the room. "They are gentle curves, you see. And what is this? Fingerprints? Monika has no trouble keeping her paper clean. Why cannot you do so as well?"

"Because we do not have French soap, Frau Haufe."

"It is not where soap comes from, but how close you put your hands to it, young man." The warning tone that adult patience was wearing thin crept into her voice. It was a relief to Monika that the ending bell sounded before either Max or Frau Haufe had further words.

She dug the chunk of chocolate out of her rucksack before shrugging its straps over her shoulders. The leather carrier, of which she had been so proud a month ago, was beginning to show signs of wear. Monika had done nothing that would damage the soft cowhide, but the older children often grabbed its flap closure and pulled.

When someone gripped the rucksack from the rear, it was hard to fight back. Monika sometimes had difficulty in merely maintaining her balance. One afternoon, she had tried putting the rucksack in front of her so that she could see its potential molesters before they struck.

"You can't do that, Monika," Heidi had corrected. "Everyone carries things on the backs."

"Mothers don't," Monika objected.

"That's different!"

But why should it be? Maybe how people carried things said what kind of value they placed on the objects. Babies were held in front. Vati's beautiful silver pots and bowls were borne on huge silver trays. Baskets of vegetables were slung over housewives' arms. And on the back, people hauled sacks of dirty potatoes, sugar beets, and trash.

"I won't walk with you unless you wear your rucksack right," Heidi threatened.

It seemed like a fine idea, and Monika clutched the container closer. Then she remembered Vati's caution to her.

"Be kind to Heidi. Her father may only be a forge operator, but Hans has it within him to be a great engraver. And it is not her fault that her mother is dead."

The warmth of the classroom had made the chocolate soft and runny. Chewing it quickly to avoid either having to share it with Heidi or endure Heidi's lecture on the treachery of East Germans who dealt in the black market, Monika managed to smear chocolate on the eyelet trim of her pinafore as well as on the corners of her mouth.

When she reached the playground, Heidi was swinging. The girl did not usually want to go straight back to the villa. Getting fresh air there meant running across the lawn, walking to the factory where the silver flatware was made, or exercising Bubi, the shetland pony. Heidi understood that fresh air was good, but she preferred getting it with a minimum of effort. Peter was at the slide. He usually walked home with or near them, although Peter was not friendly to Heidi.

Even after Monika explained her father's charge regarding Heidi, Peter was unmoved.

"Herr Groebel does not care what his bookkeeper's son does."

Monika joined the line for turns on the slide. Peter was climbing the ladder when she felt the jerk on her back again.

"Stop that." She turned to scowl at her tormentor.

"What can you do about it?" He was a tall boy, in the class of the oldest children. "Your wolf isn't here to chew my ass for you, little witch."

The only course of retreat for her was up the ladder to the top of the slide. Monika bolted for safety. But she was only partway down the slippery board when the tug came again. He was behind her and slowing her.

"Please," she screamed, letting loose of the handholds to try to reach him with her fists. "Let me go."

With a laugh, he obliged. Monika plummeted the few remaining feet, head leading so that she fell prone at the bottom. As the pain rocketed through her, she heard the cheers go up.

"Herbert hurt Monika," Heidi was screaming over and over. "Bad Herbert. Herr Groebel will get you. Bad Herbert. I will tell Herr Groebel."

"Be still, Heidi," one of the older girls snapped. "Some of you go and tell a teacher that Monika has had an accident. Sit up, Monika, and stop crying. The dirt will wash away, and the scratches heal."

As hands started to lift her, Monika let out a howl. The pain was so intense that she knew she was about to die. The light was fading. Her fear made breathing impossible.

"Be brave, Monika," said Peter quietly from the side opposite the pain. "I will bring your father."

Panting hoarsely from the exertion of running across the playground, Frau Haufe returned with the aid-seekers. Her breath was heavy with the residue of stale tobacco as she gasped her dismay.

"Poor child! Poor little child!"

"Don't touch me," Monika moaned, tensed against the great agony that helping hands seemed to mean.

"Who could be so cruel?" Frau Haufe demanded. "Who would do this to such a small child? To Herr Groebel's daughter?"

"Accident," the surrounding youngsters chorused. "It was an accident."

"Get out of the way!" Monika, still on her stomach across the throbbing arm, heard Frau Alma, the health instructor, order.

Gentle fingers rested on her elbow, then slid along the arm as she was lifted at the waist to make room for more extensive examination. Monika was surprised at how little pain there was as she was raised to her feet, her back firmly placed against the teacher's muscled thigh.

"It is broken, I think. Someone bring me an old sketch book and a towel."

"She is the Groebel daughter," Frau Haufe shrilled.

"That changes the pain not at all." The soft voice changed to near croon. "One more small hurt, liebchen, and then we shall be able to move you."

Monika stared through the distorting tears at the face bent over her from the rear. A white scarf failed to confine the teacher's curly hair. A few visible strands were flaxen, incredibly pale and beautiful. The woman's face, however, was long and bony. Its expression was deepest concern.

At last Monika was in the teacher's arms, her face pressed against the bib of a white apron that smelled of soap and sunshine. Now that her body was no longer shaken by her sobs and her arm was securely held, Monika felt her fear recede.

The cot in the health room was a lot softer than it looked. Between its comfortable embrace and Frau Alma's soft touch and speech, Monika gave in to her exhaustion.

As she awoke, both arms felt heavy. But when she opened her eyes, she realized all was right.

"Vati?" she managed, and wriggled the fingers of her right hand in his grasp.

"I have come," he told her, releasing his grip to brush her hair back from her face. "So has Hanna. I think we will go now. We three will ride together. Peter will take Hanna's bicycle back to the villa. Do you think he can manage?"

"Of course, he can." Monika managed with a misty smile. He had brought Vati and Hanna after all. And she and Peter had practiced bike-riding, the two of them wobbling all over the roadways of the estate.

"We of the staff regret this terrible accident greatly," Frau Haufe began as Vati raised Monika from the cot. "The instigator will be punished."

"There are some as would say she already has," Vati said cheerfully. "My young imp often acts and speaks before she thinks, especially around the young. We are, after all, a household of adults—I, my wife, and my elder daughter. Monika is the only child in our home."

"I have your rucksack," Hanna spoke, her voice tremulous. Monika was not surprised. Hanna often shed tears over her sister's cuts and bruises. How had they removed the sack from her back, Monika wondered before her sister added, "The straps can be resewn easily."

Hanna took her place in the rear seat of Vati's maroon Mercedes and reached out her arms to guide Monika's body into place across the cushions so that her upper torso and arm lay secure against Hanna's breast. With a nod, Vati moved to the driver's seat.

"Are we going to the doctor's?" Monika whispered to Hanna. "I don't want a shot like when I cut my hand."

"Of course, you don't, darling," Hanna agreed. "The doctor will make a statue around your arm. And then tomorrow, when you wake up, we will begin to paint it. All beautiful colors. Aren't you glad the hurt arm is your left? If it were your right, I'd have to do all the painting myself. But you are the artist of the family!"

From her place in the car, Monika would see little of the town except for the trees and a few high roofs. They would pass neither the Catholic nor the Lutheran Church on the way to the doctor's. Mostly the view seemed foggy, and it was hard to focus her attention past her throbbing arm.

When they came to the hip-roofed house where graphics proclaimed the residence of the town sign painter, Herr Wentzler, Hanna's grip on Monika tightened. Last spring and summer, the Wentzler son, Lars, came to the villa nearly every evening. Mutti would protest his presence as unseemly since the couple was not engaged.

"Lars can help to paint the statue on my arm," Monika suggested. But Hanna made no reply. Perhaps Lars was no longer Hanna's friend. Lars was very busy, of course, helping his father and brother. They were painting many signs. The Russians had ordered a large board painted where the roads entered town, telling about what good friends the Russians and the Germans were becoming.

After they halted at the curb in front of the doctor's home and office, Vati told the girls to remain in the car. A few minutes later, he came back.

"Frau Bindau says the doctor is out on calls. She will tell him that we need him at the villa," he reported.

"Maybe we should go on to Leipzig," Hanna suggested. "Cousin Kurt would be glad to take care of Monika at his clinic."

"Kurt is in Vienna at a medical seminar this week. I fear that we shall have to make do with Old Bindau," Herr Groebel replied.

"I want Cousin Kurt," Monika moaned, letting her pain show in her voice. "Kurt doesn't lie about things not hurting when he knows they will."

"Kurt is an excellent doctor, child," Vati agreed. "So he must use his time to care for badly injured boys and girls, little ones whose needs are beyond the Bindaus of medicine. Right now Kurt is learning how to be even better."

The ride in the car had not been exactly comfortable, but it had been calm. The same could not be said for next hour in Monika's bedroom. Under Herr Groebel's direction, maids were dispatched and returned with tea, aspirin, cold water, and a spoonful of sugar. Hanna fetched a vial from Mutti's medicine cabinet.

"To calm her little heart," Wera Groebel commented as she measured the tincture by drops onto the sugar.

After Monika had swallowed the medications and the tea, she lay quiet with her arm encased in cold compresses. The others hovered, maids whispering ominously until Vati's glare quieted them. Mutti sat next to the bed, her back as stiff and straight as the chair's. When Hanna changed the cloths on Monika's arm, Mutti winced.

"You do not think the arm will be crooked?" she asked her husband once again. "Or withered? It seems so swollen. And look how dark the skin is becoming."

"I would guess it is only a simple break," he told her, "much like Cook suffered last year. In a cast for perhaps a month. Then a week or so of stiffness. And finally, all forgotten."

"At least you will not have to peel the onions for me," Monika muttered. Mutti frowned at Monika's smile.

"Don't you recall, Wera?" Vati inquired. "Colonel Tamarov arrived early for the party, and you came directly from the kitchen to meet him? You had been chopping onions because Cook could not. And he immediately kissed your hand?"

Monika had to laugh, even though every movement was painful. From the top of the villa stairway, she'd had such a good view of the Russian trying gallantly to keep from sneezing after the unfortunate greeting. But her giggle ended in a groan.

"Do you think she is suffering greatly?" Mutti continued, her face stiff with concern.

"No," Monika injected herself into the questioning. It was as if Mutti had forgotten that she was present.

"Oh, but she is a brave girl!" her parent cooed.

"Here comes the doctor," Hanna announced from the window that faced the road. Her tone was laced with dismay. "Oh, Vati, he drives his pony cart. That means..."

"That means," her father cut her off, "that Doctor Bindau has been calling at the farms. The cart can go where his auto cannot."

"I don't want him touching Monika," Hanna protested. "Not when he is like that."

"I will meet him downstairs. The rest of you remain here." Vati's eyes swept the assemblage, stopping at one of the maids. "Except Marie. You bring coffee to the salon."

The maid's nod showed that instructions had been received, but she remained in place until the master had departed from the room.

"Coffee that is like a good man," she murmured to those nearest her. "Very strong, very dark, very hot."

Despite the coffee, it was nearly an hour before Dr. Bindau began treating Monika's arm. And it was another four days before she was sufficiently recovered to begin the task of decorating her cast.

Before that, Monika thrashed and moaned, remembering little except being moved from one side of the bed to the other as Hanna and the maids changed the sweat-soaked linens. Mutti came in from time to time to sing for her, soft sweet music from earlier years. But Hanna was there constantly as she always had been.

"Her little shoulder and her fingertips look so swollen," Mutti commented.

"They are. The cast was put on over swelling. It has continued, and that is why Monika is so miserable." Hanna sounded bitter.

"Dr. Bindau left some laudanum for her, in case the pain grew too great," Mutti reminded.

"That old poppy eater knows no other solution," Hanna scoffed.

"You are being uppity, miss," Mutti corrected her. "Dr. Bindau has tended many people in this town, and they are both alive and grateful."

"I'd prefer to call them lucky. We should never have permitted him to touch Monika."

When the cast was removed at last, four weeks later, it was apparent to all that Hanna was correct. Two of Monika's fingers were immobile and an enormous lump seemed to have grown just below the elbow.

"He even broke my beautiful cast when he took it off," Monika complained as they drove back to the villa after leaving the doctor's office.

"Is Cousin Kurt coming to dinner tonight?" Hanna wanted to know. The way she was biting her lip made Monika sure that Hanna, too, resented the practitioner's carelessness with their art work. It had been very pretty, even if Lars had not come to help paint the plaster.

Her week in Leipzig with Kurt was not nearly the fun Monika expected it to be. The family had accompanied her, and Kurt had indeed met them in the large entrance hall that was nowhere near as elegant as the lobby of the hotel where they sometimes went for Sunday breakfast.

"Do you really live here?" Monika asked doubtfully.

"That's the way it seems," Kurt grinned at her, lifting her in his arms. "Now let us see if we can find you a bed."

It seemed a silly thing to do in the middle of the afternoon. But it was much worse later, after Kurt had disappeared, and she learned that she was expected to stay in that bed.

"I will bring you a radio," a woman called Schwester Hahn offered. "You can have music to entertain you."

"When can I go to supper?" Monika eyed her suspiciously.

"Not tonight, I'm afraid. But tomorrow, for certain."

It was dark outside the window when Kurt came to see her. He obviously did not intend to stay because there was another man with him. Ignoring the stranger, Monika complained to Kurt about her hunger.

"Tomorrow, soon after you wake up, I am going to make your arm right," he explained. "No more hump. And all your fingers will move again. I'll even give you a new cast that you can paint. And because all this is going to happen so soon, you cannot eat tonight. Do you have other complaints, Fraulein?"

"The radio station is stupid," Monika said firmly. "I want to hear…"

"Right! We will change the station for you. Better yet, you can pick and choose for yourself." He brought the radio from across the room to the table next to her bed. "Schwester Hahn will bring you some medicine soon. It will make you ready to have your arm fixed."

The morning was dreadful beyond belief. Some men and women took her from her room without Kurt even knowing. They put her, covers and all, on a table that moved on wheels. In the hall, Mutti tried to stop them but they rushed on by her. Monika began to scream, for Kurt, for Mutti, for anyone who even cared a little. But all there seemed to be was a stinging in her shoulder and then that terrible cone covering her face.

She heard the people talking and knew they were near. It seemed to make sense, however, to keep her eyes closed. If she couldn't see them, then they might not be able to see her, either. And somehow she was sure that she had escaped from the terrible people and from that awful smell.

"Has there been nausea, Julia?" The voice seemed familiar.

"A great deal. But then you were much longer in surgery than you had planned, I think."

"It was very messy. I only wish I had been the one to handle it first. She is so little to go through such agony twice." Of course. It was Kurt speaking. The other might be Schwester Hahn.

"Was Dr. Bindau drunk that day?"

"On drugs, I think. Karl noticed no alcohol smell on his breath. Although this vodka of the Russians isn't as distinctive as our beers and wines," Kurt was explaining. "What he did to Monika was criminal!"

"You love your little sister very much, don't you?"

"God, yes. It is a miracle that she even exists."

Now that was odd. In the many times that Kurt had been at the villa—for Christmas and other holidays, for her birthday and Hanna's birthday and Vati's—he had never spoken of a younger sister.

"Does Monika know?" the woman inquired.

"We're only 'cousins,' Julia," Kurt spoke softly. "Karl paid for my university and my medical training. He still does something special from time to time. The seminar in Vienna was my birthday gift from him."

"Herr Groebel doesn't call you his son."

"Vatti has no sons," Monika piped, suddenly deciding that it was safe to be discovered. "But if he did and I had a brother, I would want one just like Kurt."

"Bless you, Monika," the young doctor smiled and bent to kiss her forehead. "As you can see, you have a brand new cast to work on, just as I promised you. Now what would you like for supper?"

Returning to school with Kurt's cast, beautifully decorated and supported by one of Mutti's handsome silk scarves, Monika discovered her classmates were glad to see her again. They had questions about her stay at Kurt's clinic and about the trip to Leipzig.

"My mother says that we might be able to go to Leipzig at Easter," the boy who sat in the desk behind her confided.

"The gardens are the prettiest then," Monika agreed before she realized that her classmate had not been to the city before.

"My brother goes to Leipzig every day," Heidi butted in. "I've been there a lot of times, too."

Monika pondered the status one received from a journey to Leipzig. Having been taken there almost weekly for as long as she could remember—to eat, to attend concerts and plays, to shop, and to visit Haus Groebel—she was hard-pressed to find anything remarkable about the short trip.

She was sure, however, that Leipzig and not her recuperation was the key. She had been back in class for a number of days after the swelling had subsided beneath Dr. Bindau's cast. No one seemed interested in her presence at that time.

Having missed a number of days made school more fun. The other first year students had increased their skills in her absence. Words to read and write were longer and more challenging; verses and phrases to memorize made more sense; numbers and processes were becoming more intricate.

Peter's lack of progress, however, puzzled her. He often stammered when called upon to recite. His papers would bear red checks on arithmetic problems much less complex than the pair of them solved at play.

"Why don't you give the teachers the right answers?" Monika challenged the boy one day after the two of them, with Heidi in tow, had turned into the estate grounds.

"Because he doesn't know them," Heidi answered for Peter. "He does not study hard enough. Hans makes me study for two hours every night so I know the right answers. It is the duty of all children of the German Democratic Republic to do their homework. How long do you study, Monika?"

Monika, already disgusted with her playmate's butting into a situation that did not involve her, stopped to glare at the child as if she was a mental deficient.

"There is nothing yet to study. But I will help you, Peter, if you want."

"I do not want," he muttered and trotted off toward the bookkeeper's house.

"Peter is a stupid boy," Heidi decided.

"He is not! He is my friend," corrected Monika. She stepped from the driveway to kick at a leafless tree.

Heidi stood waiting to continue to the warmth of the villa. Her face showed Monika that she did not realize the trunk had absorbed the anger directed at her.

"I wonder what treat Cook has prepared for us," Heidi said as Monika came to her side once more.

The following Monday arrived chill and grey, heralding a winter that was about to blanket the town and countryside with white. Lights burned ineffectively in the school room. The bulbs had been changed recently to conserve electricity. Brightness, the grammar teacher told his students, was wasteful.

The air was heavy with the odor of lunch being heated when the music master came into the classroom without his glockenspiel. Monika was surprised. He usually carried the instrument like a badge of office—the sword of a soldier, the hod of a bricklayer.

"This day will be special," Herr Schlauch announced, rubbing thin-fingered hands together. "Instead of singing together, each of you shall make music alone. Those who choose not to sing may whistle or hum. You may pick your own song. While you are considering what you will present for your classmates, let me remind you of the rules for a musician."

As he detailed standing straight, keeping hands under control, shaping tones and words, Monika tried to decide what she would do. There were, of course, the little tunes that Mutti had sung for her—first when she was a baby and more recently during her discomfort with her arm. But they were silly little things, melodic but without meaning. Better were the snatches of opera that Vati often bellowed with more enthusiasm than accuracy, even though he accompanied himself on the lacquered piano at the end of the salon. Those were, however, songs for men.

She was still undecided as the recital began. Herr Schlauch was selecting volunteers. The first selection was a poor rendition of one of Mutti's lullabies. The next was a plain chant by a boy who sang with the boy choir at the Catholic church. To her surprise, Peter's hand had shot up at the beginning. He sang third, a nursery tune about an egg.

After each performance, the master commented.

"You have a good voice, but you should not be wasting it on silly songs," he told Peter.

Monika knew she would receive no congratulations on the quality of her voice. Hanna usually stated, with laughter to take the edge from the sting, that her young sister sang lead monotone. But that thought gave Monika an idea. Her hand joined the forest of upraised arms, bidding for the master's attention.

She had to wait, however, for recognition. During the interval, she considered how fortunate it was that today she was wearing Mutti's lovely purple scarf for her sling. Her selection deserved purple, dark but vivid.

At last she was on her feet, straight-backed, with useful hand cradling the casted fingers. She waited for a moment for her classmates' eyes to turn to her. Then, with a deep breath, she began:

"Unter der Kaserne vor dem grossen Tor
Steht eine Laterne..."

Herr Schlauch came down upon her like a whirlwind, one hand hard against her mouth. The other grasped her uninjured shoulder.

"Students, get out your bowls and go to lunch," he shouted over the voices erupting throughout the room. "This troublemaker must be dealt with. We go to the principal."

She could feel anger flowing through his fingertips as he shoved her along the hall to the principal's office. She hadn't been sure Herr Schlauch was much of a musician and now she knew for sure. It was such a pretty song. It was historical, too. The woman who had made it famous was a world-renowned actress. But the music master obviously disliked it. She was sure the principal, who came from a wealthy family in Leipzig, would not feel the same.

"Monika must be expelled from school," Herr Schlauch told the principal after detailing the situation. As far as Monika could tell, he said nothing that was not fact. It was his conclusion that she could not figure out. "We cannot allow our young students to be exposed to her deviant influence."

"I find it hard to believe that the Groebels would allow this." The principal's narrow features had pinched in dismay at the beginning of the man's report. Now disgust had replaced the earlier expression.

"Yes, they would," the teacher insisted. "You must know that the chocolate she perpetually carries in her lunch comes from the Black Market."

"I think not. Herr Groebel's business takes him often to Switzerland."

"So he smuggles it in. That is no better."

The principal began to say something, then bit her lips.

"And if the Groebels buy Black Market goods and smuggle, it makes sense that they also listen to traitors to the German people on Radio Free Europe. They are enemies within our midst. This little one is poisoning our children with her filth."

"It is a song from the other war, 'Lili Marlene,'" the woman mused. "Perhaps…"

"It is the song of Marlene Dietrich, whose words and actions are filled with treachery against her own people," the musician insisted. "You know that."

The principal spread her hands in surrender.

"I will call Herr Groebel to come," she sighed. "You, Monika, will sit in silence in that corner until he arrives."

"Shall I wait with you to confront him?" the man offered.

"No, Herr Schlauch. Return to your duties. I am the principal. I shall do what is necessary."

What was necessary, in the end, was Monika's withdrawal from school. Vati had maintained a cold but proper attitude while in the principal's office.

Once he and Monika were in the Mercedes, its heater making the interior warm and comforting, he exploded.

"They take out on a child their hatred of me," he stormed. "My dear daughter, I am unable to protect you. A bad father for bad days."

"No, no, Vati," Monika protested. "You are so good and so strong."

"Not strong enough," he shook his head sadly. "And good cannot stand in these times."

"How could Monika have done as they claim?" Mutti demanded when she heard the story at the supper table. She had been visiting earlier in the afternoon so Vati had sent Hanna home from the silverware factory to supervise her young sister.

"Monika didn't know, Mother." Ever since Hanna had arrived home and heard about the scenes at school, she had been working hard to keep her laughter from showing. "We listen so much to Radio Free Europe. In fact, Kurt had to stop her from asking for it at the hospital because he had a Russian doctor with him."

"I should have paid more attention to Kurt's warning," Vati nodded at Hanna before turning to Monika. "Child, do you have any idea of what you did that was found objectionable?"

"Herr Schlauch didn't like the way I sang my song, I guess," she shrugged before reaching for the last biscuit in the roll warmer.

"You see?" Vati asked Mutti, speaking over Monika's head. She hoped they would talk some more about the trouble at school. The grown-ups, even Hanna, understood what was going on. To her, nothing of this day made much sense. Its high point had come when Heidi did not arrive after school was dismissed.

"Well, she wasn't getting much of an education," Mutti decided. "I didn't want her in class with all those children from the farm and factory families. If she weren't so young, we could send her to Hanna's school in Leipzig. The faculty there are not Russian lovers."

"After the holidays, we will get you a tutor, Monika," Vati promised.

"Perhaps Father Konrad would help her with her studies," Mutti suggested. "History and Latin at least."

"No!" Vati shouted, jumping to his feet so rapidly that his napkin dropped on top of his half-eaten strudel. "Wera, you keep him away from Monika. It is bad enough that he comes at all. If I learn that your papist pet so much as speaks to her, I shall let Harry have at his blessed tail."

"Please, Vati," Monika broke in. Usually she was content to let the adults talk over and around her, but this was too much. "Don't make Harry bite Father Konrad. Harry doesn't like being all bloody."

Herr Groebel swung his body toward her, staring at the earnest little face. Suddenly his laughter filled the dining room. Monika took a deep breath. Things were all right again, even if she still did not know what she had done that was wrong.

26

Chapter Two

Stille Nacht, Heilige Nacht

Vati and Monika made the trip to Leipzig on Christmas Eve morning so that Kurt could remove her cast. The silverware factory was closed, but Hanna elected to remain at the villa to help Cook finish cakes to be distributed to the plant workers' families. Mutti would be overseeing the maids in the last-minute cleaning of the salon. By noon, the estate's woodcutter would arrive with the family tree, and the round table near the piano had to be ready to receive it.

"We have shopping to do after we are finished at the clinic," Vati announced as the family left the breakfast table. "And when we are done, we will bring Kurt back with us."

A little snow lay on the ground, not a blanket but some camouflage. It didn't impede traffic, and the Mercedes surged through the town toward the center of Leipzig. Perhaps everything looked older in winter, Monika decided. This day the houses and stores they were passing gave an impression of eternity.

"Is Leipzig one hundred years old yet?" she asked. She thought it had to be because the city looked older than Oma Kohn who lived in the attic at the villa. Oma claimed that she was ninety-three.

"Ten times one hundred," her father laughed. "Leipzig is a very old city. That church over there has stood for eight-hundred years, even when bombs came down like rain. The university beyond Kurt's clinic is more than six-hundred years old. Many great men have studied and taught there. Many great people have come from here. The Russians took the best of Germany when they chose Leipzig so there may be no more greatness, at least for a while."

"There's you and Kurt," Monika assured him.

Her physician cousin was true to his word about preserving her cast. With a technician to help, he split the plaster into two neat halves and handed them to the attendant nurse.

"Please find a box for this item of beauty and put it on my desk," he instructed. "Fraulein Groebel wishes to keep it for posterity. And now, Monika, will you please wiggle your fingers?"

Although there was no pain, it was hard work to make them move. She grunted her hand into a fist, her face reddening with concentration.

"Enough, enough!" Kurt protested, laughing. "Now put the arm back into its sling so it can rest. Each day a little more wiggle, a little hard fist. But do not try to hurry things. Agreed?"

"We'll come back for you at two. Will that give you time?" Herr Groebel asked.

"Ample time, Karl, unless every child in Leipzig decides to celebrate the Christ Child's birth by breaking a bone," Kurt assured him. "I'll be waiting for your return."

Of all the treasures displayed at the Mart, in Monika's opinion nothing surpassed the candies. Best of all was the marzipan, formed in shapes of fruit, flowers, vegetables and breads.

Her store would sell them all. She had received the child-size structure on her fourth Christmas. As proprietor, she presided at the counter each day from Christmas to Twelfth Night, dispensing sweets to anyone with coin and desire. The varieties were displayed in small glass-fronted drawers of the cabinet behind the counter and were transferred by tiny scoop to a scale next to the cash box. After the purchase had been weighed, using jewelers' weights provided by Vati, it was slid into a miniature sack and given to the customer.

The first holiday of operation, she had earned the tidy sum of five marks, ten pfennigs. Each succeeding year, the proceeds increased under Vati's approval.

"Hanna for the factory, Monika for the shop," he would laugh. "Who needs sons when he has clever daughters?"

She knew that last year's profits could have been even greater except that twice she had given candy to Peter. There was no problem when the boy came to the house with Herr Walz. But Tante Walz had a tight fist. Vati, if he knew, would not have minded, Monika was sure. He had often altered prices on items at the shop when he knew that a customer's love for an item exceeded the contents of his or her purse.

"Not so many of the flowers and more of the fruits," she corrected Vati's choices at the marzipan stand. "Fruits sell better."

But Kurt's little sister would not be there, Monika was sure. Why did he not celebrate with the girl instead of at the villa? Perhaps he was not so good a brother as she had thought. Then Kurt grinned at her. And she didn't think any more about the girl she did not know.

Some things, Monika decided as she and Vati walked along, were changed by repetition. The terrible was not as bad, like having the second cast removed. The wonderful, on the other hand, also could lose its luster. But the Christkindlmart was different, its enchanted land of celebration bringing pleasure to every sense.

Vati and Monika were not unusual in making such a late visit. The area thronged with people who moved along shoulder to shoulder and often bumped abruptly against those who unwisely halted or attempted to change direction. There was further hazard to the children, who had to dodge the loaded shopping bags that grew larger with each additional purchase.

Monika had no fear of the crowd that often shut off her view of everything but overcoats and shopping bags. Her fingers were firmly interwoven in Vati's. When the need arouse, he sliced a course for them to follow through the mass of shoppers.

The purchase they would make Monika could already name. There would be tinsel of lead foil for the branch tips. They would also buy forty small beeswax candles to insert in the brass holders on the tree. When the candles were lit, the smell of honey would fill the entire salon.

She and Vati would choose cookies of various shapes and colors which, suspended from gilt cord, would be added to the Erzgebirge carvings to decorate the tree. They would purchase other candles as well, a set of larger white tapers whose heat would set the wooden tree with its Trachten-garbed figurines spinning.

"Before we buy too much, we should eat," Vati decided, glancing down to catch her anxious nod. "Sausage, I think?"

They never lost contact with each other as he turned toward the sausage stand. When the food had been paid for, she followed in her father's wake once more to a quiet corner where their shopping bag could be put down.

Monika bit tentatively at the crisp casing of the Weisswurstle. A less cautious approach could lead to a burnt tongue as the hot juices were released.

"You want to dip?" Vati held out the butcher paper adorned with a generous glob of hot mustard.

Monika extended the sausage to the paper with restraint. Grown-ups certainly did not have the feeling in their mouths that children did. It probably had to do with so many years of brushing their teeth. As if to prove her point, Herr Groebel thrust a large portion of sausage, covered with the golden condiment, into his mouth.

"Very good," he commented after a solid swallow. "That should keep us strong until dinnertime. And now I believe we must tend to merchandise for your store."

"It is your store," Vati shrugged. "You may determine the merchandise."

"There should be chocolate as well as marzipan," Monika pointed out.

"Alas, Fraulein, we have no chocolate," the vendor said sorrowfully.

"But we..." she stopped as Vati's grip tightened. "Cherries, not grapes, please. The maids always buy cherries. And some violets. And we need some brown rock sugar, too."

"For your store?" Vati's brows rose.

"For Bubi," she giggled at him. "It's his Christmas treat for pulling the sled when we take the packages to the workers on the estate."

"I had forgotten," he admitted, but his eyes were dancing, and Monika was sure he had not. He undoubtedly also remembered that Oma Kohn liked to suck on the hard candy. Oma, however, was never mentioned in public.

"May you have the finest Christmas ever," the man at the stand intoned when the candy had been packaged.

"Thank you," Monika grinned up at him. "It will be."

When their purchases at the Christkindlmart had been completed, Monika and Vati stopped at Haus Groebel to pick up Vati's presents for Mutti and Hanna. Monika solemnly took an oath of secrecy in exchange for a preview. She examined sapphire and diamonds, a necklace and matching drop earrings, and approved. Mutti adored blue. But the pearls, secure in tiny gold baskets, puzzled her. They had studs for pierced ears.

"Hanna is not yet twenty-one," she reminded her father. "You said she had to wait."

"I did." The sudden sadness in his eyes surprised Monika. "But waiting is not always possible. And our Hanna is growing to be a fine lady."

He forced a chuckle and put his arm about Monika's small shoulders.

"Just as you shall be. Now can we bid a Happy Christmas to the staff so that they, too, can be off to their homes?"

Holding Vati's hand, Monika went with him to the work room. He lifted her onto the long table that centered the room. Smiths and apprentices looked up expectantly. Vati squeezed her hand as a cue.

"Frohe Weihnachen," she intoned with a straight face, barely keeping from laughing at their surprised expressions.

The workers began folding squares of dark velvet around the pieces on which they worked. Each placed the cloth packet on a small tray. The procession to the vault took place under the watchful eye of an elder smith. As each employee passed Herr Groebel, a holiday wish was exchanged.

"We will be seeing you later this evening," Vati remarked as Hans Krieder made his wishes.

"Of course, Herr Groebel."

"Why will we see Hans?" Monika whispered after that workroom had cleared.

"Mutti asked him to come for the gift-giving so that he could be with Hanna," Vati told her.

"Why?" Monika repeated.

"Because the time has come when we must consider a husband for Hanna. Mutti and I feel that Hans is a good suitor. He has great talent. The designs he creates would be appropriate for silver flatware."

"But Hanna prefers Lars," Monika insisted.

"Lars is a sign painter and a younger son. Mutti feels he is not appropriate for Hanna." Vati shrugged as if he was not sure Monika would understand his explanation. "Hans will bring Heidi with him so that you and she can play together. Now that you are no longer in school, we must see that you still have time with your good friends."

She'd rather have Peter with her on Christmas Eve than Heidi, Monika thought as they moved into the front of the shop to speak with the sales staff. She was sure Hanna would prefer Lars.

The snow was sifting down slowly from a greying sky when they stopped at the clinic to meet Kurt. During the drive back to the villa, Monika nestled in a corner of the rear seat, surrounded by purchases and gifts.

Vati and Mutti were wrong. Hanna already loved Lars. Hanna had said so yesterday when Monika had watched the two of them together in the corner of the attic. But she hadn't told any member of her family. She couldn't. Mutti would disapprove of her spying while Hanna would probably skin her alive. Vati, of course, would be puzzled over why Hanna did not prefer her parents' choice.

Taking lunch to Oma had been Monika's task because Mutti was going out and Hanna was waiting for Lars to arrive with wreaths his mother made every year for certain of the village families. He'd come just as Monika started upstairs with Oma's tray. Their voices—Mutti's, Hanna's, and Lars'—had drifted through the hall and up the steps.

"The wreaths are lovely as always. Please put them in the wintergarten for now," Mutti directed, "and stop in the kitchen before you go. Cook has some stollen for your family."

A horn honked outside to punctuate her sentence.

"I'm coming, Karl," Mutti muttered. Monika smiled to herself. Mutti might sound obedient, but she would take another minute to readjust her silver fox stole in front of the hall mirror. She wondered if the animal's glass eyes could see how elegant he looked on Mutti's shoulders. There was a quick blast of chill air as the front door opened and shut again. It did not open again. Evidently the fox's tail had not been caught between door and frame. Last week it had, and he'd lost some fur as a result.

* * *

Mutti's departure was followed by silence. Monika was used to that. It meant that Hanna and Lars were kissing. With a grin on her face, she let herself through the entrance to the upper stairway.

The doorway to Oma's room was hard to open at any time. With the arm in a sling, it was nearly impossible, even after she set the tray aside. As the door cracked open, the heat of the room struck Monika's face. Poor Oma always wanted to be warm. It seemed like every day took more heat just to make her comfortable.

"Is it my lunch already?" The room was always dim, but Monika knew Oma would be in her chair, knitting. The old woman had to make the needles work by touch, Monika was sure. She certainly couldn't see the yarn.

The corner of the table by the chair had been cleared in expectation of her arrival so Monika was able to slide the tray along the surface. She reached up and pulled at the lamp's chain.

"So you can see what you eat," she explained as the woman rubbed her eyes.

"Thank you, child." Oma laid the knitting aside and examined the tray. "How good it all looks. You must thank Cook for me."

It didn't look that good, Monika decided, and Cook had been thanked many times over the years for the thick soups and mashed vegetables that Oma could eat despite her lack of teeth. Sometimes Oma talked about the days before she had come to the villa to live, before the war, when there was little money for food. Then Oma had gone without in order to feed her children.

"Will you wait while I eat?" Oma invited, gesturing to the chair on the other side of her circular rug.

Monika seated herself. Either Oma would ask her about what was going on downstairs, or she would tell a story about an earlier time. Whatever she did was fine with Monika. It meant she didn't have to do her arithmetic assignment until later.

"Has Wera bought new furniture?" Oma asked, her spoon halting above her soup bowl.

"No. Why?"

"The sounds," Oma explained, digging into the liquid once more.

Oma always heard sounds and most of them frightened her. Vati said that the old woman still listened for the sounds of trucks in the driveway and the clatter of boots on the stairs.

"Bad sounds?" Monika asked sympathetically.

"I don't think so." Oma pushed the soup plate away and pulled the pudding nearer. "Just sounds like the furniture in the attic being moved about. Perhaps the maids were sent up to clean?"

"Maybe you hear the pigeons coming in under the eaves," Monika offered.

The dessert spoon was pointed toward her, its bowl quivering in the ancient fingers.

"Those birds and I have lived up here too long together for me to mistake their noise. I heard furniture moving and a broom on the boards."

As if the spoon were a magic wand, a sneeze exploded on the other side of the wall nearest Monika. She jumped in surprise.

"There?" she gestured, dropping her voice to a whisper.

Oma Kohn nodded. She laid aside her spoon and signaled to Monika to come closer.

"Take down the picture," she whispered in Monika's ear. "There's a hole through which you can look. I made it myself."

Monika tiptoed to the picture and gently removed it from the nail. As she pressed an eye to the hole, she saw Lars disappearing into the door beside the linen closet. Maybe Oma was right. He and Hanna could be getting some holiday decorations from storage. She waited for him to reappear.

There were sounds again, over where the sneeze had come. She raised her head from the peephole and looked across the room to Oma.

"It's only Lars," she told her. "He must be helping Hanna get something from the attic."

"Helping?" Oma chuckled softly. "Is that what they call it now? Did you see your sister go into the storeroom with him?"

"No. But I can go and look."

"Better you sit down in your chair, and I will tell you a story."

Monika sat as instructed, her attention wavering between the tale the old woman was spinning and the faint sounds from the other side of the wall. When Oma dozed off, the story wasn't ended. Monika decided she was free to leave.

It was only when her fingers were on the latch of the storeroom door that she realized she could be interrupting a secret. An entire corner of the attic was filled with former toys of Hanna's. What if she and Lars were refurbishing a plaything? She decided to be extra quiet so as not to spoil their surprise. Keeping well back in the shadow, she tiptoed toward where she thought the earlier sneeze had originated. As a precaution, she pinched her own nostrils shut against the camphor odor that leaked from the linen closet.

Hanna's giggles stopped her mid-step. Whatever they were doing must be funny. Then Lars groaned. Perhaps he had hurt himself. Hanna let out a gasp. Maybe he was bleeding. Monika wondered if she should offer to help.

"Let me tell your father that we want to marry," she heard Lars speak. His voice sounded like he had a cold, too. "I want you with me like this always."

"Darling Lars." Hanna was hoarse, too. "I do love you. But I don't think Vati and Mutti will…"

Her sister was definitely catching Lars's cold, Monika decided. She could tell by the way Hanna was wheezing. And just before Christmas, too. But it served both of them right. There was no heat in this part of the attic. She was having trouble now keeping her nose pinched because her teeth wanted to chatter.

"Did you fix up this hideaway just for us?" Lars asked after several moments in which all Monika could hear was rustling. "A place to get away from the Little Mouse?'

"No, Lars. This has been my private place for years. I come up here whenever I want to be alone. Sometimes to read books that Mutti doesn't think I should."

"It certainly is private," Monika heard Lars admit. "But I want a wife, not a lover. Don't the maids ever come up here?"

"Of course, but I can hear them coming. Anyway, they usually stop at the linen closet. Besides, unless you stand up, no one can see you back here."

As if to prove it, Hanna came to her feet. From her hiding place, Monika could see her sister clearly on the other side of the stack of old furniture. Hanna's blouse was open to the waist and she was tugging her undershirt down into place. Hanna had to be crazy, Monika decided. She was shivering and Hanna was taking off her clothes. Suddenly she disappeared, laughing as she slid from view.

It was time to leave, Monika decided, waiting for an increase in the noise beyond the furniture to cover her movements. If she did not, she would either freeze or sneeze, or both.

Later in the afternoon, after Lars had left the house and Hanna had gone back to the factory, Monika crept back up the stairs and into the storeroom again. She edged around the furniture to inspect Hanna's secret place. It didn't look so very special, just an old mattress and some quilts.

She reported her discovery to Oma Kohn as she picked up the lunch tray. Oma nodded her head.

"Now that I know, I don't worry anymore," the old woman told her. "And you do not worry about Lars and Hanna being sick, either. They are all right."

Oma had been correct, Monika knew. Hanna had seemed very healthy at breakfast this morning. But she wasn't sure if her sister knew that Mutti and Vati planned for her to marry Hans Krieder. That was too bad if Hanna loved Lars.

Monika stared at the two men in the front seat of the car. Lars was definitely better than Hans. But Cousin Kurt was even a nicer man. Hanna should take him up to her private place.

The snow was falling steadily as they packed the sled with food gifts for the residents of the estate. Monika caught one large flake on the palm of her mitten and watched it melt. It was lovely, much finer than the Austrian crystal with which artisans at Haus Groebel worked.

Hanna and Kurt swung wicker baskets filled with tissue-wrapped stollen into the bright red sleigh. Vati slid the containers behind the seat and reached for more. There was so much more—rhubarb preserves and apple jelly in an assortment of glass jars saved all year for the annual giving, salted dried venison, dried and canned fruits, and Cook's marvelous pickles. At holiday time, everyone shared in the riches of the property.

Monika sat on the driver's seat, clutching Bubi's reins tightly in her right hand, as the grown-ups worked. The pony had no intention of going anywhere, but she was sure he felt more secure with a human in control.

On Christmas Eve, Bubi was always adorned in his best. His special harness had great silver bells on its straps. His headstall was laced with evergreens. Somehow Hanna had found time away from playing Cook's assistant to braid red ribbons into his mane. He shook his head impatiently. His finery danced and the bells dinged softly.

Kurt climbed up beside Monika and took the reins from her mittened hand. Lifting her up, he passed her to Vati's arms.

"Today I will be coachman," Kurt told her. "Bubi needs a driver with two strong hands, little one."

That wasn't true. Bubi could make the entire trip guided only by voice. But the driver's seat was very small. Monika was content to snuggle between Vati and Hanna with the fur rug pulled up to her shoulders. Its soft hairs tickled her nose, and the smell of mothballs that preserved the fur from one season to the next drifted into her lungs. She sneezed lustily. Vati's hand erupted from his glove to rest on her forehead.

"It's the camphor in the fur," Hanna told him, laughing before she, too, sneezed.

Bubi moved out briskly as they swung onto the road that led to the silverware factory. His bells jingled merrily and the sleigh's runners squeaked on the fresh snow. How nice it was, Monika decided as they passed through a grove of oak, that nature had decorated the trees that were outdoors, too. The orchards, however—apple trees on the right and pears on the left—were less beautiful. She shifted uneasily at the appearance of whitened skeletons reaching for the sky.

The sleigh stopped first at the woodcutter's tiny house. He must have heard the bells approaching because, woolen cap clutched in calloused fingers, he came out of the door before Bubi halted.

"The tree. Was it good?" he asked anxiously.

"Exactly what I would have chosen," Vati responded promptly. Monika frowned. She was sure Vati had not gone into the salon to examine the Christmas tree after their return from Leipzig.

Packages filled both of the woodsman's arms so Kurt climbed down to hold the cottage door ajar. Monika caught a glimpse of the fireplace and the heap that was the woodcutter's wife huddled nearby. According to Mutti, the woman was crippled by arthritis. Dr. Bindau stopped by regularly to treat her, then stopped at the villa for payment in coin and cognac for his efforts. Monika suspected that the woman would be better off to forget the old doctor and go to the baths as Mutti did.

From there it was down a slight slope to Peter's house. Here the four of them chorused a holiday wish in unison before Herr Walz, his sister, and Peter emerged. The horse's bells roused the chickens lodged in coops behind the house. Muttered clucking protested having their silence disturbed.

Tante Walz raised chickens for eggs so that she could have an income of her own. But Peter did most of the work, according to what he told Monika. Sometimes there was a turkey or two in a smaller coop, but not now.

Shadows lay about the silverware factory, its long single story seeming to sink into the snow. Metal rollo panels were closed over its tall narrow windows like eyelids shut for the evening. When the windows were covered and the doors locked, the manufacturing plant guarded its treasures well.

Outsiders coming to the estate upset every dog on the property, from Harry to the dachshund that snoozed on Tante Uschi Behlke's sofa. And the rollos were terribly heavy. Monika and Peter had discovered one not quite shut on a Sunday. In their efforts to close it, Peter's hand had been caught. It had taken all of their combined strength to ease it enough that his fingers were free. One nail had been black for weeks afterwards.

On the far side of the factory, six houses huddled together, facing each other, three on each side. When Kurt pulled Bubi to a halt, all six doors were flung ajar, and the tenants ran to the sleigh.

"Oh, look here," one woman pointed to the greasy stain on the tissue covering the stollen Hanna had placed in her hands. "So rich with butter. Such a good way to celebrate."

The road looped around the lake to the smaller factory. Here stockings were made and repaired.

"Have you heard more about the government taking over the plant to manufacture hosiery for Russian soldiers?" Kurt turned in his seat to look at Vati.

"Nothing this last month. But I have to believe it will come. Silk stockings had no place in the plan for a Communist Germany, I am sure."

Only five families lived near the stocking plant, but they provided a staff of sixteen workers. Husbands, wives, and older children all had employment there. These residents seemed pleasantly surprised at the sleigh's visit. Kurt remarked on it.

"Does Herr Mueller do nothing for the people?"

"No," Hanna supplied a flat answer. She had worked the repairing hooks during the summers of her final years in school. "He has a door that leads from outside directly to his office so that he does not even have to speak to his employees."

Vati lifted his face to the snow. In the dusk that was deepening about them, Monika could see his features in silhouette. He was exactly what he should be, she decided. Perfect nose and chin. Forehead straight, not sloped like many other men. As Kurt turned toward them again, she smiled. Kurt also had a good nose and chin, like Vati's. How lucky Kurt was.

"Don't unharness Bubi, Kurt," Vati instructed when they reached the villa once more. "I shall take the sleigh to fetch Johann and Uschi. There is no reason for them to bring out the car in this weather."

Vaulting over the sleigh's side like a young boy, he reached up to lift Monika down.

"In you go." He gave her a shove toward the steps. "Tell Cook to bring my grog to the hall. I need a little warmth before I set out once more."

"Can I tell Cook to give me hot chocolate?" Monika asked.

"You don't tell Cook anything, young lady," Hanna reprimanded.

"But you may ask," Vati chuckled.

Cook had supplemented Monika's requested drink with two cookies. It was with satisfaction and little appetite that Monika viewed the dining room from her place between Unkel Johann Behlke and Kurt. The placecard had originally been Hanna's, but while the rest of the family had been busy with the tree, Monika had shifted the markers.

Hanna did not need to sit next to Kurt. She could view him better from across the expanse of linen and silver and Meissen china. When the adults came to the table, Mutti's eyebrows rose to ask Vati if their younger daughter should be corrected. Monika had held her breath until a slight shake of her parent's head retained the status quo.

This was a good place to sit. The pyramid crèche sat on the sideboard, visible between Hanna and Tatne Uschi. Stepped layers rose from the carved holy family to the angels at the top. By turning her head just a bit, Monika could also see the tree at the far end of the salon. Tiny candies rose from each branch, awaiting the time when they would be lit.

"Do you need some help with that fish, Kleine?" Kurt spoke softly in her ear.

Monika's attention returned abruptly to the plate in front of her. A chunk of stuffed carp, oozing drawn butter and fragrant with majoram and bay leaf, filled half of her plate. She shook her head and picked up her fork. The fish was traditional for the Christmas Eve feast, and she could accept that. But the bones were a real challenge. Vati, of course, had removed the spine. Nonetheless, she had to take care.

With the tines of her fork, she began digging through the flaky flesh. Mutti was doing the same, but more elegantly. Her rings sparkled in the candlelight as she speared repetitively at the carp. The first year that Monika had been seated at the holiday table, Mutti had lodged a fish bone in her throat. Monika would still remember her own terror as Mutti, her face echoing the blue of her satin gown, rose from the table with such force that her chair overturned.

Both hands clutched at her neck as the woman ran from the room, followed by Vati and Hanna. Monika, left at the table with the Behlkes and the Muellers from the hosiery factory, had begun to rise, too. Tante Uschi stopped her with a soft hand on the shoulder and a smile that understood the child's anxiety.

There had been the sound of many feet hitting the stairs that rose to the second floor and then to the top story where the maids slept and Oma Kohn lived. Vati was shouting commands for Mutti to stop in her flight to find breath. Vati and Hanna finally returned to the table. Mutti had not come back. Several days later, Vati took Mutti to Leipzig so that doctors could remove the bone. And it had been ever so long before Mutti could sing again.

Satisfied at last that the fish was edible, Monika popped a piece into her mouth and, just to be sure, chewed it with care. She didn't really like carp. And she certainly did not wish to do as Mutti had done, vomiting out of an attic window.

The Pechamel Kartoffel looked more inviting. She turned her attention to the potatoes, piling capers that flavored the white sauce alongside the three small bones her digging had unearthed. Vati had sliced roast duckling by then, and the other diners were passing plates to him.

Monika did not. Christmas Eve dinner, always the same, had little to recommend it. She could have made a meal of croissants and honey, but not this evening. After the grown-ups had eaten their fill, the family and guests would move nearer the tree where the maids would serve apfelstrudel laced with heavy cream. Hanna, had memories to relate.

"Do you remember that year after Monika was born?" her sister asked the other diners. "There were Colonel Hoffman and his staff officers who insisted on eating with us. And Oma Kohn upstairs knocked over the Menorrah and started a fire?"

"Kurt saved us that time," Vati laughed, raising his goblet of Liebfraumilch toward the guest. "He ran out ahead of me and the soldiers to pull coals from the kachelofen in Monika's room so that the rug was scorched. The officers were so busy saving our baby and reprimanding her nurse that they never realized anything was happening above their heads."

"And, at this very time, the nursemaid is probably pouring coffee from the silver service Karl gave her for taking all that abuse," Onkel Johann chuckled before turning serious. "But what are you going to do about Oma Kohn? Is there no one to whom she can go?"

"As far as I can discover, she is all that remains of the Kohn family," Vati told him. "And she is as fearful of the Russians as of the Nazis. At ninety-three, one does not change opinions or places easily. To move her out of the attic would probably kill her. I owe her dead husband, who taught me my trade, more than that."

"And she should live many more years," Kurt added. "Oma's health is remarkable. I give her pills for her arthritis and so that she can sleep regular hours. But, considering she had not been out of the attic for more than fifteen years, she does well."

"We have persuaded her not to burn the Menorrah candles except when someone is with her," Mutti explained to Onkel Johann. "The girls go up each day at sunset and sit there while she lights the candles. After she has finished her dinner, Hanna extinguishes the flames."

"Since you are not even making an attempt to clean your plate, Monika, I suggest you go to Oma now," Vati instructed. "Cook will have her tray ready. Get a maid to carry the tray up the stairs. One of us will come later to light her candles."

"Please excuse me," Monika spoke on cue, smiling at the opportunity to be freed from the meal.

She entered the kitchen where Oma's tray lay on the counter, covered by a towel. Marie reached for it as Monika bounded in. At the same time, the knocker on the front door sounded. Marie glance at Cook.

"You had best answer it," Monika sighed. She was sure that Hans had arrived with Heidi in tow. Of course, they would come in time for dessert and perhaps a little earlier in case an invitation to the table would be given.

Maybe Vati thought that Hans would be a good factory manager with Hanna to guide him, but Monika was sure he was wrong. She could envision Hans giving sharp orders to the workers, making them angry and edgy, and then going home to criticize the way in which Hanna kept their house.

The rock sugar that she and Vati had purchased earlier in the day sat in a bowl near Oma's tray. Poor Oma's holiday menu consisted only of mashed vegetables and flaked fish. She would enjoy having some sugar, too. Monika took a handful and shoved it in a pocket.

"It was the young apprentice from Leipzig and Monika's little friend." Marie's report fulfilled Monika's expectations. "Herr Groebel asks that a place be set at the table for each of them."

Cook's mutter was low, but it brought a smile to Monika's lips. The Swiss woman was very perceptive.

Monika led the way up the stairs past the floor on which the family bedrooms lay. She held the entry door to the attic with care so that Marie could go through. But her nose already detected bad news. The Menorrah had been lit without anyone in attendance.

Quickly they moved past the doors to the linen and storage rooms and halted at the old wardrobe that disguised the entrance to Oma's area. Marie placed the tray in Monika's hands and fled.

The servants all knew that someone lived in the area, but they protected themselves by not seeing the occupant. One former maid had been positive it was Herr Groebel's insane brother. Another, clinging to the town superstition about Monika's beginnings, had determined that it was Frau Groebel's real baby, deformed and monsterous.

Peter heard these things in the kitchen when he brought the eggs, and related them to Monika. But no one, Peter included, talked about the attic resident outside of the villa walls. To do so would bring immediate separation from the estate and Herr Groebel's generous care.

Sure enough, the area was lit only by the blazing Menorrah. The room's quiet was punctuated by wheezing snores. It was not hard to find the table, even in the gloom. Once the tray had been placed, Monika reached for the lamp chain. Oma was curled in her highbacked chair, her head tilted against its cushions. Vati would have to be summoned. Monika was not allowed to blow out the candles.

Unfortunately the party was still in the dining room when Monika came downstairs. Heidi was occupying her place between the two men. Hans had a chair between Hanna and Tante Uschi. Both Krieders were eating silently and quickly in their attempt to catch up with those finishing the final course. Monika ducked around the table to Vati's side. Standing on tiptoe, she whispered her message about Oma while Kurt watched alertly.

"Please excuse me," Vati rose. "Monika tells me that a maid has broken a bottle of cognac. I shall have to bring another from the cellar."

"Allow me to come with you," Kurt spoke immediately. "She may have cut herself."

"Shall the rest of us move to the salon for coffee and dessert?" Mutti asked as soon as the men were gone. Onkel Johann nearly leaped to the back of her chair. Monika grinned at the floor. In an attempt to cover the disruption caused by the early guests, the family and close friends were creating a scene this night that was nearly as dramatic as the one that Hanna had related.

Monika's fingers touched the rock sugar that Oma had not received. It was no problem. There was plenty more for Oma. Perhaps Bubi could have the treat before he had to pull the sleigh to take Onkel and Tante home.

By the time that they had all found seats in the salon and Cook had brought the coffee service, Vati and Kurt returned. The adults, including Hans and Hanna, had coffee and alcohol along with their dessert. Monika and Heidi ate their apfelstrudel, using a low cabinet top for a table. Like the pair that flanked the immense crimson sofa on which Tante, Hans, and Hanna sat, it was glass-sided to protect the precious Meissen figures inside. Cook had spread a napkin over the surface before placing the girls' dishes.

"Be careful of the glass," Monika cautioned Heidi between mouthfuls. "Mutti's figurines are very valuable."

"What good are they?" Heidi inquired, running her fork around the empty plate and licking the tines in hope of finding more cream. "You can't play with them."

"Mutti likes to look at them. She won't let anyone else dust them."

"I dust all of our house," Heidi stated proudly, holding up her plate as Cook arrived with second helpings.

Of course, she did, Monika thought. The Krieders had no maids at all, not even a cook.

"But I think your mother's dolls are stupid," Heidi continued as she attacked the new serving. "Hans says they are obs...obstinant."

"Obsolete," Monika supplied with a grimace. That was an odd word, but she had heard Hans use it when he was talking to Hanna. Hanna didn't seem to like the word, either.

"That's right." Heidi nodded as she chewed. "You're the one that's obstinant."

"Be quiet!" Monika put up a hand to halt her companion's speech as Vati and Kurt began lighting the candles on the tree. Even Kurt had to stand on tiptoe to reach the highest lights. When all the candles burned, turning the cookies and the Erzgebirge ornaments with tiny trees stamped on the bottom to fairyland objects, Hanna went back to the dining area and returned, carrying the crèche pyramid. The hush continued as she placed it beneath the tree. Behind her came the maids and Cook.

When every adult held a glass of spirits, Vati stood up and took his place next to the tree. He raised his glass high above his head. Monika scrambled to her feet and motioned Heidi up, too.

"To Christmas and the great gifts of family love and friendship," Vati announced and drained his glass.

The spirits were replenished. Kurt took Vati's place.

"To Karl, filled with generosity, and Wera, filled with grace."

As the round of toasts continued, the adults contented themselves with only a swallow at each salute. It was finally Hans's turn.

"To our friends, the Russians," he intoned.

Mutti and Tante were pale as they sipped the champagne. Vati and Onkel brought their glasses to their mouths but did not drink at all. Kurt, standing out of Hans's view, was motionless. Monika spun around, hoping that Heidi had not seen or understood the gestures. But Heidi had disappeared.

Trying not to call attention to herself, Monika moved slowly away from the cabinet, looking first behind the red couch, then the horsehair settee. Fortunately she was not there. There were presents, however, stacked beneath disguising sheets. She finally found Heidi on the far side of the piano. The Christmas store was back there, stocked for the sale that would begin the next morning. Heidi was inspecting the merchandise, opening drawer after drawer. Unaware that she was being observed, she removed a piece of marzipan shaped like a miniature loaf of bread and dropped it into her pocket.

"Put that back," Monika ordered, and the girl spun toward her.

"I want it," Heidi retorted.

"The store will be open tomorrow. Come back then with your pfennig."

"Where will I get a pfennig?" Heidi pouted. "Do you think Hans will give me coins to buy capitalistic candy?"

Monika considered. It seemed highly unlikely. But that didn't mean Heidi could steal what she could not buy.

"Anyway, if I don't get the little bread loaf, I will tell Hans that Kurt did not drink to the Russians. And he'll tell…"

"Take it, thief! But that's all." Monika stalked away. "Come on. It is time for the gifts."

This was another of those points at which formal tradition controlled adult movements. Monika would have to wait for her presents. Knowledge that they would surpass her dreams did little to dispel her anxiety. Vati placed the rectangular case that held the necklace and earrings in Mutti's hands.

All three women gasped as the candles lit fires inside of the gems.

"Liebling," Mutti murmured as she raised the stones in her fingers. "Please."

He took the gems from her and looped them around her neck, deftly fastening the clasp. Her hands lifted the drops to her ears.

A round of applause told her how well the gems were set off by her gold lamé gown as she rose and crossed to the mirror. A glance was sufficient to satisfy her. She acknowledged their appreciation with a wide smile. As she returned to her chair, she stopped to lift the envelope and the ornate round tin that had been placed in the seat during her absence.

Mutti's fingers worked quickly, prying the lid from the tin. She murmured with delight at the Lebkuchen shapes inside as if she did not receive the same treat each year. Lifting a star from the selection, her long nails picked off the opaque obladen and deposited it in an ash tray. She bit a point from the star, then smiled.

"It's delicious," Mutti proclaimed, passing the tin to Uschi Behlke. "You must each have one."

When it was Vati's turn, he took a bell and ate it all.

"Why do you always remove the obladen, Wera?" he inquired, his eyes sparkling. "It's the same recipe that is used for your beloved wafers at Mass."

Mutti frowned at him before turning her attention to the envelope in her lap. Eagerly she tore at the flap.

"Ah," she breathed her pleasure. "We are to go to Zurich in the spring. All of us to shop!"

Monika caught Hans's expression as it changed quickly from disgust to expectation when Mutti's hand slipped between cushion and chair to retrieve her gift for Vati. As the couple again exchanged kisses, Monika felt sadness for Hanna. She was sure that, if Mutti and Vati insisted that her sister marry Hans, Hanna would never get to go to Zurich again.

"Hans engraved it for me," Mutti smiled across the room at the boy.

"And a fine job he did," Vati responded. "My journeymen will have to look to their laurels. That Greek key motif would make handsome flatware, I think." He passed case to Onkel Johann who also nodded approval.

The gifts for and from the Behlkes were exchanged next. Monika squirmed in place to get a better view of Heidi. She would not let her get to the store again.

"If Hanna does not mind, I think the little ones should see their gifts next." Mutti had caught the movements and looked at her elder daughter for agreement.

And so Heidi had a doll with porcelain face and hands to occupy her arms. Monika held a toy kangaroo, designed by Steiff, with a baby tucked in its pouch. Her fingers clutched one side of the head, then the other, discovering the button in its left ear.

"This is Kengi," she announced proudly, "and that is Rooey."

"Every good kangaroo needs a place to sleep," Mutti declared. "Look behind the sofa where Tante is seated."

Kurt met her there, waiting until she had lifted the sheet to reveal the canopied crib.

"It is just like Hanna's," Monika exclaimed as Kurt carried it to where the girls had been sitting.

"It was Hanna's," her sister told her. "Mutti and I refurbished it for your Kengi."

"Are you sure?" Monika gave Hanna a doubtful look. It was so beautiful with its organdy and lace.

"Positive! But I won't give you my dolls. I'm keeping them for my daughters."

Monika ran to Mutti, then to Hanna, hugging them both. When she got back to her corner, she looked more carefully at the bed. Heidi's doll stared wide-eyed from the pillow.

"Take your doll out," Monika whispered.

Heidi only shook her head and looked meaningfully at Hans.

Monika played with her stuffed toys, trying to ignore Heidi. There were only so many times that one could wake up the doll and put it back to bed again. Above their heads came Hanna's shriek of happiness over the earrings and the realization that finally she could have her ears pierced. It was followed by a quick fashion show as Hanna modeled the grey coat with Persian lamb trim that Mutti had given. With it she wore the black leather gloves that Mutti had insisted Monika choose for her sister and a Persian lamb muff from the Behlkes.

"What do you think?" Hanna inquired of Hans. "Am I not elegant?"

"You are beautiful, of course," he responded. "And they will wear well, I think. Now I will give you something which I crafted especially for you."

Hanna had just removed the coat and its accessories, laying them carefully over the back of the sofa when the knocker sounded. Marie bobbed off to answer the door. Hanna's fingers were pushing back the tissue that surrounded Hans's offering. But the package dropped beside her, momentarily forgotten, as Marie came back into the room.

Lars had not even paused to remove his coat. Snowflakes sparkled on his shoulders. His arms were filled with something over which a snow-laden quilt had been draped. As he came nearer, the covering slid away and Hanna squealed with pleasure.

The chest the young man held was red lacquer with brass trim. The lid became visible as he placed the box at Hanna's feet. Ornate golden letters spelled her name. Tears were sliding down Hanna's cheeks as, one by one, she opened the three drawers. The sweet odor of cedar wafted upward to blend with the other holiday smells. And suddenly she was in his arms, hugging Lars to her as if he were earth's last handhold.

"I thought..." she began

"I know what you thought," he interrupted, carefully removing her hands from his shoulders. "But I don't know any other Hanna to whom to give it. Good evening, all."

His dancing eyes swept over all of them, resting briefly on Hans who had turned as red as the chest.

"And good night. I must return to my family's celebration."

"Stop by tomorrow," Vati invited as Lars headed for the door. "We'll share a cup of grog."

"I shall," Lars promised, beaming broadly. "I have a matter I'd like to discuss with you."

"And bring money for my store," Monika chirped after him.

"That will be perfect for your lingerie," Mutti decided. Hanna managed to nod her agreement. As if in a trance, she kept opening and shutting the drawers of the chest.

"I doubt Lars meant it for such intimate use," Vati frowned darkly.

"Then I'll use it for gloves and mittens and scarves," Hanna announced airily. As if to prove her point, she placed Monika's gift gloves inside.

The silence suddenly grew awkward. Finally Tante Uschi delivered the cue.

"You were about to show us Hans' gift, Hanna."

The tissue fell away to reveal a hair brush backed in tortoise shell. Intertwined initials, HBG, were worked in inset silver.

"So that is why you have been so careful with the leftover bits of metal," Vati commented. "It's been since last spring that you have been saving, hasn't it?"

"Master Luchs said I might." Hans seemed surly as though he was being accused of theft.

"I know that, son. Is it not lovely, Hanna?"

"Oh, yes. Lovely."

The pleasure was forced. The others smiled, but Monika knew her sister too well not to recognize the stilted tones. Anyway, why did Hanna need an old hair brush of shell? She already had the complete dresser set that had been Grossmutter Babette's. And it was all silver.

"Come here, child," Vati called to Monika. When she was standing at his knee, he gave her that enormous smile that she loved so well. "Take your sore arm out of your sling for a moment."

Monika glanced at Kurt who nodded approval. Slowly she drew the sling away from her arm and extended it stiffly to her parent. And as she watched, the most beautiful wrist watch she had ever seen encircled the pale swelling. Its face was round as the moon in a golden case. There were only four numbers, but she knew them and what went between. The band was plain black leather, shining and elegant. She tried to raise her arm to her ear, but had to compromise in order to hear its ticking.

"It is a Piaget?" Tante Uschi asked in amazement.

"Yes. A very special one," Vati explained with pride. "It is their newest model. The stem sets the watch, but there is no winding. An average sort of daily exercise will keep it wound."

Monika passed from person to person, showing off her new treasure. Kurt was the last one to view it. He leaned toward her and lifted the arm back into its support.

"For the next week or so, you must take your arm out of the sling each day and swing it back and forth so that the watch will we wound." He demonstrated the motion. "Can you remember to do that?"

She nodded.

"My wife and I have something we wish you to have, Hans," Vati walked across the room to the couch, extending a book to the young man.

Hans examined the cover, a line deepening between his eyes. He opened it and stared at the title page.

"Goethe was corrupt, a toady of royalty."

"Nonetheless Hegel and Marx found great inspiration in his works." Vati's voice was suddenly frosty.

"Sir, you are incorrect." Hans was on his feet, glaring at his employer. "You allow your mind to be filled with the insanities of the enemy. I suppose Radio Free Europe told you that anathema."

Everyone in the room had fixed attention on the two of them. But Vati made no reply. With a gesture of contempt, Hans threw the book to the carpet. It spread open. His foot came down hard on the binding. Monika thought the sound of its rip was one of the most horrible things she had ever heard.

"Heidi. We must leave this place." Hans extended a hand toward his sister.

Mutti rose, regal and tight-lipped.

"I will see you to the door."

"I also," Kurt was on his feet.

"Thank you, Kurt."

Monika tagged after them into the hall. Heidi was, after all, supposed to be her guest.

Kurt drew the door open. The snow had stopped and the very air seemed to be filled with ice crystals. Helping Heidi into her coat, Mutti glanced outside.

"Monika, have Marie bring down your coat from last year. Heidi will need the extra warmth. And a blanket as well to wrap her. Otherwise the child will freeze in the motorcycle's sidecar."

But when the maid brought the garments, Heidi would accept only the blanket.

"My sister does not wear hand-me-downs," he said stiffly. "I shall return the blanket to the shop after it has been laundered."

"Do you think it is safe for the child?" Mutti asked as the motorcycle moved noisily up the road.

"I don't know, Wera," Kurt replied sadly. "It would seem that she could be in no more danger from the weather than from her family."

Monika could not help but feel sorry for Heidi as she went back to the doll bed, now vacated and awaiting Kengi's retiring. The ice would be sharp against her face. Maybe it would even cut the skin and make her bleed.

But then she didn't care anymore. If Heidi experienced pain, she deserved it. As she reached into Kengi's pouch so that Rooey could share the crib's pillow with his stuffed parent, she found that the small toy had disappeared. In its place was the bread loaf made of marzipan.

Chapter Three

✴ ✴ ✴

Going the Way of the Sun

"What's 'Go West' mean?" Monika paused in her work and turned to Cook. They were alone in the kitchen, Mutti having recruited the maids for duties in the salon. Hanna was supposed to be helping, too. Fat chance of that!

"Keep shaking," Cook ordered.

Obediently Monika put the sack containing powdered sugar back in motion once more. The doughnuts, fresh from the frying fat, thudded inside.

"What does it mean?" she repeated. "Lars' brother, Ludwig, went West the day after Christmas."

"At night the sun sinks in the West," Cook commented as she stirred the browning circlets with a wooden stick. Deftly she speared several through their holes and turned their cooked sides up. "Going West is going the way of the sun."

"Why did he do that?" Monika opened the bag and removed the contents, laying each doughnut gently on the cooling racks.

"Perhaps he wanted to seek his fortune." Cook dropped six doughnuts into the empty sack while Monika licked sugar from her fingers. "Quickly now!"

"Ludwig didn't need a fortune," Monika moved the bag briskly.

It was good to have the sling off for a while. And all this motion was winding her beautiful watch. Kurt said that shaking doughnuts would help to bring the color back into her arm. Its skin had been sadly white when the cast was first removed. "He would have had the Wentzler business. Now

Lars will be the master painter when his father grows too old. I'll bet Lars won't go West."

Cook laughed without missing a sweep through the chattering grease.

"I think going West is far from his mind at the moment. Getting a wife is what he thinks of."

"And that will be Hanna."

That brought Cook to a temporary halt.

"Little pitchers have big ears?" she asked softly.

"Do they?" Monika tried to remember a pitcher with ears. Perhaps that meant the handle, but the pitchers in the Groebel house had only one. "I don't know. But you should see Lars and Hanna. They were in the attic storeroom before Christmas, kissing and hugging in Hanna's hiding place. She had her blouse open and her undershirt pulled up. But it was very cold up there. She shouldn't have been that hot."

"She certainly shouldn't," Cook bent her head over the pan. "And you should not have been spying on her. Now, when you get those on the rack, put that sack aside and use the cinnamon and sugar instead. Or is your arm getting tired?"

Shaking her head, Monika changed sacks and stood in readiness to receive the new batch.

"Is it a crime to 'Go West'? Peter says his uncle and some Russian soldiers went to the Wentzlers' house and they took Herr Wentzler to the barracks. But they didn't put him in prison."

"The Russians wanted to know what Ludwig took with him, I would imagine," Cook supplied information and doughnuts simultaneously.

"Hanna says Ludwig took nothing except what he wore. He couldn't go West naked, after all."

"But he took his youth and what was in his head," Cook reminded. "That's what the Russians do not like. Workers are important to Germany."

"What if you went West?" Monika asked. " Would Peter's uncle come here and take us to the barracks?"

"I go West every summer when I visit my family in Basel. But the Russians have no use for old women."

Then why didn't Oma Kohn go west? Monika wondered.

"Will Lars marry Hanna tonight?" she asked. "Vati has invited the Wentzlers to Sylvesterabend."

"No, child, not tonight. Marriages take time. But there might be a surprise, just the same."

"I hope Hanna doesn't get hot while all the guests are here. Even the Muellers are coming, you know," Monika peeked into the sack to see if the doughnuts were coated properly. Pleased with her work, she moved to the racks. "Frau Mueller doesn't like to see women with their blouses open. She says it upsets her stomach. Wouldn't it be funny if she threw up all over the floor?"

"Your arm is tired," Cook declared. "Put it back in the sling and see if your mother needs you to run errands."

On her way out of the kitchen, Monika captured one of the cinnamon-coated confections. They always tasted so much better when they were still warm. If she ever had a Sylvesterabend party of her own, she'd have Cook fry the doughnuts after the guests came. Each person could have a bag of sugar to shake. And everyone would say it was the finest time ever!

As she came down the hall, she could hear Mutti giving instructions. The rugs had been rolled and the maids were tugging the heavy Persians to a hiding place behind the sofa, according to the directions she could hear. In a minute, they would begin waxing the floors so that the guests could dance. The heavy buffer, pushed around by its long handle, would whoosh across the boards until you could see yourself when you looked down.

"Hanna!" Mutti called sharply. "Can you not even fasten the streamers properly? We do not have the entire day to spend. Otherwise we will end up meeting our guests in work clothes."

Monika peeped through the double doors just to make sure Mutti was overstating the case. She doubted there was even one house dress in the big closet that held Mutti's gowns. Certainly there were no aprons, no smocks.

The aqua crepe frock Mutti wore wasn't new, nor were the shoes with narrow ankle straps and high heels. But then Mutti wasn't working either, just giving orders. Now her head turned to the door.

"Don't come toward me, Monika. Sit in the corner by the piano until the floors are done."

Monika didn't need to be told that the doughnut was verboten beyond the doorway. She swallowed the piece that remained before crossing to the little chair by the window.

In her mind, she could see that scene that had upset Frau Mueller so much. Ordinarily the Frau's outspoken opinions were accepted with grace within the villa. She was, after all, the wife of the hosiery factory manager, and that gave her prestige. But that day she had gone too far. Not that the Groebels had laughed in her face, but there had been many references to the incident later.

Guests had gathered for an afternoon party. Spirits had been high for the war was over and the Russian occupation was not as bad as had been anticipated. Mutti had been seated on this same fragile chair with Frau Mueller occupying the majority of the settee opposite. In the remaining space, sixteen-year-old Friederich Mueller, face expressionless, sat erect with elbows pinched to his sides.

Monika had been over by the dining table, picking chunks of liquor-soaked fruit from abandoned punch cups. But the goodies hadn't satisfied, and her stomach felt uneasy. And so she darted down the length of the room to her mother.

"Milch, bitte?" she requested when Mutti's attention fell on her.

Without missing a word of the conversation, Mutti opened the bodice of her dress. Pressed against her mother's firm thigh with perfume rising from the warm body, Monika took a firm grasp on the proffered nipple and nursed. The warm liquid filled her mouth as Frau Mueller had erupted. First Friederich had been sent off to join his father. Then the tirade had begun.

"But, Gertrude, I have had to nurse her," Mutti protested, completing an expressive gesture by placing a ring-bedecked hand on the child's head. "There was no extra animal milk when she was born. Even now we are allowed to keep only enough for cooking. And she is so small. I make her bones strong with cod liver oil and myself."

After insisting that her son had never before seen a woman's bare breasts, Frau Mueller had gone bustling off to another part of the room where her appetite would not be put off by the sight. Looking back, Monika suspected that, in defiance, Mutti had kept her at the breast longer than necessary. Afterward Vati had said that if it were indeed Friederich's initial experience with female anatomy, he could not have had a finer beginning.

Monika wondered how Frau Mueller felt now that the factory had been taken over by the estate. Herr Mueller was still the manager, but a Russian efficiency man stood at his shoulder, Vati said. And the product, which had been the first fine silk hosiery for women and then, during the war and after, cotton stockings and stocking soles, would now be hosiery for soldiers. Vati and Onkel Johann would not share the profits anymore, of course, but at least they still had the silver factory. Vati said it would be a while before the Russians figured out a way to use silverware to stand off their enemies in the West.

"Monika!" Mutti called sharply. "Go to the dining table and hold the streamer ends for your sister. She's in another world today, and either the lamp is going to fall or we will have crepe paper in our punch."

Whether or not Monika's intervention made any difference, she was pleased to find that both lamp and streamers stayed in place as the evening's festivities began. Hanna's announcement that she would attend church services with the Wentzlers brought a storm of protest from Vati.

"Isn't it bad enough with the Russians trying to tell us how to think and act during the week?" he demanded. "Do you have to give the pastor the same right on Sundays?"

"But the Wentzlers always go to the Sylvesterabend services," Hanna protested, pushing the stud onto the post protruding through her newly pierced ear.

"The Groebels do not!" he bellowed.

"Perhaps she is to become a Wentzler," Monika suggested softly as Mutti straightened her sashes. Vati whirled quickly.

"Is that the way it is?" His eyebrown quirked. "I suppose it is possible now that Lars stands to inherit what was Ludwig's. And the matter of Hans is settled. But the young man and I have not reached an agreement."

"Why did you invite the Wentzlers to the party?" Monika inquired.

"I think you have been found out," Mutti laughed lightly. "I hope you and Lars do work things out. When we go to Zurich, we might…"

"Oh, no!" Hanna screamed and jumped back from the mirror. "My earring."

Vati moved quickly toward the chest above which the reflective panel hung. Monika scrambled after him, untying the sash whose ends remained in her mother's hands. In a moment she was reined to a halt.

When Vati tipped over the vase that rested atop the chest, the pearl cam rolling out. So did a string of jet beads with a suspended silver cross. He handed the first to his daughter and the latter to his wife.

"At least the Wentzlers are not Papists," he growled as he left the room.

Monika was delighted with both herself and her home when, at 9 o'clock, the guests for the party had assembled. She had managed a short nap between dinner at which the Behlkes were the only guests and this hour. Sylvesterabend this year would not find her, as in prior years, asleep at midnight.

Seeing the new year in meant one was getting older. However, Oma Kohn, the eldest of all, had climbed into bed immediately after her meal.

"What is another year to this old head? I haven't stayed awake on Sylvesterabend since the war began. It seems silly to celebrate the year in which one may die," she cackled when Monika asked about her plans for the evening. Not that Oma had any plans for death. Her Menorrah had been packed with care in an immense rouge bag to await the next December.

The Groebel dining room, always beautiful in the child's eyes, was paradise this night. Mutti's cloth of Flemish lace, fragile as a spider's web in early morning, set the theme for the platters and bowls beneath the canopy of streamers. There was another carp, of course, but this reposed on a silver platter. Cook had formed the fish so that it seemed as if it were leaping within its wreath of carrot-strip flowers with parsley leaves.

A matching platter displayed venison sauerbrauten. Cut lead crystal, with edges so sharp one had to handle the bowls with care, contained herring in sour cream, sauces for fish and meat, and pickle spears. A huge circle of crystal was heaped with fried chicken livers. Next to it was the little silver vase filled with tiny Jena glass swords on which the hors d'oeuvers could be speared.

Neatly balanced on the sideboard were two matching punch bowls of silver. One held hot mulled wine, and the other had chilled spiced cider. Twin mountains of doughnuts flanked the bowls. There would be champagne when the clock chimed twelve. At present, it was being cooled, stuffed into the snow bank outside the door that led to the kitchen garden.

"Come along, Monika." Hanna guided her with a hand on her shoulder. "You must greet the Wentzlers. Your hands are clean, aren't they?"

Gravely Monika welcomed Lars's parents. She knew that many girls of her age curtsied to their elders. But Vati said that no child of his would bend a knee to another living being. When Frau Wentzler extended her hand, she gave her hand. Herr Wentzler, however, put his arms around her and lifted her to his face. His skin was like fine leather, his lids hooded over eyes that resembled deepset sapphires.

"You have welcomed me to your home," he whispered in her ear. "I now welcome you to our family."

"It's true, then?" she whispered back. "Lars and Hanna will be married?"

"I think yes. Here comes your father and my son. Look, they both smile. But you must say nothing. It is for Herr Groebel to tell."

Monika grinned at the approaching men. Almost every day since Christmas they had spent time together. She wondered if Vati had discovered that Lars liked to read Goethe as she was shifted from Herr Wentzler's arms to Lars's embrace. The younger man hugged her and kissed her cheek before passing her to Vati.

"At least I may have you for many years yet," Vati sighed before allowing her to slide to the floor.

Mutti claimed her then, leading her to the crimson sofa where Frau Mueller was seated, a lump of grey crepe. At the woman's right was a young man wearing the uniform of the new army that the Russians were building in defense of the German Democratic Republic. He blushed as they approached, and Monika realized it must be Friederich.

"Welcome to Villa Groebel," Monika spoke the expected words slowly so that she would not laugh.

"It is as I told you," Mutti said with a laugh that rang like silver on crystal. "Monika has grown up strong."

An elbow in the ribs catapulted Friederich to upright attention in Mutti's presence. The glass cup from which he was drinking skidded from his control and shattered on the floor. As he stammered his regrets, Mutti said all the right things to comfort a guest, but her tones were laden with thick honey that Monika recognized as disgust. Marie was there to clean up, almost before Mutti beckoned her.

"What good can the new year hold?" Frau Mueller regarded the scene with deep wrinkles folded into her features. "First, my son must serve as a common soldier. Then the factory is taken over. How can I bear to look ahead?"

Perhaps a mountain of food would comfort the woman, Monika thought unkindly, edging her way around the glass slivers. Kurt had just entered the room. She wondered if it would be permissible to tell him about Hanna and Lars. He was almost family, after all. But there was no need.

"Karl tells me this is a most special party," he shared as he bent to receive her kiss. "Is your arm up to it?"

When she reported on her work in the kitchen, he nodded appreciatively.

"Good for your arm and your wrist watch. You keep it up. Now shall we have ourselves a drink?"

"Can I have an icicle for my cider?"

"How could I have overlooked that?" he asked, slapping his forehead before reaching out to take her hand.

Outside the front door, he looked in one direction, then the other.

"Will that do?" He pointed to the place where the eaves angled around the corner of the house. It looked like a reasonable height. His strong hands held her above his head while she broke the piece of ice away. Monika regarded it with satisfaction. It was big enough to stir at least two, maybe even three, glasses of cider.

When they returned, the guests were beginning to break into groups according to their predilections. Some danced on the shining hardwood floors to music from the record player. Others sat or stood in clusters, heads bent to carry on conversation over the melodies. The table was popular with plates being heaped. Near the punch bowl, Herr Walz, Peter's father, was listening patiently to Herr Mueller.

"Never a moment to myself," the man was protesting between long swallows of mulled wine. "Why for everything. Questions, questions. If I want to go to the toilet even, why? And my bookkeeper. He is nearly done in. What will I do if he goes West?"

"Have you tried the sauerbraten?" Kurt interrupted. "Perhaps I can get you a slice on black bread? It is truly fine."

Herr Mueller reached instead for the punch ladle.

"I cannot. The Russians are ruining my stomach."

Monika frowned. There was a lot of it to ruin, although not so much as his wife's. Kurt shrugged and moved down the side of the salon toward Hanna.

"If I do not dance with your sister now, I will lose my chance," he told Monika. "But you and I will have the first dance after the midnight comes."

As Monika passed Tante Uschi, the woman held out her arms.

"Come sit with me, Liebchen." She lifted Monika to her lap. "It will not be much longer, I fear, that I can hold you."

Monika glanced at her own feet, dangling just above the floor. Tante Uschi was right. She was growing very fast.

"One day soon I shall hold you," she promised.

The woman's arms closed around her, and water glistened on Tante's incredibly long eyelashes.

"Oh, I hope so."

It was very comfortable sitting with Tante Uschi. After a while the woman began swaying to the dancers' melodies. She hummed softly. Despite her resolve, Monika was nearly dozing when Vati came over.

"If you will excuse us, Monika, Tante Uschi and I will waltz. And I will tell her a secret as we dance."

It seemed to Monika that the secret had to be about Lars and Hanna. But she must have been wrong for Tante Uschi suddenly stopped dancing, raised her hands to her face, and rushed from the room. Mutti paused in her conversation with the Burgermeister's wife, then quickly followed.

There weren't any tears later when Vati's announcement of Hanna's engagement to Lars was punctuated by the clock's chiming in the new year. And the wishes for the coming months were postponed long enough for all to witness Lars' placement of a ring on Hanna's finger. Then came the cheers, the noisemakers, and the hugs and kisses.

Monika had received her share, and she was beginning to flinch from the whiskered cheeks. It was a pleasure to be lifted above the forest of legs by Kurt. Mutti was sitting at the piano, running her fingers over the keys. As Kurt found a chair for the two of them, Mutti struck a heavy chord. Realizing her parent was about to sing, Monika stiffened. She did hope Mutti remembered not to sing that song about Lili Marlene.

But it was, instead, a folk song. After Mutti had sung it all once, she invited everyone to join her for a repetition. Afterwards, there was a wave of applause and pleas for more.

"What would you like to hear?" Mutti asked.

"I believe the national anthem of the German Democratic Republic would be a good way to begin the year." Friederich was standing in the curve of the piano. His hand, holding another punch glass, was wavering over the lacquer. Mutti would hit him if he spilled a drop, Monika was sure.

"No!" Herr Mueller bellowed the length of the room. "We will not sing their song."

And Mutti, right on cue, began to play a lullaby. It was followed by another childhood tune and then a third. Monika sang lustily until at last they came to a song whose words she could not recall.

"Did you see your sister's beautiful ring?" Kurt asked. "It is a fine gold band with a diamond in a golden basket. Lars' grandmother received it when she became engaged."

"But it didn't fit," Monika reported.

"Karl will size it for her and strengthen the prongs on the basket as well," Kurt told her. "But see what I have here. It needs no special work and has never belonged to another."

He uncurled his fingers to reveal the little gold ring. Monika lifted it to examine it closely. Where most rings had gems, this one had a painting. Blue and white and pink enamel described a tiny angel.

"How pretty!" she cried out.

"So give me your hand." As he slid the ring into place, he kissed her cheek. "This ring, whenever you wear it, will remind you that you are my very favorite little friend and that I love you very much."

"As much as your little sister?" Monika inquired as she regarded her new jewelry.

"Exactly as much," Kurt told her, bending to kiss her fingers above the ring.

* * *

Perhaps Frau Mueller had been correct in her dire predictions regarding the new year after her son broke his punch cup. At least the first month seemed to have borne her out.

Vati had been unable to secure a tutor for Monika, and so the chores of continuing her education had been divided among several people. He had retained her geography and history for himself. Those almost daily visits to his study to peer at maps, globe, and old pictures were wonderful.

Peter's father, the silverware factory bookkeeper, was charged with her mathematical prowess although, so far as Monika could determine, arithmetic had become a matter of making neat numbers in straight columns. Her answers were always right, but her methods seemed constantly open to criticism.

Mutti became her French mentor, teaching reading and writing as well as speaking. The reason for this second language, Monika decided, was in order to buy things. She already knew enough to buy a lot—shoes, gowns, and hats—providing she were where the language was spoken and had the money.

Reading in German was the province of whomever happened to be available. Vati assigned large portions from the books he had secured in Leipzig and the oral lessons were practiced before Hanna, Cook, the maids, and, if no human ear were willing, Harry. But the best sounding board, without doubt, was Oma Kohn who would listen patiently for long periods and provide, in ample shares, both praise and edification about words and writers.

Lars, Monika supposed, was as near to the art teacher as one could hope for. He monitored her efforts without confining her to circles, squares, and triangles. She had discovered in their early days that color, rather than media, was his strong point. Nonetheless, he had shown her how to present things by representation rather than by trying to create every last detail. She could make credible trees with a slash of the brush tip and supply the leaves by quick jabs of the brush base.

Mutti doubled as music master. It was on Mutti's latest assignment, a simple melody that required both hands, on which she was now working. But it was late in the afternoon and one could not look at both the keys and the scene outside the window. So, with Peter expected from school at any minute, she was struggling to complete her required minutes of practice.

A crash came from the kitchen, followed by loud voices. Monika sighed. Undoubtedly something was broken. These days something always was. Adults seemed to break things when they were upset.

* * *

Vati had broken many mirrors last week. But it hadn't been the shattering glass that had wakened her that night. Voices from the family dressing room first interrupted Monika's sleep.

She knew her parents had attended a reception in Leipzig earlier in the evening. Vati wore his penguin clothes. Mutti chose a blue gown that was cut so the Christmas necklace of diamonds and sapphires could rest against her skin. Monika had thought Mutti looked beautiful as her parents departed, but apparently Vati disagreed.

"...dress and act the whore, do not be surprised when others treat you that way" were the shouts that had brought Monika awake. "Even the Russians know your kind!"

"You were all swine at that point," Mutti shrieked her reply, "having swilled liquor in order to gather sufficient courage to even talk to one another. I was not the only woman offended by the behavior of you so-called gentlemen."

"But you were the only woman who danced with a comrade's hand inside her bodice," Vati hurled back. "You flaunt yourself and what is exclusively mine by right of the marriage contract."

"Karl, my love, it is the drink and the strain of the evening." Mutti's voice softened. "Let us go to bed before we wake the children."

"I do not wish to go to bed with used goods." Vati grew louder. And then came the crashes of anguished glass falling.

Monika had squeezed her eyes tight shut against the sounds, but her mind saw the mirrored doors that closed off the wardrobes on three sides of the room. And one by one, the reflections fell away to expose ugly wood beneath.

There had been sudden silence when it was over, and then another ugly sound. All she could think of was those days when old sheets were ripped to make cloths with which the maids could dust.

"Just what do you wish I should do?" Mutti spoke low, but there was a threat in her tones. "Cut them off?"

The featherbed had nearly smothered her, but Monika found that her retreat was also nearly soundproof. She spent the rest of the night in myriad nightmares within her cave. In the morning she lingered there, not wanting to see the havoc in the adjoining room. But she could not dress without getting a skirt from the closet. At last she could wait no more. She slowly pulled the door open for a peep. There was no glass on the floor at all and her heart jumped with hope that everything had been a bad dream. And then she saw that there was no glass on the doors, either.

* * *

"What in the world is the matter with you, Monika?" Mutti asked from the other end of the room. The woman had found that listening to novice attempts at scales and harmonics could be borne better when mixed with the self-assigned chore of dusting her collection of figurines.

"I cannot play this piece," Monika reported, lower lip outthrust.

"I begin to think you are right," Mutti replied with a laugh. Surprisingly, she had laughed a lot lately, even when explaining that the mirrors were gone because Vati wished to "protect us all from vanity."

"It's time for Peter to come home and I need to play in the fresh air," Monika pressed her advantage. No one had been designated for physical education instruction.

"You are dismissed then." Mutti held one of her treasures, a full-skirted shepherdress, up to the light for closer inspection. "Wear your winter coat. The sun may be shining, but this is only a false spring."

Because she was sure Mutti would not check on her, Monika opted for a heavy jacket instead. The coat was too long and clumsy for play.

Peter had not yet arrived, she guessed, as she slid through the doorway to the kitchen garden. But false spring or not, the woodsman was spading in the rhubarb patch by the pump. He would have seen the boy arrive.

"Has Peter come by?"

"Only me and your devil dog here all afternoon, Fraulein Groebel." The man paused and leaned on the shovel handle. "And the old hard earth. I told your father that the frost was still in the ground, but he would have this patch opened just the same. Never knew a man to set such a store in rhubarb. For years now it has had better tending than all the rest of the gardens combined, even the roses."

Monika nodded, drifting off to stroke the soft muzzle Harry thrust through the fence. She'd heard the old man's complaints about the rhubarb as long as she could remember. Vati's interest in the rhubarb patch was because of Cook, she thought privately. Cook made so many marvelous things from the stalks—preserves, pies and cake, even the pinkish wine that seemed so sweet as it touched the tongue and then suddenly turned sharp as if playing a joke on the palate.

"Monika!" Peter shouted to her as he came around the house. "You'll never guess what happened at school today."

She waited gravely for his explanation. School seemed like another world after having been gone so long.

"Fraulein Alma has gone West. Herr Schlauch told us at music time. He must teach our health and physical education until a new teacher is assigned.

He said she has deserted her post and made all of us suffer because of her selfishness." Peter shrugged out of his rucksack, placing it on the stone by the pump.

"I'll bet he got all red and breathless leading the exercises," Monika observed. "As red as that pin he always wears."

"No. He had each of us lead an exercise. I got to do the one where you touch your toes." Peter demonstrated the technique. "I was very good."

"I don't care whether Herr Schlauch says I'm good or not." Peter frowned. "Actually he didn't say so today. But I knew. Heidi is his favorite, you see. Hans attends meetings with Herr Schlauch."

So that was what Hans did now that Hanna spent her time only with Lars. Monika was not surprised. It had seemed like Hans was always lecturing Hanna instead of hugging her or holding her hand or kissing her. She didn't think Hanna much cared for lectures.

"Shall we climb the tree?" she suggested. The oak was so inviting when the leaves were gone. They could create a house with many rooms in the branches and fight off invaders by launching barrages of the puff balls that lingered after the acorns fell.

The French were the enemy that day with Monika supplying the challenges to their security in the language Mutti was teaching her. It had been hard to find out the words for "Surrender" and "Give up" because Mutti insisted they were never used when bargaining in the shops. She and Peter were still clambering through the branches when Vati arrived to inspect the woodsman's work.

"A good job," he observed as Monika descended into his arms. "Especially with the distraction of these two monkeys. We shall expect a good crop, I think."

Whatever the woodsman thought, he did not express. He held his shovel upright in one hand, his rough wool cap in the other, until Vati turned away.

"Tomorrow, children, you must confine your play to the villa lawn," he told Monika and Peter as he bent to put his daughter on her feet. "There has been a wolf skulking around the silver factory and, until it is gone, the danger is great."

"Will Tante's chickens be safe?" Peter was alarmed.

"I think the fenced yard will protect them. But I will speak to your father this evening."

Monika was anxious to learn more about the wolf, but Vati left the villa immediately after supper. She supposed this was his promised visit to the Walz' house. Hanna had gone with Lars to visit friends from her school years in Leipzig. Most of Hanna's time lately seemed to be filled with telling people about her engagement and making plans for the wedding, which was set for early July.

* * *

Mutti sat curled on the red sofa in the salon, looking at magazines filled with bridal fashions. They must have several designs in mind before their trip to Zurich, she had told Hanna. Monika was using the table in front of her mother to stage an imagined adventure for Kengi. Since Baby Rooey had been stolen, Kengi had become a male in her mind. He had developed several abilities, among which was the capacity to spring onto or over buildings. When the need arose, he resorted to magic, using potions and tools stored in his pouch.

"Did Vati take a gun when he went to see Herr Walz?" she inquired as Kengi set a spell against wolves. They had to be pure-bred wolves, of course, so that Harry would be safe.

"Why would he do that?" Mutti looked up in surprise from the page she had been considering.

"To protect himself against the wolf."

"Your imagination is getting control of you again," Mutti chided, her attention back on the book.

In a whisper Monika told Kengi to replace his magical aids and cease his exploits. As for the wolf, perhaps Peter could tell her more about it in the morning.

Peter had not seen the wolf, however, nor had the chickens been bothered during the night. He shared this news as he brought the eggs to the kitchen while Monika was eating breakfast. And he had no time this day for play. His father and aunt were taking him to Leipzig to choose new boots.

But the day appeared not to be wasted. Later in the morning Mutti sent Hanna to the stable to harness Bubi to the cart. Tante Uschi had invited them to lunch.

The Behlke was similar to the villa, grey stone roofed in red tile. Once Tante and Onkel had kept maids just like the Groebels. Now that the children were gone, Tante Uschi made do with a cleaning woman from one of the factory houses. There was no cook because the kitchen was Tante's domain. The meal, of course, was delicious. It seemed to Monika that Tante had to have prepared everything in her house, but the dinnerware was not her finest.

"These are very pretty," Hanna admired, running her finger along the scalloped edges of the plate. "Not as pretty as your Rosenthal, though."

"Oh, so you covet my Rosenthal?" Tante Uschi asked lightly. She was as charming as ever, but her hands trembled as she handed the tea cups around.

"Of course not," Hanna stammered quickly, "but it is perfection."

"And what's more, it is yours." Tante laughed sweetly. "I have packed each piece carefully in the barrel, and you shall take it home today. Before you leave, Johann will load it on the cart, along with the buffer that Wera let me borrow. You and Lars shall have Rosenthal for grand parties in your own home."

"Oh, Tante." Hanna jumped from her chair to embrace the woman. "But what will you use?"

"I will have new china. Johann and I are going to Berlin on Monday to visit his sister. And I shall shop there. Perhaps we shall even stop in Dresden. Who knows?"

"You'll never find anything so grand, especially in Dresden. So many of the old factories are gone." Hanna shook her head sadly. "Are you sure you should give the dishes to me?"

"My children do not need them." Tante Uschi brushed away her tears. Her son had died during the war while her daughter had married a French soldier and lived in the suburbs of Paris. "So it will make me happy to know that my god-daughter is treasuring the dishes."

"Hanna will take very good care of them, Uschi." Mutti, too, seemed to be struggling with tears.

"How are you getting to Berlin?" Monika asked practically as she followed the others to the kitchen with dishes from the table. "Can Onkel Johann get enough petrol?"

"We go by train. And we will carry our lunch so that we can eat on the way. I will pack the old wicker basket that Johann and I used when we were first married." She pointed to a counter at the far side of the room. "Come, I will show you."

She opened the container. Its lid held two plates, two cups, two forks, and two spoons. The bottom of the basket was empty except for a cloth. Mutti removed a fork and examined it.

"Very nice," she said and slid it back into its place.

Mutti was being more polite that Monika would have believed. The fork was not nice at all, even though she recognized the pattern as one from the factory. Its tines, like those of its partner's, were bent at the ends. Tarnish was deep in the flowers on the nicked handle.

"You have forgotten your knives," Monika supplied.

"You are right, of course," Tante gasped, then smiled. "I shall have to find some knives. I will do it this evening so that I do not forget. Now come into the parlor, Monika, for I have something for you, also."

The box that was placed in her hands brought delight to Monika's heart and face. She needed only to turn the handle on its base in order to hear the notes from "Die Fledermaus." This music box, in which Tante Uschi kept rings and necklaces, was Monika's favorite item in the Behlke house.

"I shall buy another jewelry box as well," Tante Uschi met the unspoken question. "And you shall have this one in which to store all your precious things. And now, Wera, perhaps you will sing for me so that I can carry the memory with me on my trip."

So Mutti sang while Monika explored her new treasure. It was a large box, bigger even than the one which Hanna had. There was a lot of room beneath the two trays that swung forward when the lid opened. Even Kengi would fit, she decided, along with her angel ring and the Piaget watch if she ever took it off.

When she finally looked up again, Mutti and Tante were both crying. Hanna was trying to comfort them.

"It's all right," Tante Uschi sniffed. "Do not be upset. Wera's songs remind us of bygone days, some very pleasant and some most sad. But now we must look ahead with hope for the future. Hanna's wedding day. Monika's growing up."

Mutti also blew her nose and wiped her eyes.

"Yes," she managed. "We look to the future."

Onkel Johann came into the parlor then and the remains of the tears were quickly dispersed. He admired the jewelry box on Monika's lap.

"If it were any larger, we could store you inside," he chuckled. "But it is nothing compared to the one my Uschi shall have. The new one will play 'Liebestraum,' I think, for she is my love's dream."

The tears, however, returned as the two women waited for Onkel Johann to load the cart. Hanna helped him, huffing and puffing, to place the barrel on board. He was so exhausted by the effort that he could hardly raise the buffer. And Tante Uschi and Mutti stood, arms around each other, and sobbed. The songs must have been very sad, Monika decided, as she climbed into the cart.

"Tante Uschi and Onkel Johann are going to Berlin on Monday," Monika told Vati when the family sat down to supper. "And Peter went to Leipzig today. When will we go somewhere?"

"There's our trip to Zurich," Hanna reminded.

"Yes," Mutti agreed. "We shall plan our trip to Zurich."

But Vati did not remain after the meal to help them plan. Again he was gone. Mutti seemed a little surprised when he told her about the wolf, but she nodded her understanding.

* * *

On Monday, Monika went down to breakfast to find Cook and the maids very upset. They kept turning to the window. Finally she pulled a chair over to the opening so that she, too, could see. A dark cloud of smoke was rising from the other side of the factory, close to where Tante Uschi and Onkel Johann lived.

"What is burning?" she asked Cook.

The woman turned to her, her face white and deeply lined.

"It is the Behlke house, Monika. I fear little will be left except the walls."

"This is the day when Onkel and Tante were going to Berlin."

"They have gone," Cook said softly.

"Oh, where will they live when they return?" Monika felt deep sadness, thinking how terrible a sight awaited her friends. "I know. I will ask Mutti to give them my room and I shall sleep with Hanna."

"That's a fine idea, my love," Cook praised. "Now eat your egg and your bread like a good girl."

* * *

How strange it was that no one had wakened her. Monika pinched her arm to make sure she was not yet dreaming, then looked at the watch on her wrist. Now she realized why she was awake. The little hand was at six and the bells of town's churches were announcing that Easter had arrived. Perhaps everyone else still slept.

If Vati were not yet awake, she could understand. Although no one had been willing to talk with her about what being in prison really meant, she was sure that it would cause one to be terribly tired. Even though Mutti had been predicting that he would be free by Easter, charges of aiding Onkel Johann and Tante Uschi to escape as well as other crimes against the state being dismissed, he had not arrived last night before her bedtime.

Monika had tried to stay awake, listening for sounds at the front door and in the hall. Knowledge that sleep had overtaken her made her feel guilty. She slid out from under the featherbed, feeling the soft rug beneath her feet and aware, although she could not see in the gloom, that her next step would bring her to the cold floor.

Monika cocked her head to check for sounds. Except for the bells, still chiming vigorously, there was nothing. In such silence, it was not wise to be alone. She reached back to her pillow for Kengi, and with her companion, she braved the hall. Besides the bells, she could hear the rain beating against the walls. That would make those who were superstitious very anxious, for sun on Easter prophesied a good planting, strong growth, and an ample harvest. With Easter coming in March, rain was almost predictable.

Beyond the dressing room was the door to the room in which Mutti and Vati slept. She approached it slowly, clutching Kengi tighter so that the soft flannel warmed her skin. What would she do if Vati were not there?

Just speaking about Vati since the soldiers had come to Haus Groebel and taken him away caused Mutti to break into tears. They were the same tears, Monika knew now, that began that Saturday at Tante Uschi's. The Behlkes had not returned from Berlin. Peter's uncle claimed that the fire had been set by Onkel Johann so that no one else could live in the house. Peter and Monika both believed it was true. The couple had left with nothing but the wicker basket. And nothing of theirs had survived the flames except for the Rosenthal china and the jewelry case. For this the Russians seemed to blame Vati.

She had to know about Vati before she opened the door to the bedroom. If he were not there after Mutti's promises that he would be, she would cry, too. She knelt down to survey the room through the keyhole. It was a large opening and had once had a large key, gone before the house had become theirs.

"You look first," she told Kengi and squashed his head against the lock plate. Then she had to take her turn. From their vantage point all that was visible was the bed with its billowing down coverings. She couldn't see whether anyone was beneath the featherbeds. But the need to know was strong. Monika summoned her courage, hugged her toy for luck, and pushed down on the door handle.

Her parents' bed dominated the room. Its mahogany headboards, highly polished, rose almost to the ceiling. It looked like a single piece of wood, but Monika knew it came apart in two sections as did the bed itself for cleaning. On each side was an attached bedside table. Vati's table always held one or more books. Mutti's had a mirror. Both had Meissen lamps with shades decorated with scenes from mythology. Only grownups would be able to sleep soundly with writhing orange dragons next to their heads.

Monika tiptoed across the floor toward Vati's side. She would surprise him this special day, welcoming him home with a kiss and a hug. But when she swept her hand across the pillow, she knew Mutti's promise had been empty. Peter's uncle said that Russians did not let many people go, not unless they promised to be good Communists. If Vati could not have borne to be known as a Nazi, he would never promise anything to the Russians, even if it meant release from prison. So she must, instead, comfort Mutti yet another time.

Pushing Kengi ahead of her, she scrambled under the featherbed. But as she edged nearer where Mutti's warm body should be, she began to realize that she and the kangaroo were alone in the room. Closing her eyes against the fear that was stealing her breath and senses, she lay very still. There was a cold around her that the featherbeds were inadequate to change. Fear would go away, she told herself, if she would be brave enough to face it. That's what Vati always said. With a resolute surge, she rolled to the other side of the bed. Yet it had not gone away.

Perhaps everyone was already downstairs. She was edging toward Mutti's bed table when she saw it. The mirror, supported by a gold filigree stand, reflected a chocolate rabbit. Extending her fingers, she knew it was true. Her Easter candy was here. Life was right again.

Monika swung up quickly to examine the rabbit more closely. It and the mirror were set on a sheet of glass that protected the table's surface. Beneath the glass were snapshots of the family, so many that the wood was barely visible. There were pictures of her as a baby and a toddler. Here was another of those with Vati's arm ripped away so that no evidence of the hated armband would be seen. Tucked between Mutti's lamp and the mirror was a note. She snapped on the light and read the message.

"Frohe Ostern, Mutti and Vati."

Monika frowned. How unusual it was to receive a note. And then she grinned. Vati was free. That's what the words said. And the reason she'd never had a card with her Easter treat before was that she was now just able to read for herself.

Stuffing the rabbit into Kengi's pocket, Monika pushed herself out of the bed and to the floor. It was time to join the family for breakfast. She felt a great deal more confident now, rushing toward the stairs. It would have been nice to slide all the way down the banister, much quicker and more thrilling. Mutti, however, had decided that it was time for her to become a lady. The newel post at the bottom now supported a huge cactus as a reminder to practice decorum in her descent.

The first door she tried was the entry to the wintergarten. Sometimes Mutti drank her early coffee there. But the room's white furniture seemed overwhelmed by the grey of the dawn. She moved farther down the hall and tried the salon door. The hall was cold, but if the dining room were in use, this section of the house would be getting warm. She could detect no light, no sound, nor aroma of breakfast, even at the long room's far end.

That left the kitchen as the only possibility. And as if to answer her question about her family's whereabouts, something dropped, clattering across the tiled floor. She could hear Hanna cry out, as if she were being tortured. Whatever was behind that door could be no worse than being alone unless she wanted to hide for the rest of her life with Oma Kohn.

The four of them—Hanna, Cook, and two maids—turned to regard her as she stood in the doorway. Even here it was chilly. Nothing was being heated on the stove. Suddenly Cook broke out of her trance and lifted Monika to a chair.

"Poor child. Your feet are like ice. What can we be thinking of to have forgotten about you?" she moaned.

"Where is Vati?" Monika inquired, raising her knees to draw her feet up inside her gown.

Hanna ran her hands across her face and looked up bleakly. The swelling was so great that her eyes were barely visible. There was a hint of a smile when she spoke.

"Vati is free and safe."

"And Mutti?"

"She has gone to join him."

"In Zurich?" Monika pressed. Perhaps, after being in prison, Vati needed a cure and Mutti was taking him to a bath there.

"No. They have gone to Berlin."

"Like Tante Uschi and Onkel Johann?" Monika asked. And Hanna laid her head on her crossed forearms and wept again. Her sobs turned to shivers, huge convulsions that rocked her body. Marie went to the closet by the kitchen door and brought back a coat to wrap around her. She, too, was crying now.

Cook slapped a plate containing a piece of stollen in front of Monika. "Be good and eat. Then Hanna will be good, too."

Hanna had only eaten a bite or so and finished part of a cup of coffee when suddenly she stood up.

"Come along, Monika. It is time for us to bathe and dress for the day." Her tone and manner reminded Monika of Mutti. Yes, she thought suddenly, Hanna was old enough to be married.

Hanna selected Mutti's bathroom for their use. Between the freshly lit water heater and the sunlamp in the ceiling, the room warmed quickly. Realizing that she still carried Kengi and the rabbit, Monika cracked the door to Mutti's bedroom enough that she could put Kengi on the other side. It would make him angry if the chocolate were to melt in his pocket.

It had been a long time since she had enjoyed a bath in Mutti's lovely pink tub. It stood out like a Burmese ruby against the black marble that went halfway up the walls. The tub that she and Hanna shared, like those of the maids and Oma Kohn, were plain white. Someday, Monika had resolved, she would paint her bathtub to match Mutti's. Maybe after Hanna was married and gone.

She and Hanna shared the tub. Hanna was being very much like Mutti, insisting on washing Monika's hair as well as her own, then drying it with a thick white towel as they stood naked beneath the sunlamp. Monika caught a glimpse of the two of them in the mirror. At least Vati had left this one, as well as the one by the bed, intact.

Once they were dressed, there wasn't much to do. Finally Lars came over, and he disappeared, with Hanna, into Vati's study. Left to make her own decision, Monika opted to go into the kitchen and was glad she had. Cook and both maids were working frantically. Bread was rising on the shelf over the stove. A pie was cooling near the window and another was waiting to be put into the oven.

Something was boiling merrily in the stew pot. Cook was browning chicken parts in grease. At the sink, Marie washed carrots and potatoes from the cold cellar.

"Just what we need," Cook exclaimed as Monika made an inspection round of the room. "Another pair of willing hands. Give her the cookie dough and the rolling pin, Marie."

The baking was nearly completed when Lars and Hanna joined them. The girl's eyes were swollen again and so was her mouth.

"I think I should stay the night here," Lars announced, looking to Cook for agreement.

"Absolutely not," Hanna gasped. "Think of your parents and the business. You probably should not be here even now."

"I will move up to the house," Cook seconded Hanna's statement, "and I shall bring with me my husband's rifle."

"You keep a gun in your cottage?" Lars looked astounded.

"All Swiss men must have a gun," Cook explained. "It is the law."

"But not in Germany, surely." The amazement had not faded.

"In my cottage it is Switzerland," Cook corrected. "And do not fear, I know how to use the weapon."

"The maids?" Lars inquired.

"Must be gone by tonight. Hanna and I have decided. That's why we are preparing so much. Can you come by tomorrow?"

"I have to finish the sign at the factory." Lars frowned. "Hanna can come down to meet me. It will now say that it is the property of the Democratic Republic. My father is very sad to be doing it."

"If you didn't paint it, some other sign painter would," Hanna insisted. "And you would be in trouble, too."

Lars insisted on helping Cook move before he left. She was given Hanna's room. The girls would share the master bed, Hanna announced. But even though supper consisted of a sampling of all of the things that Cook had made, it did little to relieve the day. The maids just seemed to melt away, not even saying good-bye to the girls. But Oma Kohn remained. Hanna and Monika went up together to feed her.

"Vati and Mutti went to Berlin," Monika reported as she straightened the table next to Oma's chair. "Just like Tante and Onkel Behlke."

"When did they go?" Oma was leaning forward, her fingers pressed so hard against the arms of the chair that the stuffing bulged below her fingertips.

"When did they go?" Monika looked at Hanna for information.

"Last night. Here is some fine barley soup that Cook made just for you," Hanna put the tray beside the old woman. "It's very good."

"Tasted it already, ja?" Oma Kohn cackled. "A fortunate woman I am to have fine barley soup and such good friends."

No persuasion would bring Cook to join the girls in the salon. The kitchen was her place and she intended to stay there. Food had to be wrapped and stored properly. So Hanna led Monika to Vati's study and fueled the Kachelofen. They stayed near the small stove until its heat began to radiate.

"Listen to me, Monika." Hanna took both small hands in hers. "You must tell no one outside of this house where Vati and Mutti have gone. You may say only that Mutti is out. Do you understand me?"

"Is their trip to Berlin a secret?" Monika twisted her fingers in the tight grip.

"Very much a secret. That means no one is to know outside of the household."

"But Lars knows."

"That's different. He is like our family. And he will not tell, even his parents."

"Is Peter like our family?" Monika looked up into her sister's serious eyes.

"Not for this. It is very important that Peter does not know. He could be hurt if he knows. Do you understand me?"

She nodded and grimaced. The angel ring was cutting into her finger.

"Does Kurt know?"

"I'm not sure. Vati trusts him. We can, too, I think. So Mutti is out. You do not know where."

"And what if they ask about Vati?" Monika finally cleared one hand and laid it on top of Hanna's.

"Vati is in prison. Remember?"

"You said he was free." She pulled her hands away and jumped to her feet. "It is Easter, and he is free."

Hanna frowned, but did not reach out to capture her again.

"I told you the truth, but you are not to tell anyone else. You must make everyone, even Peter, believe that Vati is still in prison. Monika, you must! If no one in town knows that we are alone here, we will be safe."

"Is it all right if I talk about Vati and Mutti to Kengi?" Monika countered.

The question caught Hanna unawares, and there was a pause as she considered. Then she smiled at Monika, a wide beautiful smile and the first of the entire day, the child thought.

"You may tell Kengi anything. He is family, and we can trust him, I know. What shall we do now? Would you like to play a game?"

"Checkers, please." Monika ran to get the game board from the drawer beneath Vati's bookshelf.

Monika was nearly asleep when Hanna led her upstairs to the master bedroom and undressed her. With her sister on the other side and their bodies creating a nest of warmth beneath the feathers, Monika realized it was the first time since their bath that she had been truly comfortable. For some reason, the woodsman had not taken care of the furnace this day. It felt good and reassuring and she dozed off.

The shouts and the pounding on the door wakened her. Harry was barking fiercely from his kennel in counterpoint to the sounds. Hanna was already sitting up, reaching for the dragon lamp.

"Someone knows," Monika moaned. "Someone knows."

The pounding continued.

"If I turn the light on, they will know we are here," Hanna reasoned aloud, hugging her sister tightly to her.

"They already know." Monika bit down on her lower lip until she felt the pain. It was not a bad dream, and to cry now would be wrong. She clutched Hanna and pulled herself tighter inside the protecting arms as the door across from them swung open.

"It's only me." Cook whispered as her flashlight identified the cowering duo. "What shall I do?"

Again the pounding thundered, louder now from the hall.

"I have the rifle with me."

"We can't shoot the whole police force," Hanna observed, her arms relaxing the hold on Monika. "I suppose we must go down and meet them. Are you decent?"

"I am wearing a robe if that is what you are asking," Cook said gravely.

"Then put the gun away. Hide it in case they search the house. I will find robes for Monika and me."

The dragon lamp snapped on. And Hanna, straight-backed and with a determined look on her face, climbed from the bed.

"Hurry," she directed. "We don't want the door caved in."

As Cook disappeared, Monika pulled the featherbed to her chin and watched her sister move to the dressing room door.

"I could go out the kitchen door and let Harry run loose," she offered.

"The men would shoot him, I think," Hanna said as she returned with a pair of robes. Pink flannel with satin ribbons was tossed to Monika. Hanna worked herself into a dressing gown of Mutti's, a heavy brocade with a high collar and gilt cord sash.

"Let me tie the bows," she offered as Monika's fingers struggled with the ribbons. "No shoes, I think. We should look as if we had been surprised."

"We are."

"No longer," Hanna smiled thinly. "Cook? Are you ready?"

The three of them went down the stairs together, Monika in the middle. Hanna kept adding light to mark their way. At least the shouting and pounding had stopped. At the bottom, they formed a single file, this time with Monika bringing up the rear as they approached the door.

She could hear Hanna as the girl took a deep breath before reaching for the bolt. Her sister's head was high, chin thrust out. The brocade folds picked up and moved light from the overhead lamp. Surely Hanna was as beautiful as the brave statues of angels and martyrs Vati had shown Monika in Leipzig.

Suddenly the door swung open, engulfing them in cold dampness. Fog swirled across the threshold. Yet there appeared to be no one on the far side. Cook pushed past Hanna suddenly to encounter whatever awaited. And she stumbled. As she fell, she began to laugh.

"A deer, children. Only a deer," Cook kept repeating.

Hanna was reaching to help her up. Monika pressed close, too. Her bare foot encountered the carcass. She frowned.

"Deer do not shout," she murmured. Deer also did not charge doors, she knew.

"Look," Cook pointed from her knees. "It is already gutted and bled. An Easter gift to the villa, children. That is all. A gift for our Easter from someone on the estate. Just as always. But we forgot."

"You're right," Hanna agreed. "But later than usual. We must bring it in."

"Not through the front door," Cook chided. "Monika will open the kitchen door, and we will take it around."

It took a long time for the women to get the deer to the back door and then down the long steps to the basement. When they were done, Mutti's lovely robe was laden with hair and Hanna's feet were filthy. But the girl herself was pink-cheeked and radiant.

"I shall lock up again, Cook, and you will heat some milk for us. And we shall toast our friends of the estate and our own bravery."

"To them and to us," Cook echoed, reaching for a pan.

"And I will get my chocolate rabbit so that we can share," Monika announced on her way to the hall.

Chapter Four

✴ ✴ ✴

Disposing of the Pieces

The remains of Nikki's chocolate rabbit lay in melting lumps on the desk in front of her, its mutilation barely visible in the dusk of the dormitory room. Nikki touched the parts with a tentative finger. Broken and shapeless, the rabbit seemed to represent her past.

That Monika would remember it all so clearly seemed miraculous. People and places perhaps could be understood, but the vividness of color, sound, smell, and touch was amazing. And the evident strength of the retained emotions shocked the person she had become.

Dear Hanna, Nikki thought. Brave, dear Hanna. What kind of life did she and Lars now have? Were there children? Had her sister found happiness in a place where dishwashers and garbage disposals were not available and necessities of life like blue jeans and nylon stockings rare? Did Hanna ever see Kurt? Had Hanna met Kurt's younger sister?

As far as Nikki knew, her parents' last communication with their elder daughter had come soon after their defection, an oral message carried by strangers. To write to persons in the East whose earning power depended upon the continuing goodwill of the government was considered unwise. Mail from either West Germany or from the United States would jeopardize Hanna's pretense of lacking knowledge about her family's disappearance.

Now that wall, nearly two years old, formed a physical separation. Nikki supposed she might never know anything more about her sister. How strange it was to think of the Hanna from that other Easter. She had been about the same age as Nikki now was. Nikki doubted that she would have displayed that quality of strength.

Accepting assignment with the newspaper and accompanying Paul Peterson to Germany would not provide answers about Hanna, probably not even about herself. And it would cause her to experience more of Monika's memories, the intensity of which were frightening.

Monika, after all, was German, while Nikki Fisher was the all-American girl. And there was a great deal of truth in Doro's observation, after Nikki's confirmation, about the fervor of the convert. Nikki alone had experienced the adoption of a new faith, but both young women had worked at becoming prototype Americans. That was one thing extraordinarily nice about the United States. Almost everyone had been something else as well. Elvis and Peyton Place were today's interests, but other music and literature were remembered.

The door to the room opened, and Cissy from next door appeared.

"Nikki, you are here, aren't you?"

"No," Nikki shouted as she pressed the lamp switch. She laughed as Cissy jumped back.

"There's a call for you on the 27 phone."

Was it David or Doro? Nikki tried a mental coin flip as she marched to the pay phone at the east end of the hall. The result was close enough for horseshoes.

"Have you been to confession?" Donna Fisher asked as soon as Nikki was on the line.

"Yes, I have, Mother Fisher."

"Will you come down for supper tomorrow night? David wants to talk to you, which, I suppose, is no surprise."

"Sure, I'll come. My father and mother have to be honored," Nikki agreed. "Do we call it Easter supper?"

"Smart mouth! You're supposed to remain sinless until tomorrow's mass," Donna retorted. "And we'll call it a post-Passover parandial. Be here by six. Okay?"

"Gotcha!"

"And, Nikki, set your alarm clock tonight. More Christians attend church on Easter Sunday that any other day of the year. If you don't get there early, you won't get a kneeling bench."

"Right. Set the alarm. How are the kids?"

"Just like the last time you were home," Donna responded, "except Debra has a cast on her arm. She fell off a slide over in Lincoln Park last Wednesday."

When the conversation was over, Nikki leaned her head against the phone. The cold hand of coincidence was running its fingers along her spine. Another girl and another slide, yes, but there were so many ways to break an arm. Still, Debra would enter her teens in the fall. She should have known better.

The telephone shrilled through her skull before she could pull away. In obedience to the dorm rules, she lifted the receiver.

"Davis House," she announced.

"Would it be convenient for me to speak with Miss Fisher?" The giggle gave the message that her voice had been recognized. "Or is she too deeply engaged in her studies to talk with friends?"

"If you will hold the line for an hour or two, I will attempt to locate Miss Fisher," Nikki snapped back, holding laughter at bay.

"Hey, I called you twice today and left messages," Doro complained. "Maybe your dialing arm is broken?"

"I went down to The Loop." Another broken arm? It wasn't possible. "I spent the entire day."

"What did you buy?"

"A chocolate rabbit."

"No clothes."

Nikki shook her head and then put the negative into words.

"St. Ann's has late confession tonight," Doro reminded.

"I've been to confession at Old St. Mary's."

Doro whistled shrilly.

"You really were in The Loop. How about coming out for dinner tomorrow? Max will pick you up about noon."

"Okay, but I promised Donna to be home for supper at six."

"No sweat. We'll put you on the 4:05 train for Chicago, and you can catch a bus to the Northside."

"Then set a place for me," Nikki agreed. "I'll see you as soon as your chauffeur can get me there."

"Nikki, don't forget to set your alarm tonight. The church will be really crowded."

"I know. I know," Nikki protested. "My Jewish mother already warned me."

"Good for Donna," Doro chortled. "Sometimes I think that every RC girl needs a Jewish mom. Oh, oh, got to go. There's a rug rat in my cupboards again."

Nikki replaced the receiver for the second time and stared at the phone. Not even Dore knew about the Jewish grandmother in the attic. Monika seemed unclear about why Oma Kohn had lived with the Groebels. The old woman was more like a permanent fixture about which no one commented any longer. She certainly had been in the villa as long as Monika had lived there except, of course, for those very last days.

It was the morning after Easter when Hanna had gone upstairs with breakfast to discover the old woman dead in her easy chair. And with that same practicality that had emerged the previous night, Hanna marshaled the services of Cook and Lars. Oma Kohn had been laid to rest, without marker or service, in the far end of the basement. Her grave kept her permanently in the house that she had refused to leave during life.

When she opened the door to her room again, Nikki recognized that the rabbit was exuding the heavy odor of chocolate, sugar, and vanilla. The candy was too badly mutilated to even consider taking it with her on either visit tomorrow. And she doubted that her dorm mates would look with favor upon it, either. Quickly she scraped the pieces into the greasy sack and took it back to the hall for disposal down the incinerator chute. When it had slid from sight, she let the door slam back into place.

"Shhhh!" Cissy hissed from the 27 phone. Her posture indicated less concern about the noise than about missing the words that she was hearing. It had to be the boyfriend whose fraternity pin graced Cissy's ample chest. The vacant smile on her face said so. The light danced along its thin guard chain in tempo with Cissy's sighs.

Nikki, although she sometimes sported Mark's purple letterman jacket, had never worn a frat pin despite offers of three. Nor had she allowed herself to be caught up in the anxieties of sorority rush week. Her refusal to become a wholehearted participant in the social side of higher education probably stemmed from Monika's Vati and his stand on allowing others to impose their insignia. Another more practical view, so far as sororities were concerned, was the problem that a Roman Catholic adoptee in a Jewish family might pose to those who were selecting pledges. She smiled to herself over the potential confusion and knew she could care less.

It was nearly time to go down to the lounge and view the late news. Those residents of the house who could had departed to spend Easter at their homes or, more ideally, at Fort Lauderdale. There should be, therefore, few couples to be interrupted at various stages of intimacy as she went through the process of boning up for Monday's current events quiz.

The short exam was a weekly ritual introduced by David in an effort to increase the awareness of his students. The results over the term amounted to fifteen percent of the final grade.

One more task could be completed before the broadcast began. Nikki took the shoulder bag she had carried to Chicago and emptied out its contents. The necessities—wallet, cosmetic/medication bag, note pad and pencil—were relocated to the patent leather envelope she would carry to church and on her visits. The less essentials were sorted between the top drawer of the desk and the waste basket.

She groped along the bag's bottom and pulled out the one remaining item, a rectangle of cardboard. Paul Peterson had scrawled his home telephone number on the back of his business card. Nikki examined both sides carefully.

What a problem his offer was going to pose tomorrow. At least she would get views from both sides during her time with her host families.

Doro, of course, would be violently opposed to the idea. She had returned to Germany twice, both visits at Max's insistence. And she had hated every moment of the interval away from her suburban castle.

"If my folks or Max's want to see little Max again, they can come here," Doro announced after last year's sojourn. "Everything there is ancient. Everyone is out-of-touch with reality. The food is as bad as ever. Being on time is more important than being kind. I won't go there again."

Doro's arguments to keep Nikki Fisher all-American would focus on the nature of the offer. If people would suggest such an assignment for a junior in journalism, what greater opportunity could be expected when one graduated? Beneath the suggestion and probably unspoken would be another contention. Doro wasn't really sure that Nikki should be training for a profession, anyway. Homemaking and motherhood had a lot to recommend it, from Doro's viewpoint. Days should be filled with bridge and tennis and horseback riding. The role of men was to work. If wives assumed their spouses' responsibilities, males were let off the hook.

David and Donna, on the other hand, were residents of the world. Their children had been born in Japan, toddled about London, and began school in Frankfurt. Their first complaints about American schools rested on the lack of second, even third languages, among their classmates. Summer vacations were not squandered on repeated visits to the same cottage on the same lake. They were spent in Brazil and South Africa and India.

And Paul Peterson was a long-time friend of David's. They had trained and practiced their profession together in those early years, beginning at Columbia and continuing to the CBI and Pacific theaters during the War. During Paul's convalescence after the plane crash that had cost him his leg and left David without a scar, they had co-authored an impressive book of photo essays on Navy flyers. It had been only natural that, when David accepted his position at Medill, he brought Paul on staff as an adjunct professor to teach a single section on photojournalism each year.

David's attempts at persuasion would begin with some ancient philosophy about one's talents opening doors to opportunity. He would remind her that her language major combined with her journalistic training had brought her to this rare option. The rest of her studies could, if she elected, be completed at any future time. But this chance for experience and adventure would not come again.

Between Doro and David, she would be pulled one way and then another. Her stomach would begin to cramp as it always did when others were trying to impose their ways upon her.

"Vati! I owe you for this!" she thought savagely as the pain tried to double her.

As if she had summoned up the man, she saw him again, stiff-backed in those days just before the government moved to take the factory, when questions about the crimes committed by the Behlkes had been asked again and again. And with him was Mutti, clutching the fur coat she despised. And there was Hanna, drawing the bolts on the door to face whatever lay beyond. And Cook, rifle resting across her ample forearm.

Why could she not have their strength, to make and stand by decisions regardless of those who would persuade her otherwise? Why, when her mind wanted to assert her independence, did her body protest, twisting her as cruelly as people and events had the young Monika?

Suddenly, Nikki was laughing. Relief from her present pain was available. Coins in one hand and Paul's business card in the other, she stalked to the 27 phone. She looked at the face of the Piaget on her wrist. There was just enough time before the late night news came on.

"Hello?" Paul Peterson was at the other end of the line, listening.

Now was the time to come to a decision!

* * *

Nikki rolled from back to stomach, rested her chin on crossed forearms, and regarded Lake Michigan with regret. She hated to think that, in only days, she would be on the other side of the world, far away from her adoptive family, her American friends, and even her favorite beach.

Summer had not yet officially arrived so this stretch of shoreline, within walking distance of the Fisher apartment, was rather deserted. Glancing over her shoulder, she noted one jeans-clad man throwing a piece of wood to a bouncing shepherd pup.

"Harry!" she thought. There was no way that her beloved wolf dog could still be alive. Still, since Monika's recollections at Easter, he had been living in her mind along with other images nourished by preparations for her journey.

Spring had taken a cue from early April and remained warm. Today the sun was hot on her nearly bare back. Unless she took action, there would be strap marks left on her skin by the two-piece suit's bra. She stretched her arms behind to free the clasp that secured the garment. As she fought to pull the piece of metal from its loop, she resolved that several French bras with front closures would be among her first purchases in Europe. Undoing hooks at her back always challenged her agility and tried her patience.

Mark, however, had no trouble with the similar fastening last night, she thought with a grimace. She suspected that he had plenty of practice, even though such ardor was unusual when he was with her. The evening's romantic moves, she had decided in review, were ploys to change her decision about the job. Of all her acquaintances, he had been the most troublesome, chiding her about turning away from commitments she hadn't been aware of having made. He'd cited the length of their relationship as proof of his contentions.

That first summer when she was sixteen, she and the Fisher children, Debra and Doug, had come to the beach nearly every day. In the beginning, they had kept to themselves, but as July progressed into August, they had begun to recognize and be recognized by the "regulars" at the park. Acquaintances had grown and continued into the school year.

One of these had been Mark, who lived high in a glass-fronted cliff that offered a marvelous view of the lake. At first, he was only another participant in pick-up games of volleyball or softball. She had discovered that he attended the high school in which she had been enrolled. Finally they had both chosen the university just north of Chicago. Meetings for cups of coffee changed to occasional party invitations and finally became regular events.

Yesterday's date was the last for at least a year, she had insisted. The trip preparations had tired her. There was so little time, so much to do.

Mark had taken her to a drive-in movie, something "you don't want to miss." But Nikki had missed most of the feature film, having spent the time arguing about her upcoming departure. What she was seeing, quite clearly, was the Mark was acting like a spoiled adolescent. And perhaps he wasn't "acting" at all.

"Aren't I more important to you than that old job?" he queried ungrammatically. "What happens to all our plans?"

Nikki looked at his face, lit from the picture on the screen, and wondered which plans he had in mind. She certainly had none.

Mark was her security blanket, she suddenly realized, smiling at a mental image of herself as the little boy in that popular cartoon. One hand firmly clutched Mark's shoulder. The thumb of the other was imbedded in her mouth.

He had quickly become a stereotype man-on-campus, a well-dressed athlete with a sports car and a marginal grade point average. The effort of earning the latter was made only because he had no desire to be drafted or employed. His parents were satisfied. Mark was their only son and heir, but his father was well able to manage the family firm for another decade.

Mark's family seemed pleased with Nikki, too. She was attractive, well-mannered, and had good connections. Perhaps a girl from farther up the North Shore would be a more ideal candidate for daughter-in-law, but Nikki wasn't pushing for marriage.

Of course, she wasn't! That's what made Mark so useful to her. Despite what he said, there had been no discussion of emotional commitments until halfway through the film. Suddenly she had realized that tears were shining on his cheeks.

"Nikki, let me love you just one time before you go out of my life," he pleaded as he pulled her across his body so that the steering wheel was impressed on her back. Mark's lips punctuated his request, and his fingers traced circles on her breasts.

Since she was unable to speak, she shook her head, knowing he could feel her dissent. He did, and broke the contact with her mouth.

"Why are you being like this? We mean so much to each other," he groaned, the sound ending abruptly. "Or are you planning to give yourself to some European stranger? Those men don't take 'no' for an answer."

His hand had left her breast to stroke her thigh, each gesture calculated to raise the garment nearer her hip. It wasn't the first time that his hands had explored her contours. Nor was the warmth in the center of her abdomen new. With her mental resolve at war with the demands of her body, she reached down to release his fingers from the fabric of her skirt.

"You know I like you very much, Mark," she began, speaking slowly to keep desire from introducing a quiver to her voice. "But I don't want a quickie in the back of a car for my memory of you during the year I am gone. If we really have something, it will last."

"It will last." Mark breathed his assurance in her ear, re-establishing his grasp on her breast. His fingers released the buttons on her blouse, then opened her bra. As his hand cupped a breast, thumb going directly to its nipple, she frowned at the screen. Which was breathing harder, Nikki wondered, Mark or the male star?

It didn't matter, she decided, ignoring the messages that her body was sending to her mind. Giving oneself to another was a matter of trust. Once she thought she trusted a man enough to love him. Mark, however, was not that man.

Finally she had pushed him away, refastening her bra and straightening her blouse as the film's theme music swelled to anticipate the movie's end. Now her fingers repeated the chore. It was time to get back to the apartment and her packing.

* * *

Trust was like a gift of flawless crystal, Nikki decided as she walked along the path that led to U.S. 41 and the buildings beyond. It could be chipped, cracked, or shattered easily, either on purpose or through carelessness. Experience had shown her that caution was necessity. The world to which she was going had been a place where the shards of so many trusts still lay. She hoped she would not stumble on the pieces when and if she encountered them.

At least she knew that her translating skills were up to Paul's requirements. Twice a week she had gone to Dr. Wilson's home to express in English, and to his satisfaction, the news and comment coming over shortwave radio. Mostly he had chosen stations in Bonn and Frankfurt or Paris for her drills. Once he had played a trick and given her Zurich. Another time it was Vienna. But when she followed his instructions and let her ears work before her mouth, the drills had been simple.

Wilson taught European political science. He and David had filled her with the background for what she was translating so that she knew the significance of Adenauer's departure from government and was aware of DeGaulle's maneuvers on behalf of the French. She understood the concepts behind the European Economic Community and why the continent did not choose to allow the United Kingdom to join, the problems that confronted NATO, and even the concerns of Vatican II.

Sometimes Dr. Wilson would dial in Radio Moscow and translate the "official" views of happenings in Western Europe. It didn't work as often as she would have expected. "Official" views came many hours after the occurrence that generated them.

The Berlin Wall was the hardest of all to understand. It was, first of all, a misnomer. The division ran throughout Germany. But she had known, without explanation from Dr. Wilson or David, why the great flow of humanity from east to west had to be stemmed. What was terribly apparent now was that there was a structure that was real and could be seen and touched that separated her from her sister and her previous life. Before it had been only a sheet of cold fear that kept refugees from the East properly divided from those who had remained.

The actual preparations for the journey, beginning at term's end when Nikki moved from the dormitory back to the apartment, were conducted under Donna's supervision. The woman had acted as a liaison officer, working with the newspaper and a variety of governmental entities to get Nikki's papers in order. There had been appointments with a dentist ("Do try to avoid getting work done in Europe. They have a proclivity toward steel instead of the finer metals.") and physician ("Don't buy remedies over there. Pharmaceutical standards are sadly lacking.") and ophthalmologist ("You need no lenses and don't let them say you do.")

Buying clothing had occupied three entire days. Not all the time had been devoted to Nikki's needs. Debra and Doug had to be entirely reoutfitted for their summer at camp because both were in the weedy stage. "No ironing" seemed to be Donna's motto. And her experience kept the purchases on the spare side.

"Underclothing, yes," Donna proclaimed as she motioned the salesclerk to ring up a dozen pair of nylons and two panty girdles. She'd insisted the store include spare garters. "You want a Timex to wear until you get your Piaget repaired. Although I really think we can find a watchmaker here who can be trusted."

"I want to take it back to where Vati bought it," Nikki explained once again.

Donna nodded understanding that she didn't really feel. And Nikki did not tell her stepmother that American underclothing fell far short of what was available in Europe. Most, of course, had to be handwashed, but there were always trade-offs. She would find the kind of lingerie that Mutti used to favor. She only hoped she could afford to buy it.

As a result of determined shopping, Nikki's closet contained a "little" black dress with a jacket that could also be work with a skirt; a suit for travel of a synthetic linen guaranteed "not to wrinkle much"; one white and two print blouses; a short white wrap-around skirt of cotton and a long one of nylon. Added to this was a yellow slicker with a matching Southeaster hat. Another hat (black and small), three pair of white gloves, and six scarves rested on the chest.

There was no way that these garments would jump into the suitcase by themselves, Nikki thought grimly, and that left her to accomplish the task. Donna and David were gone until tomorrow night, their return timed so that they could drive Paul and Nikki to O'Hare Field. It really had been easier, she decided, having made her farewells to the kids yesterday morning as they climbed into the car en route to Wisconsin and Debra's Camp Waconda, then to Camp Cameron, in Michigan's Upper Peninsula where Doug would work as counselor-in-training.

After her adoptive family departed, Nikki had caught the train to Arlington Heights and spent the day with Doro. A fistful of pictures, illustrating Young Max's emergence to full-fledged toddler, had been entrusted to her for delivery to Max and Doro's families. She also had six pair of white bobby sox for Doro's baby sister who, Doro informed her, was now seventeen and "would die" if she didn't get them.

Doro still did not approve of Nikki's decision even though she had met Paul at a command performance that had Nikki's twenty-first birthday as its excuse. It was, of course, a backyard barbecue although it had been rained indoors by seven-thirty. Weather in May tended to be an iffy proposition.

"Yes, he's nice," Doro admitted grudgingly. "He's also awfully old. And a cripple. What about his wife?"

"She left him after the war was over," Nikki reported. "He sort of takes the blame, according to David. He was an addict because they used so much morphine on him with his leg. But he cleaned himself up and worked in a Tokyo bureau during Korea."

"He must be at least forty."

Nikki nodded. David and Paul were the same age.

"How long do you have to stay over there?"

"I don't know. Whatever the paper decides. A year, at least."

"What a bore! Running around taking care of an old man and showing him older buildings and telling him what everyone is saying." Doro shook her head in disgust. "Think of the school dances you are going to miss."

"What would you like me to bring when I come back?" Nikki asked firmly.

"Not a thing. I need nothing from there. No little boxes with edelweiss painted on. No cuckoo clock. No scratchy wool sweater. Nothing."

Nikki kept the smile from her face. She knew exactly what she would bring. A German dictionary. If Doro wouldn't use it, perhaps Little Max would as he grew older and wondered about his heritage.

The apartment seemed strangely silent. Mostly it was clicking sounds that she missed—David's typewriter in the corner of the master bedroom that he had proclaimed as "den," Donna and her friends with the mah jong tiles, and Debra practicing her tap dancing steps in an effort to satisfy the instructor who had once been a Rockette and believed that modern dance and ballet would never replace the noisier art. That the apartment could contain such sounds without neighbors' complaints was a tribute to the buildings' architect.

This soundproofing made the switch beside the door and the air circulating fan that it activated obvious necessities. She depressed it and listened for the response. "White noise," David called it. He said that several laboratories had completed tests that indicated people worked better with a little sound around them. It also made them less sensitive to loud distractions.

Nikki knew she should have begun packing last night after Max brought her back from the suburbs. Instead she had gone to David's desk and pulled his Boedecker's from its place between the bookends on his desk. This was where he kept his most used reference. There were also a Bartlett's, a Webster dictionary, a Roget's Thesaurus, a pocket-sized atlas, and a current World Almanac. It had been nearly one in the morning before she had put aside the descriptions of the places she had known as a child. And her dreams had been filled with them again. This morning her stomach suggested that breakfast would be unwise, and she had gone to the beach without eating.

Nikki tossed her empty suitcase on the bed and opened its jaws to receive her belongings. It would stay there, she resolved, until everything was inside. So if she wanted to sleep tonight, she needed to get moving. Using Donna's formula, she began filling the space. Ten pair of nylons went into the case. One pair were laid on the pillow to begin a separate pile. The last was tossed on the dresser to be worn on the flight. Panties were divided in a similar manner. One of the print blouses and a contrasting scarf were relegated to the adjunct stack. So was a pair of ballerina flats. The other shoes were placed in the travel bag.

If she followed instructions carefully, there would be one change of clothes for the carry-on bag. It was a necessity, Donna warned. Too often luggage took a different route from that of its owner. One had to have a way of making do until reunion.

Don't pack anything when you already have something else that will serve the same purpose, was another of Donna's rules. The flats were an adequate substitute for slippers and the raincoat could be used as a robe. Perhaps that was right, but Nikki folded her favorite terry robe and found it a place. No blue jeans, Donna had insisted. But Donna was again outvoted. The pants were far from new, but they weren't frayed as yet.

Nikki frowned. Something had to go if these two additions were to travel with her. She removed the white sweater, pocketed and long enough to substitute for a jacket, and returned it to her drawer. Maybe Doro didn't want a sweater, but she did, one with traditional patterned yoke and silver fastenings.

It had been over an hour, and the suitcase was beginning to look as if travel were near. Nikki decided to reward her diligence with lunch. But when she opened the refrigerator, her stomach cramped with a suddenness that nearly doubled her. After her dreams, she had known the pain was going to come, but she was not prepared for its intensity. And yet it really wasn't bad. That taste of raspberries, a certain prelude to vomiting, wasn't in her mouth.

Ignoring the selection of cheeses and cold cuts and the container of Donna's homemade chicken salad, she reached instead for a can of beer. Again she changed her mind, opting for the resealed bottle of Rhine wine nestling in the door shelf between two containers of tonic water. She poured several ounces, using one of Donna's tulip glasses from Yugoslavia. Doro's Americanization allowed one to imbibe from paper cups, but the wine never tasted as good.

"Glass for wine makes it fine," she told herself and laughed aloud, ignoring the pain it brought. Perhaps she should send the verse to that boxer, Cassius Clay. He liked to speak in rhyme.

* * *

Leaning against the counter, she sipped the wine and waited for it to bring relief. It was a reliable remedy. Donna had spooned it into Nikki on the ship that had carried them from Europe. But there had been qualms.

"She's only a child, David. Should we be giving her this? Maybe the ship's doctor has something…"

"Nonsense," David had countered. "You're only worried because we could bring just five liters with us and Nikki is cutting into your supply. Wera let her have wine, both medicinally and for refreshment. You know that."

In her agony, a younger Nikki had wondered if her new mother actually valued wine above the recent family addition. The years since had proven otherwise. When word had come of Wera Groebel's death, Nikki realized that Donna had become her mother in truth if not by birth.

The wine, however, was slow with its healing this day. Sometimes it did not work. And so Nikki turned to the doctor's answer—those grey and blue capsules. She washed one down with the remainder of her wine, then filled the glass again. There was a label that warned against drinking and driving when using the medication.

"So I won't drive," Nikki told the container before putting it back on the carry-on pile. The capsules were in a larger container than usual. The doctor had wanted her to have enough. And she was to send back to the States for more, if necessary. Once he had suggested to David that Nikki be taken to a psychiatrist. David had refused, saying, "She's not ready for that yet."

Maybe the pain was lessening. She couldn't be sure. Usually it was more that she became accustomed to the pangs and then, in surprise, would realize they had ceased. There was no doubt that the alcohol had sped into her system without any food to block it. Her mind was definitely becoming, to quote a Donna-ism, "tipsy." This was probably the best time to tackle the jewelry box. But the phone began to ring.

"Hello?" Her voice was small and tentative. She just couldn't face another round with Doro. And if the university were suddenly seeking David, she could only supply rough estimates on his whereabouts.

"Nikki? Are you napping?"

"Paul?" She made his name sound like a plea for help. "I was packing. Then my stomach began cramping."

"Did you take your medicine?"

"I'm on pill one and glass two of wine. I think maybe I'm feeling better. Is forty pounds an absolute limit?"

"Definitely. Do you need help with your packing? And what have you eaten today?"

"Is your packing all done?" She hoped her discouragement didn't carry over the line.

"No way. But I've had a great deal more experience than you. I'll do it first thing Wednesday morning. Again, what have you eaten?" He sounded as stern as David.

"I can't eat today."

"You have to. How about my bringing over some Chinese food? It slides down easily. You can cook the tea," he told her. "And afterward, I'll give you a hand with your bags."

Paul had helped. In the hour she had waited for his coming, Nikki realized that he was becoming what Donna called "a really truly friend." The title was earned only by a person whom one could bear to have around during illness.

Nikki's jewelry box had fascinated him. Even after the mechanism had run down, he had hummed the Mozart tune.

"That box really should go in your suitcase," he told her after shifting its position several times within the carry-on.

"I can't," Nikki refused. "What if I lost it?"

"Then leave it here with David and Donna," he countered.

"I wouldn't be me if I didn't have my jewelry box," she objected.

"Where does David keep his travel gear? He must have something you can use?"

Nikki had her doubts, but Paul insisted it was all right.

"We'll leave your carry-on for him to use," he said when he returned to her room with his selection. "See how much better this is going to be? Now you can be you."

She nodded, knowing that she really wasn't Nikki Fisher despite what he thought and her traveling papers proclaimed. She handed Paul the legal-size envelope that held her documents.

"I guess we can put these inside the jewelry box."

"No. All papers go in your handbag. For the trip we fill the box with little things." He reached past her for the stockings, panties, and scarves. "Like these," he demonstrated.

Nikki watched, wishing she dared place Kengi there instead. The toy, however, was much too fragile for further travel. Her kangaroo, along with woolens from school, was tucked away in Donna's cedar chest.

When Paul had the bottom of the box stuffed, he turned his attention to the tray.

"I hope we do find your Swiss jeweler." He fingered the Piaget. "What in the world is this?"

"My angel ring." It looked ridiculously small next to his hand. She lifted it out and pushed it on her little finger. At the first knuckle it stopped moving.

"You must have been a baby when it was given to you." Amusement showed on his face.

"Not quite that small, but young." She smiled, too. Kurt, she bet, would now be a man much like Paul. He'd be a little older, of course, but just as kind and thoughtful. "A man gave it to me. He was a friend of our family—my other family. I think he was a distant cousin."

"A nice guy?" Paul asked as he replaced the ring in its slot.

"Very nice. Very much like you."

"What about this thing?" A tarnished silver medallion swung on a blackened chain as Paul held it nearer the lamp's light.

For the first time since dinner, Nikki's stomach cramped. How she wished she had thrown it away. Heaven knew there were many times when she had determined to do so. But her explanation to Paul seemed almost innocuous.

"That's a commemorative coin. It was given to me by a former pen pal and my real father, a jeweler, made the setting."

"Male or female pen pal?" Paul probed.

"He was Swiss," Nikki revealed with reluctance. "I saw his name in a Walt Disney publication. He wanted to correspond with someone who could read and write in German, French, and English."

"How long did you two write each other?"

"Until I was fifteen. Then I stopped answering his letters." She was telling the truth, but not all of it.

"So much for your Mickey Mouse friend." Paul put the necklace back in the tray. "You should polish the coin when you find time."

When both pieces of luggage were filled, Nikki carried the scales from bathroom to bedside. Its dial showed a weight of 39 pounds.

"Now we will pack your handbag. You need your driver's license," Paul told her. "And the American Express card that David got for you. Your citizenship papers. Medical record. Shot card. Traveler's checks. Passport and visa. Press card. Got them all?"

"In here." She passed the previously rejected envelope to him.

She was glad when he accepted it with a nod and dropped it inside her purse without opening it. She would have had to explain Vati's post card and tonight she did not want to. The half-truth about the medallion had been enough.

"Now that your packing is all done, how will you spend tomorrow?" he asked, brushing imaginary dust from his palms.

"In the morning I am going to get my hair trimmed. Doro's meeting me for lunch at a little place on LaSalle that makes marvelous daiquiris. And then I am going to cook dinner for David and Donna. They expect to be back at six-ish. Do you want to eat with us?"

"No, thanks. You and I are looking forward to a lot of meals together. In the afternoon I'm going to a Cubs' game with some guys from the sports desk. From there, I think it's dinner at the North Star. So I'll see you Wednesday. Mayhem in the a.m., right?"

"Right, chief." As he passed through the door she was holding open, she rose on tiptoes and kissed his cheek. "Wednesday it is!"

Chapter Five

✦ ✦ ✦

In Flight

Getting from O'Hare to Idlewild hadn't been as hard as Nikki thought it might be. There had been a brunch of sorts to enjoy. Her medication seemed to be in firm charge so she enjoyed a slice of melon along with a piece of dry toast.

Paul had briefed her on their itinerary. Their transfer in New York had to be accomplished in less than two hours and there was the possibility of being stacked over the airfield. Other than that, they should have no problems, even with a change of planes at Heathrow for the final leg into Rhine-Main. There they would be met by the head of the German bureau.

"The paper will take us to a hotel for a couple of days so we can recover from the jet lag," Paul told Nikki. "Then we find housing. By July 1, we should be getting regular assignments. The main thing is to be as relaxed during and after the flight as possible. Eat small meals. Sleep when tired."

Nikki had smiled and kept her own counsel. The Germany she remembered did not specialize in small meals.

Paul took the advice he gave. Once they were airborne on the second leg of the trip, he slid his seat back, braced his head against the edge of her seat, and shut his eyes.

* * *

Nikki stared out of the window, down at the clouds. Occasionally there were glimpses of blue breaking through. The Atlantic hadn't looked that color the last time she had crossed it. In fact, there was so little resemblance that she wondered if the pilot might have made a major navigational error. The cabin attendants didn't think so. They had already posted estimated arrival time in London.

Grey had been the color of her rite to passage, both real and figurative, from Europe to the United States. It was reflected in the sky, water, and ship's paint. The vessel was operated by the military to transport its troops and dependents to and fro "across the pond." The Army's Navy, David had explained with laughter. Their presence was allowed because he was completing a contract with the Department of Defense as one of its overseas publicists.

On the ship's lowest decks were enlisted men reassigned to stateside posts or looking forward to separation. Above them were the NCOs and the officers, traveling with families. The Fishers had two cabins on the boat deck. The females occupied one. David and his son shared the other. Deck times were enforced so that the lowest-ranking troops did not mingle with their superiors.

A Spec 5 who was acting as purser for their deck referred to her as Miss Fisher. It had taken a while before Nikki remembered to answer. She had only been Miss Fisher for two months.

Until the court had granted the adoption papers, she had continued to live with Mutti. Knowing that relief was on the way had not made the last year as Monika Groebel any easier. Herr Rennecke had not been one of her favorite people, even when he and Vati had been in partnership.

Looking back now, she had to admit he was a handsome man, tall and silvered, with a patient charm. He and Mutti were the kind of couple whose presence is always remarked upon. Herr Rennecke—Mutti called him Stefan—always displayed deep parental affection for Monika when her mother was present. His greatest and only true kindness had been to convince his mistress to allow Monika to become a Fisher.

Mistress was exactly what Mutti was even though she explained to her former acquaintances that she was "living with a friend." Perhaps the two of them would have married if there had been proof that Vati was dead. Instead Karl Groebel was classified as missing, a heading which in police circles covered thousands of Germans who, at their own behest or that of others, suddenly disappeared.

Mutti sometimes stated among her intimates that her husband had abandoned his family and deserted his business responsibilities. It was believable. Everyone knew that Karl Groebel had withstood more pressures in two decades than the average individual knew in a lifetime. But not every acquaintance believed. Greed, as often as stress, broke men who dealt in gems and fine metals.

"...probably in Argentina," Monika had overheard one cocktail hour conversation. "That's where they all go."

The same night she had heard Dubai mentioned and Singapore.

Monika had not the least idea, however, where he might be. She had allowed herself to consider that Vati must be dead, assassinated perhaps by some old enemy after returning to Zurich with Gerhardt.

* * *

For awhile, Vati's death was such a certainty that she stopped writing to the pen pal who had become her love. Every sentence in his letters after that one time they met face-to-face seemed to mask a guilt. Perhaps some powerful Russian or East German had recruited her Gerhardt as a Judas goat.

Later, however, she was sure that Vati still lived. Never was she more certain than on the day when Herr Rennecke had taken her to the office of Mutti's physician. Slowly and in simple terms, using an anatomical chart as reference, the doctor had explained that Mutti was suffering from cancer of the breast. A mastectomy would be performed the next morning. The physician had expressed his confidence in the procedure, detailing many cases in which the cancer had been arrested successfully. But Monika's eyes were fixed on the mirror on his far wall, her mind on Mutti's harsh words:

"Just what do you wish I should do? Cut them off?"

Surely Vati had found some mystical way to punish his wife for giving herself to another man. The operation was a success, but the patient died. Not right then, of course, but within two years, Mutti succumbed to the disease.

* * *

Following Mutti's discharge from the hospital two weeks after the surgery, Herr Rennecke took the three of them—Mutti, her nurse, and Nikki—to Baden-Baden. There they met Donna and David. The Fisher youngsters found in Monika a fine playmate and Donna seemed more than willing to allow the three of them to entertain themselves while she sat with the woman she knew as Frau Rennecke.

How much Mutti had spoken about the old life, Nikki was not sure. Neither David nor Donna ever mentioned the years before Wiesbaden to her. But she knew that Oma Kohn had been discussed. She overheard Donna telling the story to David when she returned Doug and Debra to their parents. Donna was crying and her sentences were muddled:

"I never considered...my hatred...so great...just treasured and protected...as we would have...God forgive...I, too, am a bigot."

Perhaps she had been the tradeoff for Oma Kohn, Monika thought when the offer of adoption was made. If so, she was content. For she was dying, as surely as was Mutti, in the presence of Vati's terrible revenge upon those he left behind. There was nothing she could do for Mutti. The woman didn't seem to want her around. Some days she would see only Stefan.

In the end, it had been that way. Herr Rennecke had sent finally for Hanna, arranging for her transportation and the necessary papers to clear the errand of mercy. But the GDR had been extremely slow with copying and rubber stamping. Hanna's arrival in the West had been barely in time for Mutti's burial. Before she returned to Leipzig, she wrote a letter to be forwarded to her younger sister. Its first words were:

"I cannot understand your absence…"

* * *

"Are we there yet, Mommy?" Paul slapped a well-manicured hand across his mouth to cover a jaw-rending yawn.

"The pilot announced the half-way point about fifteen minutes ago," Nikki supplied. "Was it a good sleep?"

"No, but I needed it all the same. Last night's party lingered on until nearly dawn. I have to believe that I am getting too old for such festivities."

"You didn't have the look of a night owl this morning," she observed. And he hadn't. His seersucker suit had been crisp and well tailored. Both suit and oxford cloth shirt echoed the blue of his eyes. She thought that her wrinkle-free linen looked heavy in comparison. But Donna had regarded the two of them with satisfaction. The woman wasn't at the match-making stage as yet, but her smile announced that she hoped things might take the matrimonial course she was imagining.

"Let's see if a little water in the face will improve things." With an effort he heaved himself past their seat mate, a tall gangling youth who had sat too far from his barber on his more recent visits. The boy did little to accommodate his fellow passenger so that Paul moved perilously around the bare knees, stumbling over immense hiking boots.

"That your dad?" He inquired as soon as Paul disappeared down the aisle.

"We work together." Nikki chose a short explanation.

"You're his secretary. Do you get trips like this often?"

She decided to ignore him.

"What's your destination? The British Isles, maybe? I'm going there to work rock faces in Scotland."

"Oh, you're a sculptor." She had meant to keep her mouth shut. Still there were lines that were too good to miss.

"I'm a climber."

"That, too? Where is your work displayed?"

Paul interrupted the conversation before it became more involved. His look of gentle chiding told her he had intercepted part of the exchange.

The cabin attendants wended their way through the aisles distributing the next meal. Nikki's watch, along with her body, was still on Central Standard Time, and she couldn't be sure what meal the entrée was supposed to represent. On the other hand, she was hungry and the pains remained at bay.

"Can I buy you and your secretary a drink?" the boy on Paul's far side inquired.

"Yes for me. But since my secretary is back in Chicago, I can't respond for her." Paul compressed his grin into a carefully controlled line and waited for the ball to return to his court.

"How about the young lady?"

"Young lady, name your poison." Paul turned to Nikki. "How about bourbon and tonic?"

"My name is Ted," the youth supplied as he distributed the glasses the stewardess was handing him.

"That's a good name," Paul commented, passing a glass and miniature bottle to Nikki.

"Ted works rock faces." Nikki fed the line.

"Oh, does he now? Just like Gutzon Borglund I imagine. Marvelous work, that!" Paul prattled on as Nikki choked over the combination of his words and the carbonation in her beverage.

How much longer they could have kept it up remained a mystery. Ted was rescued by another youth who had recognized a recreational compatriot by his bare legs. The pair trooped off toward the rear of the compartment to exchange information on carobiners and pitons. With their departure, Paul and Nikki allowed their laughter to explode.

"I trust you are not going to do that in some language I can't understand," Paul commented when they had finally sobered. "I'm told the American sense of humor is lost on most Europeans."

"As well as on some Americans," she finished the thought.

* * *

"Are you Mr. Paul Peterson?" the blonde among the cabin crew stood in the space that Ted had vacated.

"That's right."

She withdrew a sheet of paper from the jacket which fit so beautifully that Nikki thought anything in the pocket would destroy its line.

"The pilot received this message for you."

Paul unfolded the note, frowning at its contents. Nikki forced her eyes toward the window. The message was private, after all.

"I think we're being re-routed," Paul announced as he refolded the note and dropped it into the inside pocket of his jacket. "We're to 'check with the Pan-Am desk at Heathrow re: change in destination.'"

"Oh" was all that Nikki could manage before the demon in her stomach grabbed hold.

* * *

Monika jumped in surprise when Peter spoke from behind her. She had been alone for so long, playing by herself while Hanna and Cook did all sorts of things in the house. On the first three days after Easter, it had rained and she had been relegated to the wintergarten. Today, with the sun coming out, Hanna had bundled her up and pushed her outdoors.

"What are you doing?" Peter had asked.

"Kengi is hiding from the hunters." She pointed to a place in the thatch of rhubarb where the toy's head could be detected. "They want to shoot him and make shoes out of him. Do you know where Australia is?"

"Down at the bottom of the world, isn't it? All alone."

Monika nodded.

"What are you doing here? Is there no school?"

"Tante kept me home today. Onkel took Vater away last night, and we wait for him to come back. She says he is in much trouble because of your parents and Herr Behlke," Peter explained.

"Have they put him in prison like they did Vati?" Monika moved Kengi to a more secure spot.

"No. He is at Onkel's office. They know he will not escape like Herr Groebel did."

"Vati escaped from prison?" Monika swung around to face Peter. "Are you sure?"

"Onkel says so." He crouched down on the sun-warmed stones by the pump and lowered his voice. "He says that Frau Schliegel, who is one of the wardens at the Leipzig prison, let your father go free. She took him from his cell to a prison van and drove off. They found the truck in Dresden. But they did not find your father or Frau Schliegel. The Russians are very angry."

"Oh, oh!" Monika lifted Kengi and changed his hiding place. "The hunters nearly found Kengi. Do you think Frau Schliegel is with Vati and Mutti?"

"Shhh!" Peter put his finger to his lips. "Do not tell me where your parents are. Tante says that what I do not know, I cannot say."

"Kengi is going to climb up into the mountains," Monika announced. "The hunters will grow tired of chasing him then."

"But he will need shade for it is very hot so close to the sun." Peter snapped off a large leaf and stuck the stalk into Kengi's pouch. The triumphant animal now rested near the pump with his makeshift umbrella trembling above him.

"Monika, come quickly!"

They turned to see Hanna standing in the kitchen doorway. Her arm, as well as her voice, beckoned.

"Will you wait?" Monika snatched up Kengi and tossed aside the rhubarb stalk.

"No. Tante wants me to rake the chicken yard." Peter shrugged at the inevitability of the chore. "Maybe I will see you later."

When Monika entered the kitchen, only Hanna was there. Her sister came to her immediately and hugged her hard.

"You're squashing Kengi," the child protested.

"Run upstairs and wash. Then change your clothes. I have laid out what you are to wear on the bed," Hanna directed. "Leave Kengi with me."

"Are we going somewhere?"

"Yes, Liebchen. To be with Vati and Mutti. Hurry, now!"

It took no urging. Monika's small feet pounded up the back stairway. She found the bathtub filled with water, smelling sweetly of the oil that Mutti liked so much. Reluctantly she pulled off her clothes and climbed in. It would have been much faster to run a cloth over the parts of her body that showed when she was dressed. But Mutti wouldn't like that. She said that clean clothes could not cover bad odors.

When she had dried herself, she walked naked into her parents' room. She and Hanna had continued to share it since Easter. She was slipping into her jumper when Hanna came in.

"Let me brush your hair." Hanna, seen backwards and in the mirror, looked as hardfaced as she had the night they thought the soldiers had come for them. Her front teeth kept latching into her lower lip until Monika felt sure there would be blood.

"How will we travel?" Monika asked, flinching away from the pain of a tangle.

"Lars will take you to the train station. He is down repainting the sign on the factory. Cook has gone to bring him here. It will be safe."

Monika frowned as Hanna pulled her hair again. Of course, it would be safe. Lars was a very good driver. And the truck was in good condition. It smelled, of course, of sweet turpentine and fresh wood, but she liked those odors.

"Do you have your watch? And your angel ring?" Hanna examined her at arm's length. "And Tante Uschi's jewelry box. There are some little things to play with on the tray. Kengi will travel in the bottom."

"Did you pack my clothes?" Monika asked.

"Vati and Mutti will buy you new ones. Come along, now. You must meet the people who go with you." Hanna took a firm grasp on Monika's hand and scooped up the box under her arm.

"Where are the dragon lamps?" Monika pulled to a halt. "And the pictures under the glass?"

"Lars has taken them. Come now."

They descended the front stairway, and Hanna led Monika to the salon. Two people sat on the red couch. One of them came upright as the girls entered.

"Herr and Frau Gruen, this is my sister, Monika. Monika, you will be traveling with the Gruens. You are to pretend to be their niece. You will call them Onkel Josef and Tante Maria," Hanna instructed and repeated their names. "Onkel Josef and Tante Maria. They will call you Annamaria. Can you remember this?"

Monika nodded. Annamaria was the name of her favorite doll.

"But…" she began. Hanna's fingers crushed her small hand, making the next word "ouch!" Couldn't Hanna see that these were not Herr and Frau Gruen? Both people were women.

There was a knock on the door.

"It's Lars," Hanna told the couple. "I will let him in. Give Kengi to Monika so that she can put him in her toy box."

"Here is your toy, Annamarie." The woman lifted Kengi from the sofa and handed him to the girl.

"Danke, Tante Maria."

"That is very good," the woman who Hanna said was Frau Gruen nodded approvingly and glanced at her "husband." "Onkel Josef and I will take good care of you. But you must obey whatever we say. Your father and mother have said so."

"She speaks the truth," the other person agreed. The clothing was that of a man, a black suit almost shiny with age, and the voice sounded right. But the eyes were different somehow. As if "he" were a mind reader, Onkel Josef drew a pair of glasses from an inside pocket and donned them. It was better, Monika decided. Why they were playing this funny game she could not imagine. But if they were going to Vati and Mutti—and Hanna had said they were—it was enough.

Hanna went with them to the truck. Frau Gruen climbed onto the seat, followed by Onkel Josef. Before she lifted Monika to Herr Gruen's lap, Hanna hugged and kissed her sister.

"You will be good," Hanna instructed. "And tell Vati and Mutti I love them very much."

"Aren't you coming?" Monika asked.

"I can't come. I have to marry Lars, remember?" She thrust her ringed finger beneath the child's nose and a note of laughter seemed caught in her throat.

"The train," Lars growled. "It will not wait."

Monika was raised and deposited. She had been right. Onkel Josef was a woman.

* * *

Lars said nothing more during the trip. Watching him as he steered the truck past the houses of the town and into Leipzig, Monika thought he was as hardfaced as Hanna had been earlier. At the station he broke his silence.

"You have ten minutes. If anything happens, we will take Monika into our home."

Herr Gruen shifted Monika into the woman's grasp and climbed out. His arms raised to receive her.

"Good-bye Lars," Monika managed before the pair whisked her into the station. Just inside the door, Onkel Josef put Tante Uschi's box in her hands."

"You will carry it now. Come along. We go to the platform."

Herr and Frau Groen chose the first compartment in the carriage. They put Monika in the seat nearest the passageway. The Frau sat next, then her partner. Their backs were to the engine.

Almost immediately two men, white hair showing beneath their caps, took two of the seats across from the Gruen party. Monika thought they must be brothers. They looked very much alike. Almost as soon as they were seated, each opened a book and began to read. Even the covers were the same colors.

Then the door opened once more. A large-framed woman came in and walked to the window seat beyond Herr Gruen. She wore the loden worsted coat of a hiker and a snap-brimmed felt hat decorated with a feather and a band of enameled pins. She was lugging a rucksack. When it came time to place it on the shelf above the seats, the men across from her ignored the plight. Herr Gruen, however, stood and lifted it. Monika thought, from the effort, that it must be very heavy.

The train was on its way. Tante Maria let out a deep sigh as if she had been holding her breath.

"You may play with your toys if you wish, Annamarie," she told Monika.

It would have been a great deal more fun to climb up on her knees and watch the countryside through the windows on the other side of the passageway. But Hanna had said obey, so Monika opened the box. In the top tray she found three of the family's Christmas ornaments: a boy and a girl in Bavarian dress and a carved wooden tree. For a while, she balanced them on the jewelry box's top. They were Monika and Peter. The tree, although it looked like a fir, was the oak by the rhubarb patch. She was explaining the trip for Peter had never had a long train ride.

It was difficult, however, to keep the playthings balanced as the train swung along. Each time that the engine stopped, she would lose control and one of the carvings would slide beneath the feet of the reading men. The first two times Onkel Josef retrieved her toy. The next time she scrambled down herself.

"Perhaps you should play with your stuffed toy," Tante Maria suggested.

Monika stored the ornaments on the tray and pulled Kengi free. He was wedged tight. It was a very good idea taking him out, Monika thought. He needed some room to move around. Since the men did not seem to care, she probably could play in the space at the passengers' feet. As she began to slide from her place, Frau Gruen caught her arm.

"Why don't you and your little friend take a nap? You may rest your head against her shoulder."

Monika didn't want a nap. Nonetheless, she slumped against the woman. With her head that close, she could detect the odor of mothballs. It wasn't as strong as that which clung to the fur robe they used in the sleigh but she still had to sneeze. She repositioned herself with her head against the passageway wall.

To pass time, she observed her fellow passengers through squinted eyes. The men even turned their pages in unison. The woman had opened her coat. Underneath she wore a deep rose dress of wool. Its collar was trimmed in the same satin that covered its buttons. Her shoes, Monika realized, were high-heeled pumps, not at all the thing to wear on a walking tour. In time the train's motion caused Monika's lids to lower further. She finally fell asleep.

* * *

She came awake with a jerk. The compartment seemed to be jammed with people. One man wore a railroad uniform. Two more were in suits and overcoats. In the doorway stood either a policeman or a soldier, his rifle held at the ready but pointing up at a spot above the readers' heads. Beyond him were more people in the same uniform with the same guns. Monika knew why they were there and let out a moan. It gained her a brisk elbow in the ribs and a deep frown from Frau Gruen.

It was the woman in the high-heeled shoes and the hiking coat that was being pulled to her feet.

"Nein, nein," she was protesting in a high strong voice as the men in the suits grasped her arms. The trainman stepped aside for them, his body threatening to squash Monika as he leaned away from the trio. The woman screeched on as the soldiers in the passageway formed an aisle through which they could pass, but Monika couldn't see past the barrier form in front of her. Tante Marie had placed a hand on her arm, demanding silence.

When the trainman finally moved out, he pulled the door shut after him. It wouldn't close all the way. One of the woman's shoes blocked the panel. He kicked it back toward them, and the door snapped into place. But the train remained motionless. Through the window by her head, Monika saw the soldiers moving farther down the carriage. After a while, they returned and climbed back to the platform. As soon as the soldiers had departed, people erupted into the passageway from the other compartments in the carriage. Monika could see nothing but their backs. No one in her compartment moved. The men read on. Herr Gruen's head was tipped back as if he were trying to sleep.

Tante Maria dug into her purse and pulled out a round container.

"Here, Annamaria. Have a sweet." She had taken off the lid to reveal pastilles.

Monika dutifully took hold of one. The candies were stuck together and several broke loose. She thrust them into her mouth. Immediately the taste of raspberry struck her tongue.

"Keep them, my dear." Tante Maria thrust the container into her hands. "You may eat them all if you wish. We are still stopped, Josef."

"I know that," Herr Gruen snapped back. "Just sit quietly and wait."

Some of the spectators had returned to their compartments. The platform looked empty to Monika. Then a troop of soldiers marched toward the carriage once more. This time, Monika was sure, it would be she for whom they came. She would never see Mutti and Vati again. She pushed herself back into her corner, lowered her head, and waited as the candy continued to melt. She heard the door's opening but could not look up.

"You! Give me that bag." Since no hands were touching her, Monika was able to look up at the train man whose fingers brought Onkel Josef into motion. As the rucksack changed hands, the recipient's arm straightened sharply. She had been right about its weight.

"Here." Onkel Josef extended the forgotten shoe. "The Frau will require this to complete her trip."

"Not where she is going," the other snapped back. And then the door was shut.

As the train shuddered into life, Monika saw the soldiers perform an about-face. A young man at the rear had slung his gun over one shoulder and hefted the rucksack on the other. She couldn't see the woman's shoe at all.

She swallowed hard as their speed increased. Tante Maria, who had been very straight and hard, was almost crumpled soft in her place. Onkel Josef held a hand across his eyes. The men read on. Suddenly the candy lodged in her throat and Monika began to choke. After several coughs did not dislodge it, Tante Maria gave her a hearty slap on the back. The candy slid free, but Monika's breakfast was following it up. She let go of both jewelry box and Kengi, slapping both hands across her mouth.

"Quickly," Onkel Josef hissed as he came to his feet and pulled the door aside. "Take her to the toilet."

They just made it to the tiny room at the far end of the carriage. Tante Maria pulled it open and thrust the child inside so that Monika could empty her mouth and her stomach into the stainless steel bowl. It all tasted like raspberries.

The spasms would not remit and the lurch of the train drove the child to her knees. The pain and the taste were still there, but no more liquid flowed from her mouth. She felt a draft as the door opened behind her. A hand pulled on her shoulder.

"Do not touch the stool! There are germs," Tante Maria's voice was choked with horror. "Get on your feet. I must wash you."

It took help to get Monika upright. She was thankful that she was not expected to stand unaided. The tiny room was so crowded with Tante Maria trying to reach past her to the sink that the child could not possibly fall again. Tears that had filled her eyes during her sickness had been wiped away, and Monika watched as the faucet was turned. How spewing brown water could possibly make her clean was beyond her understanding. But Tante Maria was catching the water on a lace-edged handkerchief and smearing it around her "niece's" mouth. Monika was shaken by another spasm.

"Hold still," Tante Maria ordered.

"Please hurry," a man's voice called from the other side of the door. "I need to use the facility."

"Go to another carriage or use a window," Tante Maria snarled back.

He called her a name and slammed the door with his fist. When he was gone, Monika peered up at the woman.

"Where are we going?" she asked weakly.

"To your parents. To Berlin."

Chapter Six

✦ ✦ ✦

Sun and Shadows

"But I don't want to go to Berlin!" Monika wailed. Tante Maria Gruen began to shake her shoulders.

"Nikki! Wake up."

She did. The hands on her shoulders belonged to Paul Peterson.

"We'll be down at Schiphol in five minutes. Can you read this message?"

She blinked her eyes as he extended the sheet to her. He was standing in the aisle next to her, with a flight attendant hovering at his elbow. This unplanned part of their journey had put them on a crowded plane where they could not sit together.

This time the writing was French. She supposed the woman's second language—and the American overseas crew all had one—was not French.

"It confirms two seats on a KLM flight for Berlin. That's all." Nikki could have welcomed news that they could not be accommodated on a connecting flight. She forced a smile anyway.

"Now please return to your place and fasten your belt," the attendant nodded, taking a firm grip on Paul's elbow. "We are about to begin our descent."

"Okay. Thanks." He gave Nikki a warm smile. "See you on the ground."

"Just what worried you about the message?" Nikki asked when they were reunited in the terminal. "You were expecting that the seats would be arranged, weren't you?"

"Let's just say I had hopes," he chuckled. "When the President of the United States goes to Berlin, all the press of the world goes, too."

"But why us? Doesn't the bureau have someone already there?"

"Nope. The bureau uses Reuters. West Berlin is not where the action is, after all. It's only an island in a Red Sea, as someone once observed and every commentator since has copied. We are in Bonn, Frankfort, and Munich."

"So why not send someone who is already in Germany?" Nikki objected.

"To fly to Berlin, one has to exit Germany," Paul pointed out. "Usually that means coming here. To drive through the Russian zone could be difficult, especially if the Reds would rather not have the President's trip reported. I suspect, however, that our being airborne was only part of the decision. Donovan from Bonn would have been the logical selection. He was sent to Ireland before the press learned about JFK's Berlin side trip. Do we have time for coffee and something before the flight?"

"Yes. But I don't want anything. I'll take another pill instead and watch you stow the chow away. By the way, did the bureau find us hotel rooms as well as airplane seats? West Berlin is not exactly the convention center of Europe."

"You're right!" Paul nodded. "You want to help me make a long-distance phone call?"

He was nearly through his meal when he was paged. With Nikki's help, he talked with a friend in Berlin and seemed satisfied.

"Frank says it's not the finest accommodation, but we can stay with him. And he'll get someone to Templehof to meet us. Anything else we should be worrying about?"

Nikki shook her head. But she didn't feel comfortable about her lack of concern. What was going to happen, for instance, if someone found out that she had been a German citizen? Would she be allowed to remain?

This time they had adjoining seats. Nikki was glad. Paul wanted to talk, it seemed, and she certainly didn't want to fall asleep again.

"Do you think the Russians are concerned about Kennedy going to Berling?" Nikki asked once they were airborne.

"Probably," Paul allowed. "But the feeling is that Khruschev is fairly pleased with what the President had to say at American University. It was the first time in years that an American speech on Voice of America wasn't interrupted or jammed. So I suppose that Uncle Nick thinks he owes JFK something."

"It was a nice speech. The part about breathing the same air on the same planet and cherishing our children's future. It's a shame, though, that he didn't say it at Northwestern," Nikki decided. "David says that having a Democrat speak at commencement wouldn't cause the school to slide into Lake Michigan."

"But he can't prove it!" Paul laughed. "Kennedy's speech did set a good tone. Maybe, with Adenauer on the way out and DeGaulle taking the attention off of NATO for a while, the Cold War will truly end. Think what it would mean to the German people to see *The Wall* come down."

Think what it would mean to me, Nikki thought. She spoke aloud, "It can't come down. The best that could happen would be more gates. Otherwise all the talent will drain out."

"That's a little simplistic, don't you think?" Paul asked.

She shrugged. Once she had thought, as Doro still did, that Americans had all the answers. Now she recognized that what the people of the United States really had was distance. Building *The Wall* was almost exactly what Cook used to do when she canned vegetables and fruits. There was no deterioration once the ingredients were sealed tightly in the sterile jars. There was also no more growth, no increase in maturity or flavor.

The Wall meant very little to her personally. The time the Groebel family had spent in Berlin had been very short. Visits to East Berlin, of course, were out of the question. In fact, it was not often that she, Vati, and Mutti had gone anywhere. Once they walked in the Tiergarten, and several times they had shopped. Only rarely was she allowed to play outdoors.

"The President is still talking European unity," Paul announced, knuckling the *London Times* he had acquired in the terminal. "I like the sound of it."

"Sounds better in a non-election year," Nikki repeated one of David's remarks.

"You're a good newsman's daughter," Paul laughed at her. "Is your seat belt fastened?"

* * *

Their landing reminded Nikki of movies she had seen of people shooting rapids in narrow canyons. The plane dove for a runway, hedged by apartment houses. She wasn't sure that the pilot would pull out of the descent in time nor that her stomach would stay in place, for she tasted raspberries as she had in her sleep. Whatever happened, she wasn't sure that she cared.

Any fears that she had about their arrival, once the plane was on the ground, dissolved in the face of their press credentials. Frank, whose last name Nikki was never told but already knew from his bylines, was there to meet them. Their luggage, it turned out, was still in Holland.

"Welcome to Berlin's day in the sun," Frank greeted the pair. "One of the boys can retrieve your baggage later. It'll be on a press charter this afternoon."

The man's apartment was small, but there was a pair of daybeds in the bedroom.

"You get the couch," Frank pointed, "because you are the shortest."

"Do you have a dog?" Nikki asked. The last time she had been in Berlin, an animal had shared the couch with her each night.

"No." Frank's head tipped to the side as he regarded the out-of-context query. "But you might be able to entice a starling to the balcony rail if you work at it."

During dinner, which Frank prepared for them with some assistance from his guests, he gave Paul a summary of the presidential tour.

"Day before yesterday JFK was in Cologne. Went to Mass with the Chancellor at the Cathedral. Yesterday he was in Bonn for the chartering of the German Peace Corps. Quoted Dante on the hottest place in Hades going to those who maintain neutrality during moral crisis. At least he was smart enough not to say that in front of the Cardinal. I certainly hope he maintains his balance on this tightrope he has chosen."

"How do the Europeans see him?" Paul inquired. "In the States, he comes on almost like a monarch at times."

"If there's anything negative, it's the fact that he seems impetuous," Frank said after a pause to consider.

"You could say that," Paul agreed. "The Cuban missile crisis had us on tenderhooks."

"At least Cuba is in the Western Hemisphere. The Germans thought it would be a good place to fight if the major powers had to have it out." Frank poured coffee around, the offered Paul tobacco from a handsome porcelain humidor. "They have grown a little tired, over the centuries, of being the world's perpetual battlefield."

"What about Asia?" Nikki inquired.

"What about it?" Frank shrugged. "That's even farther away than Cuba."

"But it's the same land mass," she objected.

"Not in the European mind."

It was true, she realized. When she had first been with the Fishers, she was amazed at their knowledge of what lay across the Pacific Ocean. Some of their familiarity came from the time they had spent in Japan during the occupation and again during the Korean conflict. But their concerns about China and Mao, and more lately about those little countries where the French had been influential, still surprised her.

"You have to be a German to understand," Frank commented, noticing her frown.

She glanced at Paul. Catching the barely perceptible headshake, she let the comment pass. Nonetheless, it made her a bit irritable to sit at the table and listen to this self-proclaimed expert on the European mind hold sway.

It was an American problem, Donna had said once. A week in Paris made one see oneself as an authority on all things and people French. And while a resident of Illinois or Iowa might not understand the thinking process of a next-door neighbor, a mere stopover in a Scandinavian port provided more than enough contact to qualify culture, intelligence, and skills.

But Frank was not just their host in a place where beds were at premium. He had also secured their credentials for the Kennedy speech at the Free University of Berlin. Nikki made herself smile at him as if she were awed by his perception.

"Is the University his only stop?" she could hear Paul asking as she did her duty with the dishes.

"With our President, who knows? Rumor is that a caravan is ready to drive him around Berlin first. I suppose they want him to see *The Wall*. Anyway, we have a car ready to roll with them. Do you want to come along?"

"Not really. I can't imagine that he will say anything important before he addresses the convocation. And I am exhausted," Paul announced. "I have a hunch Nikki feels the same."

"Right. I'll leave the door on latch so you have only to pull it shut when you get ready to go," Frank told them.

She was exhausted as Paul had observed. Actually she was too tired to fall asleep easily. In the streets below, traffic seemed to lumber by. The building, whose foundations might well have been weakened during bombardment two decades ago, seemed to shake intermittently. And her dreams, when they came, were troubled.

* * *

There were Mutti and Vati, standing in the doorway of the apartment to which the Gruens led her. They had left the trail at a station in the Russian sector and walked to the Western side, through alleys and down streets edged in rubble. The jewelry box seemed to grow heavier with every step she had taken. At last Tante Maria had carried the box while Onkel Josef had lifted her in "his" arms.

While her parents hugged her and kissed her, the women disappeared. When they returned, both wore female attire although Josephine Gruen was sternly dressed. It was the women's home, Monika realized, not that of her parents. Mutti and even Vati helped to set the table, but Maria said where people were to sit. She took her place, next to Mutti and across the circular table from Vati, but she ate little. Instead she tried to follow the women's comments about the train trip. The men who had always been reading, it appeared, were back-ups for the escape.

"Escape" was the word Josephine used. It sounded so much more daring than "trip." It also made Monika's stomach hurt more.

"That woman…" she put in sleepily. "Why didn't she escape?"

"She tried to do it alone," Maria said flatly. "Too cheap to spend where it was needed. And look where it got her!"

Monika's head nodded against her mother's arm. Tomorrow she'd ask just where the woman was.

But the morning brought new terror instead. When she opened her eyes in the dusk of the room, Monika found a monster staring at her. He was red like the devil and had the same pointed ears. And he lay on top of her, pinning her legs against the couch. She could feel his breath, hot and vile, rising against her face. And then the devil yawned. The inside of his mouth was black as coal. Monika let out a scream. The devil sprang forward. His black tongue darted out and she knew she was about to be eaten.

* * *

Nikki forced herself to open her eyes. The room was nearly as gray as the one in her dream. Of course, there was no chow dog this time. She reached for the rug beside her bed, fingers searching for the Timex. When she held it close enough to discern the numbers, she realized it was still on Chicago time. But she could hear sounds in the apartment. It was time to be up and moving. She'd turned from political refugee to Presidential reporter (well, nearly) between Berlin visits, she thought, and it had not been so long. She reached for yesterday's blouse, then caught the impact of her suitcase resting on the floor next to the chair she had used for a makeshift closet. The white blouse, she decided, was exactly what was needed for this first day of her newest identity.

* * *

It was only an hour later that she and Paul challenged the streets. They had plenty of time before they needed to be at the University, and Frank had thoughtfully provided a map. Breakfast seemed like a logical beginning. The restaurants they passed, however, were all closed and locked. Some had cards tacked or pinned to the doors. The message was always the same. The proprietors were willing to let two Americans starve because the American head-of-state was in town.

At last they came to a small bakery where the aroma announced, before they opened its door, that some Germans were still tending to their trade. She tugged at Paul's arm.

"Let's stop for some kuchen at least. Often they have coffee available, too," she urged.

"Why not?" He followed her into the store. His stomach growled its agreement.

"So clean it sparkles" was an American advertising slogan, but for this establishment, it was the truth. She had forgotten the country's preoccupation with cleanliness and shine.

A young blonde was scrubbing industriously at the countertop. She looked up as Nikki approached, almost as if she were surprised by customers. Through a doorway at the back of the shop, Nikki caught a glimpse of a television screen. The structure shown, she knew from the past year's news, was Brandenberg Gate.

"Why haven't you gone to see President Kennedy?" Nikki asked after the girl had found two mugs of coffee and slices of kucken.

"The owner and his wife have gone. They left us with the TV. Lise watches now. It will be my turn later."

The clerk, Nikki discovered, was named Claudia and her age was fifteen. She had been born in Berlin to parents who were native. But she lived with her grandparents.

"Ask her about *The Wall*," Paul prodded, drawing a pen and paid out of his pocket. "See how she feels about it."

It had been only a fence at first, Claudia supplied, running along the street next to where her grandparents owned an entire house. "Very small, though," she qualified her boast. It had separated playmates. Annelore was now cut off from the rest of the group who had gone to school and to the park together.

"The boys would raid the garbage bins and bring rotten material to the fence," Claudia related. "They would throw it at the Russians and call them names. Most of the Russian soldiers don't know our language very well, but they did understand the missiles."

"Did you throw things, too?" Nikki translated Paul's query.

"No," Claudia laughed. "We girls climbed over the fence and went to Annalore's. The soldiers weren't going to shoot us, after all. You can't go around shooting children, you know."

"Did Annelore ever visit you?"

"She stayed on her side of the fence. You see, they put her in a new school. She was afraid that, if she came over, they might not let her go back. She wasn't old enough to work, and the Russians only like workers. Sometimes the soldiers would even help the very old and they very young to cross. Then when they tried to return, the guns would be drawn and pointed at them."

"Ask her how long she continued to visit her friend," Paul instructed.

The expeditions into East Berlin had come to an abrupt halt the day her grandfather had discovered what Claudia was doing. She rubbed a hand absently across her trim buttocks as she detailed the thrashing she had received. Soon afterwards the houses just east of the fence had been demolished. Then *The Wall* rose.

"It is too bad about *The Wall*," Claudia concluded soberly. "For my fourteenth birthday, Grandfather had promised to take me to the opera. Then I thought I would never go. But they say your Herr Kennedy has the ear of the Russians. Perhaps the opportunity will still come."

"What opera would you want to see?" Nikki asked.

"*Die Fledermaus,* of course."

Nikki nodded. "I hope you get there."

A voice came from the back of the shop.

"Lise is calling. Do you want to see the TV, too?"

Nikki looked at Paul and repeated the invitation.

"Thank her for her kindness. We must go on to the University."

Claudia nodded. There were great crowds, she gestured at the set where the President was waving at a throng who waved back. Perhaps they should hurry on to get there before the people followed him.

"He brings us good," she smiled as they left. "It is kind of you to share him with us."

At the school, Paul and Nikki ran the gauntlet of electronic wire and cabling to reach the more peaceful area in which the print journalism fraternity was assembled. Even here, however, the cues came from the broadcast side. Dozens of transistor radios followed the cavalcade's progress in almost as many languages.

"He blew it!" the correspondent for the Atlantic Coast's largest daily announced as he shook Paul's hand. "The peace of American University just went up in smoke. Did you hear it?"

When Paul explained their delay, the man pulled a tape recorder across the table, hit the rewind key, then the play button. The familiar nasal speech began.

"Today, in the world of freedom, the proudest boast is 'Ich bin ein Berliner.'" A finger activated the fast forward lever. The voice took over again. "...some who say in Europe and elsewhere we can work with the Communists. Let them come to Berlin."

The machine was silenced. In unison, the two men shook their heads.

"I suppose he was speaking from the heart," Paul finally allowed.

"The President doesn't need a heart, but a head certainly would help," the other journalist said sadly. "For a nice guy, he has repeated foot-in-the-mouth attacks."

The President certainly did, Nikki agreed without speaking. To be a Berliner was nothing to boast about. The rubble of the war had been cleared away and built over, but the debris of the so-called peace remained in the city's people. Most of the strong and usable citizens had been sent on, to the Federal Republic and beyond, much like the sorting process related to reparations at the end of World War II. Those who stayed in the city, powerless to deal for themselves, had given their destinies into the hands of others. Vati would have despised them.

Later, dining with Frank at a small restaurant he favored, they rehashed the two speeches at length. Kennedy had departed for Ireland, but the Berliners' jubilation over their brief time in the world's eye remained. The dining room staff wore red, white, and blue ribbons pinned on their uniforms.

"At least Kennedy modified his City Hall words a little at the University," Frank remarked as he twirled a wine glass by its stem. Candlelight reflected off the liquid. "Perhaps Khruschev will accept that he still believes the great powers must work together to preserve the race."

"He should," Paul decided. "Red Number One hasn't always had the best rein on his tongue, either."

"The question is," Nikki spoke up finally, "whether it makes any difference to Claudia and the other people who live here. Will things be better because President Kennedy came?"

"She does have a nose for news," Frank praised her in words and with a glance. "The immediate result should be an improvement, because he brought hope. In the long run, however, I think it has more to do with Adenauer stepping down. Ulbricht has given signs that he is more willing to deal with Erhard than with the Old Man."

"Will that mean *The Wall* comes down?" Nikki persisted.

"Not now. There are still too many people who want to leave. But the gates may be more open."

"Just think," Paul mused, "A thousand years from now tourists may walk along the Great Wall of Germany and ponder its implications."

"A thousand years?" Nikki asked, her heart suddenly heavy. "Could it really stand that long?"

"Not architects nor carpenters, but the determination of people…" Frank responded.

"Who said that?" Paul frowned.

"I did," Frank smiled ruefully. "Not all the world's thinkers are buried. If today doesn't make a difference, there is no reason for us to exist."

"I'll drink to that!" Paul raised his glass.

* * *

Nikki read the story of Kennedy's Berlin visit in German, French, and Italian as she sat in the hotel lobby. The newspaper rack in the library, actually the establishment's bar, did not contain this day's edition of an American paper. She would have liked to see one, preferably the one that was going to pay her salary.

Paul had filed not only official reactions to the speeches but also several interviews with ordinary Berliners, including Claudia. It would be interesting to see how the news editors chose to play the sidebar copy. Not surprisingly, the German and French publications picked up strongly on the "I am a Berliner" line. The Italians, on the other hand, chose to feature the speech at the university, merely noting that he had signed the Golden Book at Rudolph Wilde Platz.

She turned her attention to her surroundings. The Bristol Hotel Kempinsky had opened during those months the Groebels remained in West Berlin, continuing a century-old name. Mutti had wanted so much to dine there, but her wardrobe held no appropriate attire. What they had brought with them in their flight had a great deal of worth, but money was of little use when there was nothing to buy.

Mutti would have loved it if it looked then anything like it did this late June morning. The Persian rugs were jewel-like. The tapestries and antiques were much the same as those in the villa. Perhaps it was just as well that Mutti had not come. Frau Groebel was never sure that what she had given up was worth the freedom that Vati cherished so deeply.

Perhaps Nikki should not have left Paul alone to deal with the auto rental. Still the clerk spoke English, and Frank had lent his name to the cause. What kind of problem could there be? Somehow, in Berlin, it was easy to expect the worst. In desperation, she took a two-day-old overseas edition of the *Washington Post* to study. It was Katherine Graham's paper now. How David had been saddened by Philip Graham's death. She found some amusement in reading the *Post* predictions for the Berlin visit before turning her attention to the horoscope.

Doro had been responsible for her astrological interest, such as it was, calling her a head-strong Taurus. And she had answered by expressing doubt on the faithful who read their daily horoscopes before attending Mass. Yesterday Taureans were warned of "conflicts in family affairs."

She returned to her concern about Paul's whereabouts. He had decided to reward their Presidential reporting efforts by a short jaunt through the German countryside. His predecessor was leaving on the 29th and he thought it would be better if their arrival came after the fact.

"He's an absolute old woman about details," he had explained to Frank. "If I'm not there to get instructions on how to water his plants or empty his pencil sharpener, then some typist will get stuck with the duty. And that is fine with me. Besides, I need to see some of East Germany and the drive across will give me the opportunity for a look-see."

"Trains have windows," she had reminded him, although she wasn't sure it was a better alternative. Flying would have been her choice. Unfortunately it was everyone else's, too. And the others had availed themselves of round-trip bookings.

Just about the time Nikki was beginning to get warning signals from her stomach, Paul came limping across the carpet toward her.

"Sorry to take so long," he apologized. "I rented a car and got a lesson on auto manufacture in the bargain. But I think it is well worth it. For the next two days it's you, me, and a Mercedes diesel."

"What color?" Nikki asked with a frown. Germany was full of Mercedes, but the coincidence bothered her. Or perhaps it was just that there were so many of them in the past several days. Still, she would prefer it not being maroon.

"Muddy green. Only a woman would be more interested in color than in horsepower. Would you like to know what it has under the hood?"

"Nope. As long as it will get us safely through the corridor, I'd be satisfied with a lorry," Nikki grinned at him. Her lips felt as if she was pulling the skin to pieces.

"You've been giving too much credence to the Red press. The East Germans don't go around shooting Americans." His eyes clouded and he lifted a hand to his face. "I'm sorry. I forgot that you were once German. Were you ever in Berlin before?"

"A long time ago. Where do we pick up the car?"

The vehicle was double-parked at the side entrance. Had it not been for the tall plants gracing the lobby's windows, Nikki would have witnessed his arrival.

"Double-parked? I hope you don't get a ticket."

"No problem," Paul shrugged. "The doorman assured me that it is a common practice outside European hotels. At least, I think that was what he said. His English wasn't exactly fluent."

Nikki followed Paul outside. She gazed at the faded green vehicle, seeing a road readiness that wasn't always visible in Detroit products. Paul lifted their suitcases into the trunk and Nikki walked all the way around the car, inspecting tire tread.

"Why don't you go ahead and kick the tires," Paul invited. "What about your carry-on bag?"

"May we take that up front?" If anything happened to them, she wanted her jewelry case handy. "I want to do my nails."

"Are the roads that smooth?" His eyebrows raised.

"It's the Mercedes' shocks, not the roads, on which I put my trust," she responded.

When she slid into the passenger's seat, she laughed aloud at the interior.

"The Germans cling to their elegance," she responded to Paul's questioning gaze, pointing at the vases attached to the dashboard. "Couldn't you talk them into providing rose buds?"

"There's first class travel and then there is ostentatious. Let us not be greedy," Paul chided as he settled himself under the wheel. "The clerk said we were to go along...I can't remember the name of the street, but it had two syllables. Will you look at the map and see if you can find it?"

Nikki giggled.

"Did he say Kudamm?"

"Right. Where is it?"

"Under us. It's short for Kurfurstendam. Where are we headed when we leave the city?"

"That's your department," Paul told her. "As for me, the quicker we get to there from here, the better."

"Then as you leave here, turn right at the corner. At the very end of the Kudam, about two kilometers down the street, there will be signs directing us to the transit road. Be sure we don't miss it. Otherwise, we will end up in East Germany."

"Hey, the suspension is great," Paul announced as they halted at the Kurfurstendam intersection. "I could hardly feel the cobblestones."

"The transit road is the old Autobahn with all exits removed," Nikki continued her lecture, interrupted periodically by Paul's mutters about the number of pedestrians at every corner. "It's West Berlin's connection to West Germany. About 200 kilometers of East Germany first, though. The map says that the road takes us past Potsdam first."

"What?" Paul jammed on the brakes, narrowly missing three elderly women with shopping bags, "How did we get to Holland?"

"You must have learned your geography from drinking songs," she scoffed. "Potsdam is on the outskirts of Berlin. We reach the border at Magdeburg. Braunschweig is the first major West German city with exits we can use. We do have enough fuel to get there, haven't we?"

"According to the clerk at the rental desk, Ja. He said we must keep the rental papers with us, and we will have to pay some sort of toll," Paul related. "We have to pay the East Germans in West German money. They won't accept travelers checks, either."

"It's bad enough to be doing it," Nikki protested. "Let's not talk about it, too! Did he remember to remind you about following the speed limits?"

"Yes, he did. And he reminded me that we cannot stop once we enter the road except at those places marked on the map with a 'T,' as in 'tank.' I think they are like the turnpike plazas in the States," he reported. "The clerk also said he would never drive it."

* * *

While they were in the city, Nikki gave directions and translated signs for Paul. But once they entered the German Democratic Republic, she felt as if she were choking on her own fear. If Karl Groebel could disappear without a trace, how could his child feel safe? She tried to think whether there was a potential for real danger or if the most that could happen would be mere unpleasantness. Nothing she carried would connect Nikki Fisher to Monika Groebel and certain "valuables." Six years ago, the German government had lost interest when the missing man's family was unable to supply any leads. Was the lack of interest permanent?

Despite Paul's desire to view the countryside adjacent to Berlin, there was really nothing to see. From time to time, a cluster of buildings near the defoliated swath that edged the highway marked a collective farm. On the horizon there was an occasional hint of village as church steeple and town hall tower pointed toward an overcast sky.

She turned her attention to Paul, admiring the ease with which he piloted the vehicle. If the Mercedes had been like Vati's, with standard transmission, she supposed she would have been forced to drive. Could she have managed, she wondered, having to clasp her hands to keep them from shaking at the vision she was imagining.

"What's up, doc?" Paul intercepted her gaze. "Did I forget to zip my..."

"No!" she protested, feeling heat in her cheeks. "At least I don't think so...Oh, forget it. I was thinking how glad I was that you were driving the car."

"And that if it were not automatic, you would have had to play chauffeur to the cripple," he went on, without seeming to be offended. "But I had to pull up my pant leg to make them to agree to let us leave a car with automatic transmission in Frankfurt. Stick shift would have been no problem, but shiftless cars seem to be in great demand. Evidently German drivers are becoming as lazy in their driving habits as Americans. I sort of promised to mention the firm in a story."

"And will you?"

"Sort of. How much farther?"

"We're halfway to the border," she reported, studying the map and then the next milepost.

"Why does everything look so grey?" he asked.

"It's the mood."

She saw them ahead for what seemed like hours before they came abreast of the caravan, ten or more military trucks pulled over on the shoulder. There was a Fiat stopped in the road. A green-clad policeman was leaning down at the window. As they approached, another uniformed man waved to slow Paul down.

Nikki closed her eyes as they slid to a halt. How could they have known?

And then they were moving again.

"What happened?" she asked, turning in her seat to watch the troop growing smaller as their distance increased.

"Search me." Paul shrugged. "The policeman waved us on. Maybe he knew the driver of the Fiat."

Search, Nikki thought. Search Paul. Search me. What would they find? Addresses for the parents of Max and of Doro. Could that connect her with an escapee named Groebel? The Piaget watch was safe, but what about the ring? Were angel rings ever made in the West? Her papers? She thought not. Deep breaths, she thought, realizing that she was holding her lungs closed. Donna endorsed deep breaths for problems. There was an exercise she particularly favored, called breathing around the square. Breathe in to the count of four, then hold for another four. Four out, four without breath. Now begin increasing the count.

A few minutes later Paul reached across and tapped her thigh.

"Are you still with me? We're almost through this depressing area. How about cheering up?"

"Old fears die hard," she told him, trying to smile. "We didn't drive the last time. We rode a train. I was sick to my stomach the entire way."

"And how does your stomach feel now?"

"All knotted up."

"You took the medicine this morning?"

"Yes." She stroked his hand thoughtfully.

"Maybe a healthy belt of spirits will improve your condition. We can stop as soon as we get into West Germany," he suggested.

"Crossing the border will probably be enough. And we aren't going to drink until we get to the wine country. In the meantime, I must get my nails done." Reaching into the bag at her feet, she pulled out a bottle of nail polish.

"Nice," Paul commented on the smoky rose contents.

"Watch the potholes or you will end up wearing it, too," she retorted.

Now that she had gotten into it, she found it easy to concentrate on applying the nail lacquer. She was blowing the right hand dry when they had to slow for the boundary. The Fiat was directly ahead, and the driver was conferring with the guard. Could he have been told to see that the Mercedes was retained in the Demokratic Republic? She blew harder at the nails and tried to count her breathing again.

Traffic was getting heavier. Soon they saw a caravan of cars stopped ahead. The barbed wire along the road was more in evidence, and towers with armed guards rose every hundred feet or so. Nikki became increasingly edgy, seeing all the security around them.

The lines of vehicles crept slowly, but without apparent problems. The second car in front of them, a Volkswagen van loaded with young people, was directed to pull out of line and park alongside an official-looking building. Nikki watched, teeth clenched, as two armed guards yanked open the doors. Kids literally spilled out of the overcrowded vehicle. Backpacks and luggage were being tossed next to the van. She was sure that every nook and cranny of the vehicle were being searched thoroughly.

Nikki looked away, picking at the paint of a perfectly polished nail. Paul reached across to still her fingers.

"There will be no problem for us. Those kids didn't have papers, perhaps. Two of them looked pretty beat."

* * *

At the checkpoint, the guardhouse window was on Paul's side of the Mercedes. Nikki breathed a sigh of relief. She knew that her hands would have shaken if she had handed over their passports.

"Autopapiere, bitte!" The guard's command was harshly insistent.

Nikki nodded to show she understood. She removed the rental agreement from the glove compartment and passed it to Paul.

The envelope with the agreement was returned. Their passports were not.

"Oh, God!" Nikki breathed.

"The rental clerk said our passports would be hand-carried to where we pay our fees," Paul grinned at her. "You can pay our dues. Over there, I think, where it says 'Kasse.'"

"That means 'cash,'" Nikki agreed. "Should I get a receipt?"

"Damned right. The paper can pay tribute."

"Don't leave without me," she called over her shoulder.

"Wouldn't dream of it," Paul yelled back. A uniformed man scowled at the exchange before moving to the area where the van remained.

The man in the toll shed had no trouble taking the Deutsch Marks she passed across the counter. He did have some problem, however, in making correct change. She grabbed the stamped passports and the grey-colored receipt. So he made a little on the side!

As soon as she was back in the Mercedes, Paul pulled out into traffic. One more time they had to display their papers. Then they were across the border. To celebrate the fact, the sun finally broke through the overcast.

"A beautiful day," Nikki sighed deeply. "Just right for the Baederstrasse."

"Strasse for street. What's the Baeder?"

"Baths."

"Like get washed up?"

"No. Like health resorts. Cures. The Baederstrasse runs through several small cities and towns that boast healing baths. They've been there for centuries, from Roman days at least."

"So you take a bath and then you feel better?" Paul frowned.

"Not always. Sometimes you drink the water. My mother was big on baths. The worse they smelled and tasted, the better," she told him.

"That doesn't sound like Donna."

"I meant my real mother. Lots of Germans set great store on baths. Wiesbaden, where I used to live, is a bath city. The cure there was drinking water that smelled like rotten eggs."

"Sulfur," Paul supplied. "I didn't know where you lived."

"Wiesbaden water is popular with people who have stomach trouble. They drink it hot," she continued.

"Maybe you should have used it more often." Paul's eyes remained on the road, but he was stifling a grin.

"And it's good for sore joints if you immerse yourself in it. I always thought I'd like to go to Schlangenbad. That means Snake Bath, and you climb into a tub of mud to ease your arthritis. If we stop at a newsstand, I'll get a travel guide and read to you."

"Can't say that I'm that interested, but I just had a thought. Does Baden-baden mean bath-bath."

"Pretty close!" she praised. "That's where I met David and Donna, you know."

"I think I did know that. You were there with your mother. She had been ill."

"She was still ill. It was cancer. The surgery didn't get it all." Nikki looked out at the village through which they were passing. Soon they would be in the wine country with its vineyards, grown anew after the French had destroyed them so completely. It was the earth and the sun and the water that was credited with producing the quality fruit, but vintners knew that the secret was the wind. It brought the sweetness. Her hand went out to lower the window.

"Nice," Paul commented as he felt it on his face. "Your mother died of cancer?"

"I suppose that's what the doctor said, but sometimes I wonder if it is true. Do you think a person could die from living?"

"I don't think that's what you really mean, Nikki, and I refuse to discuss death. I want to hear more about what we are going to see."

She reached for the radio switch and turned the knob until she found a lilting German tune, with a lot of brass sound.

"That's mood music," she told him.

There was more traffic now. And then she noticed that they were again following the Fiat. Somehow, she was sure, the driver did know who she was. But there was some elaborate game in motion, and she didn't know the rules.

"Our friend again," Paul pointed ahead. "I trust we won't spend the entire day in his wake. Are you still navigating, by the way? Look, that sign says bath, doesn't it?"

"And so does the symbol. That's international, the snake and staff," she told him. "Take the turn to Bad Schwalbach to get to the Baederstrasse. Bad Schwalbach has mud baths for arthritis."

"How do you get the mud off?" Paul asked after negotiating the exit.

Nikki turned to look out the back window. The Fiat neither led or followed them.

"There's clean water from a spring to finish you off," she managed, feeling suddenly comforted by the warm sun and the bright surroundings.

"At this point, I am more interested in food and a room that in a bath," Paul decided. "Although a plain shower, if there are such things, might be welcome, too. Should we have made reservations?"

"Probably. There aren't many places that will put up a sign saying whether their rooms are taken. So we'll just have to keep stopping and inquiring."

* * *

Paul thought they should take turns at trying to secure rooms. Once, for him, however, was enough.

"They don't speak international sign language very well," he announced as he collapsed behind the wheel after his first lack of success. "Your offer to find our shelter for the night is gratefully accepted."

They had been rejected, graciously but firmly, by the proprietors of five gasthouses when Paul suddenly pulled off the road.

"I have to have pictures of that," he declared, gesturing at towers on the hillside. "The photojournalist strikes again. From here on, the camera and lenses travel up front with us."

He decided it had to be a castle and called for the telephoto lens to be sure. Whatever he had expected, he seemed satisfied, and walked back along the road to find a view that excluded telephone lines. Nikki followed, lugging the bag with the other lenses. She could see the structure far up the hillside, but it was too far away to define. Paul took one picture, moved for a second.

"It's really something," he said cheerfully, handing the camera to her for a view, "But I can't see how they got up there to build it. It is a castle, isn't it?"

"Looks more like a fortress with those towers," she observed. "But I think it's only a house. There is a television antenna, too, near one tower. They should have put it on top. The reception would be great. We had a tower like that, with stairway inside."

"Must have been some house. We'll have to go to Wiesbaden and see it. Hand me a polarized filter, if you please. I want to cut down the glare."

"It was before Wiesbaden," she said, complying with his request. He didn't seem to hear her. The rectangle in front of his eye was all that mattered.

"My stomach says that's enough. Let's pack up and get on with our quest. Even if we don't find a place for the night, I have to have some chow and a stein of beer."

"We're in wine country," Nikki reproved.

"Any country is beer country, and Germany is supposed to be the best. Anyway, what can they do except look down their noses at this ugly American with a thirst?"

"Now you're talking just like a tourist," she chided and climbed back into the car. The camera bag was stowed at her feet along with her carry-on.

It was fortunate she had small feet or "little under-standing," to quote a David witicism.

Their road wound through breathtaking curves, but it seemed to be all theirs. No trucks, buses, or cars. More important, no Fiat. Any smart German would be eating by now, Nikki decided. Even her stomach was beginning to suggest that lunch was more important than scenery. The car purred down into a picture-postcard valley filled with fairyland structures. The road sign proclaimed it to be Schlangenbad.

"This is the Snake Bath, remember?"

"Looks too nice for that," Paul retorted. "Maybe they have a restaurant for starving tourists."

"Some only open on the weekends," Nikki cautioned. "These appear to be that kind."

They had passed several with steel blinds over the windows and awnings rolled back into their recesses. There was a sanitarium, or Kurhaus, but few private homes. The road had narrowed to a bare two lanes surfaced in cobblestone. To the Mercedes, it made little difference in the ride. The church, coming up on their right, had marked the way to the front doors with urns of bright geraniums. A sculpted Madonna hugged the Christchild in her arms as she surveyed the roadway, unmindful of the offerings of flowers at her feet.

* * *

"How about this?" Paul nosed the Mercedes into a car park next to an immense structure. Each window—and there were many of them—was shaded by a bright red awning. "There must be a hundred rooms."

Nikki glanced at the vehicles around them and decided that it was entirely possible that they were all filled. She didn't care. A restroom was what she needed most at the moment.

They walked together along a stone walk flanked by more red geraniums, set off by impatiens. The lawns were as carefully manicured as golf greens in the States and dotted with willows beneath which were fishponds.

When they reached the doorway, Nikki caught at Paul's sleeve. The marquee read "Erdbadquelle."

"It's not a hotel, Paul," she whispered. "It's a sanitarium."

"No problem. We'll tell them we have come to see the snakes and take a bath. Let's go in and see what the bill of fare looks like."

"You're learning," she grinned at him as he held the door ajar. "No menu, no restaurant. At least not one that is competitive."

Immediately inside the lobby, Nikki spotted the sign she was seeking. Let Paul find the menu. She could translate better after her side trip. When she returned, she discovered him in a deep conversation with a chunky woman whose elbows seemed firmly anchored to the reception desk, but her hands danced like butterflies in a garden. It was too bad neither knew what the other was saying. Nikki put a hand on Paul's arm, which was also swinging wildly and smiled at the woman.

"Bitte?"

"Ja. Sprechen Sie Deutsch?" Hope replaced frustration on the round face.

"We were wrong," Nikki looked up at Paul after talking with the woman. "There are 350 rooms and 350 clients occupying them. Right now most of them are enjoying a recital. Can you hear the violin?"

On cue, a strain from Strauss floated down the long hall beyond the lobby.

"No food, either?" If he was trying to look as if his last meal were the week before, he was succeeding.

"Ah, but she knows of a good restaurant five minutes from here and she will call ahead. It's popular with the locals. And the owner is a cousin by marriage," Nikki reported. "She says to look for a white building with a white wine keg in front. The sign says 'Weinstube.' We stay on the road to Rauenthal."

"Regards to you and to your good cousin," Paul said, imitating the slight bow that he had observed in use among the citizens of Berlin. The woman blushed and thrust out her hand.

"Kiss it, goose!" Nikki ordered, struggling to keep her face under control.

"There's a first time for everything, I guess," Paul chuckled as they departed with the woman's best wishes. "Where did you disappear to, anyway?"

"The women's restroom."

"If there is a women's restroom, there should also be one for men. Does that make sense?"

"I'll wait out here for you," Nikki told him.

When he came out, he was wearing a broad grin.

"Pull chains on the toilets," Nikki interpreted.

"I guess they are so busy that they don't have time to modernize the plumbing." Paul shook his head. "A veritable gold mine—snakes and mud."

There was little doubt about their destination. As the receptionist had promised, there was an enormous wooden keg. Water flowed into a pool from the unstoppered vat. Lettering on the keg's sides proclaimed homemade Rhine wines, fine food, and a band on weekends. As soon as they were outside of the Mercedes, the aroma of baking and roasting welcomed them.

"How do you say 'heaven' in German?" Paul inquired, taking hold of her arm and pulling her toward the entrance.

* * *

As the number of cars outside suggested, the establishment was filled. Their host greeted them at the threshold.

"You are from Else, ja? May your meal be memorable! There is, however, a small problem."

Nikki repeated his words for Paul and her escort's face fell.

"Would you mind sharing the table of others?"

"Tell him we'll share a dish with his dogs," Paul said firmly when she passed on the query and nudged her to follow the man's lead.

They were barely seated and introduced to their tablemates when the waitress appeared with a tray on which two frosted goblets balanced.

"Please excuse my school English." She smiled toothily. "Welcome, Amerikaner. These come with Herr Acher's regards. The grapes grow on the hillside beyond our building, and their wine is the sweetest in all of the Rauenthal."

The two couples voiced their agreement, and Paul joined them after a sip.

"The word for heaven," he reminded Nikki.

"Himmel" the others chorused. They continued to include Nikki and Paul in their group, advising which choices should be made from the waitress's typed menu.

"Stop!" Nikki raised her hand in the universal sign. "We cannot possibly eat all of that. Sauerbraten and dumplings is what I want. Do you have it?"

The German families and the waitress laughed together.

"When Heinz Acher has no sauerbraten and dumplings, we will be gathered for his wake," one of the man explained after wiping his eyes on his napkin.

Paul agreed with Nikki's choice and, after another round of wine, the food arrived. The others were finished with their main course, but Nikki was certain they would make the wine and cheese last until the latecomers had also dined. The conversation lapsed in and out of German as they ate. She spoke to them in both languages so they would not embarrass themselves with remarks they did not want audited. And even she had to snicker at the quartet's amusement when Paul met red cabbage for the first time.

"It's not garnish, is it?" he asked in a low voice. "Please say it isn't. I like it."

"Enjoy it. That's called Rotkraut."

They had not eaten since morning, Nikki realized suddenly as she became aware that she was forking down everything that was available. She had brought to the table the clean palate that made food taste its best.

When the waitress removed their dinner plates, they joined the others at the cheese board. Their companions wanted to know where they had been, where they were going, how long they would stay. Each of the four had a suggestion on what should be seen and experienced. How pleased they were when Paul removed his note pad from his jacket and handed it to Nikki.

"Write everything down," he instructed. "And see if they have an idea of where we should spend the night."

* * *

They had. There was a small hotel several kilometers along. The diners knew the owners had five rooms that were available for travelers. Since it was not the weekend, surely one would be empty. One wasn't what they needed, but Nikki hoped it was merely a figure of speech.

"You did a marvelous job with your translations," Paul told her as they walked back to the car after a prolonged period of farewells. He had kept his back straight this time and shaken hands instead.

"It wasn't that good or that easy," Nikki told him, shaking her head. "They were speaking in a Hessian dialect, and I had to struggle for some of the words. It's like conversing with people from below the Mason-Dixon. Not only is the flow of speech different, but so are some of the words and expressions."

"Shall we get on our way?" Paul asked. "I suddenly realized in there that it was a long time since breakfast and longer since I last slept. Could you hear Frank snoring?"

"Oh, that was Frank?" she spoke with impudence, and then drew herself up against Paul's arm. "Paul, look. The Fiat again."

The car hadn't been there when they had arrived, she was sure, but now it occupied the spot next to the Mercedes. "Paul, that Fiat…"

"I'm sure there are many Fiats in Germany, although not so many as in Italy."

"It's the one that followed us today," she insisted. She would never forget that shade of blue. Her fingers tightened on his forearm.

"Followed us from in front?" His eyebrows raised. "No, Nikki. It is not the same. This has German plates. The other carried an international license."

They had changed the plates, Nikki was sure. She stared at it hard, trying to determine if there were people hiding inside. But Paul was drawing her away.

"Now read me the directions to wherever we are bound," he instructed once the car had started.

"Paul, let's not stop there. There will be another hour or so of daylight. We can go on for a while."

"And not find a room. It's not easy, remember? I turn right, right? No, make that right, correct?"

"Yes," she managed, keeping the panic out of her voice. But she turned and watched behind them. The Fiat was not coming.

"There is no one behind us," Paul said firmly. "There is no one ahead of us. There isn't even anyone coming toward us at the moment. And we are not actors in some spy novel. At least, I'm not. Are you, Nikki?"

"No," she admitted in a very small voice. But the admission did little to diminish her fear.

"Stop that swiveling!" Paul ordered. "If there were a Fiat behind us, I would have told you."

Nikki made a face at him before turning her attention to the road along which the Mercedes moved rapidly. She was tempted to ignore the directions provided by their dinner companions, or to make an improper translation so that there would be more distance between themselves and the suspicious car. If she told him that something had been left out of the instructions, Paul would never know. Yet, when the time came, she could not lie.

"This turn off. That must be it on the hill."

The road was hardly more than a lane, and it seemed to wind along forever. Then, as they swung left and back again, the gate was directly ahead of them. It was of the same wrought iron that decorated the top of a brick wall separating courtyard from countryside.

"Do we go through?" Paul asked.

* * *

"The gate is open and this is definitely the place," Nikki laughed. "You asked for heaven and we have arrived."

Centering the parking area was an immense scarlet wine barrel. Its lettering read "Gasthaus Himmel." Flowers nestled around it. Nikki wasn't sure just what, beyond petunias, the blooms might be.

"I'm crossing my fingers that St. Peter doesn't turn us away," Paul told her as she got out of the car.

Nikki looked for a bell or knocker, but finally pushed on the door and called out.

From a distance down the dark cool hall another door opened. A boy in his early teens came toward her.

"Ja, bitte?"

"Do you have rooms available? Some people at Herr Acher's restaurant thought you might."

"I will call my father. You will wait?" He disappeared through the door from which he had come.

When it opened again, a man in his middle years came through. He stopped directly in front of Nikki and asked how he could help. When Nikki had completed her request for two rooms for the night, he nodded gravely.

"You dress American and speak German. Which are you?"

"I am both, I guess," Nikki said before she thought. She tried to correct it. "I have lived in both countries. But I am with an American."

"I have lived in both countries, too," he confided in English. "The money to put my father's property back into operation was earned in America. Do you know Milwaukee?"

"Do you know Chicago?" she responded and allowed him to shake her hand.

"It is a good sign, I think," he lapsed back into German. "My wife turned a couple away not an hour ago because there was a reservation for the Doerfners. Then they phoned to say there was trouble with the car, and they cannot come until later this week. So I have their room for you. It has a shower and a toilet. Is that not nice? And Lotte serves you breakfast. The charge is fifteen Marks for each of you."

"I really need two rooms," Nikki told him. "My friend is male."

"There are two beds in the one room. It may be many more kilometers before you find a place so good. And darkness comes soon. You decide."

"I'll have to ask him," she said.

"Yes, you do that. I will wait to show you where."

Reluctantly Nikki recrossed the courtyard to the Mercedes. Paul was outside of the car, looking under its hood. Just how, she wondered, did she phrase the potential host's offer without making it sound like a come-on.

Paul straightened up as he heard her footsteps, striking his head against the metal. His hand went up to check his hair for grease.

"Well?"

"Sort of well," she answered, coming to stand beside him. "He has one room with two beds and a bath. To him the two beds guarantee propriety."

"Unaccustomed as I am to sharing a room with my translator, let me say that I am exhausted. I don't bite, and I don't snore." Paul responded.

"You are positive that was Frank last night?" Nikki asked, trying to lighten the moment. It might be fine for Paul, but she was terribly uneasy. Arriving at Heaven shouldn't mean having to worry about suspicious cars and compromising situations.

"You saw him this morning. Which of the two of us do you think got the sleep? Or am I treading on your morals?"

"We'll take the room," Nikki decided. Before she could change her mind, she drew out both bags from the front seat. With Paul following with the suitcases, she stalked back to the door. The man waited, a key dangling from his hand.

"Up the stairs. First door on the right. Is he from Chicago, too?"

"Yes. Where do we register? And our passports?" Nikki inquired.

"Later my wife will return. She fills in the papers." The man changed tongues and attention. "Welcome to Gasthaus Himmel."

"Heaven," Paul responded. "Let me climb those golden stairs."

The stairs were not golden and they were steep. He finally abandoned one suitcase at the landing, just beneath the telephone.

"Heaven is a two-trip journey," he remarked dryly as he reached the top with the remaining bag.

"Shall I..." Nikki began.

"No, you shan't. Just get the door open. There's a big difference between being handicapped and helpless."

Nikki had never accepted the phrase about believing one's eyes, but it became suddenly appropriate when the key had done its job. The room, despite its mismatched furniture, was completely decorated in pink and white. Her heart sank. They needed a room, one that was as businesslike as their relationship. What they had was a love nest.

"Omigod," Paul groaned behind her.

She turned, fearing what his face would show and found him doubled over in laughter.

"Is this for real?" he choked. "And just where are those two beds?"

"Here." She lifted the corners of the white featherbeds so he could see the frame that divided the structure. "It's two mattresses and two sets of bedding. But I had forgotten that the Germans join them together to save on space. I'm so sorry."

"Do we sleep under, on, or in these things?" Paul fingered one of the featherbeds. "They're like sleeping bags, aren't they?"

"Underneath," Nikki supplied, thankful to be spared all the obvious remarks. Her gaze moved from the bed, which was dark wood, to the white dresser with pink scarves across its top. White sheer curtains billowed away from the window to stroke a small table with its pink embroidered cloth. Her eye caught a white door in the far corner, and she crossed to it.

It was the promised bathroom and, as far as she could tell, there were no more unpleasant surprises awaiting. Grabbing the handle of her suitcase, she boosted it inside.

"Me first," she announced.

* * *

Since the fixtures were white, the shower curtain and the towels had to be pink. After she had pulled off her clothes, she wrapped one of the towels around her hair. Wet feathers resulted from wet hair. Pillows and bedding would smell the entire night. She remembered the odor well from the kitchen at Peter's house when his aunt was plucking chickens.

Adjusting the shower head to spray on her shoulders and the temperature to very warm, Nikki stepped into the enclosure. As her hand probed the soap dish, she realized that she had been wrong about the surprises. German inns usually did not supply soap.

"Paul," she shouted before remembering to turn off the water. "Paul, can you hear me?"

He thrust his head in the door as she put hers through the curtain.

"Did you fall in?" he inquired with a grin.

"I need soap. It's in the carry-on case. I think I put it next to the table."

He was back a minute later, pulling a soap case from his shaving kit.

"Here's mine. It's guaranteed to wash clean, although it may not smell as nice as yours."

She managed to keep the curtain discretely in place as she reached for the soap. If she were to lose control of it, she knew she would die. One of the girls in his seminar was always baiting Paul, Nikki remembered uncomfortably. Sherry managed an extra open button for copyediting or allowed her wrap-around skirt to gap. Paul had ignored the view and spoke to "Miss Talcott" in exactly the same tone as he used for other students. But Sherry hadn't ever given up.

"I never slept with a one-legged man, and I really would like to see how he'd manage to hump," the girl had declared.

Nikki wished the classmate hadn't come to mind. Things were bad enough already. With determination, she consigned Sherry to other than heaven and lathered her body. Still, as she began to dry her body, she found herself comparing her attributes to those of Sherry's. If only her legs were longer, the contest might be a draw because her breasts were definitely better. And, despite the length of the thigh and calf, Sherry's feet resembled those of a duck while Nikki's were small and well-shaped. The contest might have continued except for the sharp rap on the door.

"Don't come in," she shrieked as she tried to arrange the towel around her torso. After the third time, the lapover seemed to hold and she inched the panel open. Paul stood on the other side, a stemmed glass extended toward her.

"Wine to get clean by," he announced in a voice that was so like "Very good, Miss Talcott" or "Your headline lacks a verb, Miss Talcott."

So much for seduction, Nikki thought with relief as she reached for the drink. Even the stem was chilled. She took a sip and smiled her gratitude.

"I went downstairs and asked for a cold drink. And this is what I got. For under a dollar, too. Sure beats cola."

Beyond him she could see that the camera was lying on the bed. All the good feeling she had been developing drained away.

The alarm must have shown on her face because Paul was grinning at her.

"Just the room, Nikki. That's all. I had to have a picture of what heaven looked like for future reference. Now hurry up so I can have my turn at the water. It's not muddy, is it?"

"No, and I'll only be a minute. Just have to find my robe." She closed the door and took a deep swallow of wine. Her imagination was doing her in, and she was behaving like a school girl.

The photographic gear had been stored away by the time she emerged. Paul's pajamas and robe were stacked together at the foot of one bed. On the table was a container of ice with the bottle resting in it. A bowl of pretzels sat nearby.

"A day without beer, perhaps," Paul pointed. "But this ugly American still needs his pretzels. Have some."

"You have to be kidding! I am still waiting for the Brie to work itself out of my ears," Nikki told him.

"I think we are going to have a problem," Paul announced from the bathroom door. Nikki stopped refilling her glass and spun around to face him.

"There is no way I can continue to eat and drink like this," he told her and shook his head when she laughed. "Seriously, Nikki, my mobility depends on keeping my weight controlled. You are going to have to help me choose things that aren't so fattening."

"Okay, boss." She grinned back. It was too easy to forget that anything was wrong with him. And she could do it, although she subscribed to the theory that good and fattening were synonymous.

* * *

It was a relief to have the door shut between them, to be truly alone for just a little while. The wine was so good, she decided, just what was needed to level out the daylong push and pull on her emotions. After the third glass, she took a stern look at herself in the mirror. Without makeup the dark circles, brought on by their flight and the stay in Berlin, were prominent. But a touch here and there might make it better.

She tried a little eyeshadow, then added mascara. Perhaps a little color for her cheeks. A definite improvement reflected back at her. She stroked gloss across her lips and nodded again. Why not a bit of cologne? She withdrew the plastic container of White Shoulders that Donna had assured her was essential for flying and pushed the plunger. The bottle dropped away and the scent splashed on her, the dresser, and the rug. As the odor rose to assault her nose, she broke into tears. Now the place smelled exactly like a whorehouse!

She was still crying and trying to scrub her face with tissue when Paul came back into the room.

"What in heaven's..." he began.

She answered with a wail.

"Heaven, indeed!"

His hands turned her toward him and his shoulder cushioned her smeared face. And as his arms tightened, she gave way to her despair.

"It's all right, Nikki. Everything is all right. I am here. I will take care of you."

It was like a litany, repeated softly over and over. Nikki responded by clutching at him. Confusion, security, and pleasure melted into unbelievable comfort.

First she was standing tight against him, then sitting on his lap, and finally lying across the featherbed, with his arms supporting her head and shoulders. Her belt had come undone and the robe lay open as Paul kissed her damp eyes. His lips created a feather trail down her face and neck.

She wiggled against the sensations and pressed her mouth against his temple. She let her arms loop around his neck, then tightened them to keep this comfort close.

"Underneath the featherbed." Paul's voice was rasping. And there they were. She increased her grip. Her teeth took over for her arms, fastening firmly on his shoulder and her hands began to travel down his body as his mouth touched her breast.

Her body moved against his with total abandon. More comfort, she cried in her mind. Paul held back no more. His power was the ultimate comfort.

Afterward they lay in the dusk, still in contact. Nikki's hands felt his laughter before it came.

"I think the appropriate phrase is 'Thanks, dad. I needed that.'"

"I did need it," she conceded. "And I do thank you."

"What about 'dad'? I am old enough," he reminded, his lips moving across her forehead.

"Not to be my dad, you're not. Oh, Paul. You don't know me."

"I don't?" He came up on his elbow and looked down at her, eyebrows raised. "Are you certain of your facts?"

"Yes, Professor." The time had come to tell him and, instead of it being a trial, she found herself giggling. "My father was nearly fifty when I was born. But that's not what's important. You need to know, Paul. I escaped from the East."

"Oh, Lord!" he exclaimed. Concern crossed his face. "No wonder the zone had you so upset. And your father. Did he escape, too? Or was it just you and your mother?"

"My parents and I came out. But we left my sister behind. I'll tell you about that sometime if you want to hear. About eight years later my father just disappeared one day." Her hand tightened on him. "Paul, that Fiat. Do you think they know that I have come back?"

"Nikki, those were two different Fiats we saw, not the same car. Believe me. But I'm glad you told me about being a refugee. It may make a difference in some of the things we do. And it sure is a lot easier to understand your fears. I was beginning to think I had hired a closet paranoid. Instead I find you are a beautiful, lovable young woman who shouldn't be carrying on with a dirty old man like me."

"I guess maybe it's not recommended for a business relationship, but try me again some time." She wanted to repeat his "dirty old man" phrase, to ease whatever guilt he might feel, but the words would not come.

"Truly?" He waited to see her nod. "How long is some time?"

"Sixty minutes, later tonight, tomorrow morning. Why don't you surprise me?" She reached a fingertip out from under the featherbed to stroke his nose. Sherry Talcott, she thought, eat your heart out!

"Ah, heaven!" he sighed and pulled her to him.

Section Two

✶ ✶ ✶

Once There Was a Love

"Life teaches us to be less severe with ourselves and others."
—*Goethe*

Chapter Seven

Homecoming

The German summer was warm and soft, adding to Nikki's feeling of well-being. It was a good omen, she decided, that the grey sky had not returned since the day she arrived in the Federal Republic.

Sun had beamed down on the countryside that second day at the Weinstube Himmel. At night she had slept in her own bed. There had come an unspoken understanding between Nikki and Paul that comfort and romance were separate commodities.

She had posed many times for him, but always with scenery in the background. The son of the inn's owner had snapped both of them in front of the barrel sign so that David and Donna would know they were well. But after two days in their Rauenthal "Heaven," she and Paul had gotten down to the earthy realities of work.

Frankfurt held the office. Darmstadt, however, had become their home. Paul had a friend, Dick Dower of the military installation's public affairs office, who insisted that Frankfurt needed no new residents. At well over half a million, it was burgeoning.

"The trick is to find a spot for Nikki that is near enough the sisters' home to allow two of you to function with one car," Dick told them. The "sisters" were two women with whom Dick had roomed prior to his marriage. One was a retired school teacher, the other a widow. They liked having "a man around the house."

While Paul's landladies had known of no available residence for Nikki, their butcher had. So Nikki had taken over the room, vacated by a daughter now employed in Bonn, in the Schneiders' ground floor apartment. This casual selection of living quarters had worked, Nikki told herself as she stood in the kitchen, watching Frau Schneider stuff linens into the antiquated wringer washer. Her own task, intermittently, was hanging the laundry on the drying lines outside.

She and Paul had worked, too, both hard and well. The amount of what needed to be covered amazed her. There had been conferences, single interviews, committee meetings, photographic sessions, social events, and the constant need to verify facts. She was becoming skilled in research. Each assignment from Paul was like solving a mystery. She had begun to think of herself as Nikki Fisher, girl detective.

Today's work, however, was scheduled for late afternoon. Paul said they would stay away from the office until then. The event was a private reception for textile manufacturers prior to the opening of a week-long showing. Nikki had purchased a new dress for the affair.

Its deep rose reminded her of the first formal gown she had ever worn. The occasion was a shipboard party during her Atlantic crossing with the Fishers. Donna had taken that other gown from her personal wardrobe and altered it for her "elder daughter."

Paul was in for a surprise when he came by for her. Yesterday Nikki had stayed in Frankfurt after work to visit a beauty salon. Her shoulder-length hair was gone. Instead, a Sassoon cut exposed her ears. Although the stylist had insisted that the appendages were of exactly the right shape and size, Nikki clung to the opinion that they resembled both back doors ajar on a taxicab. To change the impression, she had invested in a pair of heavy loop earrings.

* * *

When the wringer had pulled the last pillowcase between its rollers, Nikki reached for the wicker basket into which the clothes had fallen. She grinned as she recalled the day she had attempted to wring pillowcases. Her first attempt had entered the wringer open end first. As the fabric progressed into the mechanism, it began to balloon until the bubble of water had been forced through the fabric, drenching her and half of Frau Schneider's kitchen. Now she left that work to the Frau, who knew that the sewn end always entered the rollers first.

The yard was perfumed by roses that marked its perimeters. Once the sheets were on the lines, the notched clothes poles had to be inserted to keep the linen off the grass. Before she delivered the basket back to the kitchen, Nikki picked a bouquet of small blooms with distinctive teacup shapes. They reminded her of a bush that had grown at the villa near Leipzig.

She might bring a rose when she met Paul later. In bits and spurts, during their travel between appointments and the daily drives from office to home, she had continued the practice begun in the Rauenthal of telling him about her earlier life. Now he knew something about proud Vati, elegant Mutti, and determined Hanna as well as Kurt and Peter.

Talking about the people was easy. It was more difficult, however, in describing happenings because of Paul's reportorial "why." There were so many answers that she didn't have.

"Do you shop before lunch?" Frau Schneider asked over the water bubbling merrily down the sink drain.

"If you need something, I'd be glad to," Nikki grinned. The stores of the neighborhood enchanted her.

"Then I would like a tube of Rei. Otto has a wine stain on his Sunday shirt." The Frau held up the offending garment, set aside from the rest of the laundry. "It is good for fine fabrics like your underwear and the tube, while small, goes a long way. You should buy some for yourself, too."

The errand took Nikki to the corner and then through a small park to the Lebensmittel. The grocer, Herr Braun, stopped shelving goods as she entered.

"Very good product," he concurred with Frau Schneider when Nikki ordered the cleaner. "Anything more?"

"What do you have on ice?" Nikki knew, as soon as it was out of her mouth, that she had translated an American phrase directly to German and he would misunderstand.

"The fine Italian ice, of course."

"I mean to drink. A soda?"

"Ah, yes. The American cola is cold."

"That's what I want. May I take the bottle and return it later?"

"By Friday," he cautioned. "They deliver then."

She was part of the way through the park when she heard Paul's voice:

"Can that be Nikki Fisher? The girl looks the same, except she must have caught her hair in the wringer."

"Yes, it's Nikki." She turned, smiling even though her surprise had been ruined. And then she stopped short.

Paul was seated on a green bench, the back of which advertised a local department store. Next to Paul sat a woman, young and Germanic blonde. A little girl played nearby in a sandbox.

"Come on over," Paul beckoned. "I sorely need a translator. Nikki Fisher, this is Delia Harbaum. And the resident gremlin is Heike."

Nikki spoke her greetings in German. The woman responded immediately, her speech as rapid as a cascading stream in the mountains.

"You are Nikki who works with Paul. And your hair is marvelous. Men think long hair is glamorous. My husband, who died last year, always wanted me to keep mine long. They should have the bother."

"Ask her if she will have dinner with me tomorrow night—say seven o'clock. That will give us time enough to file copy on the textile fair." Paul pulled Nikki to the bench on his free side. "I asked her in English, but I'm not sure of her response."

Leaning across him, Nikki made the appeal to Delia, adding her opinion of Paul as a good and kind person. But Delia was certain of that already. She and Heike had encountered him several times before. And Nikki's message excited her. She thought Paul had meant tonight, and Heike's grandparents had tickets for a concert. But tomorrow would be just fine. Should she be ready at seven or was that when Paul planned to meet her parents.

"Pfui, schmutzig. Pfui!" Heiki ambled over to interrupt Nikki's words Paul. The youngster's face was creased with dismay as she examined the condition of her hands.

"Please to excuse us," Delia stood and reached for the child. "My daughter wishes her hands to be washed."

As soon as the pair were out of earshot, Paul began a rapid explanation about Delia. She was, he claimed, very shy and proper. Her husband, who instructed at the University of Heidelberg, had been killed in a traffic crash. The young widow now lived in Darmstadt with her parents. How did Nikki like her?

"I like her very much," Nikki told him. "But more to the point, she likes you. She will be very glad to go to dinner tomorrow. The question is whether you mean seven o'clock to leave or to meet her father mother."

"Hey," he protested, hands rising. "I only want to feed her, not marry her."

"That may be, but her parents must protect her status as a proper widowed mother," Nikki counseled. "They need to know you just a little."

"Will they think…" he began.

"They will think you are a good man to give their daughter a nice evening," Nikki said firmly.

"I appreciate this." Paul nodded his head. "You tell her that it is fine with me. And I'll be by to pick you up about four today. The Textile Messe reception begins at five."

Nikki passed on the message with proper flourish.

"Paul will be delighted to make your parents' acquaintance at seven," she told Delia. "Do I need to explain how to find your home?"

"That is not necessary," Delia beamed at her. "He had escorted us to the house before."

"Have a marvelous evening," Nikki told her before bending to make her farewell to Heike. So Paul had been busy. She thought he had done very well.

* * *

Frau Schneider, having disposed of her mate's wine-spattered shirt, was reading a German romance when Nikki came down the hall to await Paul's arrival.

"You look good enough to eat," the woman decided after thoroughly examining the gown and the earrings. "Just like the lady in my book. And don't you think the hero tried! I like your little watch."

Nikki held out the Piaget for closer inspection. She had determined that it was better to wear the little disabled timepiece than to know the exact time.

"I was given it when I was small. But now it works only when it wishes."

"Who needs to regard time when she is young?" Frau Schneider asked with a demonstrative hand.

Their shared vehicle was no longer the dull green Mercedes but a semi-new Opel convertible, acquired from an Air Force officer transferring Stateswide. Paul had its top up when he came for her.

"Don't want all that hair blowing around," he told her dryly as he folded her skirt around her legs and closed the door gently.

"I thought it would be nice for a change," Nikki offered. "After all, I need to be in vogue for the textile fair."

"It's your head," he said shortly. "The rest of you looks just fine, though. I don't suppose that's a designer frock."

"You don't suppose correctly. I got it off the rack at a little shop around the corner from the office."

"The color is as nice as the fit. Have you ever worn that shade before?"

"For my first formal dance." She related the tale of Donna's made-over dance dress for him. "How long will the reception last?"

"Two hours, at least. Every exhibitor in the Textile Messe will be there so don't get far from me. There'll be people from all the countries in Western Europe, and I can't spend all my time with the English, Scots, and Irish."

"My ears are your ears and my mouth your mouth," she agreed.

"Once, when we were in heaven, there was more," he reminded with a chuckle.

The convivial reception extended well beyond the time period Paul had suggested. When that party had broken up, they had become guests of a French couple for dinner. Their surname, Metier, appeared on cottons and synthetics patterned in startling color and design. The plant was in Visoul. And they were Jacques Georges and Jacqueline.

"Jack and Jackie, just like your president and his wife," Madame Metier told them in heavily accented English. "Jacques had made reservations at the Henninger Tower. I do so love the way it revolves, don't you?"

Nikki smiled and nodded. There was no point in confessing that she had not been there before. The woman obviously was trying to emphasize the similarity in Kennedy style as well as name. Her "little" black dress had a

Chanel jacket, which Jackie Metier donned for the trip to the restaurant and shrugged off once they were seated. Then the short white gloves were removed. Only the black toque remained perched firmly on the pageboy coiffure.

"I suppose we must drink beer," Jacques decided. "Anything else in the Hennigen-Turm seems inappropriate."

"Please order a dubonnet for me," Jackie corrected him. "And ask for extra coasters, too."

Challenged, Nikki opted for a Christian Henninger Export. She suspected it improved the entrée, Hirschruckensteak "Diane" with spaetzle.

"Your gown is charming in a nouveau femme mode, my dear," Jackie leaned toward her as the course was changing. "Which designer is is that uses that hue so effectively."

"Donna," Nikki, emboldened by the beverage, responded.

"Ah, Do?a," Jackie repeated the name, adding a tilde. "I believe she will put Spain on the fashion map."

Nikki stared out the window into the twinkle of lights as Henniger Tower slowly revolved to give the diners a 360-degree view of Frankfurt. She knew she'd explode with laughter unless she could keep her mind on other things. Paul's face, wreathed in candlelight, started back at her in the reflection. She was sure his eyes were twinkling along with the tiny flames.

As her eyes shifted, she thought she noticed Jackie writing on a coaster. When she turned back to the table, the woman was smiling at the circle in her fingers.

"Please put this on the glass, Nikki." She passed the disc across the table.

There were other circles with messages already there, Nikki realized as she complied. "Try the champignons in crème," one suggested. Another bade the reader to taste "the Preiselberries on the pancakes." Jackie's contribution, penned in her native tongue, promoted the Ragout in French pastry.

The waiter had just poured the after-dinner coffee when Madame Metier raised her eyebrows to Nikki in the international request for companionship during a ladies' room visitation. Nikki's head swiveled in an attempt to spot the correct exit. It had to be one of the hazards of rotating restaurants, she decided. The sign on the nearest door was for the museum. According to the leaflet they had received along with the menu, it chronicled the company's 900-year experience in the brewing trade.

Jackie whispered to her husband who rose and withdrew her chair. Paul took the cue to extricate Nikki from her seat nearest the window. With the French woman's arm linked in hers, Nikki discovered their destination was to their left.

A steel stairway spiraled downward before them. Nikki led the way, Madame Metier's stached heels clattering behind her.

"Thank heaven we did not have to climb down all 731 steps to get here," Jackie observed as Nikki held open the restroom door.

* * *

Paul and Jacques were discussing textile manufacture when the women returned. Nikki supplied an occasional phrase when the jump between languages confounded the men, but they seemed to be managing well. Once, when Paul had resorted to slang, she started to open her mouth. Jacques, to her surprise, caught the words in perfect context and began his answer.

"We know the English beyond the school room," Jackie explained. "And it is a good thing, because our business takes us to New York each year."

Nikki listened, fascinated as the woman described a celebration of the lifting of the siege of Orleans by troops led by Joan d'Arc. The traditional religious and folk parade had wended its way through the town with a sixteen-year-old in armor portraying Joan. She was mounted on a white steed and six men marched behind, bearing the banner. Then came the clergy. Behind them were a variety of marching units, including American soldiers. Their rifle muzzles were filled with flowers.

"That way May 8, 1945, and the war was over," Jackie summed up.

Lucky French, Nikki thought. They had a date from which they could begin again. Frankfurt, shining up at them from across the Main River, also had a time of beginning. But there was Berlin, and there was the Germany beyond *The Wall* where the people still awaited both ending and beginning.

She was still somber as they drove back to Darmstadt.

"You did not enjoy dinner," Paul declared.

"Oh, but I did. They were overbearing, but I had to like them."

"I noticed. You liked them so much that you gave Jacqueline the name of your favorite designer."

"Maybe the ugly American symptoms are catching."

"And maybe you are working too hard. I have decided that the time has come for you to revisit Wiesbaden. Why don't you try to telephone your friends there and go up for the weekend? Make it three days if you like. We can manage without you on Monday."

She thought about it as the kilometers passed. If Paul thought it was time, he was probably right. And it was getting harder to write to Doro and Max, always apologizing for not having seen their families.

"I'll go," she decided finally. "But you must come, too. Or do you plan to spend the weekend with Delia?"

"She's going to Munich with her family. And don't you start trying to arrange my social life. Wiesbaden it is."

* * *

"The chariot awaits with its top down," Paul announced as he took Nikki's bag from her. He frowned at its weight. "Did Max and his wife send American bricks for their families?"

Nikki giggled. Most of the offerings were photographs of the American family.

"Not exactly. But I had to put in a pair of slacks and a couple of tops, plus my bathing suit just in case we get to go to the Opelbad."

"Another bath? Just like Wiesbaden?"

"You're learning," she grinned at him as they went out to the car, Frau Schneider trailing them to the threshold. "The Opelbad is a marvelous public swimming pool. We spent a lot of time there when we were kids."

"And how was your evening?" she asked, still waving at her landlady.

"Excellent. Delia is an extraordinarily comfortable person. And I licked the language problem by a stroke of genius."

Nikki knew he was baiting her. She took her time before asking the expected question. Perhaps, if she thought hard, she could figure out the answer. She was sure he wouldn't have been so crass as to drag the poor woman to the Officers Club at the base.

"*Lohengrin* sounds the same no matter where it is performed," he told her gravely when she finally had to inquire. "And it was playing at the Stadttheatre in Frankfurt. We both enjoyed it immensely. Now brief me on our trip. The Kneipps are Max's folks, right? And they live in the same house where you did."

Nikki chuckled as she reviewed the news she was about to share. The telephone connection had been difficult to make and, when the small voice asked her which Frau Kneipp she wished to speak with, she had felt unsure. It turned out that the frail tone was Frau Bruno. Frau Wolfgang was at the shop. Perhaps she would speak with Herr Bruno.

His voice hadn't changed that much, but in her excitement, she used her American name. It caught him unawares, and he struggled with it. When she managed the correction, enthusiasm flowed through to her.

"You are calling from where?"

"Darmstadt. Didn't Doro and Max tell you I was coming to Europe?"

"Yes, but then we didn't hear, so we thought you chose not to stop here on your visit."

"It's not a visit," she told him. "I'm working here. And I would like to see you and your folks this weekend. Do you all live together?"

"No. We stopped up so that Liesel could use the sewing machine. We live below, in your home. Do you mind?"

Mind! It was marvelous news. She had dreaded having to walk by the familiar door on her way up to the Kneipps. And now she could see it once more.

"Even their telephone number is the same as ours," she told Paul. "That's not unusual for Germany, of course."

"And where will we stay?"

"Bruno said he would arrange rooms in the little hotel next to the apartments. We'll be so near that we could walk from window to window across the separation, but we will still have our own privacy."

"Rooms?" His brows rose above a grin.

"Rooms," she replied firmly.

"Did Doro live in the same apartment house?" Paul asked. They were now beyond Frankfurt and the sky was becoming more blue.

"No, her house was two beyond the hotel. Ursula lived there, too. We were all in our teens, although Max, of course, was the eldest. And we did so many things together."

"The wildest of which was?" he led her on. Nikki recognized that Paul was trying to keep her excitement from overwhelming her.

"Posing in the nude, I suppose."

Paul's attention was momentarily distracted, and he glanced at her sideways, making the little car veer sharply to the right, then swerved back to the middle course.

"All of you?" His voice was distorted.

The poser, of course, had been Ursula, tall and beautiful beyond her years with long dark hair. The artist was a Rasputinish character who rented the attic in the building where the Kneipps and Groebels lived. He painted little madonnas which sold well during religious festivals.

Somehow they had reached a compromise with the man. The naked female form, he told them, was as important to art as were religious replicas. They could all be included in the sittings if Ursi would remove her clothing. For some reason that Nikki could not now fathom, they each had a voice in the decision. And so each day after school, the two boys and three girls trooped to the upper reaches of the building. Inside the loft, the boys were positioned with their faces to the small eastern window while the Doro and Monika watched the artist and his model. And Ursi took the positions he suggested, but her body remained covered by cotton panties and undershirt.

At the end of each sitting they had begged him to show the results. The artist refused. Genius did not show rough drawings.

Unfortunately, his cleaning woman was not as timid about respecting the artist's wishes. One day, while tidying up after the messy man, she discovered that the subject of his erotic painting was none other than the daughter of her other employer. She observed the young body, totally unclad and engaged in sexual activity with fictitional characters, and removed the offending painting to prove her point to Ursi's family.

"Her parents took it badly. They wouldn't even give her a chance to explain what really happened. The painting looked as though she had posed many times. Ursi refused to name the rest of us as witnesses. None of us were supposed to be in the attic in the first place." Nikki told him. "Her folks sent her away to a convent school and wouldn't even tell us where we could write to her."

"Thus breaking up the old gang," Paul sighed. "I wonder that your mad artist didn't then try to paint you. Or was he thrown out of the house, too?"

"No way! It wasn't that he painted dirty pictures. It was that Ursi posed. As for me, I hadn't begun to bloom yet."

"Then age has done wonders. Shall we stop for coffee?"

* * *

"Is that a new necklace?" Paul asked as Nikki removed her jacket in the bakery-restaurant they had selected. He reached across the table to lift the pendant, suspended from its silver chain, so that he could examine it.

"You've seen it before," Nikki leaned toward him to keep the chain from biting into her neck. "That's the medallion I showed you the day I packed, the one from my pen pal."

"Oh, yes, your Mickey Mouse friend. It looks a lot nicer now that you have it polished up. You don't still write to him, do you? What was his name? It began with a G, didn't it?"

"Gerhardt," she answered. "No, I haven't written him since Wiesbaden. The kids used to help me with the letters. No, that's not true. I wrote them myself, but Doro and Ursi—before she left—would edit. After all, he was older, and I didn't want to come off like a little kid. One time when I was sick, Bruno put together a letter for me because I tried to write every week. We girls really had to do something about that one. It was four pages devoted solely to a soccer game."

"Of all your friends, Bruno was the closest," Paul summarized as the snack was finished.

"Definitely, among those in Wiesbaden." Nikki had to add the qualifier. There had been a time when no friend could have been compared to Gerhardt. "Bruno was my brother, and I was his sister. Since we were the same age, it was almost as though we were twins. When Mutti first decided we had to live with Herr Rennecke, I hated her as much for taking me away from Bruno as for giving up hope for Vati. Now I believe Mutti would never have gone to Stefen Rennecke if she thought Vati was alive. But I could have dealt with those early days so much better if Bruno had been around to talk things over."

"I'll bet you hoped that Bruno would go to the United States with Max and Doro," Paul suggested.

"Yes, I dreamed of it, but that wasn't reality. With Max, the elder son, gone, Bruno had to stay in Germany to take over management of the shop. The Kneipps have been tobacconists for umpteen generations, ever since there were such things. Oh, I forgot to tell you. Bruno is married. Isn't that a surprise?"

"No."

"No? How would you know?"

"Max talked to me about his brother and his brother's wife when we were at your birthday party. Unless there is another brother."

"There was. He died during the war." Nikki frowned. "Why has Doro never said anything?"

"She didn't approve," Paul supplied. "She felt that enough generations had gone into the shop. When Bruno refused to emigrate, she was angry. At least that's how Max explains it."

Nikki considered the matter. Doro had never approved of small shopkeepers. Once, when Nikki had taken her along to see the Rennecke-Groebel salon in downtown Wiesbaden, Doro had been enthused by its size and grandeur. It was much better, the girl had declared, than the Kneipps' hole-in-the-wall. Doro's father was employed at one of the factories that had been built after the war. Although the girl hadn't much idea of what he did there, she approved of its bigness.

"I hope she is nice," Nikki declared.

"Who? Doro?" Paul cocked his head as the waitress brought the check.

"No, silly. Bruno's wife. I suppose you know her name."

Paul shook his head and regarded the paper in his hand.

"Will you look at this! The writing is so small and yet it can be read easily. It's almost as if it were printed by a press."

Nikki leaned across the table. She smiled at the tiny perfectly formed letters and numbers.

"Wait until we get to the car. I can show you something that makes this look like a billboard," she boasted.

Good to her word, she dug into the bag and pulled out Tante Uschi's jewel case.

"No wonder the bag felt like bricks," Paul protested. "Couldn't you have left the box in Darmstadt?"

"No way. It holds my life. Here." She handed him a post card.

He looked at the side on which the message appeared and shook his head in amazement. Flipping it over, he examined its pictured Swiss street.

"My father wrote that," Nikki told him as she took the card back. "Vati used the smallest, most precise letters I have ever seen."

"Is the size trade-related?" Paul inquired after the car was moving and the card was tucked safely away.

"You are really fabulous," Nikki declared, her eyes sparkling. "You always know the right questions. Or have you some jewelers among your many acquaintances?"

"Not unless you include a woman who sells costume jewelry at Marshall Field's in The Loop. But why does a jeweler write small? To make room for all the zeros before the decimal?"

"When a jeweler picks up stones, they are usually loose, unset," Nikki launched into her explanation with gusto. It was fun to find something on which Paul wasn't an expert. "So the jeweler carries squares of tissue paper in his wallet. When he takes possession of the stones, he folds the paper into an envelope, places the gems inside, and writes his record on the exterior: what they are, when they were received, what was paid or what the value is, who they belong to, who sold them."

"Come now," Paul glanced at her with a face filled with doubt. "I know the Gettysburg Address was supposedly written on the back of an envelope, but I think you are carrying the detail a little too far."

"It wouldn't be all words," she retorted. "There are symbols and codes. The date, for instance, is three sets of numbers with periods between them. You've seen that on letters coming into our office. But it is a full record, good enough to establish ownership in court. Of course, a jeweler makes another complete record once he returns to his shop. Just the same, my father always stapled the tissue to his shop record. In case there was an error, he retained the original information."

"Like a good reporter always keeping his notes," Paul agreed. "Do you know I have filled three pads since we arrived? And now there's that meeting in Bonn next Thursday. Since our Department of Commerce is providing English translators, we should find another assignment for you. Maybe you can stay in Frankfurt to write about the closing of the textile show."

"By myself?" Nikki blinked.

"You can do it. You are a competent observer with a good understanding of relationships and a desire for truth." He rapped the steering wheel to emphasize his words. "Want to try your wings? And then, after the Bonn meeting, we can join the U.S. delegation in Zurich. Hey, you can get that good watch fixed and find a field in which to plant your Timex."

"Burying watches is passé," she warned him. "But, yes. Vati got my watch from a Herr Haupt in Zurich. Maybe he's still in business. If so, that's where I'll go. Why are the world's commercial types so interested in Switzerland. Is it because of the banks?"

Paul laughed heartily and began naming off Swiss companies that Nikki had always considered American.

"Your U.S. Chamber of Commerce mentality is showing. The world is fast becoming one big shopping center." As if in proof, they were suddenly in an avenue of flags. Paul gestured to them. "You see. Wiesbaden is hosting a conference."

"Why aren't we covering it?" she demanded. "Or are we?"

"No way. This one is medical. Bates from the Bonn bureau is covering. You need to be more careful about keeping up on the entire log, not just our assignment."

* * *

The sign on their right read "Russelsheim." Only about ten kilometers to go, Nikki told herself. The number of flags increased as they followed roadside directions to the Wilhemstrasse and the Kurpark. Looking left, then right, she began to identify places.

"Look, Paul, that's the building where I took dancing lessons. And there is Mutti's favorite dress salon. And the candy store where we always went for my Easter chocolate."

They came to the shopping colonnade and the sidewalk cafés in front of the Kurpark. Look as she could, she could not spot an empty seat anywhere. Beyond were the emerald of the park lawns, the sapphire of the fountains, and the miraflore of the Litfasauelen on which play bills for nearby theaters and movie houses were posted.

"You turn onto Taunustrasse at that big theater," she instructed. "But we will have to go all the way to the end of the boulevard in order to park by the house. We just passed it now."

"Right," he spoke and slowed to let two children skip by in front of the Opel's hood. "What's this park?"

"That's Kochbrunnen, the hot spring where the sickly drink or bathe." She rolled down the window. "I can't smell the rotten eggs today. When we swing around to come back, we'll be at the entrance to the Neroberg. That's where the Opelbad is."

It was almost as if she were expected, Nikki told herself excitedly. When they came back up the boulevard, a car suddenly pulled away from the curb leaving plenty of space, almost in front of Number 13, for their vehicle.

"The Germans aren't as superstitious as the Americans," Paul observed as they stepped into the vestibule.

"Huh?" Nikki straightened from her examination of the brass plate where names were matched to buttons. She had just discovered that the Bockes family, as well as the Kneipps, still lived there. The slot that had once been labeled Groebel now read Kneipp, B.

"Number 13," Paul told her.

"Oh, yes. I was surprised when I found so few thirteenth floors in the States. See, Bruno has our old apartment. Isn't that great?"

She jabbed at the other Kneipp button and grinned as the response came through the intercom.

"Frau Kneipp, it's Nik...Monika. May we come up?"

"Goodness, child. Of course. Push the door at the sound like always."

Inside the lobby where stairs rose on her left, a stab of guilt pierced Nikki's excitement. The two flights to the apartment were a barrier to Paul. Then she spotted a new door just beyond the stairway.

"This way." She led Paul to the opening and jabbed the button for the second floor.

"I take it the elevator has been installed since you lived here," he commented with a grin. "And a welcome addition as far as I am concerned."

"You know it! The stairs are terribly steep. I know them intimately from falling both up and down. When no one was around, Mutti used to carry her shoes to the first floor so that she only had to negotiate one flight with her silly high heels."

* * *

The door to the Kneipp apartment was already open when the elevator stopped. An older, but very recognizable, Frau Kneipp stood with her arms wide in greeting.

"Ah, Monika, what a treat for an old lady! And welcome to your friend. Come in. Wolfgang is anxious to see you. And we must call Bruno to say that you are here."

She led them into the living room. Herr Kneipp sat in his favorite chair. It seemed to Nikki that its fabric was changed, but the shape and location were not. He did not rise to greet them.

"Welcome, young Monika. My legs grow weak, and I rise only with difficulty now." But his hands were strong upon hers. He pushed her back a bit to look at her. "A fine grown lady you have become."

"Herr Kneipp, may I present Paul Peterson? He is my employer and very good friend."

The men shook hands, and Paul presented him with the wine they had chosen for a hospitality gift.

"Good vintage. Excellent vintner," Herr Kneipp observed. "Do you enjoy our wines?"

"And your beer. And your cuisine," Paul told him. "It's all very special."

Frau Kneipp beckoned Nikki away from the men.

"You will call Bruno? He is at the shop. The number is 45627."

"Kneipp's," a feminine voice announced.

"May I speak with Herr Bruno, please?"

"It will be a moment. He is with a customer."

Nikki waited, excitement growing. His voice had been the same when she had talked with him earlier. Enthusiasm and energy had come strongly over the phone lines. But could he have changed? He was married. His Liesel could have made him different. She heard the chime of a cash register ringing up a sale.

"This is Bruno Kneipp," the voice announced.

"And this is Monika Groebel."

"You're here? With my mother?"

"Yes. Yes," Nikki managed before he broke in.

"I'm on my way."

When she replaced the receiver, she turned and found Frau Kneipp staring at her. There were tears in the older woman's eyes.

"Life is good when you two can be together again, if only for a little while, Monika."

"It is," Nikki agreed with a smile. "Could you manage to call me Nikki? The Fishers who took me to America call me that, and I've become accustomed to it."

"We can manage," Frau Kneipp put an arm around her shoulders. "Your parents were so very formal but we always called you Nikki among ourselves. You have done well, my child, overcoming your tragedy and now having such a good job. And I like Herr Peterson. Is he someone special that you have brought for us, your German family, to meet?"

"Paul is very special, Frau Kneipp, but not that way."

"You do not love him?" The woman examined her face, seeking for the truth.

"Yes, I do love him, but not that way," Nikki responded seriously. "There are many kinds of love."

"You know that? Then you have grown wise as well as pretty. Do you hear…"

"Kleine Maus?" The bellow was punctuated by the slamming of the door. "Where are you?"

But Bruno's arms knew where she was, and Nikki found herself held hard against his chest. Yes, he had changed by nearly a foot in height and many inches in breadth. Her arms did not meet behind his back as he lifted her clear of the floor and swung her around. Bruno, the bear, she thought, her heart singing.

"And where is Liesel?" he asked as Nikki's feet were on the floor again.

"Herr Peterson, this is my son, Bruno," Herr Kneipp announced from across the room. "He is the man for whom Monika works."

Bruno bounded over to take Paul's hand, but his eyes still swept the room.

"Liesel?"

"She is still upstairs," Frau Kneipp told him with a pleased smile. "Perhaps you and Nikki should go up to her."

"You want to come?" He turned to Nikki. "It is your old home."

"Very much," she laughed and took his hand.

They ignored the elevator and ran up the stairs. The wrought iron banister was now a creamy white. Nikki recalled it as being a leprous grey with patches of rust coming through. On the next floor she pulled on Bruno's hand.

"The Bockes are still here?" She nodded at the apartment across the hallway from the well-remembered doorway.

"Frau Bocke has the apartment. Her husband died a few years back. Franz-Heinrich, their son, went to cooking school in Switzerland and now is a chef at the new Holiday Inn," Bruno told her. "He is not married so he lives here, too."

"I can't get over it, how people stay where they have always been. After all this time, you and your family and the Bockes remain."

"The painter is gone," he reminded her with a grin. "There is a new one up there now, but she does street scenes. Liesel helps her sometimes with framing."

He turned to the door, inserting the key in the lock of Apartment 13-C, and Nikki caught her breath.

Bruno pushed the door open and stepped aside to let Nikki past. She smiled up at him before entering.

"Do not slam," a voice called from the kitchen. "I have just completed a cheesecake for your old friend, and I do not want it to turn to pancake."

"If you do not come immediately to meet my old friend, I will slam the door twice," Bruno shouted back. His warning caused a scurry of footsteps. "This is Monika. This is Liesel."

Bruno's gesture nearly struck Nikki on the side of the head. She ducked beneath his arm and thrust out her hand. The woman who grasped it was Bruno's opposite, a bisque fairy doll.

"Welcome, old friend of Bruno," she twinkled, "May I call you Nikki as Bruno's parents do?"

"Of course, you may, Liesel."

"And that," Bruno declared as he placed his hand on his wife's protruding abdomen, "is young Wolf or Gretel. In two more months we shall know which. Now let us examine the cheesecake."

It was a hilarious quarter hour that Nikki spent in the old apartment. How good it was to hear it filled with laughter. There had been other changes, too, mostly in décor. Old damasks and brocades, which had belonged to the diabetic woman from whom the Groebels had assumed ownership, were gone in favor of nubby tweeds. Dark wood was light.

"It really is all the same," Bruno laughed as he watched her touch some of the pieces that seemed more familiar. "We have done a lot of refinishing and refurbishing. Does it bother you?"

"Not at all. The place is lovely."

After her tour, they all joined the elder Kneipps in the apartment below. Frau Kneipp had set out pretzels, small hard rolls, cheeses and sausages. The men drank beer while the women sipped wine. It was decided that the party would dine at a Rathskeller nearby and then enjoy Liesel's dessert and coffee.

"Can you manage?" Nikki asked Herr Kneipp. "Will the steps be too much?"

"There is an elevator here. There is one there, too, although it is supposedly only for freight. I can ride both ways. These seventy-year-old legs will do what else is demanded."

She blinked. He was seventy. Yet he was nearly the same age as Vati. Did her father, if he still lived, also have trouble moving about?

"Come, Nikki and Paul," Bruno called them. "I will take you next door to the hotel."

They rode the elevator to the street and stopped at the VW to get their luggage.

"A good car," Bruno commented, his head skewed sideways as he listened to the door close. "We have one, too. They do well while the family is small."

Carrying a bag in each hand, Bruno led the way to the adjacent building. There was a sidewalk café attached to the hotel. A screen of wild grape separated the restaurant from the lobby. Suddenly Bruno stopped. Paul and Nikki collided with him.

"The courtyard back there. You see it?"

"Right," Paul agreed.

"One day, Monika and I were fighting. I knocked her into the iron bench, and she hit her tooth."

"Hardly seems like a fair fight," Paul commented, regarding the size of his host with doubt.

" I was much smaller then. About a size with Monika. Anyway, the tooth literally killed her. It ached and ached, but she wouldn't tell her mother."

"Not until I stumbled on the stairs when I was with her," Nikki recalled. "And she thought it happened when my face struck the railing. She wanted Vati to have the landlord imprisoned because it might spoil my looks."

"And they dragged you to the dentist across the street. His window was open, and I sat on the step outside and listened to you scream. I have never felt so awful, even the day your mother and Herr Rennecke took you away."

"The dentist didn't use an injection like in America," Nikki explained for Paul's benefit. "He gave me laughing gas and took out the root. It still turned black. Another dentist, in Chicago, capped it."

"No fights this time," Paul cautioned, looking from Nikki to Bruno, as they entered the hotel.

A red-haired woman, who had been operating the switchboard behind the counter, came to her feet. Her lips spread to form a carmine frame for huge white teeth. She had had no problems in her courtyard, Nikki decided.

"Well, Bruno, has your wife thrown you out so that you now seek residence at the Hotel am Kochbrunnen?"

"Not today, Ilse. These are my guests for whom you have rooms," he told her with another hearty laugh. "Fraulein Groe…Fisher lived in the apartment that Liesel and I now have. And this is Herr Peterson. He is a journalist."

Ilse's attention swung immediately to Paul and remained there. "Guten tag, Herr Peterson. Welcome. I speak English also. You did want separate rooms?"

One key came across the counter.

"Your passports, please. Bruno knows his way around, Fraulein. He will show you to your room. I, myself, will escort Herr Peterson." She collected the documents and placed them by the register. With key in hand, she came around to confront Paul. "Follow me."

"The barmaid from *The Student Prince*?" Paul whispered before he limped away.

"Your friend, Paul. Can he take care of himself well?" Bruno asked as they climbed the steps to the upper floor. He halted abruptly, and again Nikki's head bounced on his back. "Do you mind about Ilse?"

"I don't mind at all. And please keep moving," she scolded. "We have to stop running into each other like this."

Bruno's laughted echoed and re-echoed in the stairwell.

"I must remember to use that line on Liesel. She will like it. And she likes you." He turned to look down at Nikki. "Do you like her?"

"Very much."

"It's good then. My girls are happy together. I had fears."

* * *

The dinner at the Rathskeller was a huge success. Herr Kneipp knew the proprietor and between the two of them, Paul received a thorough history regarding the old wine cellar in which the restaurant operated.

They had been seated at the stammtisch, a large round table central to band and bar. Between courses and afterward there was dancing. Bruno had led out his mother, then his wife, and finally Nikki. One round of the floor had proved sufficient for Liesel, and she had settled herself between Paul and her father-in-law to continue the exchange of lore.

Later, in Apartment 13-C, Paul had explored the tobacco trade with the Kneipp menfolk. As a pipe smoker, he was anxious to visit the shop. Bruno promised a special Sunday tour of the premises.

"You will have an opportunity to sample our wares," he promised. "Father still does most of the blends, working at home. I buy tobacco, of course. We also have a fine selection of pipes. I go to Switzerland next week to pick up new stock. There is a carver near Zurich who does the intricate Meerschaum bowls for us. We are his exclusive dealer in this part of the Federal Republic."

"Nikki and I are going to Zurich at the end of the week," Paul reported. "While we are there, she hopes to get her watch repaired."

"Remember my Piaget?" Nikki asked Bruno. "I want to take it back to Herr Haupt. Vati purchased it at his shop."

"How could I forget your watch?" Bruno protested. "You were forever swinging your arm around to keep it wound. I also recall that big jewelry box that played 'Die Fledermaus.'"

"Nikki brought the box with her today," Paul laughed. "That's why her suitcase was so heavy."

"I'm only protecting what is mine," Nikki explained with a frown. Her eyes went across the room to where a bookcase rested against the wall. "Bruno, what do you keep in that safe?"

"What does he want?" Liesel followed her gaze across the room.

"In the safe. Behind the bookcase." Nikki was on her feet. She leaned against the wall, trying to see what the furniture covered.

"There is nothing there except a wooden panel that we have not yet refinished," Bruno told her. "We plan to get to it after the baby is born. The finish on it is different from the other woods."

"Please, can we move the bookcase? I will show you."

Bruno and Paul glanced at each other, then shrugged.

"Oh, do!" Liesel urged. "I want to see."

Between the two men, the bookcase was moved until the dark panel behind was exposed. The elder Kneipps watched.

"Of course," Herr Kneipp nodded. "Karl Groebel would have a safe in their home. I did not think."

"There it is," Bruno cocked his head, studying the panel. "It doesn't look like any safe I have ever seen. What next?"

Nikki stood in front of it, staring at the panel. Its wood was different, not only in color but also in age. Vati had installed both safe and its covering. Her fingers touched the wood, uncertain. She closed her eyes, trying to visualize Vati in this place, at this wall. Not his right hand, but his left reached out. His hand swept this swirl. And as her fingers followed her mind's direction, she felt the irregularity and pushed against it. Because her eyes were still closed, she did not move away from the door until it brushed her face.

"Bravo!" Bruno cried out. "Do you know the combination?"

Nikki laughed as she turned from the safe's dial to face Paul.

"Remember the post card I showed you today? Part of it says 'Remember to call home.' And that is it."

"What is?" It was like a chorus as they all responded in a single puzzlement.

"The telephone number is the combination. Vati thought like that."

"20941?" Bruno supplied. "It is the same as when you lived here."

Nikki's fingers spun out the code, one number at a time. Taking a deep breath, she depressed the handle. The inner door came to her.

"But it is empty," Liesel protested, standing on tiptoe and staring around her husband.

"Of course it is." Bruno's hand reached inside to sweep the area. "But we shall use it for the baby's birth...Hello?"

A scrap of yellow paper tumbled from the cavity to the floor. They all began to bend for it. Nikki and Bruno, being more agile, got there first.

"No. It's yours," Bruno pulled his hand back as his fingers touched hers. "What is it, Monika?"

Hesitantly she reached for the sheet. It was jeweler's paper, one of the squares that Vati always carried. She knew, as soon as she felt the weight, that there must be unset stones. What a surprise it would be to the others!

"I'll give them to Bruno and Liesel for the baby," she promised herself as her nails pried open the tiny envelope and uncovered a small key. Placing it on her palm, she showed it to those nearest, then carried it over to where the older Kneipps were seated.

"What do you think?" she asked.

Herr Kneipp lifted the key to the light.

"Does the paper say anything?"

Nikki took it to the lamp and carefully unfolded the sheet. There was writing there. Her name. And an address. She read it aloud.

Herr Kneipp frowned, but Bruno took the paper from her hand, squinting at the fine manuscript.

"I know of no such address," Herr Kneipp spoke.

"Nor I," Frau Kneipp added.

"But I do," Bruno announced proudly. "The street is in Zurich. Perhaps...Monika, perhaps a bank box. Do you think?"

"Yes," Herr Kneipp agreed. "A bank box with a legacy for our Nikki. I like that. Your father's estate."

"No!" Nikki heard herself shout. "Vati is not dead."

The faces stared at her. Liesel showed astonishment. The others held compassion.

"It is so long..." Herr Kneipp began.

"Now I shall find him," Nikki stated, ignoring the expressions. "I have a key, and I will have him. I have to go to Zurich. Right away, Paul, right away."

When Paul did not say anything, she began to cry. The key she had taken back from Herr Kneipp was burning in her hand, a hot hope for reunion. For luck she tucked her thumb inside of her fingers.

They were all around her, pushing her down to a seat on the couch, wiping at her face with a damp cloth, saying kind but meaningless words. And try as she would, Nikki could not stop the tears.

Chapter Eight

✴ ✴ ✴

Time and Money

Only Herr Kneipp agreed with Nikki about her immediate need to visit Zurich. In the end, his was the majority vote. And so, on Sunday night, she found herself on a train bound for Switzerland.

All through the day, as she had attended Mass with the younger Kneipps and then visted the Opelbad with Paul and the couple, the controversy had raged. Nikki had felt removed from it all because her decision had not wavered, even after she had conquered last night's tears. If it had been necessary, she was prepared to resign from the news bureau in order to make the trip.

When they had returned to Number 13 after their day out, she found that her host had made her reservation. And he brooked no arguments from the other men.

"Too many experiences without an end for young Nikki," Wolfgang Kneipp told them. "She must have some answers before the questions overwhelm her. Now there is no problem with her being alone for a couple of days. Bruno will be there on Thursday. He can go even earlier should she need him."

All heads nodded in agreement.

"And the telephones still operate. She will take with her a number at which Paul can be reached in Bonn. If he is not available, one of us will be. Further, there is Herr Haupt in Zurich. If he is an old friend of Herr Groebel's, he also will have a care for her. Now what more does she need?"

"Clothes," said Liesel in a practical voice. "I shall lend her some of mine. They need to be used."

Nikki cast a practiced eye over the young woman. There was a good three inches difference in their heights, and the girl's shoulders were much thinner.

"Do not worry," Liesel intercepted the look. "We will choose things that will work."

"What about Gerhardt Mehlert?" Bruno wanted to know. "He can help."

Paul looked mystified, then grinned.

"Right. That's your pen pal, the one who gave you the medallion."

"No. Not him," Nikki protested. It was with Gerhardt that Vati had left her life. She would not let Gerry upend her existence again.

"She has enough friends to help," Paul agreed. "We have a correspondent in Zurich. I'll give her his name, too."

Nikki stayed in the carriage corridor to wave at her friends until the train got underway. It was almost as if, despite their doubts, they had all come with her, she thought as she entered the first class compartment.

She lifted the small suitcase, one of Frau Kneipps and now filled with skirts and blouses from Liesel, to the overhead rack. The carry-on bag went under the seat nearest the window. She had slipped her shoulder bag, which held her make-up and papers, into the carry-on. Since getting on and off European trains was tricky, she didn't want to overload her hands. Within the handbag was an entire list of telephone numbers, everything from people to consulates.

She'd had to leave the jewelry box behind, assigned to safekeeping with Frau Kneipp. Paul, however, insisted she bring the medallion, just in case she changed her mind about Gerhardt. Nikki had mixed feelings about any contact with Gerhardt, but didn't want to discuss them with Paul. She was certain that Gerhardt played a role in Vati's disappearance and had held him responsible over all these years. And yet, he would be so close.

She sat down in the seat by the window, watching Wiesbaden disappear. Later, if she had no companions, she would fold up the dividing arms and create a narrow bed for herself. How different it was from the last time she had gone to Zurich. There had been Vati and Mutti and Monika. The car was a Mercedes, naturally, but it was battered grey and of a prewar vintage, much older than the maroon that had been left in Leipzig. She wondered if Lars and Hanna had been allowed to keep it.

The twilight was darkening, and there seemed to be stars coming out all around her as the train sped through the countryside. The carriage door opened.

"Guten Abend," the conductor addressed her. "Fahrscheine bitte?"

She pulled the ticket from the pocket of Liesel's jacket and held it out.

"Do you need my passport, too?"

"No. Passport control is at the Swiss border. If you sleep, they will awaken you."

"Thank you," Nikki's hand cupped her mouth as she stifled a yawn.

"I will not check tickets again." He smiled at her. "The sleeping car is connected next and only six passengers are booked. I would not know if you were to take a berth. There would be a blanket and how does one say it, kissen?"

"Pillow," she smiled back at the conspirator. "Thank you."

"Use the last one," he advised. "That way it will not matter if a sleeper should get on at the border."

She waited until he had completed his round of the car before moving. It seemed only fair, should he be found out, that he could protest not seeing her move. Grabbing the case and the carry-on, she was off to her promised bed.

* * *

The other trip came to her as she slept. What a joy it had been in the beginning. Mutti was elated at the prospect of being able to shop in the international shops. She seemed to have prepared herself an impossible list of needs—gowns, slippers, lingerie, and outerwear. And Monika was to have a new wardrobe as well.

"Our little miss is fifteen, Karl," Wera Groebel had proclaimed. "We must begin dressing her in more suitable clothes."

"Whatever she needs," Vati had agreed. "And you can take her to the shops. She can learn from you about that which is style."

But it wasn't the shopping that excited Monika. She was going to Zurich to meet Gerry. For three years now she had written him faithfully once each week. He knew, she suspected, more about her than anyone. She had told him about the family, about her friends, even about her former life. He knew how much she missed Hanna, how hard she tried to keep Mutti from brooding about the old life, how filled with pitfalls her adolescence seemed to be.

He was much older than she, of course, and had no sisters. But he appeared to understand much of her tumult. Sometimes the questions he asked helped her to understand a bit, too.

What he looked like when Vati brought him to the inn outside of Zurich where they were lodging was no surprise. Gerry had sent, as well as received, pictures. But she had a hard time believing her good fortune as they stood face-to-face. He was twenty-two at that time, with hair and eyes of a deep hazel shade. His skin tone was bronzed by the sun because he spent his weekends in the mountains, skiing in winter and climbing in summer. His athlete's body, lean with broad shoulders, made a snappy bow as he kissed Mutti's hand with Swiss gallantry. For Monika, he had a hug, just brotherly enough not to raise her father's eyebrows. Afterward, Gerry held her at arms' length and spoke his admiration for all to hear.

"You look just as I had imagined from all your pictures, only more beautiful and grown-up."

The four of them dined together that evening. It was very adult with dancing and proper dinner table talk. Vati seemed extremely interested in Gerry's family and his father's business. Monika couldn't believe that any two men would talk so long about plumbing.

The next day at breakfast she had pleaded to be allowed to spend the day alone with Gerry. Mutti protested, but Vati nodded his approval. Apparently Gerry had cleared their itinerary with her father. He drove her on a sightseeing tour of Zurich, using a Spartan Fiat.

"My first expenditure from my savings," he admitted. "Since I live at home, I have been able to put aside quite a bit. My father refuses to allow me to pay room and board."

They had followed the Limat River for some distance, crossing one bridge and then another. He explained to her the history connected to the bridges and to the buildings along the waterfront. But it was all lost on her. She only had ears for his voice, not his words. They had gone to the warehouse from which his father's plumbing business operated.

"Fraulein Monika, is it?" Herr Mehlert had greeted her, touching his lips to her young hand. "I shall let Gerhardt show you what we are about. He needs to review our stock."

She had been surprised at the extent of that stock. The company was larger than she expected.

* * *

In the evening, they attended the ballet at Mutti's request. The program, however, had not remained in Monika's memory nearly as strongly as the feel of Gerhardt's arm resting against hers. He crossed his arms, letting his right hand trail over hers, and held it tight. During the performance he would exert a reassuring pressure on her fingers several times.

She leaned closer, the herbal fragrance of his aftershave delightful in her nose. Her heart picked up speed at this nearness. She was conscious of the distinctly masculine shapes that dancing tights displayed so candidly. She had sneaked several glances at Gerhardt's lap, but the house lights were too dim to tell.

* * *

Gerry had taken a room at the inn. When she retired that evening, she was ecstatic to think of him so nearby. Near, in reality, was the hotel's far wing, but it was nearer than Zurich, after all. As she undressed for bed, she stood in front of the door mirror, critically examining her shape in the new lingerie Mutti had provided. The silky slip clung to her hips, its upper lacy insert stretched taut across her firm breasts. Her fingers played across her body, thinking of Gerry.

Did he think she was too young? Too immature? Too immature for what? Smiling to herself, she pulled her hairbrush through her long hair.

"I wish we had more time here with him," she told the young woman in the glass.

She removed her slip and underthings and climbed naked between crisp sheets. The scent of herbal lotion still clung to her imagination. Thinking of the evening she started to drift into sleep.

Then, just as her mind got heavy, she heard the sounds. It was as if a bird were pecking repeatedly at the window. At first, she rolled her back to it. But when it continued, she knew she had to check it out. She moved slowly to the window and pressed her face to the pane. There below, stood Gerhardt.

He had to have seen her because he began to gesture. She didn't need to think about the message. With one hand she pulled the sheet off her bed and around her body. With the other, she switched on the lamp by the bed so that Gerry could see her clearly. And then she nodded her head.

How she managed to get into clothes and out of her room, Monika was never sure. She had pulled on the pair of slacks in which she had travelled and a blouse from the stack of her new clothes. As the soft fabric touched her, she realized that she had forgotten her underthings. But there wasn't time to start again. Gerry was waiting. A quick spray of cologne, a dab of gloss on her lips, hair brushed into place, and she was ready. She picked up a pair of shoes and let herself out into the hall. Her parents were, she hoped, long asleep.

When she finally was out of the inn and into the courtyard, she let out a deep sigh. Somehow she had expected to be stopped. When his hand caught her arm, she jumped and nearly cried out. Without speaking, Gerry led her away from the building, down to a bench by the beach.

"There are things that need to be said," he told her when they were seated. Even this far away from the hotel, he spoke in a whisper. "I am not sure we will be alone tomorrow."

Monika shot a glance over her shoulder. There was an immense willow that shut them off from the inn.

"Yes?" It was a great adventure, being here with Gerhardt.

"I feel like an idiot," he spoke the words that she had been thinking. "This was supposed to be only a short meeting with the little girl who writes to me in four languages. I find it is a great deal more, but you are barely more than a child."

"I am seventeen," Monika lied.

"Fifteen," he corrected. His laughter was not louder than the sound of the waves lapping at the shore. "So young. Too young. And yet I think I love you, Monika."

"You do?" Her surprise deepened as his arm came around her shoulders. She knew how she felt. He was the dearest, best thing she had ever known. But to think that he thought the same about her. "Really?"

It was real enough, his kiss told her. At first she tried to analyze the sensations that his lips and tongue were creating, especially the small center that stirred just below her waist. As if it were the only thing she had ever known, her body instinctively took over. Her soft mouth opened under his touch, her breasts pressed close against his chest. She felt his skin warm against hers, the outline of her nipples rigid through the thin cotton shirt.

The transition from the soft cloth against her breasts to his fingertips almost went without noting until a fingertip intercepted a nipple.

Her eyes, which had been closed to hold in the dearness of his kiss, opened as she felt herself swelling to his touch. She let out a soft moan. Her hand had dropped to Gerry's lap, her fingers brushing the front of his jeans. She let her vision fall. The rise of his jeans led her thoughts momentarily to the bodies of tonight's ballet dancers. Gerry pulled her closer, his hand guiding hers to the distracting anatomy.

She touched him there, tentative, exploring. Gerry pulled away, his breathing heavy. "No, don't. Not just yet."

Confused, Monika tried to read his face, the moonlight's reflections dancing across his eyes, caressing the soft smile playing across his lips.

"I don't want us together like this." Gently Gerry turned toward her, his fingers adjusting the front of her blouse. "You deserve better than kisses and stealthy loving in the dark. Our first time together will be something for us to treasure forever. You may be young now, but each month, each year will make us closer."

His fingers stroked her cheek and he tucked her head beneath his chin. After a moment of silence, Gerry continued.

"If you think you love me I will speak to your father tomorrow. We'll decide how long we should wait until we can be married."

Monika reached up to touch his face, smoothing his hair away from his face.

"You smell so good. When I went to bed tonight, I could still smell the herbs and spices in your aftershave. Yes, I love you, too. I knew that from the moment I saw you. I know more about you from your letters than I have learned about people I see every day. All that I imagined was right. You are sweet and gentle."

His fingers were on her again, to cup her chin and kiss her softly. One hand caressed her breast, stroking a nipple.

"I have to admit something, Monika. You exceed everything I imagined. Here you are, a beautiful, near-woman, with a lovely body. Are you cold?" he asked as she shivered, touch and words both delighting her.

At last she understood why Hanna had felt so warm, even in the middle of winter. Love beat central heating any time!

"No. But it's hard to get used to the idea that you love me."

"So put your mind to it. I am yours and you are mine."

She repeated the words, not in a whisper but in a small clear voice. She would have preferred to shout it.

"And now back to your room to dream of me."

He helped her up, their bodies touching as they walked arm in arm toward the hotel. There was one last kiss before Gerry let her return to her room.

That night her dreams had been all good. The next day Gerry left the inn with Vati for the drive back into town. Monika smiled and waved them on their way, joy in her heart, knowing that Gerry would ask Vati about their future.

After that, her dreams began to disintegrate. For Vati never returned from Zurich.

* * *

As before when this particular memory had come in her dreams, she wakened, overwhelmed with regret. How beautiful the promise had been, how ugly its outcome. But tonight she did not have to worry about dreaming again. She could hear the sounds in the corridor of passport control moving through. She reached for her bag to be ready.

"Vacation or business," the official wanted to know, his rubber stamp poised above the document.

"Could it be both?" Nikki asked, doubtful about how to classify a quest.

"Why no? Enjoy your stay." He grinned appreciatively at her. Evidently she did not look as frazzled as she thought she did.

As soon as he was gone, she examined herself in the small steel mirror. The man was only being kind, she decided, and lifted the lid of the sink to pump a little water. As the brown liquid spewed out, her stomach clenched. She slammed the lid down hard. It must be time to get something to eat.

She hadn't inquired where the dining car might be, but it wasn't too hard to find out. At the end of the carriage her conductor friend was sitting, cap over his eyes. She hated to wake him, but he came to an automatic alert as she approached.

"And now an early breakfast, Fraulein?" he read her mind. "That way."

It had to be a very early breakfast, she knew as she entered the empty restaurant car. Everything was in readiness. White cloths, red carnations, gleaming silver. But no customers. She looked down at her watch. It said

11:36. By the time the Piaget was operational, she might learn to wind the Timex. It needed daily boosts to keep on ticking. Before she could leave, a waiter appeared.

"Table for one?" he asked the routine question, unmindful of the humor. At that point, all tables were. But, when she nodded, he led her down the car to a small table with two chairs and drew out one for her. "Kaffee?"

He came back with a carafe and a menu, along with a caution that the ovens were not yet heated. His advice was to drink coffee for twenty minutes or to select the cold breakfast. She did so, keeping her face straight. At the Fishers and in the dormitory, cold breakfast meant cereal and milk. Here it was hard sausage and cheese, croissant and fruit. Some difference, just like the coffee. Even its aroma was delightful!

She was lacing the brew copiously with cream when a second customer entered the car. He was old, slovenly in appearance, and a little clumsy in pace. Nikki drew her handbag onto her lap. She was sure he was looking at her as she focused her attention on the scenery outside. She could smell as well as feel his presence directly behind her. Then he moved two tables down the aisle and pulled a chair roughly toward him.

It was a relief that he had not tried to join her. Nikki was still congratulating herself on the escape when the waiter returned with her breakfast.

"Thank you, it looks lovely." Without realizing, she had addressed him in English.

"We hope you enjoy it," he returned promptly as if they had not used German earlier. He moved toward the man, just in time to intercept the shouted rage.

"Goddamned Amis. They turn up everywhere."

In quieter terms, the waited asked for his order. Nikki kept her eyes on the window, hoping the outburst was done. She had heard vituperations heaped upon the Americans many times before. It had always struck her funny that the American soldiers had not been really aware of what was being said. The German abbreviation for American sounded the same to the untrained ear as the French word for friend.

But her breakfast companion was not finished.

"Only coffee," he insisted in the same offensive tone. "I cannot swallow food in the same place when the American slut dines. Those swines lack the balls to keep their whores at home."

Beyond his hatred, she was also aware of the waiter's embarrassment. Now she was torn between her desire to leave and the need to eat. Perhaps she could use the croissant to build a sandwich. She began her work.

* * *

"Good morning, Dieter," the voice rang out as the door to the car opened again. "What is good?"

"Herr Germeyer," the waiter nearly ran the length of the car to meet him. "May I seat you with the Fraulein? This is your good friend, Herr Hans Germeyer, Miss. He will help."

She looked uncertainly at her sudden companion.

"I'm Nikki Fisher," she began before the old man interrupted.

"So the waiter is also the pimp. I should have known." His hand swept the table in front of him, sending tableware tumbling. Coffee and cream spattered in all directions. Nikki gasped as hot liquid splashed against her leg.

Her tablemate's explosion was as abrupt. He was on his feet, pulling the man from his chair. The oversized German, pushed on by his own arm folded across his back, was being hustled toward the exit by the younger Germeyer.

"See if the cold air will clear your mind and clean your mouth," he shouted from the door. His features, when he turned back toward Nikki and the flustered waiter, reflected the granite of the Swiss peaks. His smile softened his face, making it more attractive and he continued in heavily accented English: "Shall we try again? You are Nikki, and I am Hans. And this is Dieter who will now bring a cold damp cloth so that you can sponge away the spots."

The wet towel was in her hands almost before the announcement ended. Nikki wiped at her leg and the edge of Liesel's skirt while the distressed waiter explained to the dining car steward the occurrences of the past few minutes.

"The rail systems thanks you, Herr Germeyer, for your intervention in the unpleasantness," the older man, wearing a steward's key with his white jacket, declared at their table. "And we regret your discomfort, Fraulein. You will be reimbursed for the cleaning or replacement of your garment, of course. Only file when you leave the train. What is your destination?"

She answered, using German intentionally now, that the skirt was washable and the stain seemed not to have set. The steward considered this and decided that a hot breakfast was indicated for the pair.

"What brings you to Zurich?" Hans Germeyer asked as they ate. More diners had arrived so that they were no longer the center of staff attention.

"A little work, a little vacation." She gave him the same explanation that had satisfied the passport official.

"May I inquire as to your work?"

Nikki looked up sharply to see if he were serious or jesting. His face gave nothing away.

"Not what the man thought," she said slowly, emphasizing the final word. "I am a translator and researcher for an American press bureau."

"Ah, so. And you have information to gather, then." He ran his fingertips along the edges of a precision-cut beard. The ring he wore on his well-kept hands was an onyx intaglio set in gold. It was a fine piece, Nikki thought.

"And what is *your* business?" she asked after nodding her agreement. Tit for tat, and he might just have a good story in him. It would please Paul, she was sure, if she were to show that kind of initiative.

"Banking security. And that doesn't mean like your American guard, in case you were wondering." He laid aside his fork and warmed to the subject. "I work out of offices in the Zurich banking district. Perhaps you know that section?"

With a mouthful of eggs, Nikki could do nothing but shake her head. That tour so long ago with Gerhardt had not touched the financial areas. But she hoped to keep Hans talking. Perhaps he could help her with supplying information about Vati's bank.

"There is a marvelous restaurant directly across from our building. It's renowned for its authentic Italian cuisine, which is more than pizza, you know. I assure you, the place serves the best linguini in all of Switzerland."

She swallowed. Inside gourmet information was not what she sought. She opened the coin purse in her handbag and glanced at the scrap of yellow paper. Hopefully, she showed the address to him.

"Is that in Zurich?" she asked.

"Of course. That is a private bank, just a block or so from where I work. But you surely cannot expect to get a news story from them!"

"No. It is a personal matter. Can you tell me how to get there?"

"To get there from where? At what hotel are you staying?"

She confessed that she had made no plans.

"Then the personal matter is most urgent," he observed.

Suddenly Nikki was unsure of whether she cared to divulge any further information to an individual she had only just met. But his sudden grin insisted he was only being helpful.

"May I recommend a gasthaus to you? It is well considered by my colleagues when they come to the home office. And the rates are far lower than the famous hotels." He paused only a moment to see if she would object. "And to get to your bank from there you have only to take the streetcar, which comes by the next corner."

From the inside pocket of his jacket he drew out a notepad and began to write directions for her. When he was done, he passed the sheet to her.

"This should take care of getting you settled for a few days or however long you decide to stay."

Nikki reached to take the page from him. His hand touched hers, a momentary stroking.

"Look, I don't want to come across too strong. I know we have only just met, but if you need anything, I wrote my number there, too. Just give a call."

I am a well-respected business man, not Jack the Ripper. I'd be most happy only to help out a visitor in my country."

With those words he relinquished the paper and smiled at her, dark eyes warming his face. Then he pushed his chair back and got up.

"Excuse me, I'll get us more coffee."

As he walked away, Nikki looked after him thoughtfully. Something about him reminded her of Gerhardt Mehlert. The two were the same size and moved with an athlete's lithe steps. Back here in Gerry's homeland, the thoughts of their first visit seemed stronger than her dreams. She wondered if he still lived in Zurich.

* * *

Nikki firmly pulled herself back to the present. Gerry was past and done with. Hans Germeyer was Nikki Fisher's white knight. All her misgivings and reluctant feelings disappeared as her eyes followed Hans Germeyer's movements. His straight back was to her as he waited for a fresh pot of coffee. The jacket was obviously custom tailored, several shades darker than his tan wool slacks. She bet herself that there was not a speck of dust on his shiny shoes, the pointed toes of which suggested an Italian bootmaker.

Hans Germeyer did not look as though he had spent the night on a train. She was just as certain that, even without the damp cloth at her elbow, any observer would be aware that her journey had begun hours ago.

"We should be arriving at the Zurich station within the hour," Hans remarked, filling Nikki's cup from a porcelain pot before he passed the pitcher of cream.

"I am having trouble getting accustomed to your strong German coffee," she apologized, as she poured a generous amount of cream into her cup. "It is a great deal more flavorful than our American blends."

"I know. I spent some time in London. Let me tell you, I know why the British drink tea. Their coffee is abysmal." As he spoke, he pushed back the sleeve of his jacket to look on his watch. "Perhaps I'd better walk you back to your carriage so you can get your cases."

"I can find my way, and I am sure I shall be safe. Thank you very much for your help with that nasty man." Nikki rose to her feet and smiled as Hans stood up, too. "I really do appreciate all you have done."

She reached for her breakfast check, but found Hans' fingers under hers. He shook his head.

"This is my pleasure, Nikki."

It had been her pleasure, that time spent with Hans Germeyer. But he, like Gerhardt, was Swiss. She hoped she wasn't destined to like every male in the entire nation.

Hans Germeyer, it seemed, was not yet ready to allow Nikki to meet other Swiss males. He insisted on escorting her from the depot to the charming guesthouse that he had recommended, the "Weisser Schwan" in the Hallengasse.

"Don't you have to report to your office?" Nikki asked as the cab he had hailed carried them across the bridges of Zurich See. It was still early morning, but the traffic pattern told her that the work day was beginning.

"It is Monday," he told her, then elaborated to banish her puzzled expression. "Banks in Zurich do not open on Mondays. So I do not report until tomorrow."

"Even private banks?"

"I should think so. Most of them, at least. I will make you acquainted with the Wirt family who own "The White Swan." And then, if you think they speak sufficiently well of me, I shall ask you to let me take you dining and dancing this evening."

"I don't think…" Nikki began. Hans placed a hand on hers.

"Please wait until I have asked. Have you seen the many sailboats on the See? Do you sail?"

"Not often." She'd sailed twice on Lake Michigan, which had been two times too many. She was prone to sea sickness.

* * *

Appropriate to its name, the "Weisser Schwan" featured a wrought iron swan at its front door. They entered through a street-side garden with trellises from which scarlet roses reached skyward. Tiny tables, covered in red and white checks, punctuated a green lawn. The establishment's official greeter turned out to be a grey and white cat that stroked their legs with her thick tail.

Nikki petted the cat and was rewarded with a purr loud enough to drown out the other street sounds, when the guesthouse door opened. A young woman came out, broom in hand. She curtsied slightly.

"Good morning, Herr Germeyer. How nice to see you."

"The pleasure is mine, Susan." He gave her a dazzling smile. "This is Fraulein Fisher, and she is in need of a room for her stay in Zurich. I have told her that there is no better lodging than at "Weisser Schwan." Have I spoken true?"

"You know you have." Susan lifted her head proudly. "My parents and I welcome you, Miss Fisher. May I show you a room that I believe will provide you comfort?"

"Follow, Susan," Hans insisted. "I will bring your bags."

"The cab," Nikki reminded.

"It will wait until you have satisfaction regarding my character. Now go."

Susan led her to a corner room up the flight of stairs. Nikki blinked at its perfection, like a room from a doll's house, all chintz and organdy. The colors were mainly blue and white, echoing the view from the room's front window. There was a small bath attached in which sunshine had been added by yellow tiles and a bouquet of marigolds on the dressing table.

"You do like it, don't you?" Susan clapped her hands like a child. "Your face says so. Will you have half pensione, which means bed and breakfast, or do you prefer full pensione with all meals?"

"Can't she do as our fellows do?" Hans asked. "Half pensione and the privilege of eating in when it fits her schedule."

"Of course, Herr Germeyer. Does that suit you, Fraulein?"

"Very much," Nikki laughed her agreement. "Now, Susan, I have a question. About Herr Germeyer. He tells me you have known him for some time? Is he really trustworthy?" Nikki's eyes sparkled as she regarded Susan's serious face.

"Tell her the worst," Hans urged.

"He is a good man. A very good man," Susan spoke the words with conviction.

"Then I shall accept your invitation for this evening," Nikki turned to Hans. "At what time?"

"I shall come by for you at seven. Dress for dancing."

Susan moved over to the front window, watching while he climbed back into the cab. She turned to Nikki: "How fortunate you are, Miss Fisher. I would have said the same about him if he had not been present. I hope you will be comfortable here."

* * *

Knowing she was not able to visit the bank this day, Nikki asked Susan for directions to Haupt Jewelers. The watch, at least, could be taken for repair. Because she lacked the address, Susan referred her to the post office. It was near enough that she could walk.

She set out, following the instructions she had received. She had changed to another of Liesel's garments, and given the coffee-spotted skirt to Susan, who had agreed to wash and iron it later in the morning.

Most of the buildings she passed were white, like The Swan, and all had similar red tile roofs. Surrounded by green and crowned by blue sky, they looked like a painting in primary colors.

The clerk at the post office listened to her need with surprising attention for a civil servant, then nodded. He handed her a thick directory.

"Please turn to the business section. Once there, seek out the section on jewelers. Here is a paper to use for the address. Do *not* remove the pages!"

Attentive, perhaps, but hardly civil, Nikki decided as she hauled the book to a nearby table. Did she really look like the type who tore out pages? She could feel his eyes on her back. It was a relief to locate the information she needed without having to seek further assistance. She wrote down the address with a flourish, closed the book, and returned it with sober thanks.

* * *

The tables at "Weisser Schwan" were occupied when Nikki returned. The aroma of baked fish and fowl were heavy on the air.

Susan showed her to a small table, turned to her and cocked her head as Nikki seated herself.

"Have you not been to your room since your return?"

"No. I thought I would eat first."

"Ooh!" the girl sighed, and then recovered her role. "You wish the special—fish and noodles? Perhaps some wine? This white Spätle is nice."

Nikki barely had time to nod before the beverage splashed from carafe to goblet.

"I will be quick so you can get to your room," Susan promised.

Nikki's hand shot out to catch her apron.

"Why am I in such a hurry to go upstairs?" she inquired.

"There is a surprise, of course."

"What surprise?"

"I cannot tell you. He would be angry. Please, I must go."

"Who will be angry, Susan?"

"Oh, very well. Herr Germeyer." Susan hurried away.

Now she was curious! The meal seemed to take forever to arrive. Nikki knew she was not doing the excellent food justice, almost inhaling the dill-flavored fish with its creamy noodles and fresh cauliflower. She drained her glass quickly and hurried upstairs.

As she opened the door, the immense bouquet seemed to occupy the entire room. In its center were three rose buds cradling a card.

She lifted the message and smiled at the skilled words:

"These are to tell you that I wait eagerly for this night to unfold."

"So what do you think of that?" Susan demanded from the door. "You are so fortunate to have him for a friend."

Nikki turned around, tapping the card against her fingertips. She was sure the girl had already read it.

"Susan, you spoke for his character. But I do need to know. Is Herr Germeyer married?"

"Not now. He was, but it was so sad. His beautiful wife and a friend drowned two years ago during a terrible storm. Herr Germeyer looked for them for days. He was there when their bodies were finally recovered. He grieved for many months, poor man." Susan's eyes glazed with tears. "You seem to be the first woman I have seen him interested in since."

"Thank you, Susan. He seems like a good person. You see, he rescued me earlier today." Nikki summarized the situation in the dining car.

Susan nodded when she was finished.

"That is just like him. Now, you needed help with an address?"

* * *

Finding the streetcar with the proper placard had been no problem, but securing standing room was. The vehicle wove its way merrily toward the city center, swaying like a dancer around corners and barely pausing at stops. Nikki struggled to hear the streets announced. Her fellow passengers appeared not to need the words.

Instead they talked and laughed loudly. Finally Nikki asked another rider for assistance.

"The Bahnhofstrasse? What section? There is so much of it."

"I'm not sure, but I believe you'll find it farther down the street. Stay on the car for at least three more stops. Get off when you see St. Peter's Church. Then walk toward the church."

The directions helped some. There was, however, a proliferation of churches. Nikki had to inquire from another passenger to discover which was St. Peter's. But that was her final challenge.

Her feet found the shop as though she had known the way all her life. Yet the route had not been that simple. People along the street seemed to have two speeds, determined full-out and leisurely stroll.

The pedestrians' apparel differed from her simple cotton, too. She smiled at skin-hugging gold lame slacks thrust into high white boots. "Little" black dresses abounded, even though it was early afternoon. Some were topped with fur stoles or jackets. And even on this summer day, tweed and heather woolen suits, classically tailored, seemed popular.

The shop's façade had a power to it. Black marble panels framed its street frontage and rounded letters picked in gold read simply "Haupt." Gold leaf applied to glass to form Roman italics amplified what would be found inside: fine metals and gemstones.

The interior was reminiscent of Haus Groebel. Glass cases flanked a carpeted center aisle from which brooches and necklaces twinkled in their beds of draped satin. Long walls contained high shelving displaying gold and silverware. Small leather chairs were placed randomly along the counter's length for a customer's ease. On the glass in front of each chair was a black velvet pad on which pieces under construction could rest. At the back, with its twin lamps, was the higher counter where the problems of inoperative timepieces were diagnosed.

A clerk in black crepe, highlighted by white piping, greeted her, repeating the welcome in four languages. Nikki chose to respond in German.

"Herr Haupt, please."

The woman disappeared through the curtained exit behind the watch counter. Nikki was aware that two other female employees watched her without seeming to be aware of her presence. That was part of the security for fine shops. The sales staff observed but did not stare.

* * *

It was another woman for whom the first clerk held aside the drapery. She, too, wore black, but there was an earthy look to her. She strode forward to Nikki, chains of gold dancing across her ample bosom. Her hair, braided into a high crown above a broad forehead, seemed to be fine gold, too.

"I am Frau Haupt, Fraulein. My husband is presently not on the premises. Perhaps I may serve you?"

This woman, perhaps as old as thirty, could not possibly be the wife of the man she sought, Nikki decided. Herr Haupt had to be older than Vati.

"Frau Klaus?" she managed. The woman laughed in notes ascending to an irregular scale.

"My husband's mother has been dead these past five years. I am Frau Hugo. Are you seeking Vater Haupt?"

"He and my father were friends," Nikki supplied. "I am Monika Groebel."

"Yes!" The woman beamed. "I do know Herr Groebel."

"You do?" Nikki's hands pressed against the counter to give support to a body trying to go limp.

"As a customer, I mean," Frau Haupt continued. "Vater Haupt still serves your father as a private account. The only one, now that Monsieur LeFebevre is gone. But my father-in-law seldom comes to the shop. Nor has Herr Groebel that I can recall. It is all done by courier, no?"

It was difficult trying to think of words for conversation and to bring them out around the tremendous revelation she had received. But Nikki had to try.

"Would it be possible for me to visit with Herr Klaus? For just a little while? Please, it means so much."

The woman's hand, sparkling with an immense custom setting of diamonds, came to rest on Nikki's. Her smile was almost impish.

"Vater Haupt is at Lake Como this week to visit my sister-in-law. But on Sunday he will return for a party to mark his eightieth birthday. And you must come. What a fine surprise it will be for him! You will bring Herr Groebel, of course."

"I cannot," Nikki confessed, feeling very comfortable with this bright young woman. "My parents separated when I was young. I don't know where my father lives."

"But Vater Haupt does!" the woman announced with a wide smile. "You will ask him Sunday, and he will help arrange a reunion. How nice! My name, Fraulein Groebel, is Bettina. And I will tell you how to reach our home. You will come?"

Would she come! Nikki could hardly bear to think of the days between now and the festivities. Yet one had to be practical.

But perhaps she did not need to wait so long. Vati was alive. She could get his address at the bank. And then Bettina's first invitation would be in order. She and Vati would attend Herr Haupt's birthday celebration together.

Bettina's enthusiasm nearly matched hers. In the confusion of getting the address of the Hugo Haupt home, Nikki almost forgot about the watch. But a glance at the stainless steel on her wrist was reminder enough. She pulled the Piaget from her handbag and passed it across the counter.

"I believe this came from here."

Bettina's eyes sparkled as she examined the small gold case.

"But long ago. Ten years or more."

"More. My father gave it to me for my eighth Christmas. And just last May it became undependable. Can it be repaired?"

"Bring Marco," Bettina instructed the nearest saleswoman. "He will be enchanted."

The watchmaker was. He found excitement in the fact the case had never been opened, that it had run perfectly for so many years.

"Quality!" He tapped the crystal lightly with a square fingernail. "It shows. I will be proud to put this beauty to rights. But may I have a few days with it?"

Originally Nikki had wanted to have the watch tended to while she waited. Now that she had found new friendship and hope, her anxiety for letting this remembrance of Vati out of her possession eased. If it were necessary, she would be willing to sacrifice the gift to have the giver once again.

Next Monday seemed an agreeable time to return for the watch. Paul would be here, and they would be at work, but surely there would be a few moments in which she could come by.

* * *

How she got back to "The Swan," Nikki wasn't quite sure. It was as though she had floated there in her cloud of joy and anticipation. Joy should be shared, she told herself, as she put through a call to Bonn. Paul was not in the news bureau office there, so she left a message with the telephone number of the guest house and turned her attention to what she should wear to dinner.

Nikki sat on the edge of her bed and reviewed the fashions she had observed during her trip to Haupt's. From the range of apparel, she suspected that almost anything might be appropriate. But she decided to follow her adoptive mother's adage about proper dress:

"When in doubt, choose simple."

Simple, it turned out, was her own white skirt and Liesel's camisole top. The sandals she had brought along to double as bedroom slippers, if need be, had a small heel. With Susan's assistance, they were brought to glistening white.

"You look elegant," Susan declared, watching Nikki slide her feet into her shoes.

"More like ingénue," Nikki told her. It had taken two attempts to tie a decent bow in the blue ribbon threaded through the camisole bodice. She hoped Hans wasn't looking for sophistication.

When she descended to the reception area to meet Hans, she knew her outfit was right. Herr Wirt spoke his compliments while several guests nodded theirs. Hans's reaction showed in his eyes.

"You are special," he announced, "and so I have planned a special evening. We have reservations at a fine Swiss restaurant. On the perimeter of its dinner gardens is a park. There, this evening, will be a concert in which several of Zurich's finest brass bands compete for awards. And finally there will be a street dance. Does that meet your approval?"

"It surpasses my greatest expectations," Nikki murmured as he handed her into a silver Audi. It was just a little lie, she told herself. With the news about Vati, she had spent little time, even while she dressed, considering what this evening might hold.

Instead her emotions ran hot and cold over the potential reunion. Perhaps Vati would not want to see her again. He could have intended the break to be clean and permanent. On the other hand, if he had kept himself aware of the doings of his abandoned family, he might only have lost track of her. That last postcard he sent read: "I shall always love you, my smallest and dearest." Of course, he would want to see her!

"I have some information to assist you," Hans announced as he slid under the vehicle's steering wheel. "The small bank you are seeking is managed by Monsieur Ambrose DePrenger. My superior suggests that you ask for him by name and insist upon speaking only to him. There are several other employees, but none who can make official decisions."

"Monsieur DePrenger." Nikki rehearsed the name.

"Here." Hans handed her a sheet of paper. "It is not necessary to memorize. I have written it out for you."

She folded the paper without looking at it and slid it into the small handbag that Susan had loaned her for the evening. Now she resolved to put her thoughts of Vati aside for the evening. For all Hans had done, Nikki owed him attention and he would have it.

The Audi's radio was swathing them in classical music. It took only a moment to identify the overture from "Die Fledermaus." Was it another omen of this wonderful day, she wondered, as she hummed along.

"Somehow one always thinks of Americans as Elvis Presley fans," Hans mused, his voice barely audible above the music.

"I like him, too," Nikki admitted. "I have fairly universal taste music, but 'Die Fledermaus' is a special favorite."

* * *

Their route took them along the Zurich See, then across one of the bridges. In midspan, he brought the car to a crawl so that she could see the city fanned out on both sides of the water. He indicated a grove to the left. It was the park in which the concert would take place.

After seeing so much loveliness in Zurich, the building where they stopped was a disappointment. Its marquee awning was the only trim on the entire face of the structure. The walkway had no lawn fringing it.

"It's the back, silly," he told her, sensing her dismay. "The front is right on the water."

As a doorman in Swiss provincial attire admitted them and the maitre d' led them to a table by a window, Nikki discovered they were looking down on, rather than out over, the water.

"Marvelous," she pronounced, beaming at Hans across the cream-colored linen. Dark brown napkins, folded into a rose shape, bloomed beside silver and crystal sparkling in the light of three brown candles.

"On Mondays the house recommends rindsrouladen," Hans told her. "So, also, do I. It comes with potato dumplings and garden vegetables, very fresh. But almost anything is available except, perhaps, the hamburger or hot dog."

"I adore roulade, and my single source at home is an old chum from Wiesbaden," Nikki sparkled along with the table accessories.

"From Wiesbaden? Does your fine German mean that you, too, are truly European?"

"I was," she agreed, "but I have lived in the United States for a number of years. I am adopted, you see."

"Then we shall toast the good fortune that brings you back to your beginnings." He nodded to the waiter who stood by, a bottle of Mumms champagne extended for Hans's approval.

"To you and this place," Hans raised his glass when the formalities of service were over.

Twirling the stem of the tulip shaped champagne glass in her fingers, Nikki smiled at Hans and responded to his toast.

"To you and all your help, and to a lovely evening in a lovely city."

When the plate of salad was slid in front of her, Nikki was surprised at how hungry she suddenly was.

"I like this," she stated. "The marinade is kinder to the flavors than a dressing, as we use in the States."

"Do you remember the name? Gemischter."

"Right." She nodded eagerly. "My friend does not make salad like this. The marinating takes too long."

"Oh, the fast Americans," Hans sighed. "Always in a hurry and what for? The days there are twenty-four hours, just as they are here."

Nikki laughed in agreement.

As she worked her way through the main course, Nikki began to feel the generosity with which the Swiss filled one's plate. She shook her head when Hans preferred burgundy.

"I cannot assimilate another taste tonight," she protested. "Perhaps I might have a glass of water?"

After a while he suggested that they walk over to the park and hear the music. Nikki, feeling a little fuzzy, agreed immediately.

The night air, soft on her face as they strolled along without speaking, recalled another night and another man. She was glad that, when he finally chose a bench for them, it was away from the water.

Hans's arm rested on her shoulders. His hand shifted her nearer, inviting her head to rest against him.

"I hope you wear white often," he whispered during a wave of applause for one of the performing groups. "Redheads are particularly stunning in white."

Nikki blinked. She didn't think of herself as a redhead. That seemed to mean carrot-top. But if Hans thought she had auburn hair, that was fine with her. Gerhardt had once classified it as "polished mahogany." Back then she had believed him.

The musicians were still performing when Hans drew her up from the bench. The competition could continue for another hour, he told her. In the meantime, there was dancing now back at the restaurant.

* * *

The dance floor was of concrete, almost an extension of the walkway along the river. Potted plants in full bloom, however, separated the area from the common walkway. Periodically the borders were punctuated with old wine kegs from which grape vines, heavy with fruit, appeared to be growing profusely.

Of course there was a table for them, next to one of the barrels, and a bottle of wine with two glasses. Either Susan had misjudged the extent of Hans's sorrow or this was a place to which he brought business associates.

"Usually I am here in the company of men only, or at the most, their wives," Hans told her, making her wonder if he were reading her thoughts. "Tonight, however, I have you, and I would like to dance."

The tune was Mancini's very danceable "Moon River." Nikki found herself enjoying her place in his arms. As he pulled her still nearer, the scent of his cologne drifted to her.

The band continued with a medley of popular songs. Hans's arm tightened still more so that his fingertips were moving softly but steadily along the side of her breast. She slid her hand from his shoulder to pry against the offending arm, but not before she felt her nipples come erect.

"Your pardon," he whispered with a chuckle. "It's been a long time since I have done that. Perhaps I was clumsy."

"Perhaps," she giggled into his ear. "But I doubt it."

When the set ended, he kissed her cheek before taking her back to the table. His hand came up to brush a wisp of hair away from her face.

"You are hot. Is it excitement or embarrassment?"

"A bit of both," she admitted, not pleased with herself. She'd been drinking more than she ought had, and if she were not careful, she would do something stupid. Still she accepted the cognac he offered to end the evening.

Perhaps she could have used that final drink to excuse her response to his kiss in the shadows at the side of the restaurant. Granted he had been expressing passion, perhaps even longing. But she had been every bit as involved, her tongue thrusting in answer to his, her body bending itself to match his.

Yet she was aware that at this point she was using him to prolong that fine sense of anticipation that was buoying her spirits. He was merely another part of a marvelous day. Enough, she decided resolutely, pushing herself away.

Without protest, he escorted her to the car and turned it toward the "Weisser Schwan." Now the sounds of the street dance took over from the restaurant's music.

"I don't suppose you would like to dance some more..." he began slowing down.

"And you are correct," she told him. "You are also sweet and a wonderful person with whom to spend an evening."

"But not a night," he sighed, then laughed. "Do I get a chance to try again? Later this week, perhaps. My behavior or your permissiveness may change for the better?" he added hopefully.

At "The Swan," his arm encircled her shoulders briefly, the back of his hand turning her mouth to his for a good night kiss, soft and fragile. Nikki was glad. If his hand had exerted any force, she would have entered the guesthouse wearing the reverse of his intaglio on her cheek.

It took some effort to systematically prepare herself for bed. There was still enough alcohol in her blood to make her want to toss her clothes aimlessly about the room. Only the memory of Liesel's graciousness caused her to hang each item carefully. Once under the covers, she closed her eyes, trying to recapture the many scenes of the day.

Her thoughts, instead, went back many years to the other Swiss hotel where she slid under crisp sheets, thinking of another man, Gerhardt. It was his face she was seeing now, his arms she felt around her, his hand caressing her body and brushing across her breasts. She hugged her arms close to her body, trying to recapture some warmth. Zurich was Gerhardt's home. Would she be able to find him? Did she want to?

Drifting off to sleep, a sound of repeated scratching seemed within her memories at first. Finally she recognized that the noise was coming from her door.

"Who is it?" Nikki called out, but no answer came back. The scratching continued.

Pushing back the bedding, Nikki touched her feet to the floor. Susan certainly was not hard of hearing. If she were standing in the hall, she should have answered.

As soon as the door was cracked, she felt the pressure against it, not hard, but persistent. And then the silky tail wrapped itself around her legs.

There was no point in inviting the cat inside the room. She was already there, firmly planted on the foot of the bed. She blinked her golden eyes once in Nikki's direction, then began to wash herself.

Nikki closed the door and crossed the room. She apparently was to have a bedmate for the night, a clean one at that.

* * *

"When one visits a banker, one should be quite formal," Nikki explained to the cat who had left the room earlier in the morning, then returned when Susan came up with coffee and croissants.

The puss regarded her seriously, round golden eyes unblinking. She probably could not understand why humans chose not to wear fur year-round, Nikki imagined.

The white skirt had made it through the previous evening without spotting, and its night on the hanger had relaxed the wrinkles. Her blue jacket was fine after a brisk brushing, providing it and the cat did not come in contact. The blouse, daffodil bright, was Liesel's contribution to this day's enterprise. It would do fine as long as she did not breath too deeply.

"What I really need is a good luck piece."

The cat rose, stretched, and stalked to the edge of the bed as if volunteering for the assignment.

"Not you, crazy one. I meant a piece of jewelry." But her selection was slight since Tante Uschi's case remained in Wiesbaden. Only those pieces to which she was too attached to bear separation had come. Her fingers checked them now, a very small bundle without the Piaget, and settled on the angel ring. It had been years since she had worn it. The last time it had required olive oil to slide it free. So she slid it onto the gold chain along with the cross Doro had given her at confirmation and dropped both below the neckline of the blouse. She hoped she did not jingle in the banker's presence.

Being appropriately dressed was only a part of it, she decided, as she left The Swan. Her arrival also had to be considered. No streetcar today, even though she had a hunch which stop was involved, for getting there in one piece was important.

Within the first five minutes of her journey, Nikki knew that the taxicab was not the answer either. The driver handled traffic impetuously, seeming to test each lane and then to compare it again with the previous lane. She could design a new carnival ride and call it Swiss Taxi.

"Please," Nikki rapped on the glass partition. The driver removed one hand from the wheel as the other negotiated a corner. The glass opened enough that he could attend to her need.

"Please, not so fast."

The glass closed with a sharp punctuation to her request. Other than that, there was no reason to believe he had even heard her plea.

"It's there," he announced finally. Relieved, Nikki opened her eyes to find they were double-parked in front of a narrow four-story building. Nikki looked at it and then at its neighbors. She knew the place. It was on the postcard inside of her purse. Her trembling fingers pushed the fare toward him, including a tip that she hoped indicated her appreciation for not having died in transit.

It was a bank. The polished bronze plaque at the side of the door said so for those with ambition enough to approach closely. But the glass-paneled door that admitted her opened into a foyer was almost the same size as the one at Number 13 Taunustrasse. This time, though, there was a single button by the intercom. She tried the next set of doors and found them locked. So, with a grim smile, she resorted to the button. A robber here would have to seek approval even to get inside.

From somewhere a woman responded, asking her business in German, French, and English.

"My name is Monika Groebel. I wish to speak with M. DePrenger."
"Please wait."

Nikki positioned herself in front of the doors, ready to act as soon as the buzzer sounded. The wait seemed endless. Would they, she wondered, tell her if she were not to be allowed inside?

Soundlessly the panels parted. A grizzled man with gold-rimmed glasses peered out at her.

"Follow me if you please." He repeated it three times, just like the voice from the wall.

She was debating if security was also carried out in triplicate when he brought her to a small floor-to-ceiling cage that resembled the ticket booths in Chicago movie houses. The woman inside looked out at her curiously. Nikki stared back.

"You are Fraulein Groebel? And you wish to see M. DePrenger?"

"That is correct." Now the conversation was all in German.

"And the subject, please?"

Nikki debated how much detail she should furnish. It was essential she get to the man and not be fobbed off by some hireling.

"A bank key," she tried, hoping that was sufficient.

"Have you lost it?" Losing a key, the woman's expression indicated, was unforgivable.

"No, I have it."

"May I see it, please?" A drawer slid forward, almost catching Nikki in the midrift. In a moment, it slid again, returning the key to her. "It is one of ours. I will ring you through."

This time the buzzer sounded, but the man's hand caught the knob before Nikki could reach out. He gestured her forward and came through behind her. It took a moment to realize that they had not entered a hallway, but an elevator. The car began to move.

"Perhaps you will take a seat?" The man motioned to the upholstered chair in the corner of the box. Next to it was a small table. The floor was carpeted, the walls papered.

"No, thank you." But she put a steadying hand on the chair's back. It was impossible to hear the mechanical apparatus that drew them upward. Yet there was no music, either. She stifled a giggle, remembering how she and Mark had waltzed during a descent from the top of the Palmer House.

The car halted abruptly, and its door opened into an area that seemed to be an extension of the elevator. Upholstered chairs and sofas, flanked by small tables, gave the reception area the appearance of a formal sitting room. At the far corner, a good twenty steps away, a maturely attractive woman in grey crepe presided over a large reading table. She smiled a greeting and beckoned Nikki forward.

By the time Nikki reached her, both her escort and the elevator had disappeared.

"Welcome, Fraulein Groebel. M. DePrenger can give you a few minutes if you are willing to wait until 10 a.m."

The Timex ticked bravely past 9:47, and Nikki nodded.

"Then please have a seat. Would you like coffee or chocolate?"

"Coffee is fine." Nikki dropped to a nearby sofa. It seemed a peculiar routine to follow for banking, but there was comfort in knowing that Vati had come many times to this place and participated in the ritual.

What a ritual it turned out to be. A door near the sofa opened abruptly, and a uniformed maid entered. Her silver tray held a cup and saucer, along with a plate of cookies. The napkin was linen, heavy with embroidery and lace. With a curtsy, the maid bestowed the offering on the low table in front of Nikki. She drew back, waiting at attention, until Nikki thanked her.

One cup of coffee and two cookies later, another door opened. A tall man, thin to the point of being bony but beautifully attired in tailored grey worsted, crossed the carpet quickly.

"Fraulein Groebel, I am Ambrose DePrenger. Shall we go to my office?"

The room at the end of the long grey corridor was glassed at its front. The view of Zurich, sparkling in another day of sun, was breathtaking. Nikki doubted that the man really worked. Who could with so much to see? The decor—black, white, and grey—did nothing to detract from the vista.

"Shall we sit at the window?" he invited, leading her to a cluster of leather chairs surrounding a glass table. She took the seat he indicated. As soon as she was seated, the maid appeared. Her cup had been refilled, a carafe and cup added for the man, and the tray of sweets replenished.

"And now to business," he announced after his first swallow. "Since the key you have is not yours, how do you come to have it?"

"My father gave it to me."

"Did he now? Just when did this occur?"

Nikki took a deep breath, willed away the tears that were forming at the corners of her eyes, and related the story of the key in the hidden safe. M. DePrenger would have made a good reporter, Nikki realized, as query by query, he learned more about her. He must also be a good banker, for he discovered much without giving anything away. At last he was examining the postcard. Since she knew the contents by heart, it was as if she read with him.

"My child. I shall always love you, my smallest and dearest. What I have is yours. When you have need, remember to call home. This street in Zurich is a favorite of mine. It contains much of value. One day I hope to show it to you for it offers freedom and peace."

The message left M. DePrenger frowning.

"And you did not try the telephone number as the safe's combination as soon as the card arrived?"

"I no longer lived in the apartment. In fact, I had been in the United States for several months. My mother had died, and a friend of hers sent the postcard to me, along with some family pictures," Nikki explained.

"But it was mailed from Zurich nearly two years earlier."

"The day after I saw Vati for the last time. But you have seen him since, of course. And I was wondering..."

The shake of his head stopped her.

"I do believe that you are Karl Groebel's daughter, Monika. Otherwise, I would not be spending this time with you. But I have not seem him since the date on the postcard."

"But you must have at least corresponded with him, if only to accept payment for his box at the bank." Nikki protested. "Herr Haupt, the jeweler, does business with him."

"That may be," the man agreed. "Still, there have been no transactions between Karl Groebel and this institution during the period. Before that, there were several years in which he came regularly. He arranged long ago for settlement of his box lease. It has years to run."

"And you have no address for my father nor any way to make contact in an emergency?"

"Only the Wiesbaden address. We do not write our clients unless they initiate the process, and we certainly do not have emergencies."

Her discouragement had to be written on her face. She rolled back her lower lip under her teeth to keep her chin from trembling. This was not the way in which she had envisioned the day going.

"M. DePrenger, I hope that you can understand my feelings." Nikki fought for control of voice and words. "I do not know why I did not receive the postcard in the usual manner or why I never realized the significance of Vati's suggestion to call home. All I can tell you is that it happened just as I have reported it to you. My father has given me a responsibility and, for some reason that I don't understand as yet, I have been led here."

"I have the authority to open Karl's box, and I think I shall exercise it now to see if it can add to your understanding." The man reached across the table to her shaking hands. "You may take nothing from it because that requires legal proof of identity. While you say you are Monika Groebel, your papers say that you are Monica Fisher. Still, with the key that is in your possession, we shall see what is there. I share your concern about your parent's whereabouts."

He rose and went to his desk. Picking up the black telephone, M. DePrenger asked for Magda and issued a series of orders in French. The box was to be brought to him from the vault.

The man with the gold-wired glasses turned out as its escort, although a uniformed companion actually carried it. The box appeared to be heavy, nearly the size of a file cabinet drawer. When it had been placed on M. DePrenger's desk, the man in uniform extended a thick pad toward Nikki.

"We sign for this, Monika. I, here. You, there." The banker explained as he pulled a pen from an onyx holder and handed it to her.

Once the pair had departed, Nikki found herself shaking again. M. DePrenger watched her with compassion as she fumbled in her attempt to insert the key.

"It's so different here," she complained, trying to cover her embarrassment. "At home—in Chicago—you only take your key and give it to the attendant. It opens a door. The box is inside."

"I have seen American banks operate." His tone was level, but she suspected that he preferred his bank's way.

She strained forward to see as he lifted the lid. A white envelope lay on top of a covering that veiled the contents. It was a large envelope, and the small printing was nearly lost on it. Still she knew those precise letters spelled her own name. Her hand reached for it without thought, then dropped to her side.

"Although you may not take it with you, I will allow you to see what is inside." M. DePrenger lifted the envelope and placed it in her fingers. "The envelope, of course, is from the bank's stationery stock."

She carried the envelope to her chair. Whatever was inside, she needed the reassurance of furniture supporting her. Her forefinger pried the seal open.

The letterhead was also the bank's, but the hand was Vati's. She struggled with tears as she read it.

"My dear Monika—

I must hurry and cannot say all that I want you to know. There is trouble with which I must contend. I have returned Gerhardt to his home, and he is safely away from it all. He asked if he could marry you when you are old enough. I answered that, although such a marriage would please me, I would not control your decision.

If you read this, you must know that I am unable to act for myself. And, though I regret it, you must be my agent for just a little while. Much of what is here is mine and, therefore, yours. The rest belongs to people who have trusted me during the trying years in which our own and others have imposed their wills upon us. Those items should be returned if possible. I have included an inventory to aid you. You may expect help from Klaus Haupt, for he has helped me. Do not trust the son, who betrays him.

Use what remains for your future happiness. You have earned it in the sorrow of the past and by the joy I found in being—

Your father,
Karl Albert Groebel

Freedom and peace, my child."

She raised the sheet to her lips and kissed it.

"May I look now, Monsieur?" Nikki asked.

"Certainly. Raise the cloth."

She did, and immediately dropped it. M. DePrenger leaned toward the box, too.

"I believe you should make whatever arrangements are necessary to bring me your papers," he observed, looking down at the dozens of jeweler packets. "It would appear that may control a fortune."

"It's Vati's, not mine," Nikki stated.

"Perhaps. But you have the key, and there was only one. You must get those papers. And be sure that care is taken in transit. You will call me as soon as they arrive. This number rings my phone only." M. DePrenger was anxious to reassure her and to offer all his cooperation.

"You think Vati is dead," Nikki objected. "But Herr Haupt…"

"You must ask him when you see him." He reached for the telephone. "I have a meeting that I must attend as soon as the box has been returned to the vault. I look forward to your coming again."

There were questions she should have asked and had not, Nikki realized when she was finally back in her room. Even the cab ride front the bank had not been sufficiently terrifying to take her concentration from the problems confronting her. How long, she wondered, did it take papers to come from the States? A week, at least. Paul would know, if she could reach him.

This time the Bonn number paid off. He answered himself on the third ring.

"What luck, Nikki?" he asked as soon as she had identified herself.

"Not luck, Paul, fortune." She described as briefly as she could about the box at the bank and was not surprised at his appreciative whistle. "But the papers. How long will it take for them to come?"

"Where are the original papers? In David's safe deposit box?"

"I think so. I had a set of Photostats in my bedroom chest. Will they do?"

"Not hardly," he chuckled. "David will have certified copies made from the originals. If everything goes well, I can bring them with me when I come. I expect to leave for Zurich Friday night."

"Can't David send them directly to me?"

"Not in the news bureau pouch, he can't. I won't steal your diamonds. Trust me."

She told him about the party. Would he mind going with her? Paul agreed that it would be fun. Then, feeling suddenly very selfish, she asked about the conference and his stories.

"I really wish you were here," Paul told her. "There is a State Department translator, of course, and he seems to do quite well. Except…"

"Yes?" she prompted.

"Except that I know the chairman keeps talking about washing hands. I know those words, having spent so much time with Delia and Heike. But the translator keeps ignoring it. So I wonder what else I may be missing."

"Is the phrase you heard 'Eine Hand wascht die andere'?"

"That sounds right."

"Literally it is 'one hand washes the other.' But your chairman is discussing trade-offs and cooperation. Okay?"

"Makes a lot of sense," Paul admitted. "Now, what do you plan to do tomorrow?"

"I don't know. Perhaps sight-see. Bruno said he'd be here Thursday."

"Will you take some advice from a friend?"

"Of course."

"Then hang that silver coin around your neck and find your Mickey Mouse friend. I know that you are reluctant, but I think it is important. Promise me?"

Paul's words came like a slap in the face. Of course! Vati had told her that Gerhardt could be trusted. Her years of denying her feelings were past. With that realization came light and longing. She told Paul she would try.

But as she replaced the telephone's receiver, a new set of fears swept over her. What had happened to Gerhardt in the past six years? Would the man who loved Monika Groebel at fifteen love twenty-one-year old Nikki Fisher? If she could locate him now, could he forgive her distrust? Would he have even waited?

Chapter Nine

✦ ✦ ✦

Love Returned

The Weisser Schwan cat, called Muff by the Wirt family, had appointed herself Nikki's temporary roommate. She had listened patiently to Nikki's chatter about gemstones and Gerry, then washed herself until two in the morning. Then Muff wrapped her magnificent tail around her pink nose and fell asleep.

For Nikki, slumber had been more elusive. The last time she had examined the luminous dial of the Timex, its hands had passed three. Nikki's sleep, when it came, was too eventful to be classified as rest. She had been chasing after Gerry, across the face of an immense clock. He rode the hour hand, she the minute hand. But they never seemed to cross each other. At the base of the tower in which the clock was mounted, Vati and Paul stood shoulder to shoulder, urging her to hurry. In desperation, she had swung across to the second sweep. Just as it came abreast of Gerry's position, he slid down the marker and into a hole where the hands joined.

Her dream, coupled with a late awakening, did little to improve Nikki's perspective on the potential reunion. What if Gerhardt had changed? What if he had married? What if he had forgotten all about her?

As she soaped her skin under the shower spray, she washed these thoughts away. So what if he had changed? So had she. In those intervening six years, she had become a citizen of a different nation. She was a working, albeit novice, journalist. Even yesterday brought change. For Monika Groebel was an heiress. Besides, she might not even like Gerry once they met again. But knowing was important.

Nikki and Muff went downstairs together. The cat flicked her tail in farewell and turned toward the kitchen while Nikki headed for the post office once more. The civil servant of the previous visit recognized her immediately. He proffered the requested telephone books, along with a piece of scratch paper, without cautions.

There was no home listing that seemed appropriate, but the business directory—under plumbing—carried a firm list for Mehler A.G. By the time she returned the books, customers were lined up at the counter. The postal employee ignored them to repossess his property.

"I can phone from here?" Nikki asked, keeping her eyes on him and ignoring the frowns of those awaiting service.

"Of course. Take that booth, and I will provide an outside line. You will pay me after the call is complete."

"Mehler A.G., Gruess Gott," a female voice answer after the third ring.

"Gruess Gott. Herr Mehler, please?"

"Herr Mehler, Sr., is out of the country." Nikki's hopes plunged, only to bob back with the information that "Herr Mehler, Jr., is out at a site. Perhaps he can return your call."

It was suddenly important to Nikki that she control the contact. She thanked the woman and promised to phone again. There were things she should be doing back at Weisser Schwan—brushing lint and Muff's hair off the navy jacket, rinsing out underwear, writing a letter to the Fishers or to Doro. And then she could use the guest house phone.

Instead she retrieved the business directory from the man. His customers had disappeared. So had his earlier good humor. Refusing his offer of an additional sheet, she jotted the Mehler address next to the phone number. When she inquired about directions, he referred her to a wall-sized city map with a flourish of his hand and tucked the precious reference volume back on its shelf.

The Mehlert A.G. street address, when she finally located it, seemed nowhere near the place she had visited with Gerhardt that other time. The building had been on a canal. But this street was removed from the water. She re-read the map's index. The street name appeared only once. Nikki grinned to herself. This was Europe, not the United States, where the same name might be used for street, avenue, lane, and court within the same municipality.

Now that she knew where she was going, Nikki was anxious to be on her way. Advice on transportation alternatives would be helpful, but she doubted that the man behind the counter considered providing such information a part of his duties.

Instead, she chose a corner several blocks away from the Mehler address and, when she finally succeeded in stopping a taxicab, gave that as her destination. She would arrive at the establishment on foot. That provided the option of walking past if her courage failed.

Whether it was good fortune or her driver had tired of participating in the race, she was transported along at what she considered a suitable speed with judicious stops and lane changes. The glass panel between compartments remained open so that the cabbie could converse with her in Italian. Even as she responded to his comments, Nikki wondered if he thought it was her nationality since when he greeted her in his native tongue, she replied. She was enjoying the drive, even though it was taking longer than she had expected. Finally she brought up the subject.

"Did you understand my destination?" It was possible, she thought, that Zurich cabbies, like their Chicago cousins, might drive passengers for miles in order to get around a block.

He understood, he assured her, but his assurances suddenly were less vehement. The cab stopped, and he turned to stare at her. Her choice of cross streets had brought them to a vacant lot. The opposite corner and the one behind them were obviously warehouses. She wished she'd made a better selection. The intersection they had just passed featured a church.

Before Nikki could think of an explanation for this place, her driver's face brightened. He was so sorry, he told her. The cab spun about and entered park-like grounds framed by iron gate posts. He braked the vehicle before stone steps leading to a massive oaken door.

Nikki knew she didn't dare protest. Wherever they were, this was where he thought she belonged. She paid him, and he drove off with a "Ciao" and a wave of his hand. There was nothing on the building itself for identification, although she had glimpsed a plaque at the fence. As she decided that her wisest course was to walk back down the drive, the door opened.

"You are seeking here?" The voice was sweet and melodious in contrast to the speaker's ensemble, the drab apparel of a religious postulant.

"What I really am is lost," Nikki confessed. "Can you direct me to this address?" She hoped the woman would understand even though she had Anglicized it as she wrote it down.

"Mehler? Why, they have done our work. Just down the street two blocks and a bit more." The woman's eyes sparkled. "Perhaps you would like Sister Anna Claire and me to accompany you to your destination. If you are a stranger in Zurich, you may not wish to walk alone."

If arriving at the firm in a cab cut off her options, how much more binding a religious escort would be, Nikki knew. But she could hardly refuse. The woman who identified herself as Margaret Mary so obviously wanted to be outdoors. And it seemed to be as much of a treat for the nun.

Mehler A.G. was both more modern and more open than most of the structures they passed. It featured a glass show window in which an entire bathroom, replete with terra cotta tiles and beige fixtures, was displayed. The convent, the women told her as they stared in fascination, held only humble white. And they insisted upon entering with her.

"Good morning, sisters," a salesman met them at the gold-plated taps. "It is kind of you to visit."

His gaze rested upon Nikki as he waited for a cue.

"I have come to see Herr Gerhardt Mehler," Nikki explained. "I am a friend from many years ago, and I am visiting from the United States."

Her announcement set the man in motion toward the back of the showroom and excited her companions as well. Did she know where Maryhill, New York, was? Had she ever seen the golden dome at Notre Dame University?

The wares recaptured their attention before the man returned. He drew her aside so as not to interfere with Margaret Mary's explanation of a whirlpool tub to Sister Anne Claire.

"Gerry should be back, but he has not come. All I can say is that we are expecting him. You are, of course, welcome to wait."

Having solved one mystery already, the pair decided that they, too, should wait. The next item of interest turned out to be sunlamps. Nikki wasn't sure exactly how clear her explanation was. The concept of sun on skin seemed difficult for the women to follow. What would they think, she wondered, if she had told them about the sunlamp in the villa and Mutti's insistence that her daughters march around naked under its rays for ten minutes each day.

The garbage disposal was more easily understood. Both thought it would be a boon to the convent. Watching their joy, Nikki decided that, if the jewels did become hers to convert, she would buy one for their order.

Talk of kitchens reminded the women of their noon meal and other obligations at the house down the street. With words and expressions of regret, they thanked her for the adventure and departed.

* * *

Still Nikki waited. Her stomach rumbled a reminder that it was eager for lunch. Two women employees, with handbags slung from their shoulders, came from the door at the back of the showroom. From the way the purses bulged, Nikki knew they contained a midday repast. They eyed her curiously as they passed. She wondered where they would eat their al fresco meal and whether there might be enough for a guest.

Two customers arrived, leaving their Saab at the curb. The man and woman went directly to the salesman who had welcomed Nikki. The man spoke English with a British clip. The woman's French was more leisurely. But, in both languages, they sought a blue shower stall, and they needed it yesterday. Nikki had to turn her back on the group to keep her smile from showing.

The couple's original order, which had been delivered to their home last Friday, had been white. Since then the wife had made a marvelous purchase of blue towels. They would prefer all the colors to match. She pulled a sample of her new accessories from a tote bag and displayed it for the salesman's edification. He wasn't sure that their stock blue would harmonize. He led them back to a catalog. Nikki hoped, for the sake of their personal hygiene, that there was a second bathroom in the house.

To keep from laughing aloud, she forced herself to study a display of tile and marble. The written sales material appeared in four languages, and she read each one with care although they all said the same thing. As she worked through the Italian translation, Nikki became aware of an extremely disagreeable odor. It was odd that she had not smelled it earlier. Although she knew that many specialty firms had begun introducing the aromas of their wares into the atmosphere through their air circulation units, smells related to plumbing seemed hardly appropriate.

"Are you waiting for service?"

Her heart responded immediately to the beloved voice. Nikki whirled, a smile of anticipation on her face and her hand already reaching out to him. Her motion set the Mozart medallion dancing. But the coverall-clad, safety-helmeted figure jumped back from her touch.

"Monika? Are you Monika?" Still backing away, he drew off his sunglasses. From the only clean portion of Gerhardt's face, well-remembered tawny eyes gazed at the necklace, then at her face. The dusty jawline dropped as she nodded. And now his teeth, incredibly white in contrast to the grime, appeared. He started to laugh.

So many times Nikki had dreamed of this meeting. Sometimes the vision had been of a stormy session in which her suspicions had been denounced with anger, a prelude to a passionate reconciliation. And there had been those imagined meetings in which, still believing him guilty of her father's disappearance, she had ignored his presence, leaving him to either end his life or continue it in misery. Once her mind produced a tender coincidence in which they happened to brush against each other in some neutral site with love overcoming the immediate need for explanation.

Never had Nikki visualized their reunion as an occasion for long and loud hilarity. Gerry's laughter seemed unremitting. As it continued, she began to wonder if there was something about her appearance that was causing such amusement. She took a quick glance at the bathroom cabinets displayed nearby. According to their mirrored faces, she was fine unless, of course, her slip was showing. But the noise was too much. Her stomach gave one warning cramp. Nikki turned toward the front door.

"No. Stay. Follow me." Gerry strode to the back of the shop. Without even debating the maneuver's wisdom, she fell in behind him. The lighting in the hall through which they moved showed unkind stains and soil on the back of the coveralls. The garment had been white once, she supposed, but was now the source of the unpleasant odor. Dirt was streaked in uneven layers, heavier on the legs, especially where the bottoms were captured in silt-caked boots.

"Wait here!"

He disappeared through a door, slamming it in her face. From within she could detect thuds and squeaks and running water. Back in the showroom, she heard the excitement of agreement on a shower stall that was, according to the wife, "heavenly" and "acceptable" to the husband.

She was still eavesdropping on the culmination of the sale when the door where she was stationed reopened. Now things were right. Gerhardt's arms were around her, pulling her to him.

"Monika. At last. At last!" he muttered, no longer laughing. His lips met hers, then veered off to trace the shape of her face. Then, hands firm on her shoulders, Gerhardt pushed her away from him and looked down at her.

"I never thought it would be like this, our meeting again. After all these years, you come to me and I am too filthy to even touch you." The smile came back and his hands slid down her arms to capture her fingers. "Monika, Monika. Why so long?"

"I see you found your friend from America," the salesman noted as he came bustling by. "I don't suppose you want to install a blue shower stall this afternoon."

"How intuitive!" Gerhardt responded, pulling Nikki closer so the man could pass. "If it is essential, pull Tony off inventory to put it in. I have other things to occupy the remainder of the day. I'll call in later."

* * *

Their departure had been swift, through a back door into a fenced storage yard, to a white XKE. The car moved swiftly as streets of warehousing gave way to avenues of homes, and the residential areas became countryside.

"Gerry, I am so glad…" Nikki began, but was cut off abruptly.

"Don't talk yet."

They were high above Zurich when he finally halted the car and led her to a courtyard of a small restaurant. He took the chair next to her rather than the one opposite, maintaining a grasp on her hand. The waitress, after a few quick directions, disappeared.

"Now you may speak," Gerry grinned and relaxed his grip to reach for the commemorative coin.

Nikki watched his long fingers stroke the medallion. It swung free on the tiny hinges in its silver frame, a setting designed and executed by Vati before that other meeting. She had no idea where to begin. Her confusion seemed to be apparent to Gerry.

"A starting point," he suggested. "How about why you have come to Zurich? Was it only to see me?"

It took over an hour to pick and choose from the platters of cold cuts, cheeses, pickles, and fruit and similar disorganized elements of her life. Yet, when they settled back with coffee to consider the vista below them, Nikki knew she had probably not made a great deal of sense. At least Gerry was learning why she had stopped writing.

"I am very sorry that my trust in you was so weak," she concluded her fragmented report.

"Nikki, the trust I had in you isn't something of which I am proud. You cannot imagine how I felt when we finally met after all those months of writing to each other. Even before I saw you, I was sure I loved you. Being with you was confirmation." He paused to grasp her fingers, grip tightening as he continued. "But you were so very young. When your letters stopped, I believed you had found someone nearer your age to love. It never occurred to me that you might blame me for your father's disappearance."

"And I should have known better," Nikki whispered, her eyes on their joined hands.

"You were fifteen. I was twenty-one. Those years between us were important then. What was my dream for us might not have been yours. That's how I explained it to myself, but I felt like a fool for dreaming in the first place. How glad I am that you have come back to me." Her fingers were raised to his lips.

"I am sorry that I was not wise enough to shield you from so much unhappiness," Gerry continued as Nikki struggled with tears that seemed imminent. "And I rejoice that you have found joy and knowledge with your new family and in your new country."

"And you? Have you found joy as well?"

"Only this day, I think." His features grew grim and his eyes closed on the scene before them. Without looking at her, he began a recital of the years that had passed. The company had thrived and grown as he added his energies to his father's business sense. The new warehouse and showroom had opened two years ago, just after Roswitha had left him.

"Roswitha?" Nikki prompted softly.

"Former wife. She is now married to a contractor in France."

Nikki sat silent, looking down at the city. Tiny white triangles danced along the lake. She wondered, without really caring, whether Hans Germeyer was down there on his boat.

"It was not a good marriage," Gerry finally spoke again. "But there comes a practical time when the dream must be laid aside. Perhaps she had a dream, too. I never cared enough to find out. So what do we do now, Nikki?"

"I guess we go back down the hill," she suggested. "Bruno will be here tomorrow and Paul on Saturday. I want you to meet them both. Can you come to Herr Haupt's party with us?"

"Of course. Are you free for the rest of today? I would like to share with you some more of my life."

Nikki nodded and smiled at him. Gerry returned her regard with that same lovely grin that she had held in her mind over six years and half a world.

"I'd be glad to share," Nikki agreed, "but I would prefer to avoid blue shower stalls and wherever it was you spent the morning."

* * *

"So I am not perfect," Nikki told Muff during the hour Gerry had allowed her to prepare for their evening. "But Gerry doesn't expect me to be because he isn't, either."

The cat's response was a soft snore. Apparently the feline had found Nikki's earlier report on buildings in which Gerry's products were installed boring.

Now Nikki cast a critical eye over the contents of the room's small wardrobe and winced. There was little choice in the matter of dinner dress. The white skirt and sandals again, she supposed, were adequate. Add to it her own blue blouse. It buttoned down the back, and she could wear the silver medallion with it. Despite Muff's reaction, Nikki still thought the afternoon had been marvelous, an opportunity to explore the life Gerry had made for himself.

"I'm not exactly expecting immortality in porcelain," Gerry chortled as he took her through the rooms of one wing of a new hotel where construction was nearly complete. "I doubt that five hundred years from now a tour guide will point out that the bathrooms were by Mehler. On the other hand, I was a big job, bigger than my father eve bid when he was alone with the firm."

"Do you actually do the work?" Nikki inquired. "Or do you just plan and supervise?"

"Mostly the latter, but Dad made sure that I learned the trade from our people. And I like to keep in practice," he explained. "This morning, as your nose knows, I was working on a clogged drainfield."

He had shown her the exteriors of several villas on the heights over Zurich. Here, too, the Mehler firm had done its part. And they visited an excavation where a new governmental building would rise. Mehler was a subcontractor for the project.

Nikki had enjoyed the impromptu business tour. More fun, however, had been the quick visit to his home.

Because its entrance was separate and on the far side of the company building, she had missed seeing it before. This time, however, he had parked at the door instead of inside the warehouse compound. A portico protected the entry. In place of doorbell or knocker, there was a chain pull from an antique water closet.

Just inside where the small hall opened onto the stairway was an old-fashioned lavatory on an elaborate metal pedestal. Its basin was filled with a floral arrangement that rose above the marble counter.

The oaken stairwell and banisters were repeated within the sitting room. Gerry's wood, oiled and polished, retained its natural color. The upholstered furniture were done in beige and rust with accents of old gold. Several landscapes adorned the walls. Nikki moved closer, not so much to observe the paintings but to examine their ornate frames.

"So you bring your work home with you," she giggled, running her fingers over one old medicine chest.

"They're all things that I tore out in renovation projects, and much too lovely to consign to the dump," he grinned. "I had a whole storeroom filled with them when Roswitha left. So, when I moved in here, I got the best out."

It was not the only room that echoed Gerry's occupation. The bathroom contained the best that a plumber might offer and so did the kitchen. Only the master bedroom seemed removed from the work world. Here the wood was dark. The bed's head board was like the one she remembered from the villa, high and ornately carved with attached lamp stands. Nikki paused by the bedroom door, looking back. She blushed as her imagination placed her beneath the featherbed with Gerry holding her.

* * *

The Timex said that she had done very well in making her preparations. Only the three upper buttons at her back remained to receive attention. So Nikki sat down by the window, shifting the chair so that she would see the Jaguar when it arrived.

Waiting by the window had been the posture that Mutti had assumed that night so long ago. After a pleasure-filled family dinner, Vati and Gerry had left to drive into Zurich. Monika had been confident that during the journey, no more than ninety minutes each way, Gerry would have Vati's approval for an understanding regarding their future. Mutti must have sensed it, too.

"It might have been wiser if you had not met Gerhardt at this time," Wera Groebel had commented as she pulled a satin robe over her nightdress. "He is a fine young man, but you are so young. There are so many places you have not yet been, so many parties and people to meet."

"I can do all of that with Gerry," Monika protested. She was lying across her parents' bed, head propped on her elbows. "How soon do you think Vati would let us marry? Doro is eighteen, and Hanna was only a little older."

"Those were different times," Mutti had observed. And that had launched her into a monologue about their former life. Monika had not interrupted. Instead she let the words roll on as she tried to visualize herself as Gerry's wife. But the mental pictures were hard to establish.

Monika, bride of Gerhardt Mehler, came easier. It had been only three weeks since Doro had married Max Kneipp and the young couple had departed for the United States of America.

She saw herself in a wedding gown, clinging to Gerry's arm. It was quite different from the one Doro had worn. There was less lace, more embroidery. The fabric was softer, the style simple. Beyond that event, Monika imagined herself in bed with Gerry. At least, there were two figures beneath the covers. But the descriptions she had discovered in Mutti's romance novels did not seem applicable. As for a daytime existence, the wanderings of her mind held nothing.

It was when Mutti first moved to the window and pushed the curtain aside that Monika became aware of a tension. She looked at her wristwatch. It was nearly two in the morning. With a pang, she wondered if Gerry was having to argue their love with Vati.

"I'll go to my room now," Monika announced. Mutti had fallen silent. Perhaps she wanted the bed vacated.

"Don't leave me, Monika. Sleep here, please."

"What about Vati?"

"We'll wake you when he comes. Perhaps he will use your room. There will only be a few hours before we have to leave."

Monika had slept fitfully even though the lights had been turned off. And each time she roused, she could hear the whirring of Mutti's immersion heater in still another cup of water and the rattling of the foil from another bar of chocolate.

When morning came, Mutti had exhausted both the tin of Nescafe and the can of evaporated milk that she always carried. The room was heavy with the odor of the beverage, chocolate, and tobacco. It required only a glance at Mutti's face to know that Vati was not in the room next door.

"Since you are awake, please go down to the desk and see if your father has called us." Mutti's voice was husky from the hours of waiting. "I am going to bathe."

Monika retrieved the clothing she had hung over the foot board. It was wrinkled, but at this hour, only the desk clerk, emerging for the day shift, would know.

* * *

There had been no message. Perhaps Vati had tried to call earlier and the phone had been untended, the man at the desk suggested. But periodic queries throughout the morning had been no more fruitful. In between trips to the lobby, Monika had changed clothes, brushed and reset Mutti's long hair using cologne to freshen the hairline, and gathered her belongings, as well as those of her parents, into their suitcases. She expected that, as soon as Vati appeared, they would leave.

By noon Mutti was done waiting. Monika was sent to the desk to extend their room reservations for another night. After lunch Wera Groebel appealed, through the local constabulary, for a check of accident reports in and around Zurich during the past fifteen hours. Only the Mercedes was located, discovered late in the afternoon on the Limmatquai.

Using her set of keys and the hotel manager's son, Mutti took possession of the vehicle. The next morning, when there was still no message, Wera and Monika Groebel departed for Wiesbaden with the boy as their driver.

But Mutti never filed a missing person report for Karl Groebel, Monika learned after their return to Number 13 Taunustrasse. Mutti did not expect to see Vati again.

"Karl knew this would happen, but he would not stop in his crazy efforts to restore those gems he held in trust," she complained bitterly. "His honor was more important than our well-being. So now we fend for ourselves."

There would be days of peril ahead, Mutti predicted. When Monika sought details, the conversation ceased. Ignorance might be weak protection, Mutti suggested, but it was also the best available.

After that, Wera Groebel kept her own counsel while her daughter wept in private for a lost father. The predicted peril did not come until Mutti turned to Stefan Rennecke for assistance.

* * *

"Nikki? Your escort is here." Susan rapped on the door, then thrust her head inside. Muff roused, along with Nikki, and yawned her greeting. As Susan, at Nikki's request, fastened the elusive buttons at the neckline, she chattered about Gerry.

"He's a handsome one, too. Almost as gorgeous as Herr Germeyer! By the way, what should I tell Herr Germeyer if he calls?"

"That *you* will be glad to dine with him tonight," Nikki laughed. Suddenly she couldn't recall what Hans looked like at all.

This time the Jaguar carried them north of the city. Nikki had never been good about compass directions, but when the sunset was on her left, she managed. Still she was a bit surprised when she began to recognize their destination, the village of Winterthur where their first meeting occurred.

"I thought we should return. The past does have to be discussed," Gerry explained as he halted the XKE in the parking area at the Garten Hotel. But before they went inside, he led her down to the shore. They only stood, hand in hand, staring out at crimson sky, reflected as pink in the water.

Before she could think or protest, Gerry swung her to him. This kiss was not the symbol of reacquaintance as those earlier this day. With his lips he was claiming her and renewing their pledge.

"Now we have begun to catch up, I think," he announced huskily.

During their meal, she told him about the hours of waiting here and how she and Mutti had returned to Germany. There were times that her lower lip quivered. Going over the details twice in such a short time was almost more than she could manage. But Gerry's hand on hers calmed her spirit, and Nikki was able to continue.

"I can't give you the answers you seek, darling," he began when she was finished. "But here is how I remember that night.

"We had just turned on the highway when I began to explain that I wanted to marry you. I gave your father all the assurances that a young fool would, about how I would cherish and care for you so that you would never know sadness or need. And Karl laughed at me. I had a lot to learn about life, he said. He began to explain why he could not give you to me, because no one has that power over another."

"That sounds exactly like Vati," Nikki exclaimed, but Gerry seemed not to hear her.

"Suddenly Karl stopped speaking. He began varying the speed of the Mercedes. For a mile or so he would hold the car right at the red line. Then he would slow way down and we would be continually passed."

"Did Vati seem ill?" Nikki inquired.

"No. His expression was grim, almost resolute. There was one car that stayed right with us, regardless of how he drove. Because of it, your father decided not to take me to my parents' home. He said he was sorry to have involved me in his troubles and that he wanted to spare me further danger. In the city center, he stopped the car and secured a cab to take me home."

"Then he had stones with him," Nikki concluded. "Vati had a built-in alarm system when he thought he might be robbed. Do you think there were thieves in that car?"

"Perhaps. But I am sure that Karl did. 'They cannot follow us both,' he assured me. 'I will lead them away from you. And you no longer know me.' And then he got back into the Mercedes and drove off. The other car, a Citroen, pulled out after him." For a moment Gerry's eyes closed. When he looked at her again, his stare was intense. "Nikki, I wish I had stayed with him. Whoever they were, I could have helped him."

"But he must have made it safely through the night." This time Nikki reached out her hand to comfort Gerry. "I know Vati was all right in the morning. He met with M. DePrenger and wrote a letter to me."

"Who is M. DePrenger?"

That brought out another story, about the key and the box and its contents. She found that she had to tell it carefully, leaving out peripheral details in order to make it sound sensible. Even then, Gerry kept interrupting to seek to identify one of the persons involved.

"The letter that lay on top was dated the day after you and he left us at Winterthur. And it urged me to trust you." She smiled past the candle flame at the serious face she cared for so much. "Vati also said that, although he would not give me to you, he thought I should consider your proposal."

"And have you considered it?"

"Not until yesterday. Until then I blamed you for Vati being gone. I'm not sure why. Herr Rennecke thought you were involved. Mutti said not, but he kept insisting. It was an easy set-up, according to him. You were too old to be writing to children's magazines for a pen pal anyway. So what you did was to correspond with youngsters whose parents were well-to-do and then you stole. You robbed Vati, Stefan said. When we went back to Wiesbaden from Zurich, Vati was supposed to have diamonds for one of Stefan's clients."

"Did Karl carry gems around Europe often?" Gerry asked, startled.

"Of course. Didn't you know?"

"If I had known, do you think I would have left him alone to be robbed?" His face had turned crimson.

"But you knew he was a jeweler," Nikki reminded him.

"I don't know much about jewelers, but plumbers do not carry their pipes with them on vacation. I should have realized, though. Your father was right. I knew nothing about life back then." Gerry shook his head.

"About your proposal…" Nikki moved to the other subject.

He waved her silent.

"The vault box with the jewels. How large is it?"

She described it with her hands.

"And the value. What do you estimate?"

"That depends on how many of the stones have to be returned to their real owners. Vati expects me to do that. I didn't see the inventory, and I can't estimate. I've been away from the business for too long." She shrugged. "The value would be based on a gemologist's appraisal. I don't want to hazard a guess. Why?"

"If you don't know why, you also don't know much about life. Let's hold the proposal in abeyance for the time being and dance instead." He stood and took her hand.

Somehow, it was enough for the time being to feel his body, catch the beat of the pulse in his neck against her forehead, and to know peace for just a little while.

* * *

Bruno's plans changed. His supplier of carved pipe bowls would not have the order ready until Monday. Bruno, therefore, decided to drive down with Paul and to take the train back when his business in Switzerland was completed.

"We'll see you Saturday afternoon," he assured Nikki over a less than adequate telephone connection. "What's been happening down there?"

Somehow Nikki didn't feel that she could do the treasure box justice by trying to relate its story over the static. She suspected that Paul would brief Bruno on the subject before they arrived, anyway. But she did have to tell him about Gerry.

"I'm glad you located him," Bruno told her. His next sentence was lost in line noise. "...forward to meeting him."

He gave her the name of the inn where he always stayed and said he thought they would be there by three o'clock. Why didn't she ask if Gerry would join them for dinner? By the way, was there a wife?

"Not now. Bruno, can you put my jewelry box in Paul's car when you come? That way it and I will be together when we go back to Darmstadt."

"Your what?" The crackling was especially loud.

"My jewelry box. Your mother is keeping it for me."

"Right. See you Saturday."

Nikki was wondering how she would spend the day, discussing alternatives with Muff, her constant companion except at mealtime, when Frau Wirt hailed her to the telephone once more.

"Are you free for lunch and the afternoon?" Gerry inquired.

"I certainly am. Bruno just called to say he won't come in until Saturday, with Paul. And he wants to know if we can all have dinner together that night."

"Why not? I need to meet the other men in your life. But for today, dress casual. We're going up to the mountains. I'll be there in thirty minutes."

"The narrower the road, the more curves" was a David Fisher axiom with which Nikki had to concur as the Jaguar climbed away from the city. Wildflowers in profusion crowded the road's edges as though to challenge men's handiwork. Occasionally, when the treetops permitted, she could glimpse Lake Zurich far below. Deep shadowed gorges and sunlit meadows vyed for her attention. Amid the natural beauty, she found herself speechless. She didn't need to know their destination. It was sufficient just to be here.

"Why so quiet?" Gerry asked finally, putting the vehicle through yet another switchback.

"It seems appropriate," she murmured.

Without taking his eyes from the road, he nodded and smiled to himself. She knew he was pleased by her reaction.

Finally he pulled off the road and stopped under the shade of a tree. There were no buildings visible. Even the city was cut off from view.

"And now we hike," he announced, glancing down at her feet. Her sneakers seemed to meet with his approval. "But not far. It's an easy walk and well worth the effort."

She put on her sunglasses and took the basket he passed to her from the XKE's trunk. Grabbing a small cooler and a mesh bag, Gerry led the way. It was a narrow path, defined but not overused. As he had promised, the grade was easily managed. Still, as they topped one hill and looked up toward another, Gerry paused to allow her to catch her breath.

"Is this where you bring all your girls?" Nikki asked after her lungs adjusted.

"Roswitha and I used to come here on Sundays," he nodded. "That was in the better times. But I have to warn you. It's been almost three years. I'm hoping it has not changed, for I want to introduce you to Switzerland as it is and always has been. Ready to go on?"

"Switzerland, here I come!" Nikki announced boldly and fell in behind him again. The trail turned a steep corner and then leveled out again. He might consider this his homeland, but to Nikki the scene before them was what she privately thought paradise would be. A carpeting of orange, yellow, blue, and green was interrupted with occasional grey boulders. Evergreens, in conversational clusters, provided spots of shade. And in the center of it all was a small lake, competing with the sky in its blue. As they drew nearer, she saw the tiny mountain stream that fed it.

"How beautiful!" she sighed aloud when he sat down his burden on a mound above the lake. Nikki looked down at the water and smiled. "Can't we eat right at the edge?"

"It's rather marshy there," Gerry warned. "Up here the grass is drier. There's a blanket in the mesh bag. You spread it out while I refrigerate the wine."

She watched him move toward the creek with a bottle in each hand. The water, undoubtedly snow-melt, would cool the beverages rapidly. Then she turned to her assigned task. Once the blanket was in place, Nikki took over a corner of it, pulling off her shoes and turning her jeans up so that her knees were exposed. The sun was warm and the breeze was like velvet, stroking her skin.

Gerry came back to stand between Nikki and the sun so that his shadow crossed her face. As she looked up, he seemed as much a part of the scene as the hardy trees and ageless rocks. It reminded her of geopolitical arguments she had heard and in which she had sometimes participated. Was Switzerland a place or a people? Then she had spoken from knowledge gained from books. Now she knew in her heart that the two were the same.

"You were pretty when you were fifteen," Gerry told her, looking down, outlined against the sky. "I thought you would grow to be even prettier. But you haven't."

"Thanks a..." she protested, then stopped as he raised a hand toward her. Reaching out, she allowed herself to be drawn up against him.

"Instead you have become a beauty," he continued, tightening his arms about her.

"There's a difference?" she asked, nuzzling against his throat.

At that he pushed her back so that she could read his face. He was smiling—lips, eyes, and features in unison to produce an expression of joy.

"Of course. All Swiss know that. Pretty is embroidery and paint and other human additions. Beauty is nature." He let go of her now to gesture at the setting. "This is you."

He had reached for her hand again, both of his hands firmly holding hers, bringing it to his lips, caressing her palm gently. His soft touch sent little shivers of anticipated pleasures down her spine. His declaration was so different from any she had ever heard before.

Mark, as well as a couple of other boys at Northwestern, had also said she was beautiful, but it always had been in the context of proms when she had worked to make herself look her best. Even Paul's compliments had been tied to specific situations. But Gerry, she knew, was saying something different, speaking of what the heart and mind, as well as the senses, observed about a girl in faded blue jeans and an aging cotton shirt.

"Have you nothing to say?" he questioned as he pulled her with him onto the blanket. His lips continued to trace a path from wrist to arm, stopping at her neck, and coming to rest there.

"Shhh!" She purred contentedly "I am enjoying everything you just said. Please, I don't want to break the spell."

They sat there for some time without further conversation. Both were content to let the wind and trees, birds and insects, pick up the discussion. It seemed as though the years that had parted them were dissolved by the breeze that washed over them gently. Nikki, nestled in Gerry's arms, felt relaxed and at home.

Finally Gerry pushed himself to his feet and walked away. He returned with a bottle from the stream's cache. She watched him open it and fill two glasses from the basket.

"To this time and place and you," he offered when they each held a glass.

His salute opened her mind and mouth. Over picnic fare she told him about her adoptive family and her home in Chicago, about Northwestern, even about her doubts in returning to Europe.

"It had to be that way," he decided when she paused to consider which of the pastries could best complete her meal. "For I was here waiting. Probably I have been waiting for you to come back to me since I left you at Winterthur. Roswitha's leaving didn't upset me at all. My parents were angry, but I felt nothing. It was like standing on a corner and watching the traffic roll by. I was not driving or crossing the street. Therefore, there was little meaning to what was happening."

"I'm sorry," Nikki told him. She had to regret his lack of feeling as well as his loss. But he shrugged and began to pick up their leavings.

It was a relief, when he had closed the basket's lid, that he settled back on the blanket, arms behind his head. She was afraid that this special time was going to end, and she wanted it to last. So much still needed to be said. They had hardly begun.

"There's no point in asking if your feeling for me lasted," he finally said sadly. "You've already said that you thought I was responsible for Karl's being gone."

"That's right." She rolled to her side so that she could watch his profile. "Every time I saw the medallion I told myself I hated you because you had betrayed me. I even stopped polishing it. So why was it that I could never feel for anyone what I felt for you in Winterthur? I must admit I did not know that my feelings were as strong as they are right now."

Gerry was silent, the lines around his eyes deepening. She knew he was working out an answer for himself. She wanted to give him time. This was not easy for either of them.

Nikki lifted her head so that the sun could brush across her face. The delicious wine was already warming her from inside. She felt a need to hold Gerry, but could not make the first move. Not yet. She closed her eyes, thinking about the first time they were along together, sneaking time in the park behind the hotel. How close they were then, how aware of each other. How simple all their answers were that night. It was only Gerry's concern about her age that had kept him from making love to her, she realized.

That barrier no longer applied. Nikki wanted and needed Gerry now. The sun was not the only thing warming her body. Her body was aching for his touch. Her desire grew. Her eyes misted over. And one hand took its own action, reaching across the blanket toward him.

Their hands touched. Gerry leaned toward her, gathering her into his arms. He touched his lips to hers, gently at first, then thrusting his tongue inside her mouth.

His fingers, at last, were under her soft cotton shirt, circling her breasts, toying with the nipples. Moaning softly, Nikki pulled at the buttons of his shirt, intent on bringing flesh to flesh.

Gerry paused. He smiled, urging her on.

"Oh, my Nikki, if you only knew how much, since our first night together, I have wanted you. I never thought that dream would come true."

Nikki lay motionless, feeling the warmth his ministrations were creating between her legs. Then they were naked together with the sun and wind applauding their efforts. Hurry and need reversed. Her hands pressed him on. Her legs opened to him. His hands gently probed, explored, excited. His dark, strong body covered hers in hard, strong thrusts, filling her with his passion. The years of expectation were fulfilled. So was she.

Gerry rolled off of her, smoothing her disordered hair away from her face, all his energies spent. Tracing a rivulet of moisture between her breasts, he followed it around a nipple, gently pinching the silken skin.

"Effort and pleasure go hand in hand," he whispered. "You are sweating and so am I."

Nikki giggled. A picture of Hanna and Lars as she had discovered them in the attic came to mind. She shared it, and Gerry laughed heartily.

"Cook was Swiss," Nikki reminded him. "She even had her husband's rifle. She kept it in her bedroom."

"Good woman," he nodded. "I am sure she would have approved of your being warm today."

"Perhaps," Nikki allowed, searching his face. "The question is, did you approve?"

Gerry lowered his face to hers, lips brushing her eyes and mouth.

"You don't need to ask. You know! I love you, and I find your body beautiful. I can feel that you are fulfilled, and I am pleased. I want to please you always. If your love can match mine, we should have no trouble warming each other."

"There's a limit to warming, however," Nikki observed, first snuggling nearer, then pushing herself away. "I think I will use your little lake to cool off. Is the bottom safe?"

"The bottom, like yours, is just fine," he told her as she scrambled to her feet and dashed to the shore. "but the water is..."

Her shallow dive cut off his words. She came to the surface, shocked breathless by the temperature.

"Freezing," she supplied through chattering teeth.

"I suppose I have to join you," he groaned, standing and stretching his arms above his head. "It is, after all, my lake."

But he entered slowly, splashing the water against his skin and flinching from its touch. How beautiful he was, Nikki thought, her enjoyment of his nakedness and anticipation of his approach overcoming her consciousness of the chill.

They did not linger long in the meadow pool, and it took a few minutes afterwards for the sun's warmth to penetrate. She was still shivering as she sat on the blanket and wove a ring of flowers. When it was done, she placed it firmly on his water-gemmed hair. The white, yellow, and green looked appropriate atop the nut-colored curls.

"I crown you King of my Love," she proclaimed.

"Thank you, my Queen." He nuzzled her cool breasts with his mouth, speaking around her flesh. "And I truly support the concept of King's rights. We have to make up for lost time."

Gerry reached for her again.

It was hard to leave the lake, its stream, and its meadow behind later in the afternoon. Fully clad now, Nikki could feel the air cooling rapidly as Gerry pulled her up from the blanket so he could fold it.

"The mountains are not patient with those who trespass too long," he cautioned. "And they show their displeasure with cold and mist and fog and, sometimes even at this time of year, with snow. We had better leave so we may come again."

His promise swept away some of her regret over the outing's end. The remainder disappeared when he began talking about the evening meal they would cook at his apartment. He had, he bragged, an excellent touch with omelets. Nikki kept her mouth firmly shut. What she knew about cooking had allowed her to build a fair degree of competence with dehydrated soup. As Donna declared, she rarely scorched the water.

Nikki's enjoyment of the afternoon came to a sudden halt when they pulled into the parking area at Weisser Schwan. There were four vehicles already there and she recognized one. Hans Germeyer had come to call. There was nothing she could do, however, to avoid the meeting for he came striding across the gravel just as they emerged from the Jaguar. Her appearance seemed to stop the man in his tracks.

"Hello, Hans," she greeted him. His eyes narrowed, and she wondered if he could read the pleasures of the afternoon on her face. Nonetheless, she forged ahead with introductions, finishing weakly as the two men shook hands like a pair of boxers prepared to spar.

"We were up in the mountains." His penetrating look made her issue the explanation.

"Yes, I inquired for you when I brought a man from our Lucerne branch here for lodging," Hans stated grimly. "I thought perhaps you were free this evening."

"She's not," Gerry said before Nikki could open her mouth. "Nice meeting you, Germeyer."

It was all Nikki could do to control her laughter as Hans departed, his Audi's tires leaving bits of rock dancing about their feet. She held her composure as far as the inn's entrance where Gerry took a garden table to await her return. But on the stairs she began to chuckle. She climbed rapidly to share the news with Muff. Being a puss, her feline friend was sure to understand.

The animal, however, was howling pitifully when Nikki opened the door. She called out and the sound of her voice only served to make the sounds more impatient. Following the demanding mews, she located the cat on the wrong side of the wardrobe door.

"You poor thing." She held an exasperated Muff to her, stroking the soft fur. "I've been enjoying myself so much and you were locked in that awful dark place all this time."

Muff raised her head and placed her cheek next to Nikki's. Mutters of promised retribution gave way to shudders of contentment. When the purring was strong and regular, Nikki set the cat on the pillows.

"I have to change my clothes," she explained. "And you stay there so I don't lock you up again."

But she hadn't been the one who had confined the cat, after all. Nikki was certain of this as soon as she opened the drawer where she had placed her jewelry. The silver chain of Gerry's medallion was snarled with the gold chain containing the cross and angel ring. Hooked into the entire mess was the plastic-covered press pass that she used when attending government meetings.

It had to have been Susan, she decided, surprised that the girl would handle what was not hers. A look in the lingerie drawer, however, made her doubt that conclusion. A careless gesture might have caused the mess above. The disorder here, however, was intentional. Nikki stared at the chaos and felt a cold chill creep up her spine.

Gerry looked surprise when she appeared at his table, still wearing the jeans and shirt from the mountain. As she told him about the cat and what she had found, his features grew grave.

"I want to see," he told her when she finished.

Without his strength, she doubted that she could have re-entered the room. She was shaking now.

"Is anything missing?" he inquired after she had shown him what she had found.

"I don't think so." She had peeked into the bathroom. Her cosmetics, definitely rearranged, still sat on the lavatory's edge. She was reluctant all the way into the room, but the mirror only reflected her terry robe hanging on the back of the door.

"Nikki," Gerry called her back. "Where is your bank key?"

"In my purse, of course. Right here." She opened the bag, then the change purse on the wallet, and held it up.

"And that was with us," he observed. "Tough on whoever was trying to locate it."

"You think they were looking for the key?" Nikki asked doubtfully.

"We'll ask your landlords if any other guest has been bothered. What is the name? I've forgotten."

Herr and Frau Wirt, along with Susan, had to inspect the scene, too. The older couple was mystified, and Susan was upset.

"Muff climbed right up there," she pointed to a pillow, "when I finished with the bed. And I certainly did not open any of Nikki's drawers or her wardrobe. It is not done."

Herr Wirt nodded his agreement with the statement.

"I will check with my other guests immediately. And then I shall summon the constabulary. This type of thing does not occur at a respectable inn such as ours."

When he had completed his survey, Herr Wirt reported that two other guests had discovered their belongings in similar disarray. And, as with Nikki, nothing appeared to have been taken. The only person who had escaped was the gentleman who had arrived just that afternoon, the client whom Herr Germeyer had delivered. Now the proprietor was having misgivings about involving the constabulary. They were not faced with a major crime.

Nikki listened to all of this from the shelter of Gerry's arm. And as much as she liked Susan and Muff, she was relieved when Gerry announced that she would be moving to his home. She thought the changed was welcomed by Herr Wirt as well.

Section Three

✳ ✳ ✳

Once There Was an Order

"There is nothing more frightening than active ignorance."
—Goethe

Chapter Ten

✳   ✳   ✳

Birds of a Feather

"You'll have to hurry with your dressing," Gerry told Nikki as they entered the apartment. "Bruno and Paul will be here by six."

They had spent the day giving Paul an opportunity to photograph views within and near Zurich. Clean as Switzerland was, Nikki felt wind-blown and gritty and just a little sleepy. A bath would have to suffice for a nap if they were to get to Herr Haupt's birthday party on time.

The tub was filling as she stripped off her clothes. Bath salts perfumed the room with lemon. She knew the shower would be quicker, but the tub was more relaxing. And Gerry had shown her how to activate the water jets that could provide massage for muscles that ached from hefting camera gear. Paul had pressed them all into service that day so that he had a full selection of lenses at every viewpoint.

As she sank into they satiny water, she considered how well the men were getting along. It had been difficult last evening to bring herself to meet them at the commercial inn where Bruno stayed whenever he made purchases from his Swiss sources. The night and day she had spent with Gerry had been indescribably wonderful. Yet suddenly she was embarrassed to see her other friends.

There had seemed to be no difference, however, in the way they treated her. When Gerry had told them about the trespass of her room, both were pleased to know she had found a safe place to stay. Now that she was wealthy, she would need to take special care, Paul said.

He had the papers that M. DePrenger had requested. After dinner they had examined them. Tuesday they would deliver them to the bank, Paul announced. The conference schedule for that day did not start until noon, so their morning was free.

"This session could lead to something very big," Paul commented about the assignment. "The Common Market and the United States have been discussing an international trade conference."

Nikki grinned to herself at the remoteness she was feeling toward world trade at the moment. Her every waking thought had been filled with Gerry and their reunion. World affairs occupied a back seat to her life at this time.

Taking a deep breath, she submerged to dampen her hair completely. When she had splashed her way to the surface, she applied a hefty dollop of chamomile shampoo and began to massage. Piling the rich suds onto her hair, she rested against the wall of the tub so that the chamomile would penetrate the hair shafts. She closed her eyes to luxuriate in the feeling of complete contentment.

The bathroom door swung open, letting in a quick draft as well as Gerry. Wiping suds from her forehead, she risked opening one eye. He was extending a wine glass toward her.

"The nymphet wishes some refreshment?"

"Can you put it on the ledge?" She waved her soapy hands at him.

He did as she requested, then lowered himself to his knees. His fingers were in her hair.

"Allow me." When he had finished massaging her scalp and rinsing it with the hand-held shower, he reached across the tub for the soap. "And now for the rest of you."

"You're going to get your clothes soaked," she told him firmly. The observation was practical even though she regretted having to say it. She loved the feeling of his hands on her body.

"Then the clothes will have to go." He was already in action.

Nikki took delight in helping Gerry soap his body, exploring every inch of his muscular form, caressing the fine hairs on his back. As she knelt over him shampooing his curls, he sighed with pleasure. His face was buried between her breasts.

The cleansing ritual was complete. The two, like children at play, splashed water and tossed soap like the bar was a soccer ball.

"Where is your rubber duck?" she teased as water flooded the tile floor. Catching a breath, Nikki reached for the glass of wine and drained it.

Gerry took the glass from her and set it on the nearby oak shelf. His hand came back to adjust the tub's mechanism. Now they were surrounded by bubbling water, jets that enhanced and intensified the movements of their hands on each other. The water's rhythm became the timing of their lovemaking.

"What a marvelous way to drown," Nikki gasped when Gerry's arm stabilized her at last against the tub's edge. One free hand was pushing her sodden hair back from her face, while the other pursued a clump of bubbles down one breast, following it across the small mound of her belly. Gerry continued to caress her body, his lips seeking hers and prolonging the feeling of ecstasy. Nibbling on one ear he whispered, "I am so glad you came back to me. You mean so much. Saying I love you is too shallow for the feelings I have for you. You are my life, and I want to live it with you."

With those words he pulled her up out of the water, pressing his body into hers, soapy skin gliding sensuously in rhythm. Nikki, caught up in his movements, moaned and followed his lead.

Satiated at last, they sunk back into the suds. Tipping Nikki's face up, Gerry planted a wet smack onto her forehead.

"We'd better get with it. We will be late."

"I love you Gerry," was her response as she followed him out of the tub, carefully avoiding the puddles.

* * *

She was still drying herself when he disappeared into the bedroom. Closing the door behind him, she reached for her toothbrush. This time the cleansing was routine, a preparation for the evening festivities. As she rubbed the steam from the mirror an old, painful memory became as clear as the glass... There had been another time when she had scrubbed with the brush until her gums bled, and it still had not been enough.

Vati had been gone for four months when they moved to Stefan Rennecke's home. Instead of an apartment within the city, Vati's partner resided in a single dwelling outside of Wiesbaden. The house and land had belonged to his family for years. There were servants, inside and out. In a way, the new home was much like the villa in which Monika had been born, but the household staff was withdrawn as if the newcomers were unwelcome guests.

Herr Rennecke was a tall man on whom age was sat well. He had a full head of hair, silver as fine as the metal with which he worked. His clothing was of fine fabric. His manners were impeccable.

Mutti should have loved it all, this return to the elegance she had lost in the family's run to freedom. But, by then, she was too ill to care. The cancer, undetected, had ravaged her body for some time.

At last the surgery had come. For the day of the operation and the one following, Herr Rennecke had entrusted her to the Kneipps. It was the first time Nikki had been with the family since the move. The pleasure of being in their company was intensified by her fear about Mutti and the awful disease from which she suffered. Frau Kneipp had been generous in allowing the girl to cry out her distress and in saying just the right things while wiping away the tears.

The second day, Herr Rennecke's chauffeured car had arrived to take Monika on a visit to the hospital and then to the Herr's house once more. She had followed the ward nurse down the aisle between rows of bandaged women who were hooked to jars from which and into which fluids flowed. There was an undertone of moaning, like a perpetual chorus of agony. The smells of waste and the disinfectants clashed and gave her a headache. But when the curtain at the end of the ward was pulled aside, a new terror had to be confronted.

Those pain-glazed eyes that regarded her from the sweat-stained pillow could hardly be Mutti's. Yet they held recognition and fingers flexed in welcome. They had communicated by pressures of the hand during those few minutes she was permitted to remain. Monika could not find the words she wanted to say, and Mutti was incapable of speech.

Back at the house—it had never been home—the maids proceeded through the daily cleaning ritual in silence. It was a house without feelings, Monika decided, as she climbed the stairs to her room. No sound, no aroma ever escaped from the rooms in which they were created. Wood and fabric were unpleasant to the touch. The colors were all neutrals.

She let herself into her room and stood very still. It was not a bed one threw oneself upon to sob away unhappiness. The spread was a tapestry with prickly metallic thread. The easy chair by the window was upholstered in the same fabric. Both were abhorrent to the skin.

In time, she elected to take a bath. The porcelain would be scratchy with scouring powder never quite washed away. But there would be warmth at least. She took with her the little battery-powered radio that Herr Rennecke had given her as a welcoming gift. The tune was American country music, but the vocalist was German. Monika knew that the language change might be distorting the words, but the tune was laced with regret. She felt better as she turned her bath water salty with her tears.

The water had steamed the room so that she had not seen his reflection in the mirror. Herr Rennecke had entered the room silently and stood behind her when she turned to reach for her towel. He was wearing a red and black brocade dressing robe, nothing else, as the open front revealed. The gaping material showed an ugly, white skinned body, covered with dense hair. Its black curls were in stark contrast with his silver head.

He was fully erect, and somehow this triggered an enormous anger in Monika. She tried to pull the towel around her with one hand while the other shoved him violently backward. Yet she did not reckon with his strength. He reached for her arm with both hands and twisted it downward, making her scream out with pain.

He roughly pulled her against his body, rubbing her skin against his prickly, harsh hair. He reached toward the radio, turning the knob to let the music drown out her howls of agony and screams of protest. After he dropped his robe, he dragged her across the slipper bathroom tile, over the Aubusson in the bedroom, and onto the bed. Its brocade cover tore at her hot skin.

She had thought the torture was ending when he rolled off of her. The release of pressure allowed her to consider other discomforts, the harsh weave beneath her back, the warm wetness between her thighs.

But it was only an instant before his hand clawed beneath her armpit, pulling Monika to her knees in front of him. Was he really going to urinate in her face? She stopped breathing and closed her eyes tight against the expected attack. Instead, hard fingers pried at her jaw. When her tongue felt him, she bit down. Her eyes were still closed when his fist struck and blackness engulfed her.

Stefan Rennecke was already dressed and was wiping her legs with a wash cloth as she began to focus on the room once more. His face was stern, but he began to smile, an expression confined only to his lips.

"You have much to learn, child," he said, tossing the soiled cloth in the direction of the bathroom floor. "And I shall teach you when Wera is gone. What lessons those will be!"

The bath water was cooling but Monika resolved to wash herself again. The mirror above the sink had lost its film of moisture. She replenished the supply of dentifrice on the brush and opened her mouth to receive it. And then she saw the mark on her cheek. It looked like a bird pressed into the flesh.

* * *

"Nikki!" The mirror told her that the present had overcome the past. "They will be here…"

She turned and flung her arms around Gerry, resting her face against the crispness of his dress shirt.

"I love you so much," she told him.

"And I you. Just the same, we must get dressed." He gave her a smart slap on the buttocks and thrust her through the door to the bedroom.

Bruno had chosen the flowers, Paul reported, to be a token of their best wishes for Herr Haupt's continued longevity. Nikki nodded her approval of the lavish bouquet of metallic-shaded chrysanthemums. Gerry added a small book to the gift, a copy of one his father valued.

They used the Opel for transportation, she and Gerry folding themselves into the rear seats. Gerry gave directions. The house they sought was separated from the street by a fence of hewn planking behind which dahlias stood like sentinels.

"Look at the shutters," Nikki squealed with delight. "It's just like a gingerbread house."

"The illustrations are taken from one of our old children's stories," Gerry told them. "The technique is called Lueftlmalerei after the artist who is credited with beginning the tradition. And the façade is known as Fachwerk."

"I wish the light were better and that I had brought my cameras," Paul said regretfully. He had slowed the car to a stop in order to get a better view.

"Perhaps we can arrange another day for photographs, and I will take you to St. Gallen," Gerry promised. "The entire inner city features Lueftlmalerei and Fachwerk. But we had better move along before we clog traffic."

There were cars parked along the street on both sides of the residence. It was more than a block away that Paul finally found a niche into which their small sedan could be inserted. The walk back, flanked by her three escorts, gave Nikki a feeling of well-being.

Each was an attractive male. Gerry wore a lightweight suit, loden green that made his hair and eyes look special. Paul was in one of his favorite outfits, grey flannel slacks with navy double-breasted jacket. Bruno looked like an enormous teddy bear in brown corduroy. Nikki had topped her familiar white skirt and sandals with a turquoise shirt. Gerry's silver medallion gleamed at her breast.

"One day soon I am going to have to talk you into taking me shopping," Nikki smiled at Gerry, as she kept up with their stride. "I am getting rather tired of these clothes."

The bright blue door at which Gerry had knocked opened to emit sounds of laughter and gay music. But a barrier of hostility had first to be breached. A man stared at them without welcome.

"We are having a family celebration," he stated finally. "What is your business?"

"I'm Monika Groebel, Herr Haupt." Nikki extended her hand toward the man. "Frau Haupt invited me to join the celebration for your father. He was a business associate of my family."

The man frowned, making no move to touch her. His gaze moved from Nikki to the three men.

"My wife did not see fit to inform me," he said stiffly. "Since you are here, please come in."

In the hall Nikki introduced her companions. No one shook hands. They might have stood there forever, she thought, except that Bettina Haupt came bouncing down the hall toward them.

"Welcome, my friend and your friends," she called out, her plump face crinkled in pleasure. "This way, please. Most of the guests are outside in the garden. Vater Klaus will come down from his room shortly."

"My father is very old," came the voice from behind them as they followed their hostess along the hallway. "He is not strong, and sometimes memories of the past are difficult to him."

"Nonsense!" Bettina retorted. "He is having the time of his life. After all, he is only eighty-two."

As they walked through the dining room, Nikki could see into the kitchen through an open door. It looked as if Bettina were prepared to serve all of Zurich. She took the flowers from Bruno and placed them in a vase on the sideboard. It was not the only bouquet, but Nikki thought it was still the nicest. The book was placed nearby.

"Hugo, please take our guests outside and introduce them while I finish in the kitchen," the woman requested.

"This way, if you please." He was still scowling. Nikki wondered if a smile would do much to improve his appearance. Although his shoulders were wide, his head was long and thin with prominent ears that reminded her of a sugar bowl's handles. There were no relaxed planes. Every muscle seemed tight. They eyes were deep-set and cold.

"May I not help you instead?" Nikki asked as the men departed. "I would like that."

"So would I!" Bettina grinned. "Most of our guests are getting along in years and I hesitate to have arthritic women lifting trays."

Nikki found herself quickly engulfed in an apron that she could have easily shared with another body. She was pointed toward pans covered with dish towels. Doily-covered trays lay nearby, waiting for the transfer of edibles.

Bettina seated herself at the round table in the center of the room and placed a large bowl between her knees. She began to work the wooden spoon through the contents.

"It's butter crème for Vater Klaus's cake," she explained. "It cannot be done ahead. So while the guests drink wine, I stir."

The cake, Nikki noticed, was already on its decorative stand. There were several layers, chocolate dark. Thick red filling oozed from the joints.

"What flavor is the crème?" She asked.

"Mocha. His very favorite. And the layers are joined by raspberry. Just as he ordered."

"What a lot of work!" Nikki observed, watching the woman struggle with the thickening mixture. "Can you not do it with the machine?"

Bettina shook her head at the shiny electric mixer in the corner.

"I could, but it would not be as good. Hand mixing makes it creamier. Mother Haupt always mixed it by hand." She extended the spoon toward Nikki. "Will you taste it, please?"

Nikki beamed her approval as the substance melted on her tongue.

"So now we will complete the cake," Bettina announced, lifting the bowl from her lap.

As she continued with her assigned task, Nikki glanced up occasionally to watch the competent cook slather the cake with its topping. Each swirl ended in a crisp peak, even those that ringed the sides. When the pattern was complete and the bowl empty, Bettina lifted the cake.

"Now if you will please open the refrigerator for me, we will put it to cool until it is time to serve. And I hear Vater Klaus's voice. You shall meet him now."

* * *

They went out to the terrace and found those attending were formed into a line, passing before a wicker chair that served as the venerable old man's throne. Hugo, still frowning, stood at the side of the chair like a protocol officer such as those whom Nikki and Paul encountered at so many of the conferences.

"We will just cut in front of them," Bettina announced, tugging on Nikki's arm.

"No. My friends are in the line. I will join them." She smiled at Bettina. "And you be sure to call me when you want some assistance. The guys, too, as far as that goes. They are great helpers."

Bettina's brows rose at the thought of men in the kitchen, but she let Nikki go.

"Thank God you got here," Bruno grinned at her. "I was trying to figure out how to explain our presence in your absence."

"You mean Gerry has never connected a faucet in this household?" She looked at him impishly.

"As a matter of fact, I believe my father and Herr Haupt belong to the same lodge," he told her. "But I certainly don't know if Dad was invited. I don't see him here now. I do recognize some of the other lodge members."

Hugo was announcing the guests, Nikki realized, as they drew nearer. She thought it was a waste of time. The old man, although he wore spectacles, seemed to anticipate each name. His comments of welcome were precise and thoughtful.

"This person is a Monika Groebel," Hugo announced when it was their turn. "She says you know her family. And the gentlemen are friends of hers."

But the man was already leaning forward, reaching out to her.

"Ah, Monika. As lovely as Karl predicts. And you look so much like him, too. He is so very proud of his little girl. I am so glad you have come for we have much to talk about."

"Your other guests, Vater," Hugo cut in sharply. "There are many more to be greeted."

Reluctantly Monika slid her hands free of Herr Haupt and moved away.

"I get the message that we are not particularly wanted," Paul growled in her ear.

"The wife is friendly enough," Bruno countered. "And the old man was genuinely pleased."

"Did you hear him?" Monika demanded. "Vati is alive! He knows about him."

She could barely wait for the line to wend its way past the honoree so that she could talk with Herr Haupt. But as the last guest offered best wishes, Hugo helped the gentleman to his feet and led him away. By the time they followed the others to the dining room, the piles of gifts were being examined and commented upon. The little volume that Gerry had provided seemed especially pleasing.

Then the food was served. Nikki edged her way toward the man. As she approached, Hugo led him away. She turned toward her companions, shrugging. The three looked down at her, then at each other. She knew that whatever they were thinking, all understood.

* * *

And suddenly Herr Haupt was alone, sitting at a small table with a plate in front of him. Hugo, she observed, was being forced into the hall by three men in concerted effort. He kept looking hopelessly over his shoulder.

"Young Monika!" The old man looked up at her when she stood at his side. His eyes, magnified by the lenses, sparkled. "I am so glad you have come. Pull up a chair so that we can talk."

She found a footstool within reach and moved it to his side. Her troops were holding Hugo confined against the opposite wall, but she knew he was observing the meeting with displeasure.

"There is much for you to do and to know," Herr Haupt began, laying aside his fork to grasp her hands again. "Things are not as they seem, and I am an old and tired man. I cannot fear for myself, but there can be great danger ahead for you."

"Vati," she interrupted him. "Where can I find Vati?"

"Child, we have little time," the man increased his hold on her fingers. "You must take great care. Beware of black birds. Do not…"

"Come, father!" Hugo stood over them, his shadow cutting off the light. "Betting is bringing your cake now. Please excuse my father, Fraulein."

The party continued. So did Hugo's watch over his parent.

"We tried!" Bruno protested as they walked back to the car. "We explained to him how much better German soccer teams were than the Swiss. Gerry defended the Swiss, of course, and Paul kept asking stupid questions like an American should. But he would not stay. He doesn't want you near his father."

"I can understand him not caring about soccer, but I certainly don't see why Nikki alarms him," Paul added.

"Nor I," Gerry agreed. "But we will find another opportunity. Just what did you manage to say to him?"

"He did the talking," Nikki answered, shivering a little in the coolness that seemed to be building as the night progressed. "He was concerned about danger. He warned me to be careful of black birds."

"Black birds?" Bruno's face creased as he pulled the seat forward so that she could climb into the car. "Perhaps Herr Haupt, just turned eighty-two, is a bit senile."

"It's possible," Paul allowed, "but I don't think so."

Nikki slid across the seat, feeling safer as Gerry's body touched hers. She didn't think there was anything wrong with the old man, either. But she knew Vati was right about not trusting the son.

* * *

From her vantage point on the mezzanine balcony, far above the people moving through the hotel's lobby, Nikki could not help but take occasional moments from her endeavors for people-watching. She felt like a member of the audience at the performance of an opera. The stage was filled with extras and chorus. She lacked a program to tell her who the leads might be.

The people seemed to move to music she couldn't hear. Perhaps they could not detect the rhythms either, for some kept their feet moving rapidly while others halted and swayed. A few she could identify by national interests if not always by name, those with whom she and Paul had enjoyed a welcoming cup of coffee earlier in the morning before the formal sessions began. They were definitely not the stars of the trade meeting, but flunkies like herself. Some of them, no doubt, had created the reports through which she saw now paging in an attempt to find leads for interviews Paul would conduct.

There was a press room somewhere in the nether reaches of the building. She and Paul had opted instead for a small writing desk nearer the action, part of the hotel's offerings to its guests. Nikki penciled a red check on the paper she had been reading. The report spoke of increased factory capacity to produce cut lead crystal. Perhaps Paul would learn that the United States was about to be introduced to an alternative mass-manufactured containers. If so, that was great. She had personally disliked the molded glass bowls in which Doro and Donna mixed, served and stored. American table glassware, for the most part, came from the same factories that turned out canning jars. And it looked it!

Below her there was sudden considerable movement as a tour courier led his patrons to their waiting buses. He seemed to have more than one hundred people exiting in rank.

She turned to the pages that detailed pottery capacities. They were not stimulating reading. Beyond this meeting and corporation files, such reports had no life unless Paul and his colleagues featured them in wire copy. And that required a reader-researcher to pour over the statistics. But Nikki Fisher would rather have been doing something else.

"My father—how do I find him?" She had posed the question to the three men last night when they had settled back, with beer and cheese, to discuss the party.

That had involved the quartet in deep conversation as they voiced, then discarded, ideas. In the end, Gerry's idea seemed sensible. Nikki was not to seek out Karl Groebel. He would learn that she was in Zurich and initiate the contact. In the meantime, Nikki could do the job that she was paid to do, even though she now had little need to earn money.

Would she even recognize Vati when she saw him, Nikki wondered. Perhaps her eyes might fail to identify her parent, but her heart would know. She was as positive of this as she was that fine china with gold and silver edging was not going to be a hot export item to the United States. She directed an arrow toward the comment she had written in the margin: "These dishes required hand-washing." Now that electric dishwashers were replacing the dishpan and tea towel, not many women were going to return to a more primitive state just to put twenty-four-carat gold trim on their tables.

She gave her Timex a grudging glance. If she could get away at noon while the delegations lunched together and heard an official of the state express his nation's pleasure at having them in Zurich, this watch would get an official burial. It would be fun to think of a disposal on which John Cameron Swayze might comment at a later date. She suspected, however, that for the time being she would merely drop it in her jewelry box.

A corner staple joined three pages on fine linens. She frowned over it. Again she wrote along the edge. This time the message was about the need for ironing. Regardless of old craftsmanship, these tablecloths must contain some synthetic threads in order to capture a mass market. Not only were more American homemakers also participating in the work force, but those that weren't had little time left from their volunteer activities to devote to repeated applications of the iron. Even Donna, who was the consummate housewife, used laces instead of linen on the table to avoid the chore of pressing.

Nikki moved on to yard goods, suddenly finding herself on the other side of the argument. Woolens were definitely more difficult to care for than were the emerging double knits, but the latter didn't feel half so nice against the skin. She jotted a single cryptic comment—"Marketing?"—at the report's top and reached for the next sheets.

By the time Paul found her, she had skimmed through all three inches of paper on which she had been working. He shuffled through the reports, chuckling at the written asides.

"I'm going to Haupt Jewelers now to get my watch," Nikki told him, standing and brushing at the folds the extended sitting had caused in her skirt. "What do you want me to do this afternoon?"

"An interview. I set it up for four o'clock. Okay?"

She nodded. That gave her more than enough time for her errand. Perhaps she could use the extra hours to find some little gift to take back to the family that shared its home with her. She was sure that Frau Schneider would be pleased.

"You'll like the subject, I think—mass production of cloisonne," Paul told her. "And I know you'll enjoy seeing Hope Greene again."

She cocked her head, trying to categorize the name. He was barely suppressing a grin, waiting for recognition.

"That Hope Greene?" Nikki managed in a weak voice. "The Jewish girl who studied Hebrew at Garrett Biblical Seminary?"

"None other." He began to laugh at her amazement. Any person who had been at Northwestern in the past five years knew about Hope Greene who, in the late 1950s, had determined to prepare herself for residency in Israel by learning the traditional language. Obviously, she could have sought out the services of a rabbi, but she also wanted college credit. Hebrew was not on the school's foreign language menu.

In time, however, the matter had been successfully negotiated. Hope could study the tongue with Methodist seminarians at the institution, wedged between the university's north and south campus and euphemistically known as East Jesus Tech. It was a legend oft-repeated, although the language professors with whom Nikki studied averred that Hope could use any European language within the emerging nation just as well.

"She'll be waiting for you in the Ladies' Salon. Will you recognize her?" Nikki looked doubtful. The girl had been pointed out to her once as they passed on the sidewalk alongside of U.S. 41.

"Hope will be the only woman there in chartreuse, even her hosiery," Paul told her. "Now I will take these and you get to the jewelers. By the way, Gerry is coming here for dinner with us and Bruno. Then he'll take you home."

Nikki nodded. She didn't even worry about blushing anymore. Both Paul and Bruno seemed perfectly satisfied with the housing arrangements. She stuffed the red pencil into her purse and walked to the stairway. Paul went the other way to a bank of elevators.

* * *

Along the route that took her from the hotel to the shop, Nikki was jostled and pushed. It wasn't like the beating that one received at times in The Loop, she reflected. Their speed was the culprit. Here in Zurich she found the pedestrians moved with a single-mindedness. Sometimes the walkers were deep in conversation, other times thought. Window shoppers would halt in midstride to examine a display. Stern-faced executives would cut across the sidewalk traffic to reach the curb so that a cab could be hailed.

Brass bells greeted her at Haupt Jewelers, their clappers applauding her arrival. A blue-smocked girl looked up from the glass case she was polishing, cloth and spray bottle held at the ready. When Nikki announced her purpose, the young woman sprinted to the curtained entry. Her cleaning materials had been left behind.

Points off, Nikki thought. She could recall reprimands for similar infractions at both Groebel Haus and Rennecke-Groebel. Nothing except the protective glass should ever come between a customer and a potential purchase. Even the velvet and felt pads were routinely adjusted so that they did not obscure the view.

She had hoped to see Bettina again so that she could thank her for the invitation, perhaps even seek another appointment with Klaus Haupt. Nikki was sure that he was willing to reveal more about Vati if he were separated from his son. Even the watchmaker might have some bits of information that could be useful in arranging a second meeting. Instead Hugo pushed aside the drape and stared coldly at her.

"Good day, Fraulein Groebel. You grace our premises again. I have here your small watch." He was dangling it by the buckle end of the strap. Nikki was reminded of the worms that young Doug Fisher festooned from his fishing line. Reluctantly she approached the jeweler.

"It is a beautiful piece, this." A long forefinger stroked the Piaget as it lay on the counter pad. "Our watchmaker has cleaned it thoroughly. He has also replaced and resealed the crystal. It is, of course, fine jewelry. One does not take it into the bathroom when one showers, you know, or wear it while washing dishes. There was corrosion in the case."

His voice, along with his countenance, criticized her. Nikki felt her anger growing.

"I received it when I was seven. It has never been serviced until now," she spoke slowly and carefully.

"What a gift for a child!" Now the man's tone was laced with exasperation. "Only a parent who spoils his offspring would give a youngster a Piaget."

She reached out for her treasure, but Hugo's fingers were swifter.

"Your wrist, Fraulein?" He became cold and formal.

Nikki felt a chill, too. The man's touch, as he removed the Timex and replaced it with the smaller watch, turned her to stone. She told herself to stand firm, focusing her eyes on his hands. His cuffs were visible as he worked the fine buckle. The style was French, and the links that joined the sleeves at the wrist were set in black intaglio, shaped much like the ring of Stefan Rennecke's. Did all the louses of her life were similar stones, she wondered, then quickly altered the thought. Hans Germeyer had a black intaglio ring, and he certainly did not fit the description.

The Piaget was much lighter on her wrist than the Timex had been. As its circle tightened, it brought her new strength. She paid the bill very deliberately before challenging the man.

"Would your father happen to be in the shop today? Your wife said that he planned to spend a few days critiquing the shop's new designs."

"Alas, no. He wanted to come this morning, of course. Yesterday's celebration, however, has cost him strength. Perhaps there is a need to adjust his medication. Bettina will be talking with his physician." His eyes were hooded and his mouth tight. He was enjoying the denial of his father's company. "And what about your father, Fraulein? Will you be visiting him while you are in Switzerland? Perhaps you two are meeting here in Zurich? If so, please ask him to call. It has been too many years that we have dealt with him only by mail."

"I hope to see my father," Nikki responded. But when she did, this would be the last place she would bring Vati. There was no doubt that Hugo was the untrustworthy son to which the note referred.

"I, too, look forward to a future meeting," Hugo told her as she turned toward the door. She moved quickly down the aisle, certain that somehow he would come around the counter and insert himself between her and the street. She glanced back over her shoulder to see him still standing where she had left him. The bells at the door rang out then, telling her why.

"Pardon me, please," she asked as she brushed against the man and woman who were entering. The woman was wearing a grey wool cardigan, the yoke of which bore the intricate designs that set Alpine sweaters apart. Suddenly Nikki knew what she wanted for Frau Schneider's gift.

* * *

If she had been almost anywhere else in the department store, she might not have seen the man. But a male presence in the notions section was a rarity. The two saleswomen who presided over the collection of beautifully worked metal buttons and fastenings regarded him with curiosity. And Nikki joined them in their observation. He seemed intent on the display counter before which he stood. Since it was filled with elastics, stocking suspender replacements, new brassiere straps and closures, shoulder pads, and dress shields, the attraction was unlikely.

The woman from whom Nikki purchased the card of seven silver sweater hooks raised her brows and gestured with her head.

"Is he waiting for you?"

"I certainly hope not!" Nikki giggled as she took her package.

Back on the street, however, she glimpsed him again, reflected in a shop window. Her stomach gave a clutch of apprehension. He was not the only individual she recognized, Nikki realized. The large matron plodding directly ahead of him had been in the elevator on its descent to the street floor.

A block farther along, Nikki paused at another window. A study of reflections told her that the woman had disappeared. The man was still there. He had also stopped. This time he was regarding a display of intimate apparel. Two younger men smirked at him as they went by.

No great harm could come to her as long as she stayed among the shoppers, Nikki realized. Even if he were to follow her all the way back to the hotel, she was safe. But she was also annoyed. She veered off the street into an arcade of shops. If he did not follow, she could laugh at her suspicions. At the third entrance, she ducked inside. Standing near the window, she fingered blouses hanging on a nearby rack. Beyond a pair of mannequins that showed the wares to passersby in the arcade, she saw him. He stood on the far side of the walkway, watching the store.

"I would like to try on these two blouses," Nikki told the young clerk who hovered nearby.

"The fitting rooms are this way, Miss." She led Nikki down the hallway at the back of the shop and pushed back a curtain on the left. "My name is Denice. Please allow me to complete your purchase for you."

So young Denice worked on commission, Nikki surmised, as she looked around the small room. It had the requisite hooks, mirror, and single chair. Nikki lifted the curtain away from the door jamb and looked to the end of the hall. It was exactly what she thought she had seen. The door was open to provide air circulation, and the view beyond was of an alley. There was a dust bin against the next building. She had only to go up that passage to regain the street. In the meantime, her pursuer would wait patiently for her return.

There were good ideas and there were great ideas, David always said. The difference between the two was which actually worked to the benefit of their creator. As soon as she saw the figure in silhouette between herself and the alley entrance, Nikki discarded her good idea. In fact, as she admitted to Paul and Gerry afterwards, she threw out her common sense as well.

Wheeling with sudden panic, she sprinted toward the alley's far end. But running had never been one of her better sports. The sound of the footsteps behind her grew louder, audible over her own agonized breathing. And then the hand struck her between her shoulder blades, pushing her off her course and into a dark entryway. She stumbled forward from the blow. The floor, smelling of accumulated dust and mold, was much nearer than she expected. As she went down, her body seemed to strike a number of different sharp edges. A stairwell, her mind insisted, the thoughts seeming to squeeze through her pain.

The strap of her shoulder bag dug into her shoulder. Her attacker seemed to be purse snatcher, not a rapist. Nikki supposed she should welcome the difference. She pulled back on the straps with both hands, kicking out at her assailant's legs.

Both victim and attacker were scoring, but he got the higher points. He had firm footing. On the other hand, he couldn't get his hands on her while he was busy with the purse. This time she employed what she hoped was a great idea. Nikki screamed and screamed again, her sounds echoing within the cavern where she fought.

"Just what is happening down there?" a husky voice shouted down at them in French. "Can't a man sleep anymore?"

After this, Nikki hoped all of his dreams would be pleasant. The hard hands released their hold on her. She let out a sigh and relaxed against the steps.

"Who is there?" the voice repeated.

"Only me now," she responded with all the strength she could muster before she closed her eyes. "Thank you very much."

Even through closed lids, Nikki was aware that a light had been switched on. She took a deep breath, then looked around her. Bare toes were just above her head. Beyond them was raised a husky body, clad only in trousers. They were buttoned at the waist, but the fly was open. This didn't seem the time to mention the matter.

"What do you think, Hilde?" the voice of salvation queried.

"I think she has been hurt." This speaker was female. The tones were flat and pragmatic. "See how her stockings are torn. And she has lost a shoe. Perhaps you should carry her up to my flat, and I can tend to her. It will not be the first time, Waldo. You miss a great deal by working nights."

The stairway was steep and narrow. Waldo did not carry Nikki, but he did manage to support her sagging body to the landing that was an eternity away. Even though Hilde had to shoo a cat from the quilt-covered chair in order to make room for her unexpected guest, Nikki was sure it was the finest seat she had ever occupied.

It took nearly an hour before Waldo, satisfied with the quality of Hilde's care and disgruntled by Nikki's refusal to consult either medical or law enforcement assistance, stumbled back across the landing to his own rooms. In that period Nikki had been plied with coffee, laced with an additional stimulant that burned its way down her throat but was now smoldering comfortably in her stomach. What remained of her stockings had been discarded and, after cleansing, her legs had been dabbed with an unlabeled bottle of unguent that eased the smarting. The man had descended the stairs once to retrieve the lost shoe.

"You look terrible," Hilde told her as she leaned, cross-armed, against the dresser that appeared to be, except for a stained sink, the entire kitchen. A two-place hot plate occupied one corner of the counter area, its cord pointing upward to where it shared a power source with a bare light bulb. "But I think you feel better. What do you wish to do now?"

It was a good question, Nikki decided, possibly even a great question. She consulted the Piaget, pleased to discover it had survived the attack as staunchly as she would have expected the Timex would have done. Two hours remained before her scheduled interview. She could get herself back to the apartment over the plumbing shop, bathe and dress herself, and still be at the hotel before four. It was leaving this tiny space of security that frightened her.

"I don't suppose you have a telephone?"

"No, but the cutlery store across the alley does. The proprietor lets me use it when there is need. Whom shall we call?"

There was a choice. She could have Paul paged at the hotel. Back at the inn Bruno and his supplier were meeting for a business lunch. Gerry was heavens knew where, but he was the one she wanted right then. The courage that the coffee had provided was beginning to fade. New strength would be needed.

"Mehler A.G., if you please," she asked, repeating the phone number twice while the woman wrote it down on a piece of brown paper. "Ask if Gerhardt will come for me."

* * *

He was there in less time than she had expected, furious at the injuries Nikki had suffered and appreciative of the assistance the tenants had rendered. When his eye swept Hilda's room, it stopped briefly at the sink. Nikki was sure that there would be a new one soon.

With his arm supporting her shoulders, Nikki rose and slid her feet into her pumps. The right shoe went on easily. But her toes hit a barrier in the left. She leaned over, dizziness rocking her, and upended the shoe. A dark rock tumbled to the inside of the heel. She was about to discard it on Hilde's threadbare carpet, then considered her hostess and poured the stone into her hand instead.

It was then that she saw where the stone and the tarnished silver were set apart and recognized the spike of that of a tie tack. The setting was black intaglio, too.

Her hand was shaking as she passed it over to Gerry. To her it was coincidence. But there was an other meaning to Gerry. His jaw tightened.

"What is it?" she asked. "The man who tried to take my handbag must have lost it."

"Looks like a cheap piece of jewelry to me," Gerry answered, dropping it in his jacket pocket. "Just junk."

But it wasn't, Nikki knew. She also knew when protest was inappropriate. She thanked Hilde and asked the woman to pass her appreciation to Waldo. Gerry's hand was at her elbow. They were only partway down the stairs when she saw the Mehler truck standing like a fortress at the bottom.

"That's a beautiful vehicle," she spoke softly to Gerry. At this point it beat the Jaguar hollow.

* * *

Like Nikki, Hope Greene had also changed her apparel before arriving at the Ladies' Bar. Nonetheless, Nikki had no problem locating the woman. Even if she had not remembered the triangular face wreathe in black curls and dotted with freckles, the totality of turquoise would have been a giveaway.

"Of course I remember you!" Hope announced, coming to her feet at Nikki's approach and reaching out a hand. "You're David Fisher's Gentile daughter, a legend at old NU."

Nikki blinked as their hands touched. The pot was calling the kettle!

"I like your monochrome ensemble," she remarked as she took her seat. "Paul said chartreuse. Is he color blind or did you change?"

"Paul's eyes are just fine, but I need to showcase our product. This morning I was wearing leaves. But these are the pieces for late afternoon." Hope gestured to the brooch and matching bracelet of deep aqua waves. "Do you like them?"

"Very much." The jewelry brought the sea to life, and Nikki's mind held an image of water surging toward a sunwarmed beach. "Cloisonné is an old technique, isn't it?"

"That's right. So take notes because you have launched me into my spiel." Hope raised her wine glass and took a sip while Nikki gave her order to the waiter. For the next fifteen minutes, the woman summarized the process, the industry, and the market prospects. The jewelry line that Hope represented was done with enamel on gold.

"Our craftsmen probably fire the enamel more times than most producers in order to reduce pitting to a minimum. And every piece is completely handworked even though we produce a number of the same design. That includes the pumice grinding and the charcoal polishing." Hope unlatched her bracelet and passed it across to Nikki. "That's the result, a surface so perfect that the color appears to have great depth."

Nikki turned the bracelet over to examine the links from the back. Here, too, the workmanship was quality.

"Is cloisonné typically French?"

"Unfortunately, no." Hope put aside her glass and refastened her bracelet. "The art was developed by the Persians. And it spread both east and west. The Japanese and Chinese both use it, but right now we aren't worried about China in the market. Taiwan, of course, is producing cloisonné and so is Japan. There's no way we can beat their retail prices. But what they make is suitable only for mass markets. We have the fine jewelry trade, and we are going to keep it."

Nikki laid her pen down on the pad and took up her wine.

"Whatever happened to Israel?" she asked.

Hope chuckled.

"It's still there."

"But you are here."

The woman's face sobered, and she leaned toward Nikki.

"Tell me. Do you see me as a soldier? Trudging through sand and rock with my rifle at the ready?"

Nikki shook her head.

"Neither do I. Somewhere I got the idea that the Jewish people could find peace in their homeland. Instead there is war. I am willing to devote my work to a dream, Nikki. But I cannot put on a uniform and kill. Therefore, I cannot live in Israel. So I sell earrings and pins and bracelets for the French."

"And you enjoy living in Europe?"

"I love living in the world. And the key to being able to do so is knowing the languages. You find it so, too, I'll bet. It's the difference between watching a tennis match and playing. This world has too many spectators who depend upon officials to tell them how the competition is going." Hope shrugged. "God, I tend to get philosophical in my cups. What about dear old NU? I've been away for two years, and it seems like an eternity."

As she reported bits of gossip and news about the school, Nikki was amazed to find how removed she also felt. They talked about the university's construction out into Lake Michigan, faculty members they both knew, even a few of the students. The topics dwindled until Nikki decided that she should close off the interview.

"I suppose you have dinner plans, and so do I." She swung the covers of her notebook back into place. "Perhaps we'll see each other later during the meeting."

"Oh, I should think so. And elsewhere, too." Hope came to her feet. "Americans just keep meeting, it seems. Take care and write nicely about our enterprise."

Nikki took the elevator back to the balcony level. The desk she had used earlier was occupied by a man who had *The London Times* spread across its surface. But Gerry and Paul had taken over a group of chairs nearby. They rose as she approached.

"We're going back to the apartment for dinner," Gerry announced as she started to sit down. "There's been a change in plans."

Nikki looked from one somber face to the other. Whatever the reason for alteration, it was not good.

"Is Bruno meeting us there?"

They fell in on either side of her, Gerry grasping her arm.

"Bruno flew back to Germany an hour ago," Paul told her as they went down the stairs to the lobby, three abreast. "Liesel is in labor."

"So soon?" She tried to stop, but the men were urging her on. "The baby is due in late September."

"Bruno will call us as soon as there is news," Gerry assured her as they led her to the car and deposited her in the narrow back seat.

The meal on which they dined had been delivered by a caterer. She couldn't believe that Gerry had given much thought to its composition. It abounded in carbohydrates and was wanting in taste. The table discussion did nothing to improve the food.

According to what Bruno had been told by his extremely agitated mother, Liesel had been assaulted in their home. She had been taken to the hospital for treatment, and labor had begun. The injuries, apparently knife slashes, were confined to her arms and hands because she had attempted to protect the child she was carrying. There were being stitched and the lost blood replaced. Concern now focused with the baby.

"How could it have happened?" Nikki demanded. "Did Liesel come back to the apartment and find him there? It was a man, wasn't it?"

"We really don't know," Paul told her. "All we know is that she needed Bruno and he went. We'll find out more when he calls. Now, I want to hear about the attack on you."

Gerry had heard it once already. He prompted her as she told her story so that Paul would have all of the details. As she related the time she had spent with Hilde and Waldo, his questions became fewer. And when she spoke of the tie tack in her shoe, she sensed that he wished she hadn't.

"Where is it, Gerry? I want Paul to see it, too."

"I have seen it already," Paul told her.

"Then let me see it again." She turned toward Gerry and held out her hand. Grimly he removed the tiny stone from his pocket and placed it in her fingers.

Holding it by its silver post, she twirled the stone. Whatever the markings, they were very small and precise.

"Do you have a magnifying glass?"

When Gerry shook his head, she went across the room to his desk and tore a page form her note pad. Pulling a pencil from her handbag, she pushed the lead across the paper that rested directly over the setting. The men were silent as she studied the dark spot.

"It's a bird, I think." Nikki handed the sheet to Paul. "There's the head. Here's the tail. Terribly small. What do you think?"

"Possibly." He shifted the paper nearer the light. "A bird, Gerry? Or perhaps a letter. Could it be an Old English A?"

"You may have something there," Gerry agreed. "It could very well be an A."

The men were looking at each other, their eyes saying things that were not being spoken. Nikki saw it and felt a shudder go through her. Angrily she stamped her foot.

"No. It is a bird. I know it is. Herr Rennecke—" she paused, trying to think of how to define the relationship. It didn't matter, anyway. They both knew about her mother. "My mother's lover had an intaglio ring with the same bird on it."

Her hand went to the check that had once borne the mark. At this moment she could feel her skin smart again.

"The setting was platinum, and it had his initials on the side, S.R." Another thought crowded that one as Gerry and Paul stared at her. She had just told them something important, but there was more. "Hugo Haupt has the same design, onyx in gold, on his cuff links."

"Initials, too?" Gerry said softly.

"That would be H.H.," she reminded, shrugging.

"No. They would be S.R.," he said. "Look here, Nikki."

Her head nearly touched him as he indicated the tiny planes at the side of the tie tack where ornamentation appeared. By squinting, she was able to see the letters.

"Are you trying to tell me that three different people are wearing Stefan's jewelry? I can state for certain that the man would attacked me today was not Stefan. He was too young, for one thing, and an entirely different build."

"Those letters may not be Stefan Rennecke's initials, Nikki." Paul reached out a hand to draw her down to her place at the table again. "They could stand for a secret society, 'Die Schwarzen Raben.'"

He said the words in badly accented German, but Nikki grasped the meaning.

"Black birds," she simplified the thought. "Beware of black birds. That's what old Herr Haupt told me. And you are saying that Stefan and Hugo and that man today all belong to this society? What is it, anyway? Some evil sort of Elks?"

"I don't know what "Die Schwarzen Raben" stands for," Gerry told her, "but I've heard rumors about their existence and always in a bad context. It's not a large organization, I think, one of many little ideological groups that abound in Europe today."

"I can add to that," Paul offered. "I checked out the files with a news service office here. Die Schwarzen Raben membership is suspected to be international and rumors say it is anti-Zionist. But facts are lacking and, as you say, secret societies abound. There is no record of an insignia nor jewelry that members wear."

"Where can we find out…" Nikki began, interrupted by the telephone's ringing.

Bruno was on the line, and Gerry dispersed Nikki and Paul to extensions so they could all talk. Nikki drew the bedroom assignment and sat cross-legged in the middle of a sheepskin rug.

Bruno had a daughter. She was beautiful. Her name was Gretel, and she weighed just under six pounds.

"Our physician says she is very strong even though she is so small," he reported. "And Liesel is doing well. Her right hand has been taken care of, and they will do a quick surgery tomorrow to repair the cut tendons in her left hand. I am so thankful."

His voice had broken at the last comment. The three listeners jumped in with their congratulations. Then Gerry took control.

"Do you know yet what happened?"

"Father found her. He was upset by the commotion and practically crawled up the stairs to get to Liesel. Mother said that Liesel had worked that morning at the shop. At noon a mechanic from the garage came for our car so that it could be lubricated. And then Liesel decided to go home for a nap. She closed the rollos so the sun didn't shine in and fell asleep. And when she woke up, someone was in the apartment. He cut her up, my Liesel!"

"Was it a break-in?" Paul asked over the anguish.

"The police say not. Lock picks, perhaps. But why Liesel?"

It was a question still unanswered when he ended the conversation to have one more short visit with his wife before she slept. Nikki, however, was sure of the reason.

"It's because of me, isn't it?" she asked when she rejoined the men, hoping but not expecting a denial.

"That's the way it appears," Paul said bluntly. "So pack your things. We're driving back to Darmstadt tonight."

"But the conference?" Nikki protested. Damn the meeting, she thought. He was tearing her away from Gerry.

"We have enough material from the meeting, anyway. Gerry and I have decided that you are not safe here. Maybe, if we go back and mind the paper's business in Frankfurt, it will be better. Now get your clothes together."

"My papers for M. DePrenger. I have to deliver them tomorrow," she tried again.

"You will call him at his home tonight," Gerry instructed, pointing to the telephone. "I will take them to him in the morning."

"What do I tell him?" She pulled the card from her wallet and began to dial.

"That your newspaper had directed your immediate return to Frankfurt. That you will be in touch with him later," Paul prompted.

"But Vati wanted the stones returned. He left instructions."

"There will be a time for that, but not now," Gerry told her.

She made the telephone call as instructed. M. DePrenger would expect Herr Mehler at 10 o'clock. As she replaced the receiver, Gerry took her hand and led her to the bedroom.

"I don't want to leave you," Nikki protested as soon as the door was shut. "Can't I stay with you? I will be safe."

Gerry's arms were like vises across her back. His mouth closed over hers. She answered his kiss, trying to take hope from him. She twisted in his grip in an attempt to get even closer. But he was pushing her away.

"You cannot stay. One Groebel, whom I deeply respected, is missing because of my irresolution. I will not chance such a thing happening again with the Groebel that I love."

Through tears of regret and frustration, she saw the set of his jaw. Her hand went out to touch the firm skin.

To leave Gerry was to chance the survival of his affection. But to stay in defiance of his wishes would be worse. She knew in her heart that she could persuade him to back away from his decision. But she had witnessed what fear, anxiety, and guilt did to love. Obedient to the wisdom she had gained, she went to the closet and brought out her suitcase.

Chapter Eleven

✦ ✦ ✦

Dividing Lines

Her troubles in Zurich had been nothing more than that rare combination of mistakes and misunderstandings from which every person must suffer on occasion, Nikki decided as she adjusted the waistline of her skirt. Frau Schneider, on one side of her, and Delia Harbaum on the other applied safety pins to the gathered skirt of the dirndle dress.

"Oh, how my Martine would envy your small waist. Don't worry about the pins. The apron will cover our little alterations." The older woman nodded, pleased with her efforts. "You look very German now, but, of course, you really are."

"It is good," Delia added. She, too, was wearing traditional Hessian costume. Festivals, as well as holidays, were excellent reasons for returning to the old styles. Even Heike was wearing "native" dress. The youngster, during Nikki's fitting, had found more pleasure with a doll that Martine Schneider had left behind. From the corner of her eye, Nikki glimpsed the child as she thrust the doll into the waistband of her apron. She caught her breath, reminded of Kengi and the lost toy baby. Had Heidi retained little Rooey over the years? Perhaps she might have a child of her own who played with the toy.

Nikki held her place as the center of attention while her landlady adjusted a soft woolen shawl on her shoulders. Its fringe tickled her bare arms. Frau Schneider pulled the edges a bit more snuggly across Nikki's cleavage and fastened the shawl in place. The woman stepped back to observe her handiwork.

"Nice." She nodded.

"Nice," Heike echoed. They all laughed.

Laughter had been difficult in those first days back on the job. On the streets of Frankfurt and during the drives to and from Darmstadt with Paul, Nikki had nearly sprained her neck in an attempt to see whether she was being followed. Riding elevators, circulating in crowds, even standing in line with others had brought new fear. But nearly two months had passed. With each day, Nikki recognized more fully the ridiculousness of the conspiracy theory that she and the men had developed during that last night in Zurich. They had taken a series of unrelated events and forged them into a chain. And every link was weak.

The incidents were behind her. The problem, as she saw it now, was that she didn't know whether she dared to return to Zurich. Gerry seemed very positive, in his letters, that the danger was real.

Sooner or later she must go back. M. DePrenger had written to say that her papers had satisfied his needs, and the contents of the box were hers to dispose of as she saw fit. Based on her conversation with Klaus Haupt, the bank manager was making another attempt to locate Vati. He had tried to speak with the old man himself, but Herr Haupt had entered a rest home at Lake Como. Hugo had reported that his father had suffered a slight stroke following the birthday celebration and was unable to communicate.

More important than returning to the contents of the box, of course, was seeing Gerry again soon. They were back on what Paul termed "The Mickey Mouse Shift" with a letter going each way weekly. Sheets of stationery, regardless of penned sentiments, were poor substitutes for the real thing. Gerry said that he was very busy with another hotel renovation under contract. There weren't many hours in which he could feel loneliness.

Nikki knew how that was. She, too, had been laboring in assignments and research, which Paul was doling out in great measure. She was sure that her superior thought that the work would help. He was right. It had. But one tired of, as well as with, work.

An indication of how far-fetched their ideas of her danger had been was the lack of success in attempts to learn more on the subject of the black birds. Dick Dower had even taken their quest to some unnamed individual in military intelligence.

"The reference to color is quite normal for secret organizations," he reported after that meeting. "There's a lot of history to back it up, heraldry and such, with a variety of meanings ascribed to different shades. Members can establish their identity to one another by wearing the color even if the symbol becomes suspect."

"And the raven?" Paul prompted.

"Birds and beasts are popular symbols. Nearly every member of the animal kingdom has an associated legend that can be dusted off and adopted for use. The Vikings used raven figures on their standards. There are some superstitions about the birds, witness Edgar Allen Poe. And his poem was correct to the point that some ravens can mimic speech." Dick looked pleased with himself as he refilled his Pilsener glass from the pitcher they were sharing at the Darmstadt Officers' Club. "Maybe I should have been a zoologist."

Nikki's own research had discovered that the birds preferred the habitat in Northern Europe. They were omnivores. They tended to flock, making them a nuisance to whatever site they choose to rest. The peasants' suspicions about them plucking the eyes from the dead was probably incorrect. In the days when the deceased lay on their biers with coins on their lids, magpies, rather than ravens, were more logical thiefs.

There had not really been much time to look into the matter, she admitted. Frankfurt had hosted several trade shows. The grapes had been harvested in the Rauenthal. She and Paul had retraced their way through that area earlier in the month, stopping to eat with Herr Aucher but avoiding Winestube Himmel. When Paul's pictures were developed, she had written on the captions along with twenty-six paragraphs of description and tucked them into the press pouch. This weekend readers in the United States would learn about the German grape harvest.

One section dealt with the recovery of grape production since the war. Nikki would have liked to explain how the French, as part of their reparations, had torn the vines from the hillside and thrown them into the Rhein. Paul blue-penciled out her comments. West Germany and France were dealing well together at this moment. Old problems were best left alone.

This weekend was another of those working holidays. The event was the annual "Dippe-Messe," a market featuring displays of pots and crockery suitable for kitchen use. It had begun, in a country village, as a gathering of itinerant craftsmen. Over the years, the market grew from one day to a fair of several days and now had emerged as a full-blown carnival. They would enjoy the festival, but notes and pictures would be taken as well. The result was tentatively slated for use in the newspaper's magazine the Sunday after Thanksgiving.

Nikki had been a little surprised when Paul announced that Delia and Heike would accompany them. Up to now he had kept his friendship with the young widow separated from his work. Still she was pleased that they would have the extra people with them. Otherwise there was the tendency to rehash the subject of black ravens and disposition of her inheritance and both were deadened, deserving no further thought.

"Uncle Paul has come," Heiki announced from her vantage point by the window that looked out on the street. "Momma, Uncle Paul is here."

Delia needed no reminder, Nikki thought. The change in her serene face was hardly noticeable, but it said that Delia knew of his arrival in a manner removed from the usual senses.

Nikki and the child shared the back seat en route to the festival. They played a game of "I Spy," which Nikki found translated well into any language and childhood. The countryside gave way to the village. Banners and clusters of grasses and flowers on the lamp posts announced the festivities. Barriers detoured them from the main street to narrower byways. She kept waiting for Paul to shoehorn the Beetle into an occasional vacancy at the curb. Instead they drove on, emerging on the other side of the detour and climbing a rise to an inn. It was necessary, she supposed, to establish one's use of reservations early so that the host would not be tempted to give the rooms to latecomers. Still, she would have preferred to join the gala immediately.

Instead of driving past the inn to its parking area, Paul dispersed his passengers right at the door. Nikki offered to accompany him so that he would not be alone to carry the overnight cases. Delia could begin the registration process. The woman didn't require a translator.

"No," Paul refused. "You go with her. You can manage Heike."

That was ridiculous. The child was perfectly obedient to her mother. So the boss might not always be right, but the boss was always the boss. Nikki took Heike's hand and followed Delia through the door.

She blinked twice, once to accustom her eyes to the reduced light. The second time it was to make sure that what she thought she saw was actuality. The embrace that engulfed her assured her that her vision had been accurate.

"We did surprise you," Gerry stated with a satisfied smile after they had kissed.

"And how!" Nikki's voice was so weak that the words might not be carrying. But she knew it was written on her face as well.

The day, which had promised to be gay, and the weather, beginning fair and warm, exceeded Nikki's expectations. With Gerry toting Paul's heavier lens cases, Nikki had changed film repeatedly. On their visits to the market stalls, she had chatted with the vendors while Paul made notes. Actually he didn't need her. Delia would have done as well. But they followed their normal work pattern.

"That is the traditional food of this fair," Nikki explained to Paul as he sampled a waffle, dipped first in marshmallow and then in chocolate. "Every Messe has its own."

"Want a bite?" Paul offered it to each of them. Heike reached an eager hand toward him, but Delia pulled her back.

"Little stomachs do not know their limits," she cautioned Paul.

"I want a Weisswurstle," Nikki declared. "With hot mustard. Are we done with the interviews yet?"

"I think so. Let's stow the gear in the car and spend some time enjoying ourselves," Paul suggested.

"You are good with people," Gerry told Nikki as they waited for service at the sausage stall. Delia, Paul, and Heike had set off on their own. "They enjoy talking to you."

"That's because I talk to them about what they do," Nikki explained. "Speaking of work makes most people very vocal. They know their subject, and the words come easily."

"Especially when the listener makes them feel important and appreciated. And you do that, Nikki."

"Do you feel important and appreciated?" she grinned at him.

"Yes."

"Good. Because I wanted so much to be with you again. Even if it's only for the weekend."

They gave their orders to the proprietor. Nikki chuckled as he handed over their food. In this part of Germany, the Weisswurstle was nestled in a fresh crusty roll, more like the American hot dog.

"Hurry," she urged Gerry as she pushed past several customers to get at the mustard containers. Standing at the counter, with the aromas from the grill sending her saliva glands into overtime, had made Nikki realize how hungry the morning's efforts had made her.

Gerry grunted his agreement as he dabbed the hot juice from his chin. Nikki giggled and bit down on the end of the sausage that protruded from the roll. Its skin crackled beneath her teeth. Tastes rarely seemed as good as memory suggested they might be, but today her recollection of that other sausage in Vati's company understated the pleasure. By the time she had finished her meal, the mustard's sharp bite had made her thirsty.

"Gerry, let's find a place where they sell apfelwein. This will be our only chance to get it fresh. Have you ever had it?"

"Nope. But let's give your apfelwein a try. There's been no more trouble at all since you came back to Germany?" He pulled her over to a table at the wine tent.

"None. And you have been safe, too?" She pulled a pretzel from the basket in front of them. Its convoluted shape reminded her of the silly plots they had developed in Zurich. Perhaps they needed a secret organization, too—the brown pretzel.

"No problems at all. Perhaps we imagined too much. The Kneipp family has had no trouble either?"

"That's true." She put her teeth into the insignia and bit down. "Liesel has healed well, although she favors the less injured hand. And Gretel is a darling. They drove down to Darmstadt so I could meet her. Neither Paul nor Bruno felt good about my showing up in Wiesbaden at that point. But the police there have had more break-ins reported since that day. One of the thieves was seen with a knife."

226

"There doesn't need to be a connection between what happened to you and the attack on Liesel," Gerry allowed as the waitress approached with their beverage. He took a sip and his eyebrows shot up. "Wow!"

"Sometimes I think that there never was a connection except in our minds," Nikki told him, watching his face carefully. "Those eight days were bad, right from the start, except for finding you. And there's no law that says problems have to be separated by a certain number of hours. I still remember that lout in the dining car who hated me because he thought I was an American. Thank heavens Hans Germeyer showed up when he…"

"What's wrong, Nikki?" Gerry covered her hand with his. His frown deepened as her shudder was transmitted to him.

"Hans wore a black intaglio ring, too. I'm not sure about the pattern." She closed her eyes, trying to dredge up a memory. Finally she shook her head. "It is not possible. He could not have known that I was going to Zurich. I didn't know for sure until Herr Kneipp said it would be so."

"Anything's possible," Gerry allowed, "but probable, I doubt. And onyx intaglio is not that rare. My father has one. It bears the head of William tell. Father is back, by the way, and I told him about you."

"All about me?" Nikki asked in alarm.

"Those things which he needs to know. After all, it was his potential daughter-in-law that we discussed."

"Oh, really?"

"Of course, really. When will you marry me?" His face was serious, but his eyes laughed at her.

She wanted to say "Now!" but she couldn't. Until she knew where Vati was and why the distribution of his wealth had been left to her, whether there really were men with the black birds who were interested in her, she could not judge the danger she might bring to others. She had to know that the attack on Liesel had been only coincidence, that the purse snatcher had no connection to Hugo Haupt.

"I don't know," she finally managed.

His laughter faded.

"What are you really saying?" he demanded, leaning across the small table in order to see her face clearly. "Don't you love me?"

"Of course, I do. How can you doubt that? I keep telling you so."

"Then just what is the problem? Your job? Your wealth?" Even in the twilight, the flush on Gerry's face was visible.

"I don't know if I have a problem," she snapped back. "But until I am sure, I won't do anything that can endanger you. I've lost as many people who were dear to me as I intend to! Paul and I are still investigating some of the coincidence and the possibility that a black raven society actually exists."

"You are turning to Paul for help and refusing to take my protection." Gerry's response came from deep in his throat. He came to his feet and glared down at her.

"You're crazy," she accused.

"That is absolutely correct," he responded stiffly. "Thank you, doctor, for the diagnosis. But worry does that to a man. How can you expect me to go about my work in Zurich, wondering what will happen next? Either you are willing to share all of your life with me or there can be nothing."

Nikki closed her eyes, considering the alternatives. In his arms she found safety, pleasure, and love. But were those arms to disappear, to suddenly not return like Vati, she could not live at all. Yet, the bitterness of the choice she was being called upon to make faded in a flash of understanding for what Mutti had really done. It was not love or riches that drew her mother to Stefan Rennecke. It was solely a hoped-for, but unrealized, protection for herself and her child. For Mutti's life, officially ended by cancer, had actually stopped that night in Winterthur.

This was what she had to say to Gerry, that as long as they were apart, she could hope for something better. If they were together, she could only live in fear of the worst. She stared at the table top, searching for the words that had the power to make him understand. And when Nikki looked up, Gerry was gone.

* * *

Trying to find him in the festival crowds would be stupid. In time he would have to return to the inn. And the walk, the time alone, might make him more reasonable.

When the waitress stopped at the table, her words properly humble but her demeanor speaking concern for the absent male, Nikki ordered another drink. After the glass was empty, she walked slowly back to the inn, rehearsing in her mind the words she had to say to Gerry.

Paul was at the reception desk as she entered the lobby. His gaze, when it fell upon her, was filled with questions. Instead of queries, however, he gave an order.

"Get freshened up. We're going to the mayor's reception, and it started ten minutes ago."

"What about Gerry?"

"Gone. Something came up business-wise, and he took off for Zurich."

She ducked her head to hide her distress. Paul's arm encircled her shoulders.

"Look, Nikki. I don't know what happened between you two. You can tell me later if you want. But things will be better. You have to believe that." His grasp tightened before he pushed her away. "Now hurry. Duty calls!"

Paul had arranged for the innkeeper's teenage daughter to stay with Heike, leaving himself and Delia free to provide companionship and consolation to Nikki as well as fulfill the sudden social obligation. Nikki suspected that the invitation was related to Paul's being the only foreign press representative at the festival. And the mayor proved her correct.

With a firm grip on Paul's arm, their host led him from one municipal dignitary to the next. She and Delia drifted behind the men, nodding pleasantly as introductions were made. Finally, when the official was drawn aside to give an opinion concerning a civic need, the trio found their way to a table every inch of which was taken up by some delicacy.

Even in her misery, Nikki noticed that Delia had taken over explanations of foods and their combinations for Paul. She was certainly more effective than Nikki had even been in limiting his caloric intake. In fact, although Nikki hadn't really noticed until now, her colleague looked more fit and healthy than at any time since she had known him.

She chose very little for herself, then carried her plate across the room to a set of chairs Delia and Paul had chosen. Getting the food into her mouth was an automatic reflex. Swallowing it was a chore. And there was little doubt in Nikki's mind that she would have to dig into her handbag sooner or later to find the pills to quell her stomach spasms.

"Did you try this, Nikki?" Delia gestured to a mound of pinkish crème on her plate. It looked like raspberry mousse, but in time of stress, Nikki found many things reminded her of the hated taste of raspberry.

She shook her head and looked away toward the entrance to the room. Only a quick movement kept her plate from falling to the floor. Nothing stopped the gigantic cramp that seized her.

"Paul," she gasped weakly, interrupting his comment to Delia. "Look at the white-haired man in that group with the mayor."

Both Paul and Delia swiveled their heads to observe the newcomers.

"I see the man you mean. Who is he?"

"I think it's Stefan Rennecke," Nikki managed over the pain that bent her forward. "My mother and I were living with him when David and Donna adopted me."

"Right!" Paul's fierce whisper matched hers. "Another of the black birds. We'll have to get you out of here."

"He does not recognize Nikki," Delia supplied. "He has looked all around the room, including directly at us. And his eyes never stopped."

"Nevertheless, we aren't taking any chances," Paul growled. "As soon as he is away from the door, you two go to the ladies' room. That will give me a chance to see if anyone has been stationed in the lobby to watch Nikki. If, when you come out, I am talking with someone, go directly to the car and lock yourself inside."

Delia gave Paul a stricken look, then rose and placed her plate on the seat of her chair. She held out her hand for Nikki. The mayor's party was approaching the table, and their backs were turned. Nonetheless, Delia kept her larger form between Nikki and the group.

* * *

It was fortunate that Paul had consigned them to the rest room, Nikki realized as soon as they were safely inside. She reached the toilet just in time. When she had retched up what seemed to be everything she had taken in for the past week, she turned herself over to Delia's concern. Her face was washed with care.

"We cannot rinse your mouth because we do not know the source of the water," Delia muttered regretfully. "But you will suck on this."

From her handbag, she brought out a tin of lemon drops and her laughter turned Nikki's protest aside.

"I find they do wonders to settle Heike's tummy troubles. But if they do not do the same for you, at least it will taste better next time."

Her hand was firm on Nikki's arm as they exited the room. It was a relief to find Paul stationed at the front door of the hall, awaiting their arrival. He joined them as they descended the steps to the street. At the car, Nikki stopped and looked around. No one appeared interested in their departure. A group of revelers on the corner kept on dancing, without missing a step, to the beat of the three-piece band.

"Paul, if we were to lock ourselves inside the car, would you go back and find out why Herr Rennecke is here?" Nikki requested.

He considered for a moment, then nodded. But he waited until the doors were secure before leaving.

"I am so sorry to involve you in this," Nikki told Delia after Paul had disappeared back into the hall. "And I can't even tell you what it is, because I don't really know."

"Don't you worry," Delia consoled her. "Shared troubles improve friendships, and friendships do not demand explanations."

Why couldn't the same thing be said for love, Nikki wondered. Perhaps she had been wrong. Her selfishness in wanting to protect Gerry from harm might be as great a selfishness as her refusal to share the dangers. Still, it was better that his emotions, rather than his body, be hurt. There could be no future for Gerry Mehler and Nikki Fisher until the past of Monika Groebel was put in its proper place.

Delia's relief at Paul's return was expressed in one quick kiss. It surprised Nikki nearly as much as Paul. The widow had always seemed glad enough to have the man's attention, but she had never been expressive when Nikki was a witness.

"Wow!" Paul chuckled. "I will have to attempt espionage again soon. Unfortunately, I don't think much of this attempt. Herr Stefan Rennecke is here to visit an old friend. It was the friend who was invited to the reception. Without either of my translators, I couldn't talk with him very effectively. But he does speak enough English to tell me that he is retired from the jewelry business and that he is writing a book. He will be here for a week, I think he said, to gather some background material."

"He didn't happen to say exactly where," Nikki prompted.

"I don't think so. He kept lapsing into German," Paul continued as he brought the car to life. "But it doesn't matter. We're leaving for Darmstadt tonight. Again!"

* * *

A note was hanging on the spindle hook by Nikki's desk. According to the time noted on it, the phone call had been received while she and Paul had been at lunch. There was no name for the caller, but she recognized the Wiesbaden number immediately.

"Who took this call for me?" She held up the paper for everyone in the room to see.

"I did. No one else was here when it came in." It was the American clerk who fed the wire, his manner suggesting that answering telephones as women's work.

"Who was the caller?"

"Some Kraut." He shrugged and Nikki's shoulders stiffened. "A man. Not too bad an accent. Said he'd wait at that number for your call."

It had to be important for Bruno to stay in the apartment during shop hours, Nikki was sure. Her fingers shook as she requested the connection. When he came on the line, she was even more positive. Bruno's tone was hushed, almost secretive. After the greeting, he changed to German to deliver the message.

"A call came this morning for Karl, from Berlin. It was a nurse at Sankt Gertrauden Hospital. She said it was an emergency. A Dr. Schmidt has requested that she ask Karl to come to him."

Dr. Schmidt? Nikki frowned. She had known several persons named Schmidt and imagined that Vati had known even more. Schmidt. A doctor. Vati.

"Kurt," she gasped.

"I am sorry, Nikki. I didn't hear what you said."

"No matter. Was the call from West Berlin?"

"Of course. Sankt Gertrauden Hospital is in West Berlin. It is very old. I told her that your family had moved but that I thought I could reach someone. And she said it was essential that Herr Groebel come immediately. Do you know this Dr. Schmidt?"

"Yes, Bruno. He is a distant cousin. I will go to him. Thank you for calling." After the call was disconnected, Nikki realized she had not asked about Liesel and Baby Gretel.

Paul, who had stopped for a haircut after their meal, came in just after she hung up. He was placing his sports jacket on the back of his desk chair when her look caught his attention.

"Don't tell me that the young traffic engineer you are planning to interview is giving you trouble over an appointment," he laughed at her across the desk.

"Paul, I have to go to Berlin," she exploded.

"Fine. Give me a couple of days and I'll find us an assignment there."

"I mean now."

"Nikki, be reasonable. I can't just..."

She raised her hand and he fell silent.

"You don't understand. I don't mean us. I mean me, today. An old friend needs me." When the words were out, Nikki suddenly felt weak. The chair at the side of his desk provided welcome support.

"I didn't know you had friends in Berlin." His left eyebrow climbed his high forehead, almost disappearing under the lock of hair that hung down.

"Nor did I." She put her hand on his arm to enforce her words. "But he is there, and he has asked for me." She knew she was stretching the truth, but to do otherwise was to reveal too much.

"What is his name?"

"Kurt. Dr. Kurt Schmidt. When I was a child, he fixed my broken arm."

"And for this you are willing to go to Berlin again?" Paul asked doubtfully. "I had a broken arm, too, and I can't even remember the doctor's name."

"Kurt was a family friend as well. He used to spend the holidays with us. Please, Paul. I must go. He may be hearing from my father." Lie was stacking on lie in order to establish credibility. She hoped she was not blushing, but the cold that was within her clutched her heart like a steel fist. Surely the heat and chill would counteract one another.

Paul's features oozed compassion. He was sure that no one was hearing from Herr Groebel. His expression changed to a sympathetic grin.

"If you must, then you shall. Take the car to Darmstadt and pack up. When you get back, I'll have it all arranged."

* * *

It was amazing how well Paul had done. On her return, she was hustled to an Italian news office and turned over to a writer who was driving to Berlin immediately.

"You have your passport, visa, and press credentials," Paul summed up as he passed her another envelope. "This says that we are loaning you to Enrique Rossi to act as his translator. If you run into any difficulty in Berlin, you call Frank. There's a card in there with his home and office addresses and phone numbers."

Paul's encouraging smile was almost more than she could bear. Standing on tiptoes, she put her lips to his cheek.

"You are a dear person," she whispered.

"Aren't I though?" he responded, hugging her.

Signor Rossi voiced a comment filled with innuendo that Paul couldn't understand. But Nikki did and pushed him away. Flanked by the two men, she walked to the car and handed over her suitcase to be placed in the trunk.

"You take good care of her, Enrique," Paul told the man. After Nikki translated the instruction, the Italian broke into smiling assurances that had to be translated back.

* * *

Then they were on their way. Signor Rossi drove his aging Fiat as if he were in Rome, leaving Nikki with little time to worry about Russian soldiers on the corridor into Berlin. The Fiat seemed to nip at the bumpers of the vehicles in front of it like some fierce little dog. Each time it overtook and passed a car, the driver's acclamation of success nearly drowned out the sound of his horn.

It was late afternoon when they entered Berlin. Rossi offered to find her a hotel room, but, after several hours of sliding away from his wandering gestures, Nikki was sure it was not a single he had in mind. She asked him to take her to the hospital.

"Your friend, the doctor, works there?" he asked.

She hadn't thought of that. Of course it was possible. And what was Kurt going to think about her wild journey then? If he was on the hospital staff, he might not be in the building now. But they would know how she could reach him.

As they drove along Paretzer Strasse, Nikki looked around her. St. Gertrude's Hospital was a dominating structure. The statuary on its front designated it as a religious hospital. In the dusk it was difficult to determine whether the figure was the Holy Mother or the building's patroness.

One thing was certain. The original cut-stone building had been added to in later years. The six-story structure's entry was flanked by cheery geraniums.

"I appreciate this very much. I hope bringing me here didn't take you too far out of your way," Nikki spoke her gratitude as she shook Rossi's hand. He had left the driver's seat to get her suitcase from the trunk, but the engine was still running.

"Are you sure you don't want me to go in with you?" Rossi asked, maintaining his grip on her hand. When she shook her head, he bent his head to kiss her fingers. "You will call me if I can assist further."

"Of course, I will." In view of his gallantry, Nikki felt the need to be gracious. But as soon as he was back behind the wheel, Nikki dashed for the hospital lobby, dropping her luggage in front of the reception desk.

"I have come from Frankfurt to see Dr. Kurt Schmidt. I am a friend. Can you tell me how I might locate him?"

The woman's manner changed radically, from concerned helper to someone suddenly alert, the kind of change a policeman directing traffic shows when a driver makes an illegal turn.

"Wait, please. Right here."

She disappeared through a door behind the desk. Nikki felt suddenly lonely. The woman returned.

"Come through here, please," A broad hand with no-nonsense fingernails lifted a section of the counter as the other shoved a panel ajar. Nikki complied.

* * *

The man who rose from the far side of the desk was certainly not Kurt, nor even a physician, in all probability. The white of his clerical collar contrasted with his ruddy neck.

"Good afternoon. I am Father Braun, assistant administrator for St. Gertrude's. How can I serve you?" The words were those of a bureaucrat. Still Nikki suspected that the offer to help was sincere.

"My name is Monika Groebel. I have to come to visit a cousin, Dr. Kurt Schmidt. Is he on staff or is he a patient?" Nikki took the forward edge of the wooden chair to which the priest had gestured.

"Groebel? Yes." He had tried the name for sound and was satisfied. "But it was a man that we expected."

"The call came for my father, Karl Groebel. He is not able to come so I have been sent as his delegate," Nikki knew she was hedging, but it was often better when officials were not burdened with too much fact. "Please, tell me about Kurt."

"It is sad." Father Braun steepled his fingers in front of his pectoral cross. "Dr. Schmidt is a brave man, but, alas, his days remaining are few."

Dismay swept over Nikki. The errand was as she had expected. Kurt was dying. But his death could not be natural. He was still fairly young, somewhere between forty and fifty, according to her quick calculations. She nodded to the priest, signaling her readiness for more information.

What she learned caused her distress to grow. Her cousin was suffering from serious injuries received during his recent escape from the East. He had lost a foot in a mine explosion in addition to having been hit in the shoulder by a rifle bullet.

"Perhaps specialized treatment, even another hospital," she suggested. This was a worthy use of some of her fortune, one that Vati would certainly applaud. "I...my family can handle the financial arrangements."

"You are generous and well-intentioned," the priest told her, managing a grave smile. "However, Fraulein Groebel, there are many complications. Dr. Schmidt was suffering from leukemia prior to his escape, living on borrowed time before he came to us."

"There is no hope..." Nikki's teeth captured her lower lip to hold her chin firm.

The priest reached for a black-bound book on the corner of his blotting pad. His fingers found the page he sought as if from memory. And he began to read:

"Then shall the King say unto them on his right hand, Come, ye blessed of my Father, inherit the kingdom prepared for you from the foundation of the world: For I was hungered..."

His words went on to the end of the familiar passage. He raised his head and regarded her across the desk.

"Come and inherit the kingdom sounds very hopeful to me," Father Braun spoke slowly and his smile became radiant. "Dr. Schmidt brought with him four children in need of medical treatment not available on the other side. They came through unscathed and are already under care. I believe the words of our Lord Jesus are for him, don't you?"

Nikki nodded through her tears, not trusting her voice.

"Dr. Schmidt is conscious. In fact, he has refused more than minimal medication. And he will be pleased to see you as soon as you have recovered yourself."

She dug a tissue from her purse and began to wipe her eyes. Composure would come hard, Nikki knew, but it had to be accomplished. The priest walked around the desk, his hand catching hers.

"You must take time to deal with your grief," he cautioned. "A few minutes will make little difference in the outcome, but your attitude must be strong. The doctor has little strength anymore to give others."

And he had given so much, Nikki realized, even as her sobbing continued. Kurt was more than just another family member. Vati had relied upon his judgment. They all had valued his counsel as much as his presence. Her fingers drew the golden chain from beneath her blouse. The tiny cross and the angle ring tinkled against each other as they greeted her with their warmth. Unaccountably, Nikki felt better. Holding the objects on her palm, she showed them to the priest.

"The little ring was a gift from Kurt. It was on Sylvestersabend when I was seven."

He nodded.

"I think perhaps, Fraulein, you are now ready to visit Dr. Schmidt. I will take you to him."

* * *

As they walked through the halls and up the stairways, Father Braun gave her guideposts so that she would be able to find her way again. They slowed from time to time so that he could greet staff members and ambulatory patients. The respectful smiles and the eager replies to his queries told her a great deal about the man's position. But the number of nursing sisters and the variety of their habits surprised her.

"Sankt Gertrauden-Krankenhaus is operated by the Diocese," the priest answered her query. "We have, therefore, a reservoir of trained nurses and medical attendants from many orders upon which we can draw. We provide extremely good care to the injured and the ill. We have continued the work of St. Gertrude, even through the war when the bombs fell all around and yet miraculously spared us. Like the good saint, we give excellent care to all who are in need. Your friend, Kurt, is in good hands with us. He has done so much for mankind, and we will do no less for him. I want you to understand that."

"I'm sure you are doing your very best," Nikki responded as the tour continued. Then, finally on the fifth floor, he drew her to a halt before a set of double doors.

"We will be entering a man's surgical ward in order to reach Dr. Schmidt. What you will experience inside is appalling, even terrifying, to those of us who are hale and whole. Should you feel faint, you will pull on my arm, and I will take you away."

Nikki was grateful for the warning. Some medieval torture chamber seemed to be re-created in the room through which they were passing. But no sight, sound, or smell was going to keep her from Kurt's side. She followed doggedly in the priest's wake, even managing to smile at those who greeted him.

The route he took was the length of the ward. At the other end, Father Braun opened a door and held it for her. They were now in a narrow hall with partitioned cubicles on each side.

"Second room on your right," he instructed in a low voice. "Stay strong."

A woman in nurse's uniform, rather than a habit, rose from her chair as they entered. She had been holding the hand of the man who lay on the bed.

"Good evening, Father Braun. You are working late," she told the man, but her curiosity was focused on Nikki.

"Escorting a visitor for your husband, Frau Schmidt. This is Monika Groebel, daughter of the gentleman for whom you sent." His hand, firm against Nikki's back, propelled her forward.

"Monika? Kleine Maus?" The voice from the bed was Kurt's and she ignored the woman—could she really be his wife? —to respond. Nikki felt a moment of doubt, even though she knew the words were right. The body that lay there, attached to bottles and protected by a semi-circular frame, was not familiar. It seemed to require great effort for the man to raise his lids. When she saw his eyes, she knew. This grey-skinned, drawn figure was her beloved Kurt. And she reached for the fingers the nurse had loosed.

"Hello, Kurt. I can hardly believe this is happening," Nikki told him, able to smile at her joy in having found him, regardless of condition. "To be with you again seemed almost too good to be true."

She felt a feeble squeeze of fingers against her hand.

"Will you come to the end of the bed so that he can see you properly?" The woman was pulling her away from the grasp. "The surgery on his shoulder prevents Kurt from turning his head."

It was worth letting go just to see his face as he looked her, Nikki decided. And his expression matched her emotions exactly.

"Julia, my dear," the words were softly, but easily, spoken. "This is my younger sister, Monika. Monika, meet my beloved wife."

The nurse's smile reflected that of her husband's, but Nikki was unable to answer. Her hands gripped the foot rail until her knuckles turned bloodless. Should she make the correction in front of him, she wondered. The priest had said there was some medication, and the illness could be clouding Kurt's mind as well. No, she would explain later to Julia Schmidt, in private. At this point she would only enjoy this time with Kurt.

When she loosened her grip to hold out a hand to the woman, the nurse stepped forward and hugged her.

"But she does not look at all like Hanna, Kurt." The woman pushed her away from the embrace to look at Nikki closely. "But Hanna resembled Wera. This is definitely Karl's daughter."

"You know my family?" Nikki asked in surprise.

"Of course. I remember you as a tiny child with a broken arm. Kurt had to rebreak it and set it. Do you recall? I was your special-duty nurse as you recovered."

"Has it given you trouble since?" The question was a doctor's, not a patient's, and Nikki turned back to him. Those veiled references to the little sister returned and she had to know.

"You are my brother? Truly?" Nikki held her breath, wanting affirmation.

"I am Karl's son," Kurt told her. "But not Wera's. I was born before they met and married."

"And your mother?"

"Died when I was born. Do you remember Oma Kohn? My mother was the governess for the Kohn grandchildren before Hitler's rise to power. I lived in their home for several years. Then, when the persecution came, Karl took Oma and me away."

"I never knew," Nikki thought, then realized she had spoken the words.

"There is much you did not know then," Kurt agreed. "But has Karl not told you? And how is he? I want very much to see him once more."

"Vati is gone," Nikki managed, returning to the chair and reaching for his hand again.

"Dead? And Wera?"

"Mutti died several years ago. Vati disappeared before that. It is a long story, and very complicated. Do you want to hear it all?" Nikki looked doubtfully at him, then at Julia. She had expected that Kurt would be giving her answers, that perhaps he even knew where and why Vati had disappeared. Instead, Kurt was seeking knowledge. Nonetheless, she would maintain her smile.

"He wants to hear, of course," the woman laughed softly. "He has been waiting all these years to learn about you and the family."

"At least for the past seven years. That's when Karl stopped communicating. And you have heard nothing, either? What did you do when your mother died? Who took care of you?" The questions became progressively softer, slower.

"Like you, I became part of a Jewish home." How odd it was that the same thread had run through the tapestry of both their lives, Nikki thought.

"Kurt, I think you two have talked enough for the moment," Julia interrupted. "Monika can return tomorrow after you have slept."

"Of course. You will stay in Berlin for a few days, won't you? I have things to tell you as well as things I want to know." Kurt's fingers tightened on hers.

"I will stay, of course," Monika promised. "I need to find a room, though. Perhaps Julia can help me."

"Keep Monika with you, darling." Kurt was speaking barely above a whisper, his energy spent.

"Of course. She will use the folding bed. I will take her home now and come back later for the night."

Kurt nodded, even though his eyes were closed. His pinched lips were softened by a smile.

* * *

"Do you stay with Kurt all of the time?" Nikki asked after they were seated on the bus that Julia said would take them to the corner nearest the house where she had her room.

"As much as I am able. You see, he helped me escape four years ago, and we have been apart ever since. He was afraid that the officials would realize that he was arranging escapes and would imprison me along with them."

"Was he ill then?" Nikki couldn't imagine any woman deserting the man she supposedly she loved when she knew he was ill.

"He says not," Julia told her sadly. "But he would not tell me if it were so because he would spare me guilt. Let us say that it is possible that the disease was not manifested at that time. This type moves swiftly."

"Do you think he arranged our escapes, my parents' and mine?" Nikki needed to change the subject. A discussion of Kurt's prognosis would do neither of them any good.

"I know he did. Hanna should have also come, but the decision was left to her."

"Did he know the Gruens?"

"Softly," Julia warned. "We do not discuss those things in public. Although neither of them are active anymore. They are too old."

"Did they bring you out?"

"I came out with a patient, a man who was a paraplegic. The East had no use for him anymore."

"But they did for you," Nikki objected. "What did they do to Kurt?"

Julia shrugged.

"What could they do? I was merely a nurse in the hospital, not even in his clinic. They never knew we were married. Our tenth anniversary was last weekend and, until now, we have never been recognized as husband and wife. There have been only stolen moments in which we could share each other. And yet, with Kurt, it has been worth it. The next stop is ours."

* * *

When Nikki came out of the apartment's one bathroom the next morning, she was confronted by the owner. Apparently Julia was not the only sub-lessor, for the elderly woman did not seem surprised to encounter a stranger.

"You are visiting Fraulein Karsch or Frau Schmidt?" She enquired after exchanging wishes for the day ahead.

"Frau Schmidt. She is my sister-in-law." The explanation a novelty, but Nikki liked the words.

"That is good." The greyed head nodded. "She needs to have kin with her at this sad time."

Poignant, Nikki corrected in her mind, not sad. Since she wasn't sure whether she would see Julia before she reached Kurt's bedside, she sought directions to the nearest post office.

"Use the telephone here," the woman urged. "You can pay me the rates."

Paul sounded angry when she reached him.

"For God's sake, Nikki, why didn't you call before?" he scolded as soon as he heard her voice. "You are all right, aren't you? You didn't contact Frank like I told you to do."

She provided a digest of the situation as well as she could, adding elaboration when Paul's grunts indicated it was needed.

"I have to stay here with Kurt," she told him when the explanation was complete. "Shall I send you a written resignation?"

"Why should you? The paper's policy covers serious illness within the family. You said Kurt is your brother. But what I really want to know is whether you are safe. Bruno and I talked earlier today, and he is concerned, too."

"I'm sure that I am, but even if I'm wrong, I have to take my chances. I owe Kurt that. Do you want the telephone number here? It's the apartment where Julia has a room."

Talking to Paul was, Nikki decided, like touching a rock, firm, and sensible, and eternal. She promised to call Frank, which she did immediately. The reporter was happy to hear from her and offered whatever assistance she might need. Having done her duty, Nikki dressed and went to the corner to catch the bus.

Both Julia and Kurt were delighted with her return. Once she was seated, Julia left to get some breakfast.

"Tell me about your life, Monika," Kurt requested. "Start with now and work back to when we were together."

That wasn't where she began, of course. The logical starting point, although it surprised her to realize that, was with Vati's disappearance. She had never before seen it as the pivot point in her life. So Kurt heard about Donna and David Fisher, the new identity, Chicago, Northwestern, the job, and Paul. And finally they had reached the point where she was in Zurich and saw the contents of the safe box.

"Karl bought many stones, both before Hitler led us into war and after the Russians occupied our land," Kurt told her. "Most of the money he paid went to allow the former owners to establish themselves in new lives. What he gave for the gems was fair, in fact generous. Sometimes, however, he only kept the stones safe. That is why he provided the list for you. Did you know that he also bought and held precious metals?"

"You mean like gold and silver chains and coins?"

"And plates and candlesticks, even crosses. Do you remember where the rhubarb grew?"

Nikki nodded.

"By the pump. Across from Harry's kennel. Kurt, do you know what happened to Harry?"

"The police shot him. When they took over the house."

"They had no use for him, either," Nikki said bitterly, her eyes stinging, tears rolling down her cheeks. "And he wouldn't have behaved for Hanna and Lars, poor dog. Death is often the answer for true love. He was mine, and he cared deeply for me. In a way, I guess you could say he died for me. And the rhubarb?"

"A lot of the treasure was gone before the GDR took over the property, of course. Your mother left Leipzig with a mesh handbag that Karl made of gold links and painted black. The buttons on her coat were covered gold coin with diamonds enclosed in their shanks. Other precious stones were sewn in the hem of the fur. And when Johann and Uschi left, they carried gold as well."

Nikki began to laugh.

"I know! The silverware in the picnic hamper."

"Poor grade silverplate applied to gold," Kurt agreed. "Loose gems in the hollow handle of the knives. Not a lot, but enough for a beginning."

"That was why Vati opened the rhubarb patch so early that year. Peter and I were so puzzled by it. And the rest?"

"Ah, yes." Kurt was smiling now, too. "When Karl stored the metal away, he cast it in plaster of paris, painted and waterproofed, to resemble rock."

"And the treasure is still there?" Nikki stared at him in disbelief.

"As a matter of fact, no. Your friend, Peter, has it. He is the groundsman for the property. And when the rhubarb was dug up so that the well could be capped, he received permission to take the rocks. There is a very handsome rock garden in the rear of his home."

"Does he know about the rocks?"

Kurt's head nodded "yes," but it was a weak gesture.

"He is involved in all this? Quiet Peter?"

Kurt nodded again, his movements getting slower. Nikki reached out for his hand, softly cradling it in hers. When she looked over to him, she realized that he had fallen asleep.

When Julia returned to the room, Nikki drew her into the hall.

"Is all this talking good for Kurt? He tires so easily."

"It's probably not good for his body," Julia admitted, "but his mind and soul require it. Please, Monika, keep talking with him until there are no more words."

* * *

In the next several days, Nikki learned that Peter, a more shrewd observer than she was, had seen Vati working at the rhubarb patch. Apparently Herr Walz had, also, but he went to his grave without sharing the secret, even with his son. Under Kurt's direction, Peter had become involved in the business of aiding the hunted in finding freedom.

Some of those Peter helped escape had become politically suspect. Others were of Jewish heritage. And, after all these years, there were those whose intelligence and creativity required less restrictive environments.

"Did Hanna and Lars know about you?" Nikki asked Kurt. "Do they know what Peter is doing?"

"No. It was essential that they never suspect my connection with the escape network. Hanna doesn't even know that I am her brother. And they certainly will never think that Peter is involved. He has been very clever about keeping his activities secret."

Hanna and Lars had no children, Kurt told her. He had not seen them in years, but he was sure that their lack of family was intentional. They lived a very quiet life, keeping Frau Wentzler, now bedridden, at home with them.

"I felt it was safer for them if I did not visit," Kurt explained.

"What about Tante Uschi and Onkel Johann?" Nikki inquired. "Do you know where they went after they got to Berlin?"

"Johann is dead. Julia can tell you about Uschi, though. She still lives here. I wish you would visit her."

* * *

Julia was pleased to arrange the meeting. The next day she explained it to Nikki.

"You can see Uschi Behlke tomorrow, at eleven. She will wait for you near the exotic birds in the Zoological Gardens."

"How will I know her?" Nikki objected. "Wouldn't it be better if I went to her house?"

"She will not see you there. It is only a small, dark room in an old house. I have been there once, and it is very bad. So you will do what is necessary to save her pride," Julia insisted. "Perhaps you will take a small strudel and some cheese as a gift. She needs the extra food. I will tell you where to buy it."

"Be patient with her, Monika. Uschi is very old," Kurt counseled in a whisper. His voice, as well as his strength, was failing.

That evening, as Nikki sat with him, Kurt was more alert.

"Be sure you see Uschi Behlke tomorrow," he insisted.

"Yes, I am going. Julia showed me where to buy the gifts for her. You are sure I will recognize her?"

"I don't know," Kurt admitted. "Julia has not told her about me being here so I have not seen her. And Julia never knew her in the other days. But I think your heart will know even if your eyes do not. She loved you."

"But she loved Hanna better. Kurt, tell me what you know about Hanna. She came across to see Mutti at the end, and she sent me a note of reprimand. I have to believe that she disapproves deeply of what I have done with my life."

"It wouldn't by just you," Kurt said after a hesitation. "Hanna is a very bitter woman."

"Bitter? But she was always so lively, so full of fun. And in those days when it was just the two of us, so firm and brave."

"Yes, she was brave. I'd go as far as to call her courageous. Did you know that she and Lars took Oma Kohn down to the basement and buried her there in order to preserve the secret? But once she and Lars were married, Hanna no longer had anything to challenge her. And the system that the GDR has imposed is eating her up." Kurt's fingers clutched hard at Nikki's. "Monika, when I am gone, she will be your only blood relation. If ever you can go to her, do so. And whatever happens, whatever she says to you, do not think too harshly of her. You were both very young when you had to make choices beyond your experience."

"Of course." His references to the end of his life were more frequent, even if they were spoken in matter-of-fact tones. Nikki could hardly bear to think ahead toward the time of his death. And yet, because it was necessary, she smiled down at him. "Somehow I will see Hanna again."

If all other means of reaching her sister failed, there was her legacy. Money could usually do what all else forbade, she was sure, especially in the GDR.

* * *

Morning came cool and crisp, but with sunshine. It was a good day for meeting old friends, Nikki decided as she boarded the bus to the zoo. The tote bag, slapping periodically at her thigh, held the cheese and confections plus a box of chocolates she had added on her own. She wasn't sure that Tante Uschi really liked chocolates, but there had always been a supply when Mutti and her daughters visited at the Behlkes' home.

Nikki had visited Berlin's famous zoological collections during those months that her family had been in the city. Even though she detested Berlin, Mutti always left the room that the Gruen women had finally found for them to walk her daughter to and from school. On pleasant days, she and Nikki often spent a part of the afternoon at the zoo or the aquarium. After all, it served to fill those long, dreary hours while Vati attempted to re-establish himself in business.

Unlike later in Wiesbaden, Wera Groebel accompanied her daughter everywhere in Berlin because of the murders. According to both press and rumor, an unknown fiend accosted young girls, slaying them and leaving their bodies on the city's rubble heaps. And each victim had a red ribbon tied in her hair.

Vati, of course, traveled outside of Berlin. He made repeated trips to cities in the West, seeking employment. Yet, oddly enough, it had been right there in Berlin that Herr Stefan Rennecke had sought out Karl Groebel with the partnership offer.

Monika had seen Stefan as he arrived, an elegant man with silver hair, climbing out of the Diamler that was so out of place in the neighborhood.

The car's high gloss reflected the sun back into her eyes so that he seemed to be coming out of a spotlight into her life.

"You may take Kengi down to the doorstep and sit in the sun," Mutti had finally permitted after her daughter's behavior became increasingly unbearable. "But not one step away, do you understand?"

"Mutti misses Hanna," Monika had explained to the stuffed toy as they descended the long stairway to the beckoning warmth below. "And we have to do exactly as we are told. We don't want to end up wearing red ribbons."

* * *

How long they had been there before the car arrived, Monika was not sure. The cement of the doorstep was hard against her young bottom but to move would mean having to return to the little room in which everything, even Kengi, had to be put away in order to have space to move.

So the man's presence was exciting. When he came to a stop directly in front of her, she was looking at beautifully polished black shoes. The sun danced off of their surface, just as it did off the car.

"Good afternoon, child." His voice had a gloss, too, and his fingertips rested on her head. "Does a Karl Groebel reside here?"

The last word had been emphasized as if there was doubt. And it brought a quick response. This fine gentleman was the kind of person with whom Vati did business, Monika was sure. She supposed she should even offer to lead him upstairs, but that would mean going indoors, and the sunshine was far too precious, especially now that the elegant car was part of the scene.

"Up the stairs to the very top. It's the door on the right," she directed. A week later, the Groebels had climbed aboard the train for an uneventful, but to Monika, terrifying trip to Wiesbaden. She had spent a great deal of the journey in the carriage lavatory.

* * *

There were enough evergreens in the zoo gardens to keep the setting verdant even though most of the trees had lost their leaves. A kiosk supplied direction toward the aviaries. As Nikki stepped quickly along the walk, she passed many elderly people in ones and twos on the benches that lined the way. Some read. An occasional duo indulged themselves in checkers or chess. Others only stared.

Nikki was nearly to her destination when she realized that a change would be necessary. A frail old woman, wrapped in a black wool coat several sizes too large, was holding court to a flock of pigeons.

Perhaps it was the hands, showering bread crumbs upon the expectant heads, that told her this was Uschi Behlke. It certainly wasn't the face or body. All of the healthy roundness was gone, replaced by sharp planes and sagging skin. The blonde hair had faded to snow. And no rings except a plain gold band bedecked the graceful fingers.

"Tante Uschi?" Nikki breathed, her voice barely carrying above the comments of the pigeons.

"Monika!" The woman's tone and sudden movement sent the pigeons scurrying away. The arms came out uncertainly in the gesture of embrace. The hold that Uschi Behlke had on her was feeble, Nikki realized with dismay. Worse than that, the breath was laced with stale alcohol. But Nikki held her breath and returned the greeting.

The hour that the two women spent together was unbelievably difficult for Nikki. She wanted to cry out against the injustice that had left Tante Uschi in this condition. Kurt, for all of his suffering and medication, was a thousand times more lucid.

There were moments in which Uschi confused Monika with Hanna, once even with Wera, but her words never stopped. Perhaps the older woman spent so much time in conversation with the pigeons that talking to another human was hard. Nikki thought she sounded much like the birds. As Uschi chattered on, her hands moved on Nikki's arm, knees, and face as quickly as the words.

"Look what I brought for us to see," Uschi stopped at one point to delve through the bread crumbs to an object below. Once it was brought to light and the crumbs blown away, Nikki realized it was a photo album.

They went through it page by page. Many of the pictures Nikki could describe better than Uschi, but she bit her lip against the incorrect identifications. Other shots were older, taken before she was born, when Hanna was a small child. With these, she often doubted the names that accompanied the pointing finger. Still they were worth seeing, sights from a place and time to which return was not possible.

The sun's strength waned early, and Nikki realized that the woman was beginning to shiver. She drew herself nearer to Uschi and put her arm across the thin shoulders. A breeze reported to her nose staleness beyond the alcohol.

"Perhaps we can meet again, Tante Uschi. I still have your jewelry box, back in Darmstadt. Would you like to see it again?"

"No." The old woman's firmness shocked Nikki. "I have no need to see it. That life is passed and, soon, this one will be, too. I want to be with my Johann. Nothing more."

Yet, as Nikki was about to leave, firm fingers grasped her sleeve.

"One thing, if you please, child. I thank you for the fine cheese and candy and strudel. But a picture, perhaps. For the book?"

For a moment Nikki was uncertain. Then she pulled her wallet from her handbag. There was that terrible monstrosity that every girl on the Northwestern campus seemed to have, the portrait with diffused lighting, slightly out of focus, bare shoulders draped. For her the stole choice had been Malibu. She had hated it, but had taken the "special" package, lowest in price. Donna had the enlargement on the piano in the Chicago apartment. Doro carried one of the wallet-size prints. Mark, she guessed, had the second. This was the last.

When she passed it into Uschi's fingers, the woman smiled.

"Thank you, Hanna. I shall take very good care of it."

* * *

Nikki went directly from the zoo to the hospital, intent on reporting to Kurt that her promise had been kept. As she stepped into the cavernous lobby, Father Braun and Julia approached her. She recognized the stole he was folding away.

"It's over." Julia reached out to her. "Our dear Kurt is free at last."

The women stood together, arms intertwined. Just beyond them Father Braun was praying aloud, in German rather than in Latin. His informal supplication was that they, too, would find freedom and peace.

"But it really isn't over," Nikki objected later as she and Julia sat together in Julia's room. "The war has stopped. The escapes are successful. Yet everyone keeps dying. Tante Uschi hasn't much longer, either."

"It is hard on those who live through the uncertainties. Their spirits and their bodies are stressed beyond reason," Julia replied. "With some, it is disease that strikes from within. Their hearts fail, or their own cells destroy them. Others become ill from whatever is contagious around them. And there are also those, like Uschi Behlke, who seek recourse from the bottle. A whole new branch of medicine, Kurt said, needs to be developed to help people who must bear beyond their strengths."

"A whole new kind of living is what is needed, not just treatment after the diseases take over," Nikki mused. "Julia, what kind of living keeps people well?"

"A peace-filled life, of course," Julia answered promptly with a sad smile. "Isn't that what you have in the United States of America?"

Nikki smiled ruefully at the woman's innocence. She thought of union troubles, of the rebellious youth already beginning to identify San Francisco as their new Mecca, the soldiers moving in and out of Indo-China on temporary assignment, the political skirmishes.

"Would you like to go there, Julia?" Nikki offered. She was sure that David and Donna could make the arrangements. Julia had skills that were valuable.

"No, not now at least. I am on staff at Sankt Gertrauden. For now, I will stay. We will bury Kurt here. I want to be near him for a while. And Uschi still needs me." She reached out her hand to Nikki's fingers. "But we will stay in touch, won't we?"

Nikki nodded, looking down at their joined hands. She felt comfort flow. Still holding Julia's hand, Nikki suggested that Julia rest before the arrangements for Kurt's burial were begun. While her sister-in-law napped, Nikki phoned Paul.

"I'll be back in Frankfurt as soon as the funeral is over," she promised at the end of their conversation.

"No. You stay until Saturday," Paul insisted. "I'll come and get you then."

Later, Nikki and Julia were in the apartment's kitchen brewing a cup of tea when a knock sounded at the door.

"Yes, please, come in," Julia called out.

The door opened inward. Two women, the landlady and the other tenant, came into the room. Both were in tears. Nikki regarded them with surprise. Neither had known Kurt.

"Have you heard?" the older woman sobbed, reaching out to Julia. "He's dead. They shot him in Dallas."

"Who was shot?" Nikki demanded, trying to make sense of the message.

"Kennedy." The younger said it Ken-ned-dee, just as the people had chorused when he appeared at Rudolph Wilde Plaza.

"The President of the United States is dead," Nikki interpreted slowly, in English, then in German. It seemed only natural to stand up and go to comfort the women.

"And now there is no more hope." The landlady spoke bitterly. "He gave us hope, but it has died with him. And I shall die without knowing peace."

Julia broke away from the women to turn on the small radio next to the sink. There was no doubt that they were speaking the truth. Somber voices, some barely controlled, were reporting on the happenings in Dallas, Texas. The story, according to Nikki's reportorial training, was filled with "whats" and lacking in "whys."

At last the other women trooped sadly off to prepare themselves for the coming day, a November morning grey and chilled by weather and despair. Nikki turned to Julia as the reporters gave way to Bach in order to collect new details on the assassination.

"Julia, why is peace not possible?"

The woman shrugged.

"Perhaps because we are willing to place more trust and money in war and open conflict."

"Do you place your trust there?"

Julia was silent for a few minutes. Nikki wondered if she had forgotten the question.

"I suppose I do. I have never known anything else."

Nor, thought Nikki, had she.

247

As the song insisted, it was "beginning to look a lot like Christmas," especially at the Wiesbaden Bahnhof. With her handbag slung over her shoulder, a suitcase in one hand and a shopping bag overflowing with gifts in the other, Nikki suspected she was trying the holiday goodwill of other travelers as she attempted to reach the train station doors.

She found herself repeating a litany as she moved along, alternating apologies and wishes for the season. Finally she found her way blocked by a tour group that was forming up around a placard that read "Garmisch Parten-Kirchen." Rather than challenge the would-be sportsmen with their skis and poles, she found a pillar where she could set down her burdens until the throng marched toward the platform.

In spite of everything that had happened, she found herself buoyed by the approach of Christmas and grateful to the Kneipps for allowing her to share in their celebration. Spending the holidays with three generations of a loving family to anticipate, just like the old days in Leipzig, and being a part of the christening of Gretel Monika Agnes Kneipp should ease her feelings about her recent losses.

* * *

Finding, then burying, her beloved brother had bonded her once again to the past. Nikki knew now that she could not leave Europe until she had answers to all the questions which she had ignored during her years in America. Her new found resolve was so strong that she had hardly been aware of her surroundings as Paul drove her back to the West from Berlin. Vati had existed for a purpose greater than boundaries and officials. These became minor when compared to people and their freedom.

And there had still been no word from Gerry, not at her home in Darmstadt or at the office. Sometimes Nikki thought it would be wiser to let him become a part of the past also, one for which no more answers would be sought. She certainly didn't have a good track record with those she especially loved. Kurt was dead. Perhaps Vati, too, although that she still could not believe.

She had even questioned the wisdom of involving herself further with the Kneipp family after having caused, at least in her mind, what might have been disaster. Paul, also invited to share in the holiday visit but opting to be with Delia and Heike instead, had insisted that she not only could do so safely, but also that she must.

"We don't know that Liesel's attack was related to the assault on you. It was only the timing that was suggestive," he pointed out. "Besides, there has been no trouble since we left Zurich."

"What about Stefan at the festival," she reminded.

"Nothing happened there, did it?"

"It might have if we hadn't run. But I certainly had no trouble in Berlin," she allowed.

* * *

And it was true. Nothing suspicious had transpired, even after Kurt's death. Paul had come to Berlin for the burial service so that he could drive her out through the Eastern zone. It had been a small, nice service, taking place on the same day that the world's attention was focused on a larger ceremony taking place in the other hemisphere.

Father Braun had said the prayers over the coffin at Julia's request, not the full Mass for the Dead, since Kurt was not Catholic, but the words of a friend who respected the integrity and courage that surprisingly enough, Tante Uschi, although Nikki wasn't sure the woman knew who was being buried. Josephine and Maria Gruen also came, the former still looking very masculine even in her wheelchair. They were accompanied by a bent and wizened man that Nikki could not identify. Later Julia explained.

"The old people were part of the escape network with which Kurt used to work. The younger men and women who have taken on the duties did not dare come, of course, for fear of breaching their security."

So the man might have been one of the two readers that had shared the carriage when Monika was brought to Berlin. Nikki wasn't positive because no one of the trio acknowledged her presence.

Frank sent a message of sympathy to Julia and Nikki through Paul. He was unable to be present at the burial because he had to file copy on how Berliners were coping with Kennedy's death. If Julia's landlady and co-tenant were to be taken as examples, the people of the city were not managing well at all. Fraulein Karsch had roused Julia from bed the previous evening to make an emergency diagnosis of the landlady's chest pains and Julia had been sufficiently alarmed to recommend, with concurrence from the woman's physician, hospitalization. The younger woman was suffering from a sudden head cold and Julia had insisted she not come to the cemetery.

* * *

The skiers finally began to move along. Nikki hoped they would find the snow that they sought. Winter, thus far, had been kind to Europe. In the United States, it was a different matter. Heavy snow was the rule throughout the nation. The day before the Americans in the office had been marveling over the blizzard that dropped fourteen inches of snow in Memphis within twenty-four hours.

As soon as the barrier of skis and poles dissolved, she hoisted her load again. If she were not in Wiesbaden, she supposed she would be in Berlin. She had offered to go to Julia, but her sister-in-law had refused.

"I shall work double shifts over Christmas in order to free up other staff members so they may spend more time with their families," the nurse reported. "And I will visit Uschi. She will be pleased with the gifts you sent for her."

Nikki plunged forward again, hoping this time to reach the cab stands without further obstruction. But as she neared the doors, two nuns suddenly stepped in front of her like a pair of expectant penguins.

"Good afternoon, Fraulein," one greeted her in a voice, low in tone and pitch. "Aren't you Monika Groebel?"

She was about to deny her identity as she realized that habits did not necessarily mean religious conviction. With all the surplus cloth, any number of weapons could be hidden. Then she glanced from face to face. Those expressions of serenity were not easily counterfeited.

"I was," she admitted. "Although I use the name of Fisher now."

"Oh, good." The speaker's face creased in a lovely smile, and behind unframed spectacles, the brown eyes sparkled. "I use the name of Sister Magdaline. I was Ursula Hofer."

Nikki found herself lost in folds of black worsted as the former chums embraced. Ursi always had been the taller, and her vocation seemed to have added to her height.

"What brings you here?" she finally asked when they stepped back so that Nikki could meet Sister Elisabeth. Nikki had expected no welcome at the station. The holidays meant that the entire Kneipp family dedicated every possible moment to sales at the shop.

"Bruno, of course. He suggested that I come, and Sister Elisabeth was willing to accompany me," Ursi told her with a bright smile.

"But I thought Bruno had lost track of you." Nikki found herself answering smile for smile.

"True. You should have seen his face when Sister Elisabeth and I walked into the shop last week." The chuckle was familiar, too. "I guess he thought we had come to buy tobacco at the request of a priest. Anyway, he ignored other customers to come directly to us. And polite. You would not have believed!"

"Are you reconciled with your family?"

"Regretfully, no. But the order sent me here to teach, so perhaps, in time..." A shadow crossed her face.

"Sister Magdaline is our new art teacher," Sister Elisabeth supplied, looking surprised as her companions dissolved in laughter.

There would be no one at the apartment at this hour except Herr Kneipp, Nikki knew, and he would be working furiously to complete special orders for blended tobaccos. She invited the sisters to join her for coffee and

Christmas stollen at a café near the station. Sister Elisabeth seemed more puzzled than shocked as the old friends exchanged memories. She had been raised from infancy in an orphanage managed by her order.

"I used to blame the war for having taken my parents from me," she said during a pause late in the conversation. "But now I see that war is only one of many terrible things that break families apart."

The taxi delivered the sisters back to their convent before dropping Nikki at Taunustrasse 13. She was late, but even so, her coming surprised Herr Kneipp. Before she even had time to put her bags in the room in which Max and Bruno used to sleep, she was recruited to assist in packaging the tobacco mixtures.

* * *

The following day Nikki spent in the stockroom at the shop, resupplying displays and shelves from which wares seemed to disappear whenever she turned her back. She also helped care for Gretel, whose bassinette had been wheeled over to the store. For the most part, the baby slept through the bedlam. Then, at one in the afternoon, Bruno locked the shop door against further customers.

"I officially proclaim Christmas Eve as of right now," he announced, turning to face his family members and Nikki. "Let's go home and get to work on Gretel's first tree."

The holiday ritual didn't seem to impress the infant much. She slept through the decorating and the supper her parents hosted. In addition to Nikki, Frau Bocke was a guest at the table. Her son, of course, was busy with diners at the hotel. Herr Kneipp kept Gretel with him while the rest of the group attended Midnight Mass. Afterwards Frau Bocke returned to her apartment and the others presented their gifts to each other in the glow of the elder Kneipps' Christmas tree.

"It is very different from your Christmases in America?" Frau Kneipp inquired as she stroked the mohair stole Nikki had given her.

"Very!" Nikki agreed. She went on to explain that Hannukah, which her adoptive family celebrated, was a relatively minor Jewish holiday. The Christmas tree in the apartment had always been in the corner of her bedroom. But the Fishers had joined her in exchanging presents in order to honor her beliefs. Christmas Day she would spend with Doro and Max, of course. Details of a Christmas tree that stood on the floor and tickled the ceiling fascinated Nikki's listeners.

"But to use so much space," Frau Kneipp frowned. And Nikki had to take a few minutes to explain again about the size of Doro's house. She knew that her description made it sound like a mansion. She wondered what the reaction might be if she compared the Fishers' apartment to those of the space-frugal Germans. Both Kneipp flats would fit easily into her home in Chicago.

Christmas was a recent memory of good food and good friends when the day of Gretel's christening dawned. Nikki helped Liesel and Frau Kneipp prepare brunch for the family, after which they would go to the church. Following the ceremony, Bruno was hosting a larger meal at the Opelbad restaurant.

* * *

Paul's arrival brought such amazing news, however, that for a little while Nikki forgot her anticipation of the remainder of the day. They were going to cover IX Olympische Winterspiele in Innsbruck.

"The paper liked your sidebar interviews with the designers and models at the Frankfurt Fashion Fair," Paul told her. "They want you to do some of the same thing with the female athletes, coaches, and officials."

He had already begun the logistics for their stay in Austria. They had reservations at a hotel for five days prior to the opening until two days after the closing. And if Nikki wanted, they could go on to Vienna before flying back to Frankfurt.

"I don't know," Nikki told him doubtfully. "I keep thinking that someone is going to question my passport sooner or later."

"Not with the Olympics going on," he insisted. "It's not the size of the games next summer in Tokyo, but they figure on at least three-quarters of a million spectators. This will be the greatest number of outsiders that Innsbruck has known since the Romans invaded before the birth of Christ."

She nodded. It was highly likely that no one would notice the presence of Nikki Fisher among such an influx.

"Besides," Paul added, "Gerry will be there."

"He will?" Nikki frowned. "How do you know?"

"I talked to him on the telephone. He was calling for you, of course, to wish you happy holidays. And he said that he would definitely join us there. So I guess he has forgiven you or wants you to forgive him for whatever it was that happened between the two of you at the festival."

"I don't know that there is really anything to forgive on either side," Nikki told him. "He wants me to marry him, you see."

"Yes, that's exactly what I thought I was seeing on the face of your Mickey Mouse friend," Paul agreed with a grin. "But I thought your face said about the same thing."

"Except that I seem to be dangerous to love, and I didn't want Gerry endangered, too. But he couldn't understand that." She shrugged. "So he left."

"Oh, Nikki, Nikki," Paul groaned. "That is one helluva way to treat a man. Giving protection is a part of love to a man."

"But not to a woman?" She looked up skeptically at him.

"You may be right," Paul allowed after a pause to consider. "Well, it all starts anew next month. And just maybe you two can do it right this time."

"If at first, you don't succeed?"

"Exactly!"

Because she was godmother to Gretel, Nikki had the privilege of holding the infant at the baptismal font. After the sobering pledges regarding the child's upbringing, Gretel's expression of surprise when the holy water dripped through her fine hair to her scalp nearly brought Nikki to laughter. The prayer of blessing was aptly named. It allowed her to recover her demeanor before she disgraced herself by chuckling. Yet when she raised her eyes to the priest after echoing his "amen," she found his eyes were sparkling, too.

Bruno held out his arms to receive his daughter. For a moment, Nikki was overwhelmed with reluctance to release her hold on Gretel. So much of her return to Europe was focused on the past. But this little child was the future, and she wanted so much for her. Raising the infant's head, she brushed the small cheek with her lips and whispered a blessing, using Vati's words:

"Peace and freedom."

* * *

The day of the christening was fair, making the water in the Opelbad swimming pool an aquamarine that contrasted with the sapphire of the sky. The tables provided for the party lined the windows of the restaurant, overlooking the pool. Halfway through the meal, Paul let out a gasp that caught Nikki's attention.

"Will you look at that!" His hand gestured to the pool deck.

A group of individuals, mainly men, were marching out from the dressing rooms. All were wrapped in heavy robes and some wore rubber bathing caps.

"Isn't the pool closed?" he asked. "This is the end of December, after all."

Herr Kneipp began to laugh.

"It's sort of a tradition, either to end one year or begin the next with a swim."

"The German equivalent to Chicago's Polar Bear Club," Nikki supplied. "But instead of Lake Michigan, the hardies of Wiesbaden use the Opelbad. Vati used the pond on our estate."

"If that kind of insanity is carried on the genes, Gerry is in for a shock," Paul sighed. The swimmers had begun to drop their robes at the pool's edge. One gentleman, sinewy and totally bald, was swimming laps.

Nikki found herself shivering as she watched them.

"It skipped my generation," she grinned at Paul.

Gretel had fallen asleep long before the time for presentation of gifts to her. Many of the guests were long-time customers of the Kneipp boutique, and their presents reflected their interests and trades. There were books and pictures, toys and clothing, utensils and jewelry.

Nikki handed a jar of honey accompanied by a silver spoon to Liesel, grinning at her friend's surprise.

"My adoptive mother sent it," she explained. "You put a spoonful of honey in Gretel's mouth to make her words sweet. It is a tradition in Donna's family."

"How nice!" Liesel beamed. "What a beautiful idea that is. Can we do it as soon as she wakes up?"

Max and Doro had sent a gift, too. It was a lamp for a child's room, the light held up by the elephant's trunk. Nikki suspected that rewiring might be necessary to make it functional.

"Little Max has one just like it," she told Frau Kneipp as the gift was passed around for the guests to examine.

Nikki's gift for her godchild had cost a good portion of her prior month's salary. It was a garnet, contained in a gold basket and placed on a thin gold chain. Next year's ruby, however, would come from the treasures of the safe box. And for the succeeding four years, there would be one stone a year until, at age six, the initial letters of each precious gem in the necklace would spell her goddaughter's name. It would be, Bruno declared, a wonderful legacy.

Paul listened to Nikki's explanation with his head cocked, amazement and pleasure crinkling his face.

"Is that a German thing, Nikki?" he whispered to her when the guests' attention turned to the next presentation.

"I don't think so, but it is definitely European. Vati dated it back to the Love Court of Alinor of Aquataine. Why?"

"Look at this." He drew a second pipe out of his inside jacket pocket. It appeared brand-new. Around the bowl was a band of silver with four mounted gems.

"From Delia?" Nikki asked as she turned from diamond to emerald to amethyst to ruby. There was no point in looking up at the man. Delia was telling Paul that she found him "dear."

* * *

After all of the excitement of the day, Nikki expected sleep to come easily. But, after an hour of tossing about in her bed, she pulled on the robe that Frau Kneipp had loaned her and went to the kitchen. Her fingers brushed the wall next to the door in an attempt to locate a light switch.

Finally she remembered that the nearest lamp was over the table to her left, and a pull cord brought it to life.

"Would you be willing to join an old man for a glass of brandy?" Herr Kneipp spoke softly from the living room. "If so, there is a decanter and glasses on a tray near the pantry."

"I didn't know anyone was still up," Nikki answered in a low voice. "It sounds like a great idea."

When she pushed the living room door open with her foot, Herr Kneipp laid aside the book he had been reading and made room on the table next to him for the tray.

"There are still three suspects, and the detective can't decide which is most likely," he told her, gesturing to the chair on the far side of the table. "Use Agnes' spot. It is the most comfortable."

Nikki poured the amber liquid into the snifters, passing one to him. She lifted her glass, cupping its broad bowl with both hands. As the liquid swirled, she smiled across the table.

"Vati always did it this way."

"There is much of Karl in you, my child. Has this journey of homecoming been what you expected?" He took a sip of liquid before turning to stare at her. "Better? Worse?"

"Both, I guess. I thought I was only coming to observe what Europe has become. Instead I have become a part of Europe again." She raised her glass to her lips. "It's hard. I'm afraid because I am having to deal with the past."

"Your past," he corrected. "But you are staying? You could run back to your other life."

"No!"

"Just like Karl. Stubborn."

"I hope so. I want to be more like Vati, strong and able to continue those things which are important to him."

"You believe Karl lives?"

"Yes. I have to believe it." Nikki's hand came up and her back stiffened. "If I do what he left unfinished when he disappeared, we will meet again."

"Do you really know what your father did?"

"Some of it. Kurt told me before he died." She clutched the stem of her glass tightly. "But, more important, Kurt told me why Vati was so involved in the lives of others, even when it meant danger for him. I am sure that Vati left us that night in Switzerland to protect us from harm. It wasn't that he had stopped loving us or that he didn't want to be with us. Herr Wolfgang, did you know Stefan Rennecke?"

"I saw him when he came here. I knew his reputation. Agnes and I tried to get Wera to leave you with us. That man was conniving, and we were afraid for you." His face grew red as he talked.

"You were right." Nikki was shocked by how easily she said it. "He is a thoroughly evil man. I saw him again last fall and my hatred made me sick. Why did Mutti agree to live with him? Especially after loving Vati?"

"I suppose she thought she had no choice. Wera, who had always had Karl's strength to protect her, was left to fend for herself and, more important, to take care of you," he said slowly. "And the cancer was probably already growing within her. She did what she thought was right. Remember, at the end, she did give you up to keep you safe."

He pushed himself forward in his chair and refilled both snifters.

"You really think Mutti knew about..." Nikki began before he shook his head at her.

"I am sure she knew she did not love Rennecke. And if there was no love, there was probably also no trust. He came at a time when Wera was vulnerable and took advantage of the situation. But she made sure he could not keep you. Remember her kindly, Monika."

Nikki stared down into the liquid. If it were as Herr Kneipp was saying, Mutti's concern for her daughter had been late in coming.

"Kindness? I don't know. But with sadness, definitely. I am sad for her, for Kurt, for Onkel Johann and Tante Uschi, and all the others who have been literally killed by a war that does not end. That's why I have to do it Vati's way. He helped many people to find freedom. Did you know?"

"Know? No." There was a near smile on Wolfgang Kneipp's face. "But I suspected. It was easy to see that he dealt in wealth and yet claimed little for himself. And it is very much within his character. Sometimes at night he and I would sit like this and discuss philosophy."

"Goethe," Nikki spoke.

"Ah, yes. Especially Goethe."

"Today, when I was holding Gretel in the church, I could hardly bear giving her back to Bruno. If I can't help those who are gone, I must do something for those who are being born. I am very rich, after all." She smiled. "I must use my inheritance from Vati to carry on his legacy of caring. Since I can't help everyone, let me at least give peace and freedom to the children—the innocents."

"Freiheit fur die Unschuldigen." Herr Kneipp raised his glass.

"To freedom for the innocents," Nikki repeated, and they both drank deeply.

* * *

The mattress was lumpy and the air still smelled of yesterday's cabbage, but Nikki awoke on her first morning in Innsbruck feeling at peace with herself and marvelously alert. That was, she knew, because the last voice she had heard the previous evening was Gerry's.

Making telephone calls, especially long distance, from the resort town was a challenge, she had discovered. Three attempts to get through to Zurich had been unsuccessful. The fourth time, her efforts had been rewarded, and she had settled into the elderly overstuffed chair next to the upstairs telephone. Gerry's number had been logged on the sheet beside the instrument and now the timer was running.

"Did you have any trouble on the way?" was the first thing Gerry wanted to know. The second was "Do you still love me?"

"Of course, I do." She beamed as if her expression could carry over the line. "I miss you terribly. You'll still be here on the twenty-eighth? There's so much we have to talk about. And plans to make. I still like Herr Kneipp's name for the project—Freiheit fur die Unschuldigen, don't you?"

"So long as you don't try to turn it into American vegetable soup," Gerry chuckled. "If you ever abbreviate it to FFDU, I shall strangle you!"

"But we could call it 'The Innocents' for short, couldn't we?"

"Sure, we can, Nik. It would fit the headline space better." He was still laughing, but she heard his merriment fade. "Seriously, Nikki. Don't dream too big. There are so many innocents and only one woman I love."

"Paul said the same thing on the way up from Vienna," she answered before she thought.

"Paul said what?" The words of the query were slow and suspicious.

"That it would be an overwhelming undertaking and that it had to be shared." Even Gerry's jealousy made her feel warm and wanted.

"Right! And now that you are willing to share, there are many of us who can and will help. We'll talk about…"

"Gerry, I can't hear you!" The roar of the shower reverberated the wall next to her chair and a water pipe banged.

"Never mind. I'll say it all again when we're together. That and a whole lot more," Gerry promised as another guest of the inn, his striped flannel robe stretched taut across his ample midsection, came shuffling toward Nikki.

"How much longer?" the man whispered loudly in French.

"A minute, only," Nikki replied, holding up a finger to illustrate the point, before returning her attention to Gerry. "There's a guest waiting to use the phone. Shall I call you tomorrow evening, honey? I don't think you can get through to me, even at the press room."

"Not tomorrow. I have a planning council meeting starting in the afternoon, and I expect it will run until all hours. How about the next day? Anytime after four-thirty, but before seven. I'll be home and waiting to hear your voice."

"So long as it doesn't interfere with your date at seven?"

"That's right, Green Eyes. I don't get dinner at the mayor's home very often."

Watery Eyes was more like it, Nikki decided as she wiped away the tears caused by the cigar smoke the Frenchman was exhaling impatiently. His hand wiped a collection of ash from his robe.

"Fini, Cheri?" he inquired.

"Gerry, I *have* to hang up," Nikki insisted before she broke into a fit of coughing. "I'm about to go up in a cloud of cigar smoke. But I love you anyway. Dream of me."

After the connection was broken, Nikki took her time in completing the log of time used. As she surrendered her place to the man, he grabbed at the receiver. From the scowl on his face, she decided he spoke German as well as French.

* * *

"I cannot believe how warm it is," Nikki marveled as she sat with Paul at the outdoor table, its umbrella tilted to shade the occupants from the sun. Steam rose from their cups of coffee to dissipate quickly in the comfortable breeze. "Mid-January in the Tyrolean Alps isn't supposed to be like this."

"And they couldn't agree more!" Paul gestured to the trucks rumbling, like a line of marching elephants, along the street behind them. The vehicles' beds were heaped with snow.

The weather, they had discovered upon their arrival from Vienna the previous day, was the biggest news in Innsbruck. At that time, early evening, the balmy afternoon was gone. With the sun's departure, roads and walks had become treacherous sheets of ice. Their last few miles in the rented car had been hard driving, and Paul had been white-knuckled behind the steering wheel.

Even worse had been walking the short distance from car to inn. Nikki, alarmed over Paul's ability to balance himself, had insisted on having their bags carried in by man from the hostelry staff. And her concern had caused her partner, already stressed by the drive, to growl at her. Morning, however, had brought more nice weather on the "foehn," Austria's answer to the chinook wind, and the melting had begun once more.

"I can't see how the imported snow is going to do any good." Nikki shook her head at the noise of the trucks. "It will melt away again."

"But maybe not all of it. What's left will give something to build on tomorrow." Paul slid a stack of papers across to her. "The press office sent these over to us. I found them at the desk this morning."

"Is there an announcement about how and by whom the games will be canceled?" she asked bleakly.

"Not that I could find. There is a release, however, about the whereabouts of the athletes. A number of them are finishing their training at other European resorts and won't arrive until later this week." He pulled a set of stapled pages apart from the pile and handed it to her.

Her eyes skimmed the information. It was in English.

"Why don't you ask the press office to give us releases in another language as well? German or French. Then we can compare them."

Paul nodded agreement over the rim of his cup.

"Just look at this." Her finger crossed a paragraph. "In the Olympics the world is still able to recognize the German people as one. It's rather nice."

"Also rather short-lived, I'm afraid. The question of the single German team was a hot subject at the meeting of the international committee. I read a summary of the minutes last week. There's agreement to field the single German team in 1964, but I think the sentiment is for two, come 1968."

"That's sad," Nikki observed.

"But realistic," he told her. "Both sides want to showcase their successes, after all, so they can boast that their way is best. And two teams mean twice as many athletes get to compete. To me, that may be the best argument. Taking part is supposed to be the reason for the games."

"Sure, it is." Nikki laced her agreement with sarcasm. "But we, like every other news correspondent, will herald the number of medals our country's competitors win. Since I've come over here, I have been having a hard time remembering who 'we' are. Does the U.S. have a chance for many medals?"

Paul shrugged.

"I'm not really into sports. That's why the paper is sending a man from Chicago to cover the actual competition. But when I talked to him last week, he thought it would be iffy. Figure skating has always been our strength, and we lost the whole international team in that crash. Our best are a couple of youngsters."

Nikki continued paging through the press packet. She drew another set of sheets out.

"At least we start out fairly even with judges," she observed. The names, she found, meant little to her. Pulling a pencil from her handbag, she circled the several who came from the Midwest. The might be interview possibilities. Having finished that task, she paged through the other sheets. At the German list, she stopped.

"Paul, look here!" She thrust the pages into his face, nearly colliding with his coffee cup.

"I'm looking," he agreed. "What am I seeing?"

"Nordic cross-country. Lars Wentzler."

"Okay. Got it. Who's Lars Wentzler?"

"I think that's my brother-in-law. They list his hometown as Leipzig. Not exactly accurate, since he and Hanna live in a village on the outskirts, but I'm sure it's the same person. Lars used to compete in cross-country as an amateur racer."

"Looks like there will be two reunions then." He pushed his cup away from him. "Gerry and Lars."

Anticipation stabbed at her. Up to now, seeing Gerry again had been a future event. But time was getting short. She had to begin to think of what she was going to say. Face-to-face was going to be a lot different from the almost nightly telephone conversations that had begun after her talk with Herr Kneipp.

Beyond throwing herself in Gerry's arms—not a very plausible way of initiating a meeting in public—she hadn't really planned how she might greet him. Her life had changed so much since that day of disagreement last fall. Now she was almost positive that she would not return to the United States when the assignment with the newspaper ended. Two things held her in Europe: Gerry and The Innocents. Life without either was impossible. And there was still the chance, and even she had begun to admit it was slight, that Vati was alive.

With Lars, however, she could visualize the encounter. Lars had always been kind to the child, Monika, but that seven-year-old remembered him mainly as an appendage of Hanna. And Hanna still believed that her younger sister had deserted Mutti during a period of desperate need. Would she be able to explain to Lars those horrors that only a woman could understand? Even trying to find words would be embarrassing. And then there was the question of his taking back the message and delivering it in the spirit it was meant.

She walked slowly, following Paul to the little car in which they were to make an inspection tour of the competition sites. As he held the door for her, he voiced the thought that had suddenly entered her mind.

"Perhaps your sister is accompanying her husband."

They stopped at the press headquarters before beginning their trip. Her questions about the judges brought immediate anxiety to the clerk to whom Nikki spoke. She fond her query bucked up to a more senior official who expressed concern over the possibilities of bribery. If an American reporter thought there was something newsworthy about a German judge, the Olympic press staff wanted to know what it was.

Nikki tried to think of the proper words to explain her interest. To tell the truth, that she sought a brother-in-law that she had not seen in fourteen years, might alert the Austrians of her status. The conscienciously neutral nation, who held to its situation zealously, could easily expel her, claiming fraud in her credentials.

"I believe he is a relative of a close friend," she finally lied, with an anxious smile at the man. "I only want to introduce myself to him."

He was considering the request, his round and ruddy face screwed up around a bulbous nose. Nikki was positive that he was trying to decide whether he could become a party to a bribe. The fact that no American had ever been a contender in the Nordic events should be on her side, she thought. But reality apparently was not sufficient.

"The judges are in meetings this day," he told her. "I am not empowered to give out the meeting sites. However, you could take your request to the office that manages the judging. The people there should make the decision."

* * *

"It might be easier to call around at the inns," Paul observed when she reported on the referral. "Would you like to do that?"

"No. In this, I want to go by the book. I'd hate to give anyone the idea that I am not the Nikki Fisher with the American press pass."

Surprisingly, the judging office was not particularly upset by her request. People wanting to make or renew acquaintances with judges seemed to be routine. The woman with whom she talked suggested that she also might want to interview a former Austrian skier who had excelled in Alpine events. There was no need to ask with which nation the woman's loyalty lay.

"I have Lars's hotel, and the meeting he is attending is expected to end no later than three," she told Paul with a grin of conquest when she returned to the car. "So let us tour away."

Except at the indoor ice arena, they met furious activity at every stop. At the bobsled run, stern-faced officials were glaring down at the surface that glared back. Nikki was able to translate their wrathy comments about the waterslick that covered the ice.

"It's a shame," Paul said when she had turned comments into fairly unprofane English. "The Army built this run and the toboggan course. It took twenty-thousand bricks of ice carried in from the higher peaks."

"You've been reading more of the IOC flack," Nikki accused.

"Damned right. It makes impressive sense." Paul stumbled, and for a moment, Nikki held his weight. He recovered his footing, patting her shoulder in gratitude. "The problem with the Winter Games is that everything is on a hill."

Later he stopped the car in front of the Olympic village. Considering that the opening ceremonies were only a few days away, activity there was minimal.

"It looks just like an apartment complex," Nikki complained.

"Which is what it is destined to become."

"Wouldn't chalets have been pretty?"

"Someone already thought of that," Paul laughed. "He was voted down."

"Being in the majority doesn't mean you are right!" she shot back.

Nikki turned down both of Paul's offers, first that he accompany her to Lars's hotel, and second that she take the little car. At three-thirty, it was becoming markedly cooler, but she wanted to walk, using those last steps to think of what she wanted to say and the order in which her thoughts should be expressed. If it were possible, Paul suggested, she should invite Lars to have dinner with them.

"And what if Hanna has come?"

"Then both of them. I'm sure I will like your sister. Blood runs true."

* * *

All of Nikki's potential plans, however, fled from her mind when she walked into the lobby of the inn to which the Austrian patriot had directed her. Right in front of her, on a couch in the lobby, sat Mutti. It was the Wera Groebel of Leipzig, austerely elegant and at ease with her surroundings.

The woman glanced up. Her composure shattered, to be replaced by an expression of astonishment. Beautifully manicured fingers dug into the upholstery, the rings they bore sparkling beneath the chandeliers.

"You look just like Mutti," Nikki exclaimed, running across the lobby to reach her sister.

"And you have Vati's face," Hanna returned, tears rolling down her cheeks. Nikki, standing before her, began to cry with her.

Without being aware of it, the two women had collected a ring of spectators who were not sure what action should be taken to deal with these hysterical females. Lars arrived to disperse the crowd.

"If you are going to flood the premises, why not do it in private?" he demanded. His persuasion continued until he finally led them, sniffling and snorting into tissues that Nikki had supplied, upstairs.

In the hotel room, he brought sanity at last. Each woman was given a glass of schnapps with which to compose herself. After he had slid out of his overcoat, he turned to face them again.

"What miracle brings you here, Kleine Maus? We thought you were in the United States."

It was dark outside before Nikki had completed her story. And her stomach told her that Paul was probably waiting to hear from her about dinner.

"Can you eat with us?" she asked. "I mean, officially, will it be permissible?"

Lars frowned, considering the matter.

"Perhaps it is not wise." Then he brightened. "But if we were to be in the same restaurant at the same time?"

Hanna looked hopeful.

"There is your identity to protect from the Austrians," she explained unnecessarily to Nikki, clinging to her sister's hand. "And we are undoubtedly watched. The GDR has a long memory when it comes to defectors."

"We should have these days together," Nikki said stubbornly. "All the governments of the world should not be able to deny us."

"So we will take a little care," Lars decided. He named the restaurant and the time. "Hanna and I will go first. It is very popular with the judges, also very crowded. Perhaps we shall need to share our table with you and your journalist friend. After all, you have established that you know kinsfolk of ours."

* * *

Nikki left their inn to return to hers, pleased with the plan and eager to tell Paul about her joy in being with Hanna again. There was a light rain. She wondered if it would wash away all the snow that had been imported during the day, or if it might, itself, turn to crystals. The official word, according to Paul, was that the Olympic hosts no longer hoped for snow, feeling that what man had made would be spoiled if nature unexpectedly contributed fresh powder.

If only Hanna hadn't talked about the East German knowledge of the Groebels. The thought of observation was spooking Nikki as she marched from one pool of street light to the next. She could be followed so easily and the thought made her shiver. It wasn't really paranoia, she told herself. The rain, not yet changed to sleet, was very wet. The shoulders of her jacket were chillingly damp. She fought to keep her teeth from chattering.

The encounter was as casual as Lars had predicted. Nikki and Paul arrived at the planned time and were told that no private tables were available. She left her bright yellow rain slicker with a dismayed attendant. She should have worn the more sedate cloth coat, Nikki realized, but she didn't want it, like the ski jacket, soaked through. She only hoped the jacket would be dried by morning. The inn at which they were staying turned off the heat at eleven o'clock.

When she and Paul observed the dining room over the shoulder of the maitre d'hote, Lars rose and gestured to them. His greeting as they were led over to the end of a long table where he and Hanna were seated was totally correct.

"We meet again so soon, Miss Fisher. My wife and I would be glad to have you and your friend dine with us."

"Thank you, Herr Wentzler." Nikki introduced Paul to Hanna and Lars.

The conversation during their meal was what would be expected of people who were only casually acquainted. Nikki feigned a lack of knowledge about Leipzig. Paul didn't have to do so. He was thoroughly enjoying Lars's commentary of the history of the area. Hanna spoke about their daily lives, expanding the knowledge of their circumstances.

"My husband is kept very busy painting signs," Hanna remarked. "He does a great deal of work for the government. And then, of course, he works with the committee to promote cross-country skiing."

"And what do you do?" Nikki asked eagerly.

"I am an overseer in a factory that makes stockings for the national security forces," Hanna stated. "It is a very old plant. Once, silk hosiery was manufactured there. The manager, Herr Friederich Mueller, succeeded his father. Many of the employees remember the older man. In fact, many of us have lived in the area since birth. One of our long-time friends, Herr Walz, said that he was going to come to the games for a few days. He is a well-known gardener and takes care of the grounds at the factory. Perhaps I can arrange for him to meet you. He was a good friend of our little sister, and he would enjoy hearing about her."

Nikki would have been content to remain with her family all night. The restaurant staff, however, had other ideas for the use of the space which the quartet occupied. At last it was necessary to give up their places to waiting diners.

When they reached the foyer, Nikki could see that the rain was now pelting down. Since Hanna and Lars had walked over from their inn, she insisted her sister take her coat. She and Paul had only to dash to the car. Hanna, realizing that this was another opportunity to meet, agreed to the loan only if Nikki would take her coat instead. The woman's face was straight, but her eyes danced as she watched Nikki take the Persian lamb that Mutti had been forced to leave behind on that long ago Easter. An Nikki was not at all surprised when the whiff of mothballs assaulted her nose.

She and Paul departed first, crossing the parking area toward their car. Paul had her door open when the explosion came. They both swung around to see what had occurred.

The man who stood in the light from the restaurant was unmistakably Lars. At his feet was a bundle of vivid yellow.

Section Three

✳ ✳ ✳

Once There Was a Dream

"Live dangerously and you live right." —Goethe

Chapter Twelve

✶ ✶ ✶

The Ravens Flock

"**B**ut you can't do that!" Paul insisted. "Your keeping vigil over the sick bed of a casual dinner companion won't be regarded as normal behavior. Someone is going to ask questions and, immediately, your identity is suspect. I'm not even sure that an observer couldn't see the relationship between you and Hanna just by looking."

"You know what?" Nikk's jaw jutted with her words. "I don't care."

"You don't care about The Innocents?" Paul's eyebrows rose.

"But Hanna is my sister, the only family I have left!" Nikki protested.

"Then consider her," Paul pleaded. "Your continued presence in the hospital will endanger Hanna and Lars, raise questions within the GDR. It's one thing to come by the hospital to see how she is doing. It is quite another act to remain."

"I suppose that is true." Nikki looked across the table at Lars who seemed completely absorbed in his coffee cup. Hanna was in surgery, and there was nothing he could do but wait. Earlier the three of them had talked with a policemen regarding the shooting. There hadn't been much to tell. Nikki changed to German and recapped Paul's comments. "I don't want to do anything to hurt you, Lars."

"What more could be done?" He stared bleakly at his sister-in-law. "My wife has been shot. Is that not enough?"

"The bullet struck her upper leg," Paul reminded patiently when Nikki finished the translation. The discussion as to whether the wound was going to prove fatal had been held already. And Lars came back with the same statement as before.

"It is not where she was hit, but the fact that she was fired upon that makes the difference. There was no reason. We have always obeyed their law." He looked apologetically at Nikki. "In fact, we have been extra careful because Hanna was Karl Groebel's daughter."

"Is this the first time Lars and Hanna have been out of East Germany?" Paul asked after considering Nikki's repetition of Lars's words.

"It is for Lars. Hanna was in Wiesbaden when Mutti was dying."

"Then Stefan Rennecke knows Hanna's identity?"

"You think..." Nikki began, forgetting to translate.

"It's possible. We don't know what's on Rennecke's mind, but he may not want the two of you spending time together."

"But he's not here," Nikki insisted, then provided a digest of the conversation for Lars.

"Herr Rennecke is in Innsbruck," Lars reported. "He is staying at our hotel. We had cocktails with him the night before last. In fact, Herr Rennecke asked if we corresponded with you."

"He's here," Paul guessed, using Nikki's expression as a clue. His coffee mug struck the table for emphasis. "Hanna was wearing your raincoat. You were the one who was supposed to be shot. Damn it. We should have seen it coming. But all that blackbird stuff seemed so remote."

Nikki grabbed at Paul's fingers, needing to maintain a grasp on stability. The blackbird, suddenly the symbol of incredible evil, was casting a malevolent shadow over her life. It seemed only fitting that Stefan Rennecke would operate under such a sign.

"Stefan Rennecke hates me, more than you can imagine," she told Paul. "You are right. I am a danger to Hanna. But what do I matter to Stefan? Why can't he leave me and mine alone."

"I'm not sure. But I have a gut feeling that the contents of your safe deposit box has something to do with it. There was no trouble with Rennecke before you found the key." Paul stood and waved across the room. "Here comes the doctor who was working on Hanna."

* * *

Despite the good news the surgeon brought them, Nikki was not particularly pleased when Paul led her away from the hospital. Hanna had done well in surgery, and there was no reason why she should not be recovered sufficiently to return to the hotel within seventy-two hours. Lars was going to stay at Hanna's bedside. But, with Paul, he agreed that Nikki should come by only as a casual visitor, perhaps early in the evening or the next day.

If Nikki hadn't been pleased at the men's decision, she was even more discouraged on her return to the inn. The man at the desk had handed her a telegram. She'd been expecting Gerry to notify her when he would arrive so her fingers tore eagerly at the yellow envelope. But the words froze her hopes as surely as the night temperatures in Innsbruck turned the water to ice.

"COMPLICATIONS KEEP ME HERE STOP PERHAPS DARMSTADT NEXT MONTH STOP GERHARDT" the paper read.

Disappointment made her eyes sting and her hand tremble. Sure that she could not control her voice, she thrust the wire at Paul.

His softly spoken "I'm sorry, Nikki," didn't help either. He was only a darkness in a halo of light as she followed him up the stairway. If she could only reach her room, she would allow herself the luxury of a good cry.

At her door, however, Paul stopped her with a firm grip on her arm.

"You have exactly five minutes to bawl your eyes out," he insisted. "Then we are going to get down to work. The black birds seem to leave you alone when you are about our boss's business."

Nikki found that all she could do in the set interval was to mop up her eyes. Work, she supposed, was a good idea. That was, after all, what the paper was paying her to do. Her fear of Rennecke was turning to furor at his black birds' attack on Hanna. But the abruptness of the telegram still rankled. "Gerhardt!" His failure to sign Gerry made her wonder if he had really understood and forgiven her earlier intransigience. And the word "Love" had been missing as well. Surely he could afford to pay for the word. Maybe the love wasn't there anymore. That thought made her shiver.

"Well, what do I do today, boss?" she asked briskly when Paul arrived at the promised time.

"Here's a list of competitors. I am going over to see about U.S. television coverage. You are going to start doing interviews. There's a young skater from Ohio who may be worth a story. Her name's Fleming. Maybe you could pair her story with the boy from New Jersey. He has a fun name—Scott Ethan Allen. They're both under sixteen," Paul told her. "It might be interesting to see how they are responding to the pressures."

"Figure skaters, right?" She looked up for agreement. "At least they should be practicing in town. Anyone else?"

"Why not talk to a couple of the American judges?" Paul suggested. "Maybe you can contrast their views with some of the Europeans. That would give you a reason to have talked to Lars. Just in case anyone cares."

She jotted down the idea on another page of her folded interview sheets, plain white paper creased vertically.

"By the way, have you seen a pencil sharpener anywhere?" She frowned at her yellow pencil, its graphite worn down to the wood.

"Give it here." Paul pulled out his pocket knife and pried the blade open. He walked over to the waste basket and began shaving at the pencil. "Any more? One is hardly enough."

She pulled three more pencils from her handbag, none of which had been used. Deftly he carved a point on each.

"Be back here by six," he told her as he folded the blade. "We'll find some place for dinner, maybe somewhere where the locals sing and swing their beer steins."

"Maybe this once," Nikki said doubtfully. "But I can't afford many lapsful of suds. I only brought a few clothes."

After Paul left, Nikki crossed to the window to check the weather. Today, at least, the sun was shining. She wondered what had become of her slicker. It might have been discarded at the hospital or perhaps the policeman who had talked to them about the attack had borne it away as evidence. Either way, it was probably gone, which was just as well. She didn't want to see the garment again. That left her duffle coat and Mutti's Persian lamb. And she doubted that the latter was an appropriate garment for a reporter on a sports beat.

Her choice was correct, she decided, as she walked toward the ice arena. Short wool coats and ski jackets were *de rigeur*. From time to time she found people turning to stare at her. She wondered if the observers thought she might be a competitor. Not hardly, she laughed to herself.

If she were an athlete, it certainly wouldn't be a cold weather report. She remembered grimly accompanying David to Fox River Grove one weekend for a Midwest speed skating competition. It had snowed the entire time. If there was anything worse than being a winter athlete, it was being a winter sports spectator. She smiled broadly at the thought as the attendants at the arena checked her credentials.

The next hours were spent in getting her story. Some of the time Nikki just sat near the rink periphery, watching the coaches work with their pupils. Several skaters were on the ice at once, some accompanied by their mentors. Other coaches leaned over the rail, calling instructions. The practice was confined to single movements or what one woman, shouting in French, termed "flow." It was obvious that no contestant was giving away big items from his or her competitive programs.

By moving around the rink, Nikki was able to speak with a number of persons connected with the skaters: parents, school figure coaches, costumers, and friends. Each gave her some fact or insight. Many bemoaned the air crash that resulted in death for most of the U.S. skating team. Neither American child had a chance for a medal at this point, she was informed. But the Allen boy, given more experience, might just make it in international competition.

The Fleming girl was doubtful. She was too much the ballerina, a Swiss coach confided. Figure skating demanded vigor. As he was talking, Nikki looked across the ice at a blond Russian couple, admiring their grace and elegance. Perhaps, she thought sadly, the man was right. But the pair's effortless movements seemed so appropriate, artistry matching medium to message.

She finally got an opportunity to speak to each of her young targets. Neither's comments surprised her. To be young and in the Olympic Games was beyond expectation. They were trying to enjoy and absorb. One thing was certain. They felt no great pressure upon them.

It was mid-afternoon when she took a lunch break with a British reporter. They ate a small café near the arena. He had been in the press office earlier, dealing with the death of his country's fifty-year-old tobogganer. Nikki listened quietly to his story for she had missed out on the news the prior day. The athlete had been killed in an accident on the Mount Patscherkofel run.

"I think they should cancel the competitions for both tobogganing and bobsledding." His expression was stern. "Those runs are just too fast for the skill and equipment. But don't tell our sledders I said so. Tony Nash would strangle me for even thinking it."

His comments turned to bobsledding. Didn't she think it was a marvelous sport? Nikki shrugged as he went on without awaiting an answer. The only bob run in the United States, a relic from the 1932 Olympics according to the background material she had read, was at Lake Place. Could it be, she mused, that Britain had so many more runs? His next statement answered that.

British bobsledders spent their winters in Switzerland. Smart men, she applauded. Despite all the excitement here, she wasn't at all sure that she would not rather be in Switzerland with Gerry and his "complications." It certainly would have been better for Hanna if she had not come.

When she described her assignments, beyond translating for Paul, he nodded. And the reporter laughed as he made his suggestion for a good interview.

The Mongolians, he told her, had just arrived to compete in the games. And they had not gone through the rigamarole of filling out entry blanks. The person to whom she needed to talk was that nation's female cross country specialist. He consulted his notepad.

"Jigjigy Jazvondulem." He pronounced the name slowly, then spelled it out for her. "How do you like that for a terrific name?"

She declined his invitation to visit the bob run when the meal was over. And since Nikki doubted that she could talk with Jigjigy even if she could locate her, she decided to visit the hospital on the off chance that she could see Hanna.

* * *

Nikki was at the reception desk, waiting her turn for attention, when the familiar figure entered the lobby. Hans Germeyer, carrying a bouquet sheltered from the elements by a cone of cellophane, stopped abruptly when he recognized her.

"Hans, what in the world brings you here?" she asked, smiling broadly as she crossed to where he stood. His face showed no greeting, only surprise.

"I thought I had come to visit you," he managed, recovering to smile back at her. The flowers were transferred to her grasp and Nikki was enveloped in an enthusiastic hug. "I heard that an American woman reporter from your paper had been injured. Your friend, Gerhardt Mehler, told me last week that you had been assigned to Innsbruck so I just assumed...I'm glad I was wrong."

"It was the wife of a German judge," she told him. "I had lent her my slicker." Someone else, besides Paul and herself, must have witnessed the shooting, Nikki realized. She wondered if the police were aware. "How did you hear about it?"

She pushed the covering back from the edges of the flowers. Most of them were roses. His generosity amazed her.

"The manager of the restaurant where the shooting took place told me during lunch today. And I just added up the numbers wrong. How delightful to learn of my mistake! Have you time for a drink?"

"I'd like that," she told him. Hans Germeyer was a charming companion. If it hadn't been for finding Gerry, she might have spent more time with him in Zurich, she knew. "But I came over to see how Frau Wentzler, the woman who was injured, is progressing. Let me ask about her. And, if you don't mind, I'll send up the flowers."

"You had better remove the card first," Hans cautioned. "It would make no sense to the lady, I fear."

Hanna, according to the receptionist, was resting comfortably. Her husband was with her. And the flowers would be welcome. Nikki handed them over, knowing that Lars would need an explanation for the bouquet later. At this point, he was probably too worn out physically and emotionally to see anything odd in its arrival. Nikki resolved to cut dinner short this evening to come back to the hospital. Paul would have to do his singing and swinging alone.

* * *

There certainly was no shortage of places to eat and drink in Innsbruck, Nikki decided, as Hans escorted her to yet another establishment. Except for the inn where she was staying, she'd not been in the same place twice and there were many more, just waiting for her presence.

The tavern he chose surprised her a little. It was not one of the elegant dispensaries that attracted the village's winter guests, she guessed. Most of the customers seemed to be Austrian natives. Its patrons, mostly men, lined the long tables that ran through the center of the room. She and Hans sat apart from them, at a corner table that could seat four.

He didn't ask her what she preferred, but ordered two mugs of hot spiced wine from the waitress. The drink, when it came, was full-flavored, its aroma carrying her momentarily back to those early days in Leipzig. As they chatted about what had occupied each of them since their summer meeting, another round of the wine was fetched. The contents of the second cup seemed more potent than its predecessor.

"Do you see Gerhardt often?" Nikki asked sleepily, chewing on a pretzel in hopes that it would make her feel less muzzy.

"Who? Oh, you mean Herr Mehler. On occasion. We do not move in the same business circles, of course. He did some work, I believe, at one of our branches during the fall," Hans reported. There was something in his tone that suggested that bankers and plumbers did not move in the same social circles. "Have you heard from M. DePrenger lately?"

It was Nikki's turn to hang up on a name. Finally she connected the query with the private banker who held her fortune in security.

"Only by post," she murmured, frowning over her difficulty with getting words from mind to tongue. "I suppose I must visit him again soon, now that I can..."

She was aware that Hans was staring at her, waiting for her to finish the sentence. Nikki tried to remember what it was she had started to say. Perhaps if she began again, it would come to her.

"I shall go in..." What was the name of the month she wanted? Her mind was numb. So were her fingers, she realized, as she reached for another pretzel. Her hand fell into the dish, scattering its contents across the table and onto the floor. Embarrassed beyond explanation, she reached down to recover some of the errant pretzels. The floor rushed up at her.

* * *

She was wakening again, becoming aware of sounds around her, although her mind was still clouded and the words being used made no sense. Nikki kept her eyes tightly closed, unwilling to look into Hans Germeyer's face and witness his urbane disgust at her drunkenness. He was standing nearby, she knew, because she heard his voice saying, with some distress:

"It should not be taking her this long to recover."

"She is not very big," came the response. Nikki's muscles tensed as she recognized those oily tones as belonging to Hugo Haupt. "The problem is that she drank too much."

Hugo was right, of course, but he didn't need to be so candid about it, Nikki thought almost sulkily. The second mug of mulled wine had been beyond her capacity.

"So the dose was incorrect. It matters not. She is a healthy girl." That voice came from a time much earlier than its companions, from days of doubting and distress when Vati was gone and Mutti was ill.

Hans Germeyer and Hugo Haupt and Stefan Rennecke were together. She was with them. Nikki's imagination conjured up scenes of crows picking at the remains of animals killed along the highway. The black ravens, carrion birds, surrounded her. But she was not yet dead. And what were crows anyway but garbage collectors, genus Corvus? Very good, she applauded her memory, giving herself a mental A on the zoology pop quiz. But the real question for which she needed an answer was what they wanted with her. And she probably was not going to learn that by playing owl in daylight.

Nikki opened her eyes and looked about her, slowly moving from expected face to face, then examining what lay beyond. She was positive that this was Stefan's room. The furnishings resembled those in the room where Lars and Hanna were staying.

"She is awake," Hans reported unnecessarily. Both Hugo and Stefan had noticed and were moving nearer to her.

"Very good," Stefan agreed. "It had been a long time, Monika, unless we count your running from me this fall. And you are progressing well through the womanhood to which I initiated you. But we cannot pause now to discuss our more pleasant relationships. You do not need to suffer at all, just as you did not need to do so then. In exchange for your freedom, you will help us get all of the Jews' jewels which your father denied me."

"The what?" Nikki tried to ask. The attempted movement of her mouth told her that somehow she had been gagged. Pain from the tiny facial hairs said that tape shut her lips.

Stefan Rennecke nodded at her attempt.

"So we do understand each other, don't we? Your life for those riches that the Jews left with Karl. The gemstones are in the box in Zurich, aren't they?" He stood over her, looking down. When she did not move, he grabbed at the hair on the crown of her head. His fingers tightened on the strands, winding them until she thought the skin on her face would tear away.

Savagely he lifted her head and swung it back and forth. Nikki could not stop the tears of pain. When he released his hold, her head thumped back against the mattress. She wanted to cry in her agony, but that was impossible. Her only source of breath was through her nose. There was no choice. She nodded her head.

"But only the gemstones are in Zurich," he continued. "The box is too small for the precious metals. And you will tell us where those pieces are, as well. But not yet. We have a small journey to make. Then we will negotiate. Hugo, prepare Monika for the trip."

She smelled the danger at the instant she saw, from the corner of her eye, the quick movement of his hand and the wad of white gauze. There was no time to try to avoid taking a breath. After that, it didn't matter.

* * *

Her stomach was rebelling as she swam her way to the surface of what had to be a cold, choppy sea. Its waters tumbled her back and forth against the rocks.

But those weren't rocks that she was striking. They were shoes. And the movement had to be a car. Her hand fastened on an ankle. As the pain tore at her insides, her grip tightened. A harsh hand came down to brush her off and she changed her grasp to the fingers, feeling the metal and stone of the blackbird ring as she squeezed. It was only a matter of seconds now. She was going to throw up.

She raised her eyes in the dimness of the early dawn to plead with Stefan Rennecke. He groaned as the meaning of her motions became clear.

"Stop the car," he ordered. "She's going to be sick."

"On this ice?" came a mutter from the front seat. "If we get off the road, we'll never get back."

"At the top of the hill, then" came a suggestion. "Just stop. No one is out at this hour, anyway."

Nikki was too concerned with controlling the muscles of her throat to protest against the sharp pain of having the tape jerked free. She was towed out of the space between seats and supported on weak legs as she spewed vomit along the edge of the road. The tape, still hanging from her cheek, flapped in the chill wind. As soon as her stomach stopped retching, Stefan again slapped the covering over her mouth, shutting in the bitter bile. She was dropped back into place and the car moved on.

Dramamine, she thought, as the motion initiated another cycle of nausea. How she wished she could get at the supply in her handbag. Then, just as certainly, she hoped she had left it in her room. If Stefan remembered her stomach this well, she might have a slight edge. But could there truly be an advantage when she was the captive of three strong men. No, it was four, even though she had not seen the driver. Stefan and Hans were in the rear, Hugo and another up front.

"How much longer, Hans?"

She frowned. The speaker was Hans Germeyer.

"About a kilometer to the turning. Then several hundred meters to the chalet. All is in readiness. I have had a man open the house."

"You are sure there will be no trouble?" Stefan asked.

"None. The owner is sympathetic to us. And he is vacationing on Majorca. We will be alone for as long as it takes," the unfamiliar voice boasted. "I have arranged it all."

Alone! The thought of it caused Nikki to shiver, along with Stefan as on that day when Mutti was in the hospital. But with the others around, would he rape her again? Somehow, she doubted the numbers gave her much protection. Hugo, she was sure, would not only acquiesce, but probably watch as well. With Hans Germeyer, she wasn't positive about the reaction. She knew so little about him, expect that he was not the white knight that she had thought.

Stop it, her mind ordered, sounding to her mental ear like Paul handing out advice that must be obeyed. If she allowed fears of what could be to control her, she would be victimized by all that she could not imagine. Relax, she told herself. But letting the muscles soften on the hard floor, with the transmission tunnel poking at her back, was no small trick. Perhaps she could get her body to one side of the hump.

The sudden away of the car helped, dropping her on top of Stefan's feet as the driver cursed an unexpected patch of ice. She drew her knees up to her chest, curled like an unborn infant. There was a stream of heat coming from beneath the seat, warming her back.

The vehicle lurched to the left, this time under control. They had reached the road to the chalet, according to the driver. Nikki closed her eyes and prayed. The car was struggling over the frozen slush of the driveway. The men also were invoking God's name. Nikki hoped her unspoken words were audible to the Power over the din.

* * *

Cold wind, heavy with moisture, lashed at her as the rear doors were thrown open. Stefan's fingers pulled at the hair on her already abused scalp.

"Get out," he ordered. "And do not try to run away."

Nikki pushed her legs unelegantly out of the car, levering her body above them. How could a man be so suspicious? She could barely stand after the trip, let alone run. She started to put her hand on the car to steady herself, then pulled it away. She didn't want to adhere to the vehicle. Hans Germeyer's hand came to her elbow. Wasn't he the courtly captor!

Just then the door of the chalet opened, and a stocky figure stood silhouetted in the light.

"Hello, Fraulein," the driver greeted Nikki as he turned toward the others. For the first time Nikki saw the face of the other Hans. He was older, of course, and age had eroded his blonde hairline. Still she knew him, Hans Krieder, her father's former apprentice. "Herr Rennecke, this is my sister's betrothed, Peter Walz. Herr Germeyer, Herr Haupt. Peter perhaps remembers Monika. He and Heidi were in the same class with Monika at school."

The man at the door leaned toward them. The overhead light flashed from the lenses of his thick spectacles. The older Hans pushed past him, followed by Hugo. The younger Hans shoved Nikki along in Stefan's wake.

As each passed Peter, he bid them good morning like a well-trained doorman. There was no change in tone or emphasis when he addressed Nikki.

Kurt must have been wrong, she decided as she was pushed through another door beyond the box-like entry. The man who had greeted them was little more than an imbecile. Peter who had been her friend was clever and wily, imaginative, loyal. He would not be going to marry the selfish little cat that Heidi had promised to become. Nor would he have become a flunky for her brother.

This individual would not have risked his life to build a rock garden of the encapsulated candelabra and other precious metals that had been buried in the rhubarb patch. Judging from his greeting, he couldn't have recognized the significance of the repeated cultivation of the plants. And he most certainly would not have become Kurt's replacement as the Leipzig connection for the escape network to the West. The only problem was that the man Hans Krieder called Peter Walz looked exactly like she had remembered Peter's father, the nearsighted bookkeeper whose excess weight had clustered about his waistline.

As if Peter were aware of her thoughts, his magnified eyes rested on her. He was the last to enter the room, slamming the entry hall door behind him. Then his attention slid away, and he stalked to the grate in the cavernous fireplace. His movements were almost awkward as he used the poker to encourage the glowing coals.

"Tie her to that chair for now." Stefan gestured to a rough hewn ladderback seat halfway between the entry door and the heat source. She wasn't sure who he expected to perform the task, but the elder Hans nodded toward Peter. Hans, the younger, nudged her toward the chair, standing over her until Peter returned from some other room with a hank of clothesline.

The restraining rope was sufficient to hold her in place but not constricting. When Peter was finished, Stefan inspected the knots. With a brisk movement that Nikki misinterpreted, he snatched the tape from her face. The sudden pain brought tears to her eyes and she saw, through a mist, that he was standing over her.

"Now we shall get on with the subject at hand. Karl put gemstones that Jews and other political suspects gave him in the secured box in Zurich. He was doing it before the war began, and he continued to do so for those who sought escape after he became my associate in Wiesbaden. As his partner, I have a right to those treasures, don't you think?"

Could the jewels be what was driving Stefan Rennecke? Nikki tested it as a hypothesis and found a certain relief in deciding it was possible. If this were a movie, the heroine would bravely pretend that she did not understand what information was desired. But Nikki felt neither brave nor heroic.

"My father took those stones to hold in trust," she protested. "The Rennecke-Groebel partnership did not pay for them."

"That is incorrect," Hans Krieder objected. "Herr Groebel always advanced escape money. The Jews were supposed to redeem the stones later. I know. I saw it done in Leipzig."

"If money was exchanged in Wiesbaden, it would have been the firm's funds," Stefan insisted. "Karl did not have that much money of his own. He and Wera brought nothing from the East with them. She told me so."

Nikki saw the doubt rising on Hans Krieder's face. He couldn't prove what wealth had been moved. He didn't know, for instance, about the plating that covered silverware of cast gold in Tante Uschi's picnic basket. Nor was he aware of Mutti's mesh pocketbook or the hollow buttons on her old fur coat, or of the immense diamond that had replaced the button in Kengi's ear. But he suspected, nonetheless.

"Some of the stones in the box are mine." Nikki put a pride of wealth in her voice, certain that Stefan would understand. "You can't have those."

"Ah, but there is a list that determines which are which," Stefan reminded.

She frowned. How could he know of the list? If M. DePrenger were so untrustworthy as to have revealed its existence, Stefan would be dealing directly with the banker. But there were others who knew, too—Paul, and Bruno...and Gerry.

"Yours to you. The rest to me...to us," Stefan appealed. "Magda says there is sufficient to satisfy all."

The reference to a Magda puzzled Nikki. The name made her think of grey, filmy grey. And then she recalled the woman in M. DePrenger's reception room. Had he not referred to her as Magda?

"Why do you need the gems?" Nikki countered. "You have all the wealth you can use."

He smiled benignly down at her. Her recognition of his status pleased him.

"It is not for him," Hans Germeyer stated flatly. "It is for us, for the movement."

"What movement?"

"Die Schwarzen Raben. We are brothers who will stop the Jews from taking over the world," Hugo shouted as he whirled from the fireplace opening where he had been warming stubby fingers. "To keep funds out of Israel until the Jewish homeland is bankrupted. It is necessary. Otherwise, those filthy Zionists will end up in control of all nations, even your beloved United States of America."

"Is that true?" She looked first at Stefan, then at Hans Germeyer. Perhaps if they talked long enough, she could begin to understand what had brought these men of her present and past into alliance under the sign of the raven.

"Of course, it is true. The Nazi movement recognized that the Jews were dangerous to all free people. Under Hitler's direction, much was done to stop the threat. But it was not enough. Too many Jews escaped to infiltrate the power structures of other governments." Stefan moved away from her to take a seat on the scuffed leather couch across the room. His voice rose in volume and emotion so that it reached her filled with venom, hatred, and even fear.

His fear dominated the explanation that followed, a fear based on legend, suspicion, and envy. He presented a positive picture of every valuable that Vati had held as being the final piece that would bring Zionist domination. The Jews, his words suggested were conspirators plotting world domination. It might not be that bad a world, Nikki thought suddenly, if it were left to her foster family or to Hope Greene or, most especially, to poor Oma Kohn.

She consciously creased her forehead. He needed to believe she was considering the truth of his argument.

"And you must know that we speak the truth." He had observed her change in expression. "Those Jews who took you away. Why did you think they wanted to be burdened with an obnoxious little orphan, especially one who was a German? It was to get the jewels. That is why they have come to Innsbruck, to force you to give up your wealth. And do not believe that they, like us, will be satisfied with only what came from the Jews."

It required great effort to keep the surprise and hope from showing.

"The Fishers came to the Olympics?" she asked, her voice flat. "Both David and Donna?"

"They arrived last evening. Your newspaper friend, Herr Peterson, met them and took them to your hotel. It was because of this that we had to remove you from their presence. To save you and your wealth from Zionist exploitation."

And the bullet the night before, Nikki wondered. From whose presence was that supposed to take her?

"But you will leave me what is mine?" She looked across at Stefan and waited for his nod. "How do I get the stones for you?"

It was difficult to act as if she were cooperating, but she wanted to know their plans. Until she did, she was without a clue as to how she might protect her wealth and the cause of The Innocents.

"Wait a minute!" Hans Krieder pushed past the other Hans to confront Stefan Rennecke. "Ask her where Herr Groebel cached the gold and silver in Leipzig."

Now she attempted to look puzzled. If this all worked, perhaps she should return to Northwestern as an enrollee in its school of speech and drama. Never mind journalism! If she could just be convincing...

"Do you know of your father's hiding place in your former home?" Stefan inquired.

Nikki shook her head slowly.

"Perhaps a safe or a vault? A basement?"

She tried doubt. If she were forced to reveal something, she would opt for the basement. The vision of Hans Krieder digging up Oma Kohn's remains appealed to her in a bizarre way.

"I don't think so," she finally said with deliberation. "But I was never allowed much in the basement. There were rats, I think."

Let them make what they would of that, she decided.

"She could have been too young to know," Hans Krieder allowed. "And if Herr Groebel gave her control of the stones, he could have meant for Hanna to have the metals. I always thought Hanna would get a part of the fortune. That's why I was going to marry her."

"Then why is she not here as well as this one?" Stefan glared at him.

"Hanna Wentzler is in the hospital," Peter said suddenly. "Hans shot her."

"You meant to shoot the sister?" Hans Germeyer asked, amazement on his face.

"No. I mistook her for Monika. You know that," Hans Krieder barely controlled his anger. "And since I did, it freed up Peter to get this place ready for us. He was supposed to be watching the Wentzlers. I arranged for the assignment with GDR security in order to have Peter here. But that was before you told me who the woman we wanted was. Perhaps he recalls something about the villa. He spent enough time there as a child.

"Monika is right," Peter stepped closer to Krieder. "We were never allowed to go to the basement."

"We need the sister, too," Stefan decided.

"There will be time. She was in surgery yesterday," Krieder told him. "But if she does well, they will discharge her soon."

"And you think we are going to sit here that long?" Stefan frowned. "I want to get on our way to Zurich."

"So why don't we go?" Hans Germeyer asked. "All we really need from Nikki is a letter stating that we are to be given the contents of the box. We can be there tomorrow, get the stones, and return in time to question the sister. Krieder and his associate will keep in touch with the hospital and, should the woman be released, they can bring her here."

"Perhaps you are right. Monika can remain here with Hans until then. Having both Groebel sisters should give us leverage."

"You said we'd be at this place just for one day," Krieder objected. "What if someone decides to search for Monika?"

"We can do just as we did before when we created the false telegram from Mehler," Hans Germeyer decided. "In addition to her letter to M. DePrenger, Nikki will send a note to Herr Peterson. The letter will say that she has gone to Zurich to join her beloved Gerhardt."

"Peter can leave it at the desk in the inn when he returns to Innsbruck to see that all is well with the Wentzlers," the older Hans added. Both turned to Rennecke for approval.

Nikki closed her eyes to disguise her joy. Gerry would come to Innsbruck. Those cold words had not been his.

"How do we know that her friend had not already gone to the police?" Stefan asked.

Nikki roused and looked around at the faces considering the problem. Should she tell them, she wondered?

"Because of her background," Hans Germeyer finally decided. "It would not do, in the present political climate, to let the Austrians know that this reporter with American passport is actually an East German. I am sure that Herr Peterson knows."

"That's why they never reported the attack in Zurich," Hugo supplied. His sudden intervention into the conversation surprised the men as much as it did Nikki. She looked into the shadows at the back of the room and saw him, leaning against a high cabinet. He held a bottle in his hand. With their attention focused upon him, he raised it in a salute, then tipped it to his mouth.

"Get some paper," Stefan ordered. "We will give her the words, and Monika will write."

The four other men looked at each other, waiting for someone to begin the search. Finally Peter clumped off to the desk on the far wall.

"Hugo, you and Herr Walz carry her over to the desk," Stefan ordered when he saw Peter lay the sheets on the blotter pad.

As Hugo fumbled with his side of her chair, breathing alcohol fumes into her face while grinning at her helplessness, Nikki tried to think of phrases and words that would indicate her plight, especially to Paul. Losing the gems was less important than getting someone to intervene before Hanna was endangered further. There were still the metals that Peter held. If she got out of this mess, she'd find a way to obtain them.

Stefan himself, untied her hands and forced a pen into her stiffened fingers. As he drew back, prepared to dictate, Peter reached across him to stroke an arrangement of dried flowers at the corner of the desk. Dust billowed up, making Nikki sneeze in unison with Stefan's cough.

"I have such as these in my rock garden," Peter announced as if nothing had happened. "They grow well when the time is right, and they are not forced."

Stefan turned and frowned at him.

"Go to the truck and warm its engine. We will do the note for Innsbruck first."

Nikki sneezed again.

"How do you stand that idiot?" Stefan demanded as soon as Peter was out of the room.

Nikki lowered her head to keep the men from seeing that a message had been exchanged.

"I have little choice," Hans Krieder confessed with a sigh. "I have told you that my sister is the mistress of Comrade Schiller, who is very important in our government. It was thought necessary to arrange that Heidi have a husband who will not know he is being cuckolded."

"That one wouldn't," Hugo agreed, bringing his bottle with him as he joined the group. "Not even if her body were still sweaty from other hands."

Nikki wrote the words as Stefan gave them to her. That was what she understood Peter wanted. She hoped that her instincts and Kurt's information were correct, that Peter was playing the stupid man for reasons of his own.

When it was all done and only she and Hans Krieder remained in the chalet, she could not help but wonder. He found the liquor supply that Hugo had left, punctuating his drinking with venom about his memories of the Groebel family. How clearly he recalled the past surprised her, especially the depths of his hatred for Vati.

"He was scum," Hans declared, "a slavemaster. He lived like a king on our sweat. Do you know what I did with that stupid book he gave me that Christmas? I tore out its pages one by one to wipe the shit from my ass. And that was only right! The stupid Bolsheviks wanted that man, your corrupt father, to have an important place in government. They were upset when he refused. But I knew better. A man like that would have ruined the government, just as surely as he ruined every other thing he touched."

There was no reason to playact anymore. Nikki pushed her back straight, proud to think that someone perceived Vati as a man of such strength. And, of course, he was.

* * *

Later, another bottle of Kirschwasser gone, Hans told her about Heidi. He was not pleased with his sister's sexual activities, but he recognized the power it was giving him. He began to boast of his importance.

"But you are also 'Die Schwarzen Raben?'" Nikki asked. "Is that approved?"

"Of course it isn't." His hand came to his chin to wipe away the liquid that was spilling from the bottle. "But that gold and silver your father left hidden is none of the government's concern. Our aim is to keep if from helping the Jews. I shall see that it does not."

"And enjoy every pfennig it produces?" she suggested. "How?"

He scowled at her question.

"I suppose I shall have to escape to the West, too," he finally decided. "Otherwise, there is little upon which I can spend it. Where do you live now? Is it New York City?"

"Chicago," she told him.

"Not Chicago for me. Those gangsters would try to take my riches and then the FBI would become involved."

So much for Elliot Ness, Nikki decided, suppressing a grin.

"Los Angeles would be good. Yes, I think I should live in the city of the lost angels."

Nikki was thinking so, too. Perhaps the time had come to test the depth of his inebriation.

"Hans, I am thirsty. May I have a drink of water?"

"Of course. I'll share my wasser with you."

The bottle's neck was jammed against her lower lip. Some of the liquid flowed into her mouth. More trickled down over her chest.

"Now you need wiping up," Hans choked in delight, a hand coming forward to swipe at the moisture, then lingering to fondle her breast. "You are not much compared to my Heidi. My sister is built like your mother was, and Comrade Schiller dresses her in only the finest, not cheap cotton like this."

Hans' fingers froze on the neckline of Nikki's blouse when the noise came from the entry hall. He had managed one lurching stride toward the door before the threadbare Persian carpet that centered the room tripped him up. He let out a yelp as he fell.

Calling out seemed like a good idea to Nikki. Perhaps it was only the three Zurich travelers returning, or Peter back from Innsbruck. But a good scream never hurt anything, and then one good scream deserved another and another…and another.

Chapter Thirteen

✦ ✦ ✦

Beginning Again

"What are all of you doing here? How did you know I was in trouble?" Nikki finally was able to choke out her query in both English and German when her screams subsided. It was ever so much more comfortable in the corner of the old leather couch even though Gerry's arm about her shoulders held her as tightly as the ropes he had torn away.

The rescue party that had burst through the door from the entry hall included, in addition to Gerry, Paul, David and Donna. While Gerry had undone her bonds and tried to quiet her, the other men had pushed her captor into an upholstered chair on the far side of the room. They hadn't tied him up, but he was sitting quietly. Perhaps it was the thick walking stick that David held at the ready that was persuasive.

"Since your note said you were going to meet Gerry in Zurich, and he was standing next to me when I opened it, it was obvious that you were not." Paul, stirring the coals to warm the chill air, grinned at her from the fireplace.

"And how did Gerry get next to you?" She tilted her head so she could see Gerry's face. He couldn't possibly have shaved in the past twenty-four hours. His chin showed a healthy beginning of a beard. "You were supposed to come this morning, weren't you? This is the day of the opening ceremonies?"

"You didn't call me when you said you would. So I finally managed to get hold of Paul. When he didn't know where you were, I got in the Jag and drove." His hand pressed her closer as he lowered his head to rest his cheek on her hair.

"The note," Nikki recalled. "Stefan Rennecke forced me to write it while Hans Germeyer and Hugo Haupt stood by. But Stefan dictated the words. How did you know I was here?"

"The map and directions on the bottom of the page," Gerry supplied.

"What map?" She glanced at each of them for explanation.

"They weren't written in your hand," David Fisher told her. "And they were in German, but Gerry provided a quick translation, and off we came with directions from the landlord at the inn. By the way, who is this individual?"

"He's Hans Krieder, from Leipzig," Nikki explained. "He was an apprentice to Vati's shop, and he is another black bird."

The quartet listened with interest as she detailed her captors and what she had been required to do. As she talked, she began to shiver. Gerry's hold on her tightened, and Donna scooped a tapestry off the wall to wrap around Nikki. Paul limped over to where the remainder of Hans's last bottle of goldwasser sat. He wiped the bottle's neck on his sleeve and passed it to Nikki's trembling fingers.

"Take a big gulp," Donna instructed firmly. "If I had known you were playing around with creeps like that oaf, I would have come sooner."

"This Hans is the one who shot Hanna," Nikki choked out after swallowing the liquid she did not want. "And they plan to kidnap her, too, as soon as she is released from the hospital. But first they are going to get the gems. I don't care about that as long as we can keep Hanna safe."

"Don't worry about your sister," Gerry told her. "She will be safe. As for your gemstones, I think a phone call to M. DePrenger will take care…"

He was interrupted by more noise from the entryway.

"Hans…Hans, it is I."

"That's Peter," Nikki whispered as David's walking stick began to shift toward the door. "Don't hurt him. He is a good friend of mine. He drew the map on the note."

"Hans!" The door to the living room was flung open. Peter stood there with another man. "Here is Comrade Schiller. He insists on seeing you."

Watching Peter's entrance, Nikki was sure that her efforts at acting were of very poor quality. Here was the expert. Peter's face changed from earnestness to confusion to dismay.

"I did not realize that these were the friends with whom you were planning to meet." Peter's words came with an effort, clearly indicating his distress. "Why, some of them are Americans?"

Peter had played out his scene just inside the door. Now the other man pushed past him, crossing the room to stand in front of Hans Krieder. David, immediately aware of the ploy, lowered the cane and stepped aside.

285

Krieder's jaw hung open and his eyes darted around the room as he began to realize how he was being compromised.

"So this was the meeting that was so important that you would cease surveillance on the Wentzlers!" Comrade Schiller growled. "And now they are gone to the West because of your dereliction. The Party will act, I assure you, Herr Krieder."

Nikki risked a glance at her companions to see if the information about Hanna and Lars was true. Every face reflected surprise. Under the tapestry, however, Gerry gave a squeeze of agreement.

"But that woman is her sister," Hans came out of his chair, pointing across at Nikki. David's walking stick began to rise until Paul stopped the movement with a barely noticeable shake of his head. "We can hold her as a hostage for Frau Wentzler's return."

"There are five of them and only three of us. How can we possibly take them all as hostages," Peter wailed from his place by the door. "Besides, she is not Hanna Wentzler's sister."

Hans lunged toward Peter. Schiller's arm dragged him back.

"Yes, she is. That is Monika Groebel. I knew her when she was a child." Krieder's face flushed as he struggled against the restraint.

"No," Peter stated firmly. "I knew Monika Groebel better than you did. We played together on the grounds of the estate and were in the same class at school. Monika had blue eyes."

"What about that?" Schiller dragged Hans across the room with him, over the rug that had earlier been Hans's undoing. "This young woman has brown eyes. Did the Groebel girl have blue eyes?"

"No," Hans managed, without sounding certain. "I am sure they were brown."

"I am afraid you are wrong," Peter said with compassion, finally moving toward Hans. "Please, do not do anything more. There is more than enough trouble already. Hans, I am very sorry. To think that your own sister's betrothed should bring this upon you...I have been..."

"Never!" Hans grabbed at Peter's neck. Schiller used his superior height and weight to break the grasp.

"Enough! We shall return to Innsbruck now. Herr Walz, take Herr Krieder's other arm to help him to the car." The man turned briefly to look at the room's other occupants. "I do not know what you and this man have been plotting against the government of the German Democratic Republic, but I shall discover it. And I warn you, whatever it is, I shall stop it."

The five people who were left behind stared at each other as the outer door slammed shut.

"Is he for real?" Donna looked at Nikki, her unbelief apparent. "That stammering fat fool! Were you really playmates?"

"Very much for real." Nikki giggled as she considered the immensity of the role that Peter had designed for himself. Her listeners joined her laughter as she detailed her reunion with Peter and Kurt's story about Peter's rock garden.

"Knowing that there are people like Peter on the other side of *the Wall* certainly makes these days easier to live with," David declared. "But can he maintain his pose?"

"He's done it since we were children." Nikki smiled as she remembered Peter, the schoolboy. "Peter has chosen Vati's way of being free. He will not wear the mark of another. Vati would be so proud. And I think it is the way that I must go, too."

She sensed the release of Gerry's arm on her shoulders and realized that he was misunderstanding. Nikki grabbed for his hand.

"Let me explain, Gerry. Please."

"But let her do it back in Innsbruck," Donna insisted. The coals in the grate were mostly ash, and the room was beginning to chill.

Gerry's grip tightened again. Nikki smiled up into his face.

"Making contact with M. DePrenger before Stefan arrives is another reason for getting back to Innsbruck," Paul decided, scattering the remaining heat with a sweep of the poker. "Let's close this place up as best we can and get out."

They were working on the latch of the outer door when the farm truck chugged to a halt behind Paul's car. The occupant tumbled out of the cab, arms gesturing wildly.

David, Donna, and Paul stared at the seeming madman in amazement while Gerry and Nikki tried to follow his words.

"What about it?" Gerry turned to Nikki. "Is the chalet's telephone operating?"

She stared at him blankly, too involved in the farmer's report to even recall whether there had been a telephone. Finally she shook her head.

"If there were a phone, I am sure Stefan would have used it instead of dispatching Peter. A call to the inn desk would have sufficed." She turned to the farmer. "What color was the car?"

"Dark, Fraulein. Blue or so."

"Gerry!" She tugged at his hand. "It was them."

"We'll alert the police as soon as we get back to town," Gerry told the man. "They will take care of it."

The farmer seemed satisfied, hoisting himself up to the bench seat again, and backing his load of straw through the narrow turnabout. When he was pointed toward the road once more, he waved a hand at the group.

"He came upon a sedan that had gone off the road and fallen many meters," Gerry reported to the puzzled trio. "There were three occupants. Two are dead—an older man with silver hair and a younger man. The third appears paralyzed. The farmer could not help him because of his great size. Medical assistance will be required."

"Those three men? Rennecke and Germeyer and Haupt." Paul's eyebrows rose.

"Apparently so," Gerry agreed.

"Hugo lives," Nikki observed, then shrugged. Sometimes one did what one had to do. Sometimes it was done for one. Perhaps God's help came more freely when humans made the first gesture. "But he can no longer hurt us. Nor can Hans Krieder. I think that Paul and I had better get back to work."

"You bet," he assured her. "The Games open in a few hours."

"But bath, food, and nap come first," Donna stated firmly.

"And a shave for Gerry," Nikki teased.

* * *

Somehow they managed it all, making the change from the rescuers and the rescued to become the spectators and chroniclers of the IX Winter Games. Nikki knew she would always remember this time as, wedged in among others at the ski jump bowl and clinging to Gerry's hand, she watched the tradition acted out again.

She blinked back the tears when the German athletes marched in behind their makeshift banner. One day, perhaps, they could walk together under a real national flag. But that time was probably far away, for the governments of these who were her first people had done much to earn the world's distrust. It wasn't the governments, however, that seemed important at this spectacle. The flags flew bravely but attention focused on the people whose sign was the flaming caldron. Its fire reached now to the skies and would keep darkness at bay during the coming days.

"They are all my people," Nikki told herself, feeling a hilarity growing within her and flashing a smile at Gerry to let him know which of all of them—spectators and athletes—was dearest. What Vati had given her would be theirs to help them stand, just as the participants now stood for just these few days, proud and free and at peace with each other.

The shout of surprise, coming as it did in an unprogrammed second of the ceremony, turned every eye to the ski jump. A photographer, having lost footing, was sliding down the in-run, legs and arms flailing as he sought security for himself and safety for his camera. The thousands who filled the seats and the area bowl watched in silence as he hurdled forward. Around her Nikki could see lips moving without sound, but she could read the lips of many. The words were "Our Father" or "Pater Noster" or "Oh, shit." Before he reached the brink, his movement ceased. Then, as if he were aware of their concern, he waved a hand to signal he was all right. A howl of laughter filled the arena.

288

More than anything else, this unplanned event symbolized what it was that Nikki really sought. Living at peace with one another a goal. Laughing with one another was a first step.

* * *

"Here we all are," Donna summarized that evening as the meal the Fishers were hosting reached its final course. The waiter had just brought hot apfelstrudel with cream to the table.

"And here goes the diet," Paul groaned.

"I haven't had this in ages!" Nikki smiled across the table.

"Since this dinner was supposed to be last night and a surprise for you, Nikki, dig in. It turned out that we were the ones who ended up surprised because our daughter had disappeared. By the way, young lady, you never were surprised to see us."

"Stefan Rennecke told me you were coming, just after he took me prisoner," Nikki explained. "He said you and David were going to take all of my wealth and give it to the Zionists. He was going to protect me. He wanted to keep me safe."

"Keep you safe under the black bird's wing," Gerry jeered. He took her hand and squeezed. "From here on in, anyone who wants to protect you will have to get in line behind me."

"We're there, young man," David said firmly.

"I don't want protection. I want help," Nikki insisted. "I have decided what I shall do with my inheritance. Gerry and Paul already know about this."

"You know you can count on us for anything," Donna spoke quickly. "So tell David and me, too."

Nikki quickly summarized her relationship with Kurt and the events and people she had seen since her return to Europe. The words flowed easily, and even she was amazed at her depth of feeling for her land of birth and its people.

"So much has happened and in so short a time," David marveled when Nikki paused for breath. "You have dealt well with it. But your legacy from your father, it must be valued in the millions."

"I just hope it will be enough," Nikki told him and smiled as she watched his eyebrows climb. "I got the idea from Kurt's wife, Julia, after Kurt died. That was also the day that Kennedy was killed. She said that people are not willing to put the amounts of money and effort into peace that they are into war. But I, for one, am."

There was momentary silence at the table. Then everyone was speaking at once. David's voice rose above the rest as he came to his feet with wine glass raised.

"To peace," he proposed. The party rose with him, Gerry and Nikki echoing his words in German. And suddenly there was the sound of clinking glasses all about them as smiling diners at adjacent tables joined them.

"Magic words, in any language," Nikki commented when they resumed their seats. "But you have to help me get started. I want to use the wealth to continue the work that Vati and Kurt have done and Peter is carrying on. Bruno's father calls it 'Freiheit fur die Unschuldigen,' freedom for the innocents."

"I like the name," David nodded. "But we live in a world filled with innocents who seek freedom. What a challenge for a young woman to face!"

"Not just a young woman," Gerry objected. "A young couple. Nikki and I are in this together."

"Does that mean..." Donna began hopefully.

"Are you proposing..." Nikki stopped her.

"Father Fisher, may I?" Gerry looked across the table.

"Yes, yes, and yes," Paul answered before he leaned across to kiss Nikki's cheek.

"Wonderful!" Donna clapped her hands. "I love planning weddings."

"Shall we adjourn this planning session until morning?" Gerry suggested. "I would like to dance with my bride-to-be."

Sun streamed through the window of Nikki's room at the "Weisser Schwan," turning its blues to sapphire. Dust motes danced cheerfully along the beams while Muff, the cat, drowsed in a warm spot on the carpet.

Nikki stood in front of the oak armoire, regarding the airy lacy gown hanging from the padded silk hanger. The train was so long it had to be looped over another hanger and suspended from a hook on the wall. The garment's sleek satin was overlayed with dainty embroidered openwork on fine Swiss cotton. She suspected the material had once been white, back when Agnes and Wolfgang Kneipp had exchanged their pledging kiss at the altar.

Certainly it had been the present antique ivory as Liesel wore it to speak her vows to Bruno. On this latter occasion, Liesel had used a hoop to raise the hemline. But in an hour, when Donna and Frau Kneipp would dress the newest bride, only crinoline petticoats would provide fullness for the gown's bouffant skirt.

"Nikki, are you ready for me?" Susan called after tapping on the door. "I've come to do your hair, and look what I brought with me?"

She came inside, holding out an immense bouquet of spring flowers.

"Last time I brought you flowers they were from Herr Germeyer," Susan recalled. "What a shame about that awful accident."

"Put them here," Nikki cleared a spot on the table near the window. "Are they from Gerry?"

"Here's the card. Let me put more water in the vase." She stepped carefully around Muff. "So that's where my lazy cat got to. She's not had her breakfast."

"We're both fasting," Nikki said as her stomach rumbled. She lifted the envelope's flap with a freshly manicured nail.

"Beste Wuensche and Liebe, Dein Klaus Haupt," the card proclaimed. "Best wishes and all my love."

Susan was still adjusting Nikki's curls around the wreath of miniature roses and baby's breath when the "mothers-of-the-bride" arrived. Muff took one look at the newcomers and scrambled out before the door closed.

"Liesel will be here in a few minutes," Frau Kneipp reported. "She's just finishing Gretel's breakfast."

"I don't want to discuss breakfast," Nikki protested.

"It's just as well that you have to fast before communion," Donna remarked unsympathetically. "Agnes has let out every seam to its fullest. And even with that, it will be close."

"Not too close, I hope," Nikki sighed. "With that fantastic menu that Herr Wirt is preparing, I intend to stuff myself. Can't you smell the bread?"

"And you should see your wedding cake," Agnes Kneipp told her. "The butter-crème frosting must be an inch thick."

"I have to go and help him now," Susan announced. "Nikki looks splendid, doesn't she?"

"Thank you, Susan," Nikki hugged the girl. "And thank your parents again for everything—the rooms for my friends, the reception dinner, all the kindnesses."

Liesel arrived with Gretel in her arms as Susan departed. The infant, dressed in crisp primrose yellow, sucked her thumb happily.

"Bruno has gone to the church to meet Gerry. Father and Hanna are resting in the lobby. She didn't think she could manage the stairs. Lars is with them. David and Paul are bringing the cars to the entrance." Liesel frowned at the women. "So why isn't the bride gowned?"

"Give us ten minutes," Donna promised. "The man can wait."

Laughter pealed through the courtyard as people halted in their pre-holiday bustle to regard the wedding party on the church steps. Among the observers were sisters from the convent next door.

Nikki beamed at Sister Anne Claire and Novice Margaret Mary as she moved from David's arms to the embrace of Gerry's father. She knew she was the focus of attention, both that of her friends and the curious onlookers.

She suspected that some sharper eyes had caught the fact that the parents of the bride, as well as her younger brother and sister, seemed to be Jewish. These same people might have wondered about that other woman who walked with the aid of a cane. She, too, looked old enough to be the bride's mother, and the flowers she carried suggested that she had taken part in the ceremony.

A long line of men seemed intent upon greeting the young wife with a kiss. There was another elderly man besides the groom's father. He also wore a rose on his lapel. He was supported by two woman, one carrying a baby girl gowned in yellow.

And there were the two men who seemed on the brink of middle age, one of whom escorted the crippled woman. The other had a limp of his own. After he had kissed the bride, he rejoined a tallish blonde woman and took the hand of a fidgeting pre-schooler. His place in the bride's embrace was taken by the bearish younger fellow with the dark curly hair and beard.

Judging from the formality of the kisses he placed on the bride's cheeks, the last gentleman in the line had to have French blood. That was right, because the bride called him "Monsieur" when she introduced him.

At last the newlyweds met each other once more in an eager embrace before they climbed into a white Jaguar. The guests began to follow. The spectators moved along smiling to finish those necessary tasks in anticipation of Easter.

"Well, Frau Mehler!" Gerry regarded his bride, eyes filled with pride.

"Paul called me Mrs. Mickey Mouse," she told him as she patted the skirt of her gown into place.

"And Bruno's father still calls you 'Kleine Maus,' Gerry retorted. "It must be your resemblance to a rodent."

"At least I don't look like a crow," she told him after his kiss took the sting out of his remark. "I am glad that Bettina Haupt decided to come to our wedding. She is so busy now with the business and both Hugo and his father to care for. Herr Klaus sent a bouquet to me this morning along with his best wishes."

"The old man is doing his share with the shop," Gerry observed. "But I do regret that the accident did not kill Hugo. I suppose it was your friend Peter who loosened the brake connection. It was done so carefully that the Austrians believed it was mechanical failure."

"Wasn't that a marvelous card that Peter sent to us?" Nikki chuckled. "The picture of his rock garden and his promise to transplant when the climate was right?"

"His innocence has great depth," Gerry announced, eyes sparkling, as he stopped the Jaguar in front of the Weisser Schwan. "But Peter learned to stand alone from a master."

"I wish Vati were here," Nikki murmured.

"So do I. But who is to say that he is not?" He held her off at arm's length, staring intently at her face. "Perhaps we can find him anywhere that people stand proud and free. That's where Karl's place is."

"And we will tend each place as carefully as we would care for his grave?" She managed the question without faltering.

"As best we can, beloved." Gerry pulled her to him. "And we will have a lot of help. Here they come, now."

"Just another conspiracy," she giggled.

"And conspiracy means to breathe together. Let's go inside."

Herr Wirt's reputation as a chef certainly did not suffer from the nuptial meal that he and his family proudly served. Despite having missed breakfast, Nikki was too occupied with moving among her friends to eat much.

The guests were all elated. It was not only the marriage, Nikki thought, but the beginning of the new venture. Every person here knew about it in some way or other. And each was enthusiastic, even those who recognized the outcomes would not be realized in their lifetime. Herr Kneipp had put that in perspective.

"As long as the governments of the world are controlled by those who fought in the war, true peace will be impossible. Loving one's enemies is perhaps the hardest charge put upon us by our faith. But when those who do not have those difficult memories take over, the people will have an opportunity. The Innocents may be but a small step, but I will pray that my granddaughter may benefit."

"I want to be part of your glorious scheme, Monika." Ursi had told Nikki the previous day when she had arrived for the wedding. Her companion, a different sister from the woman Nikki had met at Christmas, looked surprised, but not particularly shocked.

"How would that be possible within the vows you have taken?" Nikki inquired.

"Much is changing for those of us who have chosen the religious vocation because of Pope John," Ursi told her. "By the time you have assignments for me, it will be allowed."

As Nikki stepped around her guests to reach the place where M. DePrenger and Bettina Haupt were conversing, she thought with regret that Julia's fears had kept her from being present. If she were to leave Berlin, she might not be allowed to return to St. Gertrude's and her work.

It was midafternoon before Donna and Hanna led her off to her room so she could change from her wedding gown. The two women worked as a team to unfasten the tiny hooks at the back of the dress, but Donna had to lift it alone.

"What does the doctor say about your leg?" Nikki asked her sister who, sitting on the edge of the bed, was putting Nikki's gloves and prayer book into a suitcase. Except for an overnight stay in Munich, this was the first time she had been with Hanna since Innsbruck. She knew that the Wentzlers had chosen a small town in Odenwald for their new home. Her first expenditure from the gems had been the purchase of a painting firm for Lars.

"He says it is healing well," Hanna told her with a broad grin. "He says it will be strong enough to carry the baby that is growing within me. Another innocent, but this one will be born free."

With a shriek, Nikki threw her arms around her sister.

"I am so pleased for you and Lars," she sighed.

"No more than we are for you." Our children, yours and those of Lars and mine, can grow together." Hanna's arms tightened. "We will see you often, will we not?"

"Of course we will," Nikki assured her. "We have fifteen years to make up for."

Donna touched her shoulder.

"Slip into your shoes. Gerry is waiting."

Nikki never felt the floor beneath those shoes—a pair of Bally pumps like Mutti used to prefer—as she went to join her husband. They were going home, a choice that Gerry had accepted although they had discussed a variety of potential wedding trip sites. She needed to go home, she had explained, because tomorrow was Easter. It would mark a decade and a half since the end of that other life had happened. It was well within the tradition of the resurrection to begin a new life in a new home, she thought with pleasure, as she passed down a line of farewells into Gerry's arms again.

Dusk came early to this afternoon late in March. It was necessary to use driving lights immediately as they drove home. On the way, they talked of the wedding and the reception, of those persons dear to them who had been present, of the interest shown in the project that united them as surely as their vows. It wasn't until they stopped outside of the entrance to the apartment above the plumbing shop that they became really aware of what was in the rear seat of the car.

"What are those?" Nikki asked, pointing at the several boxes lying behind her.

Gerry shrugged, stopping to look inside the car's back compartment.

"I thought my father was bringing all of the gifts with him. If you can get some of those, I'll bring the suitcases from the boot."

After everything was inside, Nikki and Gerry stood at the dining room table, looking down at the collection of boxes. He had already discarded his jacket and tie. His shirt was open at the collar. She tried to read the expression on his face as she stretched up to kiss him. Her fingers moved lightly about his features as their lips clung, then slid to his neck and inside of his shirt. When his hands gripped hers and pulled them from their contact, she made a face at him to cover her disappointment.

"We should open these, I think," he told her.

"They'll be there tomorrow," she retorted. This was hardly the scene she had imagined. Why would Gerry suddenly become the reluctant bridegroom?

"I know, but let's see what they are," he insisted. "Come on. Get it done."

How peculiar he was acting, Nikki thought, as she finally reached for the first of the boxes. They were roughly similar in size although some were white while the others were gilt-covered. As she opened the first, her nose told her, before her eyes, about the contents.

"Look," she pulled out the gift and held it toward Gerry. "It's a chocolate rabbit. For Easter."

Snatching the card that had lain with the confection in a nest of shredded paper, she handed it to him.

"It's from Hanna and Lars."

Gerry's jaw had dropped as the candy was placed in his hands. Nikki frowned. Surely he knew the significance. She had told him the story of that other Easter.

By the time she had liberated the second candy rabbit, this one from the elder Kneipps, he was beginning to smile. This replica was of an animal crouched on all fours while the first had been rampant.

The third package held another rabbit, from Paul. That bunny had a chocolate basket suspended from a front paw. Tiny candy eggs in green and yellow and pink filled the container.

What fun this was, she thought, reaching for the fourth, another rabbit—Bruno and Liesel's. The ceremony of opening the packages no longer was bringing surprise. Now each was contributing to a sense of awe at the special friendship and understanding that the offerings represented. The fifth was from Donna and David.

Nikki stopped before opening the final container.

"Perhaps we have created a counter organization to Die Schwarzen Raben," she considered. "They had their black bird. We have chocolate rabbits."

"Open the last one," he told her sternly. She thought he was having trouble controlling his voice. It was about time, after all, that he should begin showing some impatience.

And so she did.

"I wanted it to be something special," he told her as she clung to him, "something that would speak of my love for you. But I guess I overlooked how many people there are who share in that love."

"Shall we go to bed?" she invited abruptly, pushing herself free to scoop up the six chocolate figures.

Tomorrow they would be wakened by the church bells. It would be Easter once more.